A PAINTER IN PENANG

A GRIPPING STORY OF THE MALAYAN EMERGENCY

CLARE FLYNN

CRANBROOK PRESS

Copyright © 2020 by Clare Flynn

Cranbrook Press, London, UK

ISBN 978-1-916469-7-3

"Come out of the dangerous and malignant jungle to see the light again"

Extract from a propaganda leaflet dropped from the sky over the Malayan jungle by the British.

∾

"The mistake is that though we lived in Malaya, we didn't understand the real situation in Malaya."

Chin Peng, leader of the Malayan communists in a television interview with the BBC in 1998

*Dedicated to my fellow members of The Sanctuary group –
Alison, Amie, Carol, Debbie, Helena, the Janes D and DS, Jean,
Jessica, Jill, Karen, Laura, Linda, Liza, Lorna, and Roz. Thanks
for keeping me sane!*

1

JANUARY 1948, NAIROBI

Evie took another sip of mango juice and gazed towards the distant Ngong hills. Arthur had been right when he'd said all those years ago that she would love Africa. He had promised the majestic continent would seep into her bones and possess her, so that afterwards everywhere else would be a poor substitute – smaller, less significant. He'd also been right that she would sense its age, its primeval history, a land where if you were to see a dinosaur lumbering towards you it wouldn't surprise. After only nine months living here, Evie didn't want to be anywhere else.

She leaned back in her chair, letting the sun touch her face, bathing her skin with its dry sensuous heat. Still only ten in the morning and it was already hot. Instead of making her lethargic, the heat revitalised her, endowing her with strength and energy. Evie loved quiet moments of reflection like these when she would count her blessings and recognise that, after the years of sorrow, loss and war, she had so much to be thankful for. She'd lost her first husband after forgiving his infidelity, been forced to flee her home as the

Japanese invaded Penang, endured years of loneliness, refusing to accept that Arthur, the love of her life had not survived the war. But he had and here they were.

At the edge of the paved terrace a lizard stretched out on the stone wall, basking in the morning sunshine. Evie watched its heavy-lidded eye open lazily as its tongue darted out and snagged a passing insect. Turning her head, she could see Gichinga, the houseboy, was hanging sheets out to dry, their whiteness blinding under the power of the sun. He flipped the sheets with a snapping action to get the creases out as he pegged them on the line. The name Gichinga meant firebrand, but the boy was gentle and shy, like a young deer.

The sheets flapped gently as the breeze caught them. Laundry dried in moments here, unlike in the sultry humidity when she lived in Penang, Malaya. There the heat had been oppressive, like a steam bath, and she'd had to change her clothes several times a day.

Thoughts of Penang made her think of her stepdaughter. Jasmine had loved her island birthplace in a way that Evie was only now beginning to comprehend. Here in Africa, Jasmine was like a young plant, pulled up and replanted in ground too shallow for her roots to gain purchase. She appeared to be wilting, listless and etiolated, despite the constant sunshine.

Evie's own love affair with Kenya made it hard for her to understand what her daughter was going through. While Evie had loved Penang, her connection to East Africa was deeper, almost visceral. Living anywhere else would never come close. Jasmine had been born in Penang, spent four years in Australia and several months in England and appeared unmoved by the majesty and vastness of Kenya. Her brother, Hugh, eight years younger, had adapted immediately – all previous mentions of his desire to go to boarding school forgotten, as he marvelled at the zebra grazing at the end of the lawn, gazelles and impalas jumping over the hedge and nibbling at the garden plants, and brightly plumed birds chirruping as they patrolled the terrace in the early morning. Hugh had been a baby when they left Malaya, so had known nothing of the tropical island his half-sister still yearned for.

It was not that Jasmine had ever complained about being in Kenya. Jasmine never complained about anything. She rarely voiced her own needs or aspirations. Evie had tried to coax her stepdaughter into telling her what was amiss, but Jasmine only smiled and said she was perfectly happy.

Arthur suggested that Jasmine might prefer to finish her schooldays in England as a boarder. When Evie had mooted this idea to the girl, Jasmine's eyes had widened in horror.

'No thank you!' she said emphatically, shivering to underline the point. 'I can picture it – cold draughty buildings, inedible food and being surrounded by strangers. Please don't ever make me go back to England.'

She now attended a convent grammar school in Nairobi, half-heartedly serving her time.

Evie swatted away a fly as she gazed out over the open grasslands beyond the extensive lawns of the property. Everything here was so huge. Big skies, with clouds casting shadows across the enormous landscape as heat haze distorted and blurred the outline of the distant hills. She could happily sit here for hours, sipping her freshly pressed mango juice, listening to the birds singing in the nearby trees. But she also had tasks to do: menus to plan for the frequent dinners she and Arthur were obliged to host as a consequence of his role in the colonial administration, lists to draw up for a charity event she had been roped in to help organise, name labels to sew into the new sports kit she had just bought for Hugh – who grew out of his shorts so fast she could barely keep up.

Her reverie was interrupted by Gichinga, bearing a silver plate with the mail on it.

'Many letters today, Ma'am.'

She smiled at the servant and took the letters from the tray. Thumbing through, she saw most were household bills, with one or two stiff white envelopes containing invitations to official functions or social events. An envelope caught her eye. It was embossed with the name of Jasmine's convent school.

Evie frowned. She sliced the paperknife across the top and unfolded the contents, her frown deepening as she read. This was so much worse than she had feared. Her eyes welled up as she tried to focus on the words – repeated complaints from Jasmine's class teachers...habitual truanting...refusal to accept the necessary rules of the school... failure to undertake homework...It couldn't be true. Jasmine had always been a well-behaved and compliant pupil. Yes, Evie was all too aware that she showed little interest in her schoolwork but that was a far cry from refusing to do it at all and skipping lessons. What had happened? She read the final paragraph with mounting distress.

It is with much reluctance, and after a great deal of thought and prayer, that we find ourselves with no choice but to insist on Jasmine's removal from our school immediately. Please make alternative arrangements for the completion of her education. Her continued presence would serve as a bad example to the other pupils and her lack of discipline has become a disruptive influence.

There were no examples offered to illustrate this disruptive behaviour. It was so out of character with the Jasmine she knew – a warm, caring and gentle soul who always thought of others before herself. How she must have hated the convent to have rebelled so strongly against its constraints that her expulsion was necessary.

Jasmine was not yet seventeen and had been studying for her School Certificate. Evie and Arthur had both wanted to ensure she had a full education before she followed her own path – whether that was into a career, further education – or marriage.

Neither she nor Arthur had for even a moment treated her in any way other than as their beloved daughter. Jasmine was the child of Evie's late first husband and his former wife. Her mother had died when Jasmine was small. Evie and Arthur loved her as if she were their own. Her heart constricted. Arthur would be devastated. He was so proud of Jasmine – and as a senior member of the colonial administration, he would now have to face the shame of his daughter being expelled from school. There was no possibility her disgrace would escape the inevitable gossip and rumours.

Agitated, Evie left the remaining pile of letters on the table and went to pace up and down the garden. Had the nuns already told Jasmine? Was she at school now – or wherever she went when she played truant? Why had Jasmine felt unable to confide in her that she was so unhappy?

2

It had been three days since Jasmine had been hauled before the school principal and she'd still not summoned up the courage to tell her mother about her absenteeism, let alone that Reverend Mother had warned her that further infractions would lead to her expulsion. Every morning, she left the house and took the school bus to the convent, but didn't attend classes, hiding out in the grounds until it was time to go home again.

Jasmine knew it was only a matter of time before the school contacted her parents. Her guilt was compounded by the exorbitant cost of the school fees. All that money going to waste while she frittered away her time lying on her back on the empty hockey pitch staring up at the sky or hiding out in the disused potting shed at the rear of the school grounds if a game was being played.

Jasmine was not a natural rebel but she couldn't face being in class any longer. What had begun as the occasional skipped lesson had now become wholesale truanting. Right now, she should be listening to the droning voice of Sister Angelica as she bored her pupils to death with an uninspiring explanation of the Long Parliament and something called The Grand Remonstrance. What possible relevance did the politics of Stuart England have to a sixteen-year-old's life? To anyone's life, three hundred years later? It was all so pointless. So meaningless. So tedious.

The sun was getting hotter, so she rolled onto her side, and shuffled into the shade of a sausage tree. Fallen red blossoms carpeted the ground underneath the tree and Jasmine watched a procession of ants moving over them like a well-drilled regiment advancing into battle. Above her, dangling down were the as yet unripe 'sausages', the eponymous fruits which were much loved by baboons.

Jasmine gave in to an expansive yawn. She'd forgotten her sketch book. Not that she'd be drawing ugly old sausage trees. Besides, she was too anxious to concentrate right now.

School had been bearable at the beginning – when Katy Grenville had been there. Jasmine and Katy had both been new girls and formed an instant bond – possibly because they both felt like exiles who didn't belong here. Katy had grown up in Bombay and missed India with the same nostalgic longing that Jasmine felt for Penang. Perhaps it was Katy who had incited Jasmine's dissatisfaction and growing unhappiness, but over time they had each fed off the other's misery, adopting a sense of superiority towards Kenya, their daily life at school and their fellow pupils.

And then, without warning, two months ago Katy was gone. Jasmine had never got to the bottom of exactly what happened. Never had a chance to ask Katy. The rumour circulating at school was that Katy's parents, Nigel and Gwendoline, had been mixed up in a scandal. The sort of thing spoken of in hushed tones and causing uncontrollable smutty giggles. One of Jasmine's classmates claimed Mrs Grenville had been having an adulterous liaison with several other men while her husband had been carrying on with the wives. Funny how the wife's crime was widely acknowledged to be more heinous. This arrangement had apparently ballooned into a regular free-for-all among a group of married couples, who spent weekend house parties hopping in and out of each other's beds. Knowledge of exactly what this bed-hopping entailed was, to say the least, patchy among the members of the Lower Sixth and the subject of much fevered debate.

According to one of Jasmine's classmates, who had over-heard her parents talking about it, the whole sordid busi-ness had blown up in the Grenvilles' faces when Katy had walked in on them one afternoon. Katy, like the majority of girls at the convent, was a boarder and wouldn't normally have been at home during the week, but she'd been running a temperature and the school, suspecting chickenpox, had sent her home.

That was the last time Jasmine had ever seen her friend. They hadn't even had a chance to say goodbye. Jasmine couldn't begin to imagine how mortified Katy must have been if the stories were true.

Jasmine had written daily to Katy, begging to know what was happening and when she would be returning to school. After a fortnight, her letters were returned to her in a bundle, marked 'Gone Away'. Desperate, she had asked Arthur whether he knew what had happened to the Grenvilles. Her stepfather, being something important in the colonial government, knew everyone. He had lowered his eyes, coughed and muttered something about Mr Grenville being recalled to his firm's London office. There was no point asking Mummy as she never paid the slightest attention to gossip and, while never overtly criticising Jasmine's friendship with Katy, always gave the impression that the Grenvilles were not the sort of people she chose to socialise with.

After Katy disappeared, everything went sour at school for Jasmine. The other girls made catty remarks about Katy and when Jasmine rushed to her absent friend's defence they started to pick on her too. Jasmine became the target of a relentless campaign of bullying and ostracism. Her friendship with Katy had been an exclusive one – they'd so enjoyed each other's company that they never sought the company of others. But now, without the mutual protection they had afforded each other, hitherto invisible resentments surfaced in plain sight.

Jasmine's misery and isolation mounted until it transferred into her feelings about Kenya in general. It had become a place where she knew only misery, where she felt an outsider, a misfit, a broken-winged bird.

Jasmine sat upright, brushing the dust off her uniform cotton dress. It was time to face the music. Time to go home and find the courage to tell Mummy and Arthur what was going on. What choice did she have? She couldn't run away. There was nowhere to run to. No one else to turn to. Jasmine glanced at her wristwatch. Double Maths would be finishing in ten minutes. If she left now, she'd be able to slip through the convent gates unnoticed while everyone was piling into the dining room for lunch. It would mean walking the five miles home in the hottest part of the day, but that had to be better than waiting around all afternoon and braving the school bus.

EVIE SIPPED HER COFFEE, savouring the rich flavour. Only since being in Nairobi had she begun to drink coffee, finding the locally-grown beans so much more to her taste than the ersatz bottled Camp coffee everyone still had to drink back in England.

The hot liquid sent a rush to her head – she only allowed herself one cup a day in the late morning. It made her heart race, but she felt better for it, stronger, more able to face whatever problems confronted her.

Remembering she hadn't finished going through the post, she pushed her anxiety about Jasmine to the back of her mind and picked up the stack of envelopes, sorting them into piles: bills to be paid, invitations to be answered, items for Arthur. She pushed the letter from the Reverend Mother into a position on its own, as though she were quarantining it. Leaning back in her chair, she noticed another envelope had fallen onto the ground so she bent down to pick it up. With a joyful cry, she saw the Malayan postage stamp and the familiar handwriting. A letter from her friend Mary.

My dear Evie,

It's been a while since I wrote, and I mislaid your last letter, so please forgive me if I fail to answer any questions you had. I'm bursting to know how you are all settling into your new lives in Kenya. How long is it now? It must be almost nine months? Are you finding plenty to do? I imagine Nairobi is quite the social whirl. I picture you at parties, looking as beautiful and elegant as always! Reggie and I live like hermits here, so I'd never be able to cope were I in your place – but you've always been frightfully skilled at entertaining people and looking after them so well. I was often grateful for your particular skill in seating people at dinner next to others they'd find congenial company.

Frances is teething at the moment, so I am enduring many a sleepless night. No complaints though as she is generally such a placid and happy-natured baby and I can't begin to tell you how much joy she has brought to me. It's hard to credit how much my life has been transformed by Reggie and our unexpected family.

Reggie sends his love. He works so hard but couldn't bear to be anywhere else or doing anything else. And as long as he's happy, I'm happy. When I remember how I pushed him away, it makes my blood run cold. I can never thank you enough, dear friend, for helping me realise that he and I were right for each other. What kind of miserable existence would I be living now were it not for him?

Please pass on my thanks to Jasmine for the beautiful water-colour drawing she sent me of the Waterfall Park in George Town. Tell her that, yes, the monkeys are still there. No doubt much smaller than your African baboons! I will drop her a line of proper thanks as soon as I get a moment, but I am scribbling this long overdue missive in a rare interlude while Frances is asleep, and I expect her to wake any minute! I do hope Jasmine is enjoying her new school and has made lots of friends. I'm so glad – as I'm sure you are – that you decided against sending her away to boarding school in England.

I'm still teaching the estate workers' children in the little school I set up in the kampong. One of the mothers takes care of Frances while I'm teaching the class. I'd like to have the time to teach the women as well – they are all very keen to learn to read – but single-handed, it is too much for me. I'd hoped to lure one of the teachers from my old school in George Town to help out – but what young woman would be willing to be stuck up here so far out of town and having to lodge with us – at least during the week? I can do only what I can. Such a pity and a missed opportunity.

I've just heard the dulcet tones of my darling daughter – quite a pair of lungs she has too! So, I will end here and get this in the post as it could be weeks before I get another chance to write. I miss you so much, Evie, and think of you all the time. I am

enclosing a snap of Frances for you, as you have not yet had the
chance to meet her.

   With fondest love – and to Arthur, Jasmine and Hugh
   Your loving friend, Mary

EVIE LOOKED at the photo of the baby and smiled. If only
Mary were here and she could seek her advice about
Jasmine.

BY THE TIME Jasmine arrived home her uniform frock was
soaking wet with perspiration and her knee-socks were
grubby and sagging around her ankles. Five miles was a
long walk in the middle of the day and with few trees to
offer shade. Her feet dragged when she stepped into the
house her shoes covered in dust from the road. Her plan to
creep to her bedroom, wash and change out of her dirty
clothes was foiled when she heard her mother calling her
from the long stone terrace that wrapped around three sides
of the house. Jasmine crossed the entrance hall, her dirty
shoes in her hands and stepped out onto the terrace where
Evie was sitting at a table.

   'I thought you'd be having a nap,' Jasmine said, lamely.
'Don't you usually after lunch?'

   'Well I'm not today.' Evie sucked her breath in and
studied her daughter's dishevelled appearance. 'How did
you get home?'

   'I walked.'

   'In this heat! No wonder you look such a state.' Evie
stretched out a hand and gently pushed a stray strand of
hair away from Jasmine's eyes. She gave her a sad smile. 'I
got a letter from the Reverend Mother this morning.'

'Oh.' Jasmine lowered her eyes. At least she wouldn't have to break the news to her stepmother herself.

'Come here. Sit with me.' Evie took the girl by the hand and drew her into a seat beside her. 'You've been very unhappy, haven't you? I'm sorry I hadn't realised things had got so bad. I've been so wrapped up with so many other things when I should have encouraged you to talk to me about it.'

Jasmine had been preparing herself for anger, for disappointment, for reprimands, but had not allowed for the possibility that Evie might instead offer only sympathy. Overwhelmed, she burst into tears.

Evie leaned forward and wrapped Jasmine in her arms, stroking her hair. 'Oh, my poor darling. I wish you'd felt able to tell me about it. I must have seemed very preoccupied. I'm so sorry that I wasn't more sympathetic.'

Jasmine tried to sniff back her tears, as she breathed in the familiar scent of her mother's lily of the valley perfume.

'It's not your fault, Mummy. It's me. I know I should have told you I'd been skipping school, but you and Arthur and Hugh are all so happy here and I didn't want to complain, but... but... I'm utterly miserable. I hate school. I'm glad they've expelled me. The girls are mean, and they talk about me all the time behind my back. And I miss Katy so much. Now she's gone I can't bear it anymore. Not only school, but everything. I don't think I can bear living here anymore.'

rthur Leighton came into the house with Hugh at his side. The boy had only recently stopped demanding a piggy-back from his stepfather as soon as Arthur stepped out of the car each evening. At eight years old, Hugh was balancing a Tigger-like exuberance with the desire to appear more mature.

Evie looked up, smiling, as she moved across the room to embrace her husband. Not a day passed when she didn't feel thankful that, at last, they were together after their previous marriages, and then separation by the war. She had never stopped believing Arthur was alive, despite evidence to the contrary, and now here they were, living a life Evie had once only dreamed of.

It had already turned dark outside, the sun plunging suddenly behind the hills as it did each day in this equatorial region. One moment daylight, the next almost instant darkness. As was their custom, the Leightons sat outside on the long stone-paved terrace for a pre-dinner 'sundowner', gazing across open plains towards the distant hills, a sweeping panorama that took the breath away. Beyond the low hedge that defined the property's extent, zebra moved slowly towards the nearby water hole, their white stripes illuminated by the moon, forming ghostly patterns. When she and the children had first joined Arthur here in Kenya, Evie had experienced a mixture of awe and nervousness at the proximity of wild animals, only ever seen before as a child when her father had taken her to London Zoo. How easy it was to become accustomed to such novelties – but she would never tire of the sight.

Hugh was bursting to tell them both his news. He had today come second in the hundred-yard dash, a practice run for his school sports' day in two weeks. 'I know I can win it on the day. I was only the teeniest microsecond behind Roger Cunningham and I'm getting faster all the time.'

The boy beamed at his parents. How like his father he was in his looks and his love of sport – but how different in nature. Douglas Barrington, Evie's first husband, had been a quixotic character, his unpredictable moods swinging from cold aloofness to a desperate affection for Evie that he struggled to express – revealing it rarely and only fully on his death bed. Evie wanted to ensure her son would not develop the bleak, gloomier side of his father's personality. On the other hand, the heavy dark hair and fine features were going to be assets to Hugh as he grew up and made her think with tenderness of Doug and how hard she had tried to love him and be a good wife in spite of her growing feelings for Arthur.

'Maybe Roger's getting faster too,' said Evie gently, wary of Hugh's expectations being disappointed. 'And we're very proud of you, anyway, aren't we, Arthur?'

'Bursting with pride.' He tousled the boy's hair. 'Perhaps we can do some training together at the weekend. See if we can shave that teeniest microsecond off your time.'

'Thanks, Dad! That would be topping.' Hugh's eyes widened in delight. The boy was revelling in having a father. It was less than a year since his mother had married Arthur. He had been a baby when Doug died.

'Don't we have a tennis game with the Hendersons?' asked Evie, concerned that there wouldn't be time for Arthur to keep his promise.

'Hugh and I can get up early on Saturday and get some practice in before breakfast while it's still cool, can't we Hugh?

Evie laughed. 'We'll all get up early. We can watch you race and then have breakfast on the terrace here. We don't have to be at the tennis club until ten.'

Arthur looked around. 'Where is Jasmine?'

'She had a headache and decided to have a lie down before dinner.'

'She's been looking rather pale lately. Is she all right?' Arthur's eyes were full of concern.

Evie sighed. Nodding her head almost imperceptibly in the direction of Hugh, she mouthed the words, 'We'll talk later.'

They sipped their drinks, the croaking of tree frogs and the buzz of cicadas competing with the sneering calls of a group of squabbling go-away birds in the trees beside the house. As they were about to head indoors for the evening meal, Jasmine stepped onto the veranda.

'Hey!' called Arthur. 'We missed you, Jazz.' He flung an arm around her with casual affection.

Jasmine jumped away from him as though she'd been burnt and Evie saw the hurt register on her husband's face. She sent him a look that said not to ask, so Arthur said nothing, and the family went into the cool of the dining room.

Jasmine's mood coloured the atmosphere, and they ate

their light supper in silence, punctuated only by the ticking of the clock and the occasional chatter from Hugh about his running training and the form of his rival, Roger Cunningham. Eventually, the boy asked to be excused in order to finish off his homework.

As soon as Hugh had left the room Jasmine released a long sigh. She looked across the table at Arthur. Speaking so softly it was hard to hear her words, she said, 'I've been expelled from school.'

There was a moment's silence. Jasmine stared down at her plate and Evie looked anxiously between her daughter and her husband.

Then Arthur burst out laughing. 'What did you do? Blow up the chemistry lab?'

A smile flitted briefly across Jasmine's face. 'They don't have a chemistry lab. The nuns don't hold with that sort of thing. Not suitable for girls. The only science we do is Domestic Science.'

Arthur glanced at Evie. 'Then it's a good job they've expelled you. I'd no idea they believed in such old-fashioned nonsense. We'll find you a better school. Maybe back in England.' He looked again at Evie. 'What do you think, Evie? You're very quiet.'

Before Evie could answer, Jasmine spoke again. 'I'm not going to England. And I don't want to go to another school. I don't want to go to school at all.'

Evie put a hand on Arthur's arm. 'The other girls have been ganging up on her. Ever since Katy Grenville left.'

Jasmine interrupted. 'I hate them all. They're stupid and shallow and petty-minded. And I hate being here in Nairobi.' She began to cry. 'I've tried. I've really tried, but it's no good. I can't stand it. The dust. The endless plains. And I miss the sea so much. It's nearly four hundred miles away!

In Penang we could go to the beach every day and the sea was all around us.' She gave a loud sob. 'Oh, Arthur, can't you ask them to give you your old job back? Please!'

'Jasmine!' A sudden anger seared through Evie's body. How dare she ask that of Arthur? How dare she assume that her wishes should be paramount? 'Stop that at once. You've no right to ask Arthur that and I've already told you it's out of the question. You need to grow up and show some common sense.'

Jasmine pushed back her chair and got up from the table. 'I hate you too. Nobody understands me. I wish I were dead.' She ran out of the room and her bedroom door slammed a few moments later.

Evie let out a long sigh. 'She's impossible.'

'She's unhappy.' Arthur placed his hand over hers. 'At sixteen there were probably times when you thought the whole world was against you.'

'No, I didn't. Not until seventeen. That was when my father took his own life and my mother abandoned me and I realised the whole world actually *was* against me. Jasmine is behaving like a spoilt brat.' Evie cringed. The last thing she wanted was to quarrel with Arthur.

He took her hand in his and stroked it. 'Jasmine is neither spoilt not bratty. And to be fair to her, she's been through a lot. Apart from anything else she's had to get used to me butting into your family and–'

'Jasmine adores you. She's certainly not unhappy about us marrying. That's one thing I have got right in her eyes.' Evie looked up at him, aware that her eyes were welling up. 'I've been a bad mother to her. I should have seen the signs of her unhappiness and tried to talk to her about it before it got to this stage.'

'Stop being so hard on yourself, my darling. You've been

an exemplary mother to her. But she's sixteen and that's what they're like at that age. Moody. Unpredictable. She'll get over it.'

'But she's due to sit her School Certificate next year. We can't let her throw it all away. Jasmine's far too intelligent for that.'

'Better not to rush into any decision. If she stays home with you for a while it will give her time to think and make up her mind what she wants to do.'

'That's not the problem – or rather it is. Her mind is well and truly made up. There are two things she wants to do with her life. Become a painter and return to Penang.'

'The painting I understand,' he said, thoughtfully. 'She's very talented. But Penang? She was so young when she lived there. I imagine she's feeling nostalgic for her childhood not for the island. Besides, nothing is the same in Penang anymore. Not since the Japs ruined it all. And then the British Military Authority made a right mess of things.' A cloud passed across his face, darkening his features and Evie felt a twinge of pain. She knew he hated to be reminded of the war and whatever he had gone through, fighting behind the lines and then during his subsequent capture and imprisonment by the Japanese.

'She's been back there with me since. She's seen how it is now. It hasn't deterred her.' Evie turned her face up to his and kissed him softly on the lips. 'Besides, I remember someone sitting beside me on a beach once, telling me how Africa was in his blood and how much he missed it and longed to return there.'

Arthur pulled back slightly and looked into her eyes. 'Do you feel like her too? Do you want to go back to Penang?'

'No!' She could hear the explosive strength of her. 'Although I'd go anywhere if it was with you, my love. Even back to dirty old London or boring Perth. But I can honestly say that I have never been happier than I am now. Here. I have no wish at all to go back to steamy Penang. If we stay in Nairobi for the rest of our lives, I couldn't be happier.' She kissed him again. 'Now why don't you go and sort us out a nightcap and I'll join you in a minute on the veranda. I want to look in on Jasmine first. Try and make my peace with her.' She turned to go, then called back over her shoulder, 'The post is on the table in the study in case there's anything you need to look at urgently. Mostly invitations though, apart from the letter from the school. And there's one from Mary you may want to read.'

Jasmine was already asleep – or possibly feigning it – when Evie looked in on her. Evie eased the sheet up over her daughter's shoulders and dropped a kiss on her brow, pushing back a strand of hair from the girl's eyes. 'Everything will seem better in the morning, darling,' she whispered, in a rush of tenderness.

When she returned to the veranda, Arthur was reading Mary's letter, so Evie picked up the drink he'd prepared for her and sipped it while he finished. The sounds of the African night wrapped around them – the frog chorus, the distant soft rumbling and bellowing of animals at the water-hole and the occasional bark of a hyena. Above them the clear inky sky was peppered with stars. She shivered and reached for the shawl Gichinga had laid out for her.

Arthur looked up, folded the letter, put it back in its envelope and handed it to her. 'Well there's your answer,' he said.

'Answer to what?'

'To what we need to do about Jasmine.'

'What do you mean?'

'Send her to stay with Mary and Reggie. Sounds like

Mary would love some female company. Jasmine could give her a hand with the baby and the village school. And if we arrange for a correspondence course, she can even keep up with her own school studies. And who better to support her with that than Mary, as a teacher.'

'But how can I possibly send our daughter across the ocean, thousands of miles away from us? And what if Mary isn't prepared to take her on?'

'You can let her go because you love her. It doesn't have to be forever. It will help her get whatever it is she feels about Penang out of her system or if not, it will give her what she truly wants. Would you deny her that?'

Evie let the thought play around her head. 'Of course, I wouldn't. But, Arthur, she's only sixteen.'

'She'll be safe enough with the Hyde-Underwoods.' He reached for her hand. 'And you could always make the trip with her. To settle her in. Make sure she's not having second thoughts. It would be a chance for you to catch up with Mary and meet the new baby. And weren't you saying there were still some matters outstanding on Douglas's estate? You could see the lawyer at the same time. You and Jasmine could stay in George Town before you drop her at Bella Vista. Enjoy a few days at the beach.'

'I can't abandon you and Hugh.'

'You wouldn't be abandoning us. It would just be for a few weeks. Hugh and I will get along famously together. He'll be at school, and at the weekends he can come along to the tennis club and the pool. Not to mention all the running training we can get done.' He grinned at her. 'We'll have a wonderful time together. Even though I'll miss you like crazy.'

Evie was starting to weaken.

He pressed home his advantage. 'And, of course, Mary

would be thrilled to have Jazz staying for a while. Wasn't she her teacher?'

Evie nodded.

'And Mary would do anything for you, my love. It's a perfect solution.'

Evie leaned forward and kissed her husband. 'You are a clever old thing, aren't you, Arthur Leighton?'

He pulled her onto his lap and kissed her again. 'Right. That's settled then.' Smiling, he added, 'Now, how about we have an early night?'

4

Three weeks later, Evie and Jasmine boarded a ship from Mombasa to Colombo in Ceylon, where, after a short layover, they were to transfer to another vessel coming from Bombay and finish the passage to Penang.

Over breakfast on the first morning, Jasmine asked Evie how many times she'd been to sea before.

Evie did a quick mental calculation. 'Nine, I think.'

'Not much more than me then.'

'That's because you were with me most of the time. Not the first time though. When I came out to Penang before the war in '39 to marry your father.'

Jasmine tilted her head to one side. 'Did you even know Daddy before you came to George Town? I don't ever remember hearing about you.'

Evie felt herself blushing. 'We'd met only once, so no, I barely knew him.'

'That was either brave or bonkers then.' Jasmine spread marmalade thickly on her toast. 'I mean, ... what made you do it? Marry Daddy when you barely knew him?'

Evie gave a tight-lipped smile. What had caused Jasmine's sudden interest in her past life?

Jasmine winced. 'Sorry, Mummy. I know it's none of my business but I've always wondered and never liked to ask you before.'

Evie drew in a breath. 'I suppose I wanted something to happen in my life. I was stuck in a bit of a rut. Living in a small English village in a job I didn't like and with no prospects.' She smiled again, still blushing. 'And I'd met your father and remembered how handsome he was. When he wrote to ask me if I'd marry him I came to the conclusion I'd nothing to lose and everything to gain.'

'That's incredibly brave then.' Jasmine looked at her with wide eyes.

'No. Not really brave. You were right to suggest it was bonkers, as you put it. I doubt I'd have the guts to do it now. I'm so pleased I did as otherwise I'd never have had you and Hugh. Besides, you're equally brave, heading off on this adventure on your own.'

'Not really. I'm going somewhere I know. Penang's the only place that's ever felt like home to me. And I know Miss Helston – I mean Mrs Hyde-Underwood. It's you who'll be having to travel back on your own.' Jasmine's lip trembled. 'I want you to know how grateful I am, Mummy, that you're doing all this for me. I'd have felt overwhelmed if I'd been alone on this ship. When you came out before the war to marry Daddy, you were entirely alone.'

'I was nearly ten years older than you. And anyway, I wasn't entirely alone. I travelled with Arthur and Veronica.'

Jasmine pulled a face. 'Ghastly Veronica. She was always horrid to me when I was small. I heard her telling you and Daddy once that you should pack me off to boarding school "as it must be such a bore having a kid in the house".'

Jasmine mimicked the drawl of Arthur's first wife. 'And I know she used to call me a brat.'

'Don't speak ill of the dead, darling.'

Jasmine rolled her eyes, shrugged, then turned her attention back to her breakfast.

EVIE STOOD at the starboard side of the promenade deck, gazing out at the expanse of ocean. The conversation with Jasmine over breakfast had caused her mind to return to that fateful first passage to Penang from England, with Arthur and Veronica. It had been a journey into the unknown. She had been within a hair's breadth of declining Douglas Barrington's marriage proposal and now was so grateful she had not. Otherwise she might still be in the claustrophobic Hampshire village at the beck and call of her employer, Mrs Shipley-Thomas, instead of standing here on the deck of a ship crossing the Indian Ocean, with her daughter close by.

Glancing behind her to where Jasmine was sitting on a deck lounger, under a parasol, immersed in her sketch book, Evie acknowledged that her daughter, at sixteen, was no longer a child. Where had the time gone? That first voyage to Penang seemed simultaneously a lifetime ago and like yesterday.

Evie leaned against the metal guard rail and turned her attention to the flying fish leaping out of the water. They rose into the air, gliding gracefully above the surface of the sea, before skimming and diving below it again.

The sun was hot on the back of her neck, so Evie adjusted the tilt of her straw hat and moved into the shade, to sit on a deck chair. Beside her, Jasmine looked up and smiled. Her sketchbook was open on her lap and Evie realised she had been drawing her as she was watching the fish. She leaned in to look closer.

'That's awfully good, darling.'

'It's not finished yet.'

'Do you want me to go back there?' Evie jerked her head towards the rails that encircled the deck.

'No need. The drawing's done, but I'm going to put a wash on it. When it's finished you can have it. Give it to Arthur as a present from me.' Jasmine's eyes were bright, all the stress of the past weeks gone.

'You need to do a self-portrait – so we'll have something to remind us of you every day.'

Jasmine gave her a playful smile. 'You think you'll forget what I look like?'

Evie put her arm around her daughter's shoulders and looked into her eyes. 'Never in a million years. But we're all going to miss having you around.'

The girl had bloomed as soon as Evie and Arthur had mooted the idea of her going to stay with Mary Hyde-Underwood. The old happy Jasmine had emerged from under the dark cloud that had enveloped her. Colour returned to her skin. Her eyes shone and she had been bubbling over with barely contained excitement as the day of their departure had come closer. Now, on the ship, she was a picture of peace and serenity, attentive to her mother, polite and engaging to the passengers on their table at dinner, and spending her afternoons reading – or more often – painting and sketching. How could Evie begrudge her the idea of leaving Kenya when the prospect of being in Penang had so evidently made her happy again?

'Remember, you must make sure you don't outstay your welcome. Mary and Reggie are incredibly kind in agreeing to let you stay, but it's only until you've sat the school certificate. After that, we need you to come home to us so we can talk about the future. Art school maybe? Who knows how you'll feel by then? And besides, Hugh, Arthur and I are going to be lost without you.' She bit her lip. 'By then you may be sick to death anyway of being in Malaya. And remember – any time you want to come home all you need to do is tell me.'

'Never!' Jasmine's eyes were fierce. 'I can promise you that, Mummy. I will never be sick of being there.'

Evie felt a lump in her throat and her mouth trembled. Was she losing her daughter forever? While Jasmine was not her biological child, she couldn't imagine loving her more if she were.

Jasmine put the sketchpad down and wrapped her arms around Evie. 'I promise once I've done the exams, I will come back to Nairobi to talk about what happens next.'

But the hollow space in Evie's stomach remained. Tears threatened and she didn't want Jasmine to see them, so she jumped up. 'I'm going to go back to the cabin to lie down for a while. I think I've caught too much sun.' As she hurried back along the deck, Evie knew in her heart this voyage marked a permanent end.

Their layover in Ceylon was for four days and, since this trip was to be the start of a long separation, Evie decided to treat them to a stay at the Galle Face Hotel.

When they disembarked from the ship, Jasmine's face lit up in a broad smile. 'It's so like Penang and Singapore!' she cried. 'It smells the same! It feels the same.'

As the taxi conveyed them from the port to the hotel, they passed white, colonnaded, colonial-style buildings and drove along tree-lined avenues, thronged with rickshaws and bicycles, as well as ox carts carrying wooden chests full of tea to the docks. The city of Colombo was built along the coast and waves crashed against the shore as the sun blazed down, intensifying the whiteness of the buildings and the vibrant splashes of colour of the saris worn by passing women.

The hotel was a grand Victorian building, a colonial palace looking out over the sea and over Galle Face Green, an open park area. With its terracotta-tiled roof, white stucco and broad colonnaded terrace, it reminded Evie of the Eastern & Oriental in Penang. Unlike the E&O, which had been used by the Japanese military during the occupation, the Galle Face had come through the war relatively unscathed, the island of Ceylon remaining under British control.

To Jasmine's delight, they were shown to a room with an ocean view and she flung her arms around Evie. 'Thank you, Mummy. This is such a treat.'

'Well it could be months before we see each other again.' She stroked her daughter's long hair, praying that it would be months and not as she feared, years. 'I want us to have some special time together.'

Jasmine plonked herself down on the end of the bed. 'I'm sorry I've been such a disappointment to you.'

Evie sat beside her and drew her daughter close to her. 'A disappointment? Never! Don't ever think that, my darling.'

'But getting expelled. Causing so much trouble. Hating being in Africa.'

'All I want is for you to be happy, Jasmine.' She held her gently above the elbows and looked into her eyes. 'Seeing you so happy now shows me how miserable you've been in Nairobi. I should have paid more attention. I was so wrapped up in getting us all settled in, I didn't notice that you were struggling so much. I was more worried about Hugh as he's so small – but I should have known little boys adapt to anything as long as they've plenty to do.'

'I simply didn't fit in.'

'I know. I do understand. But it's all behind you now. You'll have a wonderful experience in Penang. And then afterwards, we'll see. You may feel completely differently by then. You may want to go to teacher training college or university. Who knows? Let's take each day as it comes.'

Evie felt a sudden rush of sadness. She was losing something precious – the remains of her daughter's childhood and the last stages of Jasmine's transition to womanhood. That would be for Mary to witness. Evie bit her lip. 'I don't know what I'm going to do without you. I'm going to miss you so much.'

'Me too. I'll miss Hugh and Arthur too – but mostly you. And I promise I'll write.'

Evie kissed the top of her head, breathing in the fresh scent of her daughter's recently washed hair. 'You'd better!' she said.

THE NEXT FEW days passed rapidly. They took rickshaw rides around the city, did a little shopping – and sat on the terrace of the hotel drinking tea as the waves lapped the shore in front of them. Evie read while Jasmine sketched or painted, and they took long early morning walks along the beach, fascinated by the fishermen in their wooden *oruwa* catamarans. Jasmine relished painting these long narrow boats with their outriggers attached with coir ropes to the main hull.

They sat for hours watching the toddy tappers: barefoot, loin-clothed men who shinned up the trunks of tall palm trees, a bag of tools strapped to their waists, to collect the sap of the coconut palm for fermenting into a spirit known as *arrack*. At the invitation of a smiling toothless tapper, they both tasted the freshly collected sap. Sweet and slightly fizzy, it was refreshing and tasty.

All too soon for Evie it was their last evening in Colombo. Seeing the impatient excitement in Jasmine's eyes that they would soon be in Malaya, Evie vowed to be happy for her daughter. Most of the British in Penang before the war had sent their children away to boarding schools, as did the majority of Arthur's administrative colleagues in Nairobi. She needed to think of this separation in the same way. As a small child, Jasmine herself had been a boarder until Evie married Doug and convinced him she should be at home with them. Perhaps that early separation and the death of her mother had caused the girl to develop an independent streak?

During dinner, Kuttan, their young Indian waiter, regaled them with stories of Colombo during the war, when the city was awash with allied service personnel, intelligence officers and wartime administrators. He recounted with relish how he had witnessed a Japanese aircraft crashing in front of the hotel. As they were about to leave the table, he said, 'Very sorry you are leaving us tomorrow, ladies. I hope you will return to The Galle Face so I might have the privilege of serving you again.'

The smiling waiter indicated a table across the room where a middle-aged couple and a younger man, were dining. 'One of those gentlemen is also going to Penang tomorrow. You must be on the same ship.'

Evie looked across the dining room, curious, but turned away again when the woman glanced up and saw her watching them.

Rather than go straight up to bed, Evie suggested they sit out on the terrace for a while. She ordered a brandy and Jasmine a mango juice. It was a beautiful evening, the sky cloudless, inky-black and star-studded. A soft cooling breeze wafted in from the ocean. A perfect end to a magical few days.

'Do you mind awfully if I butt in for a moment? Only, Kuttan, our charming waiter, mentioned you're heading to Penang. Are you joining the *Rosebery* tomorrow?'

Evie looked up in surprise. 'Oh, yes we are,' she answered. But the man wasn't looking at her. His gaze was fixed on Jasmine.

'I say, would you mind awfully if I joined you both for a nightcap?' he asked. 'Only it's such a beautiful evening and the Parentals have already turned in.' The question was intended for Evie but his eyes hadn't left Jasmine, who appeared to be studiously ignoring him by staring out to sea.

Glancing quickly at her daughter, Evie told him that by all means he was welcome to join them although they would soon be going to bed.

'Yes,' he said. 'We have an early start tomorrow, don't we?' He asked for a whisky and soda from the barman and insisted on ordering another brandy for Evie. Jasmine refused a second fruit juice.

As the drinks were being served, Evie studied the young man. He appeared to be in his mid-twenties, with a shock of thick light brown hair and an engaging smile. He was tanned by the sun and had a healthy outdoor look about him, despite his formal dinner suit. To Evie's surprise, Jasmine looked bored or possibly irritated by his intrusion.

Once the drinks were served, he said, 'Do forgive me. You must think me awfully rude. I haven't even introduced myself. I'm Howard Baxter.' He stretched out a hand to shake Evie's as she introduced herself and Jasmine.

'What a beautiful name. It's perfect for you,' he said to Jasmine, who blushed and mumbled something before turning away to gaze at the sea again.

Embarrassed by Jasmine's behaviour, Evie asked the young man, 'Do you and your parents intend to stay long in Malaya?'

'Oh gosh! The Parentals aren't coming.' His voice telegraphed his feelings. 'They live up in the hills here in Ceylon, at Nuwara-Eliya. Pa's a tea planter. They're only in Colombo to wave me off – or as it's turned out – to stage a last-ditch attempt to get me to stay on here.'

There was an almost undetectable flicker of interest from Jasmine, before she turned her eyes back to watch the crashing waves. But Evie knew her daughter was listening.

'The old boy wants me to work here in the tea business. Thinks I'm mad to be going into rubber. But I want to make my own way, not always be in his shadow. And Ma's a sweetheart but she suffocates me. Just between us, I can't wait to have the Indian Ocean separating us.' He gave a little laugh. 'Sorry, I'm blurting again. I always end up telling people too much too soon. How about you?' He looked from one to the other. 'I hope you don't mind me saying this, but you don't look very alike.' He smiled at Evie. The breadth and warmth of his smile cancelled out his tactlessness and disarmed her.

Jasmine spoke for the first time. 'That's because Mrs Leighton is my step-mother. Not that it's any of your business.'

Evie gasped, mortified. Before she could respond, Jasmine got to her feet. 'I'm going to bed, Mummy. Good-night.' She bent down and dropped a kiss on her mother's cheek and moved rapidly back inside the hotel.

'Me and my big mouth. I'm sorry, Mrs Leighton.'

Evie turned to the young man. 'I think my daughter's feeling rather tired, Mr Baxter. My apologies for her abruptness. It's completely out of character.'

Howard Baxter looked relieved. 'I haven't offended you?'

'Of course not.'

'Mum's always telling me I have no tact. I open my mouth and put my foot in it.' He smiled at Evie. 'As for Jasmine, I like a bit of spirit. I look forward to getting to know her on the way to Penang.' He looked towards the doorway as though hoping Jasmine might return. 'Have you been to Penang before?'

'We used to live there. Jasmine was born on the island and is desperately keen to go back. We're in Nairobi now and an opportunity arose for her to spend some time in Penang, staying with friends. I decided to make the trip with her but I'll be returning to Kenya in a couple of a weeks. It's going to be hard saying goodbye.'

'I can well believe that.' His expression was wistful. 'Will she be staying on the island or travelling elsewhere in the Straits?'

There was something about Howard, maybe his smiling eyes, that made Evie feel relaxed in his company and comfortable telling him about their circumstances, despite the short acquaintance. 'On the island. My late first husband, Jasmine's father, was a rubber planter and had two estates, one on Penang and the other an hour from Butterworth. I sold them both after the war, Bella Vista on Penang to the manager and the other one to Guthrie's.'

'Maybe I'll end up there! I'm going to be working for Guthrie's. They're posting me to a place called Batu Lembah as an assistant.'

Evie smiled. 'Batu Lembah was my husband's estate.'

'Goodness! Is that where you lived?' His face lit up.

'No. We had a house in George Town. My husband lived at Batu Lembah during the week.' But Evie didn't want to talk about Douglas and their brief marriage. She hated to be reminded of the sadness and grief. 'My best friend married a rubber planter, and Jasmine will be living with them at Bella Vista. She adores Penang.'

'So, she and I will both be living on rubber estates.' Again his eyes drifted towards the main hotel building.

'What made you choose rubber over tea, Mr Baxter?' Evie wanted to steer the conversation away from Jasmine.

'Please call me Howard.' He proffered another wide smile, which lit up his eyes, showing he was an exceptionally handsome man. 'It's less about the crop and all about being my own man. I didn't want an office job. I went to university in England but I'd hate to live there. Lousy climate. I wanted to join the Colonial Office but I wasn't clever enough to pass the exams. They're frightfully picky. And I didn't get into Oxbridge. I was a Durham man.'

'A good university, I hear. Not that I'd know.' She smiled at him apologetically. 'Although I have to tell you, my husband works for the Colonial Office. And you're right. No offence, but he has a brain the size of the planet.'

Howard returned her smile. 'None taken. I'm reconciled to my fate and know my limitations. Of course, I'll have to learn the ropes. Work my way up the ladder. The pay's awful but it does improve once you get to be estate manager. And I'm a quick learner and a hard grafter.' He placed his hands on his knees. 'What will Jasmine be doing while she's in Penang?'

'My friend runs a school for the estate workers, so Jasmine will probably help out with that. And Mary, my friend, has a small baby and needs all the support she can get. But most of all, Jasmine will be studying for her exams through a correspondence course.'

'She wants to be a teacher?'

'No. At least not as far as I know, although I'm rather hoping she might eventually. Her passion is for painting.'

Howard's eyes widened. 'Painting? Really?' He shook his head and smiled again. 'Is she any good?'

'I realise I'm biased, but yes, she's frightfully good.'

'Marvellous. Talented as well as spirited.' He sighed. 'I must say, Mrs Leighton, I'm rather taken by Jasmine but I appear to have got off on the wrong foot with her.' He took a gulp of air then expelled it rapidly as though trying to build up his courage. 'Can you offer me any tips on putting things right with her? I was rather hoping to get to know her better...'

Evie gasped. Surely, he wasn't suggesting he was considering Jasmine as a possible girlfriend. He'd been in her presence for no more than five minutes.

'How old are you, Howard?'

'Almost twenty-six.'

'That's ten years older than my daughter. Jasmine is still a schoolgirl and the last thing she needs right now is a boyfriend.'

Howard Baxter looked abashed. 'There I go again. Jumping straight in. What's that old saying – "Fools rush in where angels fear to tread"? Me and my big mouth. He gave an ironic laugh. 'Please don't tell her. Let me have a chance to make a better impression first.'

He appeared oblivious to Evie's concerns, so she voiced them again. 'I'm going to make an assumption that it's the drink talking.' Evie nodded at his almost empty glass. 'I'm certainly not going to encourage you in any attempt to form an attachment to my sixteen-year-old daughter. I happen to think ten years is a significant age difference but, more importantly, Jasmine needs to concentrate on her studies and preparations for her School Certificate.'

He was still smiling, refusing to be discouraged. She reminded herself that Douglas had been fifteen years her senior and now Arthur was twelve years older than her. She sighed. But she'd been twenty-seven when she'd married Douglas. Yes, she'd had a crush on him ever since meeting him at fifteen – but the reality had proved quite different from the girlhood memory. Jasmine was still a child, for heaven's sake! There was no chance Evie was going to countenance this young upstart trying to sweep her daughter off her feet.

Howard remained undeterred. 'I don't get deflected when I set my mind on a course. Ask Dad. He's tried hard enough to bend me to his will without success. I know it's mad. I accept that I haven't exchanged more than a hello with Jasmine, but I do believe I'm smitten.'

Leaning forward, he pushed a heavy lock of hair away from his forehead. 'You think I'm crazy, don't you? Perhaps I am. And I've no idea why I'm telling you all this.' His eyes were an intense blue and they held hers.

'I know exactly why you're telling me! You've probably had one too many *stengahs* tonight.' She indicated his tumbler of whisky and soda. 'Go to bed, Howard Baxter. A good night's sleep is what you need.' She got up. 'And don't worry. I won't say anything to Jasmine. And if our paths should cross on the *Rosebery*, I hope we won't need to mention this again. As far as I'm concerned, this part of an otherwise delightful conversation never happened. Goodnight.'

5

When Evie got back to the room, she found Jasmine sitting up in bed reading.

'I thought you said you were tired, Jasmine.'

'And I thought you were never going to stop talking to that obnoxious man.'

Evie raised her eyebrows, surprised at the strength of the reaction Howard Baxter had provoked in her daughter. 'You were rude to him. I'm surprised at you making such a snap judgement.'

Jasmine said nothing, so Evie decided to let the mood pass and started to get ready for bed, folding her clothes and slipping on her nightdress. 'Are all your things packed?'

'Yes.' Abrupt.

Evie moved to the basin and began cleaning her teeth, keen to avoid risking a row with her daughter.

She climbed into bed and switched off the lamp on the bedside table. 'I think you should turn your light off too now, darling, and get some sleep.'

Jasmine did as she was told.

Evie was drifting off to sleep when her daughter's voice penetrated the dark of the bedroom. 'Is he really going to be on the same ship as us? I hope we won't have to speak to him again.'

Evie turned over on her side to face Jasmine's bed, even though she couldn't see her in the dark. 'It's a big ship. But really, Jasmine, all the poor chap did was offer to buy us a drink and join us for a chat.'

'Exactly. He ruined our last night here.'

'What?'

'I was enjoying it being just you and me. Then he came along and butted in.'

Evie sighed. 'Go to sleep, Jasmine.'

'What were you talking about for so long?'

Evie felt a rush of alarm. While Jasmine was affecting to despise Howard Baxter, she was evidently as obsessed with him as he was with her – even if in her case the reaction was negative. But was it?

Belatedly, she answered her daughter's question. 'This and that. He's going to be a rubber planter. He's starting out at Batu Lembah as an assistant manager. His parents live here in Ceylon, where his father's a tea planter. That's all.'

'Well, you took an awfully long time. I thought you were never coming back.'

Evie jerked upright and flicked on the bedside lamp. 'What's the matter, Jasmine? Is there something particular you wanted to talk to me about? Is that why you were annoyed at Howard joining us?'

'No. Nothing. It's just him. I don't like him. I know his type. You see them at the sports club in Nairobi. Full of themselves. Cocky. Wanting to be the centre of attention.'

'He wasn't like that at all. He was very polite. In fact, he was rather self-deprecating.'

An arm shot out from the adjacent bed and Jasmine switched off the light, plunging them back into darkness. 'I'm going to sleep now. See you in the morning.'

Evie turned over and tried to tip into sleep, but it was proving elusive. Was she doing the wrong thing in leaving her daughter in Penang? Would she do that were she Jasmine's real mother? Was she wrong to leave a vulnerable sixteen-year-old in another country an ocean away?

At least being up at Bella Vista, Jasmine would be distant from the social activities of George Town and the Penang Club. It was highly unlikely that, with a small baby, Mary and Reggie would be spending time there – and Mary hated the Club anyway. And Howard Baxter would be more than occupied with his duties at Batu Lembah. Knowing how little the juniors were paid on a rubber estate, there would be little risk of Howard being able to afford to run a motorcar yet, so he would be unlikely to run into Jasmine on Penang. But first, there were almost six days to cross the Indian Ocean. Evie hoped Jasmine's expressed wish to avoid Howard was genuine.

THE *SS ROSEBERY* was a passenger liner that had seen better days, having spent the war years as a troop ship. While it had undergone some refurbishment, it was unlikely to return to its past luxurious status and now mostly plodded back and forth between various outposts of the British empire, carrying planters, traders, administrators, engineers, and their families.

It was with a mixture of pleasure and concern that Evie discovered Howard Baxter had been assigned to their table in the dining room. He jumped to his feet as mother and daughter approached on the first night, pulling out a chair on one side of his own for Evie. He was in the process of doing the same for Jasmine when she went to sit down in a space on the other side of the table, giving him a look Evie could only describe as contemptuous.

Their other dining companions were a young married couple, heading to Singapore, an army officer, a land surveyor working in road construction, and an elderly widow visiting her son in Kuala Lumpur. The widow, Mrs Clark, was the last to arrive and took the seat on the other side of Howard.

Jasmine talked animatedly with the army officer and the married couple, avoiding casting so much as a glance at Howard Baxter throughout the entire meal.

Evie was puzzled. Why had Jasmine developed such a strong aversion to the young planter?

On Evie's other side was the land surveyor, who responded to her attempts to converse with a bored expression and a series of one-word answers, making no attempt to initiate conversation himself, so she gave up trying and talked to Howard and Mrs Clark.

Her initial assessment that Howard was a likeable young man was reinforced, but so too was her concern that the more Jasmine gave him the cold shoulder the keener on her he appeared to become. His eyes constantly moved beyond Evie and the elderly widow, to try to catch Jasmine's, who resolutely avoided all attempts to engage her and was absorbed in conversation with the army lieutenant.

After dinner, there was to be dancing. Jasmine got up from the table and was attempting an escape, heading towards the door, but the military man reached for her hand and swept her onto the dance floor. Evie watched as her daughter started to jerk her hand back as if about to refuse, but as she turned and saw her mother standing beside Howard Baxter, she began to dance with the lieutenant.

Howard and Evie sat down at a table on the side of the small dance floor. Mrs Clark and the land surveyor had presumably gone to bed and the married couple were also dancing. Howard sipped his scotch and fixed his eyes on the officer and Jasmine, his face set in grim concentration.

'I was too slow off the mark, wasn't I?' He turned to Evie, his eyes full of concern. 'Do you think he's after her? Do you think she likes him?'

Evie rolled her eyes. 'I've told you. Jasmine is sixteen. She's not old enough to like anyone, let alone grown men.' She motioned with a bend of her head towards the army officer. 'He looks like he's seen the back of thirty. Honestly I didn't expect to have to be fending off so many young men on my daughter's part.' She sighed. 'Thank heavens I came on the trip with her. What would have become of her if you'd all had a free rein?' Bending her head slightly in the direction of a party of more young men on the other side of the floor, she added, 'That lot too, by the look of things.'

Howard turned to look and gave a little groan. 'They're Guthrie's men too. We were hired at the same time. I was meant to be seated on their table.' He gave an apologetic grin. 'But a generous tip to the maitre d' secured me a place on yours.'

Evie shook her head gently, half frowning, half smiling. 'You have got it bad, young man, haven't you? But you don't even know my daughter.'

'Perhaps not, but I find her intriguing. She's one in a million. I knew it the instant I set eyes on her.'

'Jasmine could be a thoroughly unpleasant girl for all you know. A veritable monster.'

Howard grinned and gave a half laugh. 'She could be, but she isn't. Is she?'

Evie was forced to acknowledge that no, her daughter was far from being a monster.

'Indulge me, please. I want to know everything about her. Tell me.'

Was the man serious? Evie frowned. 'You're being ridiculous. You need to stop this nonsense. There's nothing to tell. Jasmine is a schoolgirl. An ordinary girl.'

'That's not true. She's exceptional. Ordinary schoolgirls don't leave their family and go and live in another country – particularly when you obviously adore each other.'

'What makes you say that?'

'I can see it. It was one of the first things I noticed about you both last night when you were having dinner together in the hotel. Dad was hectoring me about tea planting being much more of a gentleman's career than rubber. I tuned him out and watched you both instead. Dad didn't notice – he's too keen on the sound of his own voice. But Mum did. She could tell I'd got it bad. Mentioned it over breakfast this morning.' He stretched his mouth into a rueful smile. 'So take pity on me, Mrs Leighton and tell me more about Jasmine. Tell me anything. Her favourite colour. Her favourite tune. What makes her laugh? What makes her sad?' He fixed his deep blue eyes on her, his expression sincere.

Evie shook her head. 'I'm sorry, Howard, but you're going to have to find that out for yourself – if my daughter is prepared to tell you.' She rose to leave as the band finished. 'It's time Jasmine was in bed. Goodnight, Howard.'

She strode across the dance floor as the band finished the number, and tapped Jasmine on the shoulder, telling her it was time to leave.

The officer threw Evie a dirty look. 'If you want to stay for another dance, then why don't you?' he said to Jasmine. 'I'll see you safely back to your cabin.'

Evie decided she didn't like the man at all. 'That won't be necessary. It's already past my daughter's bedtime.'

Jasmine glared at her and walked rapidly from the room.

Evie looked at the army man. 'Do you make a habit of trying to pick up schoolgirls, Lieutenant? You need to forget any ideas on that score as far as my daughter is concerned. At sixteen, she must be half your age.' Without waiting for a reply, she hurried after Jasmine.

'YOU HUMILIATED ME!' Jasmine was standing, hands on hips, her back to the porthole, eyes flashing fury at Evie as she came into their cabin.

'That wasn't my intent at all. And you can only be humiliated if you choose to be. That snake of a man is old enough to be your father. And since when did the waltz-hold reach almost to your bottom rather than stopping at your waist?'

'That's ridiculous!'

'I could see him. He was trying to paw you like a piece of meat.'

Jasmine's eyes narrowed. 'You can't talk. You and that awful Baxter chap. Yet again monopolising each other. What would Arthur think? How could you?'

Evie was shocked. So shocked she started to laugh. 'Don't be ridiculous, Jasmine. I'm sure Arthur would like Howard too.'

'You're old enough to be his mother!'

Annoyed now, Evie flung her evening bag onto the bed. 'No I'm not, as it happens. But seriously, Jasmine, you're being ridiculous. I have no interest in Howard Baxter at all, and I can promise you he has absolutely no interest in me either. That is certain.'

'Then why are you flirting with him all the time?'

So that was it.

'I'm not flirting. Merely making conversation, which I'm sure he'd rather be doing with you, if you weren't so blooming rude to him.'

'I know his type. He's the sort who likes older women. I heard all about that kind of thing from Katy. Her mother was always carrying on with young men at the sports club. She asked her dad about it and he laughed and said it's a rite of passage for young men to spend time with experienced older women. I could tell at once that's what Howard Baxter was after.' Her face was solemn as she said, somewhat pompously, 'He is looking to be educated in the art of love-making.'

Evie's hand went to her mouth to suppress her laughter – the last thing she needed was for Jasmine to think she was making fun of her. 'I hate to disappoint you, darling,' she said, trying to shape her face into a serious expression, 'but that young man has no such intentions. He spent more time last night talking about why he wants to go into rubber planting, rather than tea, and telling me about his domineering father. And I'm not even going to comment on the sort of thing the Grenvilles apparently talked about, but while I'm sorry that poor Katy had to go away, I'm not at all sorry to see the back of her mother and father.' She looked up and saw that Jasmine was genuinely upset. The desire to laugh left her. 'The high jinks they got up to was not the sort of behaviour decent people should indulge in and I'm glad you're now safely away from their bad influence.' She sank down on the bed. 'I'd no idea Katy was filling your head with such nonsense.'

Jasmine was shaking, her eyes filling with tears. 'I hate all this kind of thing. I don't understand at all how adults behave. I feel stupid. I wish I were dead.'

Evie jumped up and wrapped the girl in her arms, then drew her down to sit beside her on the edge of the bed. 'Oh, darling, most adults don't behave like that at all. Do I? Does Arthur?'

'I'm sorry, Mummy. When I saw how nice you were being to the Baxter chap I ... well... I thought he was trying... and you were encouraging...oh, I feel so stupid. I'm so sorry. I feel a twit.'

Evie gave her a squeeze. 'You're not a twit. Nor the least bit stupid. It's very hard when you're young to always see people in their true colours. Come to think of it, it can be hard for all of us at times. We can form a first impression and then end up revising it completely. It's the same for everyone. When you're older you sometimes get there a bit faster as you've met so many different people. You get better at reading the signs. But sometimes even we oldies get it wrong.'

Jasmine pulled out a handkerchief and blew her nose. 'Sorry, Mummy. I didn't want to quarrel with you. And I don't think you're old at all.'

'No need to apologise.' She stroked her daughter's hair, tenderly. 'But I'm interested to know what you thought of Lieutenant Ellis.'

Jasmine gave a conspiratorial giggle. 'I didn't like him at all. I only danced with him because I was cross with you. He's a creep.' She wrinkled her nose. 'He has terrible bad breath. I was jolly relieved when you rescued me.' Leaning her head against Evie's shoulder, she said, 'And I don't want a boyfriend, Mummy. I don't feel ready for that. And certainly not an old man like Lieutenant Ellis. Not anyone at all actually.'

'Thank goodness for that.' Evie beamed at her. 'We are in accord, dear girl. Now, let's get to bed.'

LYING in the dark of the cabin, Evie listened to the soft breathing of her sleeping daughter. It was a relief that the tension between them had broken and that Jasmine had no interest in the unpleasant army officer. By the sound of it, Howard Baxter wasn't going to get very far either. And Evie certainly wasn't about to encourage him in his pursuit of Jasmine.

She didn't know whether she ought to be offended or amused by Jasmine's misapprehension that Evie was flirting with the rubber planter. Clearly the Grenville girl had been more aware of the behaviour of her notorious parents than Evie had previously supposed. Although Katy was in Britain now, perhaps it was no bad thing that Jasmine was removing herself from Nairobi and the goings on among some members of the sports club. She wished Arthur were here with her now to talk all this over and to take a firm hand with Jasmine's admirers.

Thank goodness there were only four more days to get through before the ship was due to dock at Penang.

6

I
t isn't easy to avoid people when you're on a ship. Not unless you hide out in your cabin all day and skip meals. Jasmine couldn't do that – and anyway she loved sitting on deck, feeling the sting of salt on her cheeks and watching the ocean slip by beneath them. But she had managed to find a little hideaway where she could paint and draw undisturbed. It was a small deck at the stern of the ship, tucked behind the library and the writing room. Few people realised it was even there, tending to stick to the main promenade decks along the sides of the vessel. There was a wide ledge extending from the bulkhead, wide enough for her to sit on and set out her painting materials beside her. Partially shaded by an overhang, it was her quiet sheltered haven.

Every day that brought her closer to Penang, the more she wanted to be there. Mummy was sweet and kind but she didn't really understand the strength of Jasmine's feelings. How Penang represented a warm cocoon that would wrap around her and protect her from all the things she didn't want to confront. The things Katy had witnessed and then reported back to her to their mutual disgust. The things the other girls at school whispered and giggled about. The things that for a horrible twenty-four hours she had even thought her mother was getting up to with Howard Baxter, that big-headed, self-satisfied rubber planter.

Penang was far removed from all these sordid concerns. Jasmine luxuriated in the thought of scything through the salt-water pool at the Swimming Club, sitting propped up against the trunk of a casuarina tree, toes in the warm sand of the beach as the waves caressed the shore. Or taking the funicular railway up Penang Hill and gazing out across the Straits of Malacca to the heights of Kedah Peak on the mainland. She imagined painting the scenery in changing light, her mind playing with the effect of light and shade as the sun made its slow progress across the sky.

Right now, she was experimenting, creating an abstract impression of the sea and sky around her, using loose watercolour washes. She let the paint and water guide themselves and enjoyed the different effects the pressure of her hand on the brush caused, applying the paint in varying levels of intensity. Painting always helped clear her mind of the rubbish that crowded into it, erasing everything but the scene in front of her and the impact of each brush stroke. She'd read somewhere that art was a form of meditation, but as she'd never attempted to meditate, that comparison didn't mean a lot to her. She preferred to describe it as an escape. When she painted, nothing could reach her, touch her, harm her. It was just her, the paper and the paint. Complete concentration on that and nothing else. It was all she needed.

She turned her head slightly to watch a frigate bird

soaring over the ocean on the starboard side of the ship. There was an illustrated book of birds in the ship's library that she'd happened to look at earlier so she knew from the large white flash on its breast that this was a female. Entranced, she watched the elegant bird glide on her long, narrow, outstretched wings, deep forked tail behind her, its two prongs opening and closing to help her steer the course. The bird swooped to snatch a flying fish as it broke through the surface of the water, soaring skywards to eat it in flight.

'They don't dive under for the fish. They're not great swimmers.'

Jasmine twisted round as Howard Baxter eased himself onto the ledge beside her.

'Lucky for them there are plenty of flying fish and squid on the surface, otherwise they'd starve. Lazy creatures.' He looked at her and smiled. 'You've found a good spot here.'

Jasmine glared at him, anger bubbling inside her. How dare he invade her special private territory? How dare he sit down uninvited and spoil her afternoon? She said nothing. Maybe if she ignored him, he'd give up and go away.

'Your mother told me you love painting. May I have a look?' He edged closer to her.

She snapped the cover closed over her block of paper. 'No. I don't like people seeing my work. And anyway, it's not finished.'

'What's the point of doing it if no one gets to see it?'

'It's for me.'

He seemed to accept that and nodded. 'Well, if you ever change your mind I'd love to have a look. Mrs Leighton says you're very talented.'

Jasmine grunted. Why didn't he go away and leave her in peace?

Howard leaned back against the bulkhead, legs stretched out in front of him. He was wearing shorts and she could see the dark hairs against his tanned skin. She shuddered and turned away to look for the frigatebird, but it had gone.

'We've got off on the wrong foot, haven't we?' He balanced one heel on top of the toe of his other foot. 'I must have said something to upset you. I'm a bit of a clod that way. I've tried to think what it was but I can't come up with anything, so I hope you'll forgive me anyway.'

'There's no point in forgiving you for something you don't even know you've done. And I don't either so we might as well forget it.'

His face broke into a wide grin. 'That's good news. I can't believe my luck in running into you in Colombo. I'll have the chance to get to know you by the time we get to Penang. And then–'

'And then we'll say goodbye,' she said firmly. 'As I'm going to do now. I have to...' She tried to think of an excuse for leaving.

'Have to what? It's hours before dinner. And I have no intention of saying goodbye when we get to Penang. Didn't your mother tell you? I'm going to be working on one of your father's estates.'

'My father is dead.'

'I know. I'm sorry about that.'

'So, it's not his estate anymore.'

'I know that too. It belongs to Guthrie's now. I'm going to be working for them.'

'So? What's that got to do with me?'

He pondered. 'Well nothing, I suppose, when you put it like that. I really have upset you, haven't I?'

'It's not you. I like being on my own. I'm not fond of conversation. Particularly with people I don't even know.'

'Exactly. That's why we have to get to know each other. Then I can make sure I can protect you from all the other chaps who want to get to know you. I can be your personal anti-pester protection.' He shot her another broad grin.

Jasmine stared at him. 'I don't know what you're talking about.'

'I mean that army fellow on our table. Absolute slime ball. And you must have noticed all the other Guthrie chaps, eyeing you up whenever you walk into a room.'

Jasmine's mouth felt dry. 'That's not true.'

'Of course, it is. I should know.'

'Why? Why should you know?'

He gave a dry laugh. 'Because I can't keep my eyes off you for a moment either. When anyone else looks at you, my natural instinct is to jump up and knock his block off. Last night, when Lieutenant Slimeball was dancing with you I'd have dragged him off you if it hadn't been for your ma stepping in and wresting you from his clutches.' He turned to look at her, his eyes smiling.

'You're mad,' she said, simply.

'Mad about you.'

Jasmine laughed. 'Well, I'm sorry to hear that, as there's nothing I can do to help you. I'm not in the least bit interested in you, Howard Baxter. In fact I'm not interested in boys at all. Now, if you won't stop pestering me, I'm going back to my cabin.'

He raised his hands. 'Don't do that. I'll shut up. Why don't I go over there so you can get on with your painting in peace? I promise I won't breathe a word.' He got to his feet and strode across the small deck area and took up a position opposite, his back to the ocean and his eyes on her.

'I can't concentrate if you're going to stand there watching me.' She sighed in irritation. 'Look, can't you go and find something to do? Watch the birds. Look for dolphins. Anything. Only stop looking at me.'

His lips tightened but he did as she said, turning to lean against the white metal railings and staring out across the blue expanse of ocean.

Jasmine picked up her pad, but the paint had dried before she could finish the idea she'd been exploring. Turning the paper over, she reached instead for a piece of charcoal and began to sketch the outline of Howard Baxter. She drew the stick over the paper, using broad bold strokes to capture the angles of his body as it bent forward, the back of his head and his shock of unruly hair, his broad shoulders. He was an ideal model, barely moving, his body tall, muscular under his cotton shirt and his bare tanned legs shapely below khaki shorts. It was like drawing a Greek statue. Only Greek statues didn't try to talk to you or tell you they couldn't keep their eyes off you.

Gradually, Jasmine began to relax, seeing Howard only as a collection of shapes she needed to bring to life on the paper. She forgot the way he had intruded on her and instead lost herself, as she always did, in the pleasure of creating something from nothing by making marks on a blank sheet of paper.

Her concentration was broken when she heard a match strike. A soft plume of smoke spiralled into the air above his head and she heard him draw the smoke down into his lungs. 'You don't mind, do you? Would you like one?'

'No. It's a filthy habit.'

He pulled the barely smoked cigarette from his mouth and flung it out to sea. 'I'd been looking for an excuse to stop.'

Jasmine gave a little gasp. 'Seriously? You're going to give up smoking because I said I don't like it?'

'Of course.' He turned to face her. 'There are enough reasons you've decided to dislike me without me adding to them. I can't change how I look or who I am, but I can change something like that.'

She pushed her hair back from her brow and stared at him. 'I don't get it.'

'It's quite simple. I'm nuts about you.'

Jasmine spluttered in disbelief. 'Please stop it. You're giving me the creeps. You don't even know me.'

'I feel as if I always have.'

'I'm only sixteen.'

He began to hum a tune, his eyes still on her.

'What's that?'

An old song that became popular again last year when I was doing my National Service. It was on the radio all the time. Perry Como sang it. *When You Were Sweet Sixteen*.' Howard began to hum the tune again, occasionally adding words where he remembered them. 'I'll get a copy of the record for you. I imagine you'll have a gramophone where you're staying?'

'I've no idea, but please don't.'

'Well, I shall certainly buy it for myself and play it until it's worn out, while I think of you.'

She rolled her eyes.

'Have I mentioned that I love your name too? It's so perfect for you. A fragrant flower of the east.'

'Now you sound really corny.'

'Another thing wrong with me. I'm compiling a list. I'll tackle them one by one until I've removed all the obstacles and worn down your resistance. Corny is going to be a tough one though. How will I stop sounding corny when I talk about you? I'll have to think about that one.'

He pulled himself up to sit, perched on top of the guard rail.

'Be careful!' she cried. 'If you lose your balance you'll end up in the ocean.'

'So you do care? You'd mind if I fell in the sea?' He swung his legs up under him and slowly, arms outstretched, rose to stand balanced on the narrow wooden top of the rail.

Jasmine dropped her charcoal. 'Stop it! Get down before you kill yourself. I'd mind if anyone fell in the sea. Even Lieutenant Slimeball.'

He leapt off athletically and landed safely on the deck, arms outstretched and took a bow. 'You are looking at the former three times champion of the English Inter-schools' Gymnastics Competition. Haven't done that in a while but I'm glad to see my balance is still as good.' He came and sat down again beside her on the ledge. 'And I can't tell you how pleased I am that you think Ellis is a slime ball too.' He grinned at her, then took a large white handkerchief out of the pocket of his shorts and gently rubbed her forehead with it. 'You've got charcoal all over your face.'

Jasmine felt the blood rush to her cheeks. 'I'm always doing that. Comes from pushing my hair back. Mummy gets cross with me.'

'Well, I promise I never will. I think it looks quite charming, actually. It shows how absorbed in your art you are. I'll be sure to always have a clean handkerchief on me so I can save you from walking into a crowded room looking like a coalminer.'

Jasmine felt herself smiling, then her annoyance resurfaced. 'You think you know everything, don't you? Well I find you too clever by half. Now I *am* going below.' She gathered up her art materials and stuffed them into the leather satchel she used to carry them around. 'I suppose I'll see you at dinner.'

He reached for her wrist and held it. 'Please sit next to me tonight, Jasmine. I don't want you near that snake of a man.'

She didn't reply. Removing herself from his grip, she jerked open the door to the companionway and walked quickly away.

WHILE DRESSING FOR DINNER, Jasmine told her mother an edited version of her encounter with Howard Baxter that afternoon.

'I've never been so embarrassed in my life. Do you think he's playing a joke on me? Because if so I don't find it very funny.'

Evie sighed. 'I don't think it's a joke. All he ever wants to talk to me about is you.'

'What?' Jasmine was aghast. 'He told you he has a crush on me?'

Evie nodded. 'I've tried to explain to him that you're too young to be thinking about a boyfriend but he won't be discouraged. You've become an obsession for him.' She put down her hairbrush. 'And to be honest I'd rather a nice young man like him has a crush on you, then that creepy Lieutenant Ellis. But don't worry, darling, in a couple of days we'll be off the ship and you can forget all about him. It's most unlikely you'll run into him in Penang. Especially since he's over on the mainland.'

'I feel stupid. I can't understand why he says all that stuff. I don't like it at all.'

Evie put her arms around her daughter. 'I'm sure he's the

first in a long line of handsome young men who will be desperate to gain your affection.' She smiled, but it was a sad smile. 'My little girl is growing up. And I must say you look beautiful tonight.' She stepped back and looked at Jasmine, who was dressed in a pale pink silk gown.

'I don't want to grow up. And I don't ever want to have a boyfriend.'

'One day you will. When you meet the right person. But you're still very young. I didn't marry your father until I was twenty-seven. You don't even need to think about all that kind of thing right now. Howard Baxter is much older than you. When men get to his age all they want to do is find a nice girl and settle down with her.' Evie opened her jewellery case and put on a pair of pearl earrings to match her necklace. 'That young man will soon find a girl nearer his own age and will be married before you know it. Once he's got his first manager's job.'

'Can I ask you something, Mummy?'

'Of course.'

'Since this is our last night on the ship, do you mind if I sit between you and that grumpy man next to you. Only...I can't bear to sit beside ghastly Lieutenant Ellis and Howard says he wants to sit next to me. Please, Mummy. I want you for myself since we've so little time left together.'

'Of course, my darling. If that's what you want.' Evie reached back into the jewellery box and pulled out a pearl ring. Taking Jasmine's hand in hers she said, 'Let's try this on you and see if it fits.'

Jasmine's eyes widened. 'It's beautiful. Exquisite.' She slipped it on.

'Perfect!' Evie looked at her daughter, her heart twisting in a mixture of love and loss. 'I've always intended for you to have it. It was given to me by your father. He told me it belonged to your grandmother. She died when he was a small boy. Take care of it, my love, it's very precious.'

Jasmine stretched her hand out in front of her to admire the ring. 'I absolutely adore it, Mummy. Thank you so much. I will take such great care of it. I promise you.' She flung her arms around her mother's neck.

'Come on then or we'll be late for dinner.'

7

W hen the *Rosebery* arrived in George Town, Evie couldn't help wishing the ship could turn around with her and Jasmine on it and sail straight back to Africa. Now they had reached their destination, the pain of their impending separation was biting.

Crowds were gathered on the quayside: people there to meet returning family and friends, uniformed soldiers, policemen, traders, hawkers, drivers, porters, rickshaw men. Evie had told Mary there was no need to come to meet the ship as she and Jasmine intended to spend several days in George Town before she brought Jasmine up to Mary and Reggie's house up in the hills. But as her eye drifted over the throngs of people, she saw Mary standing amid the crowd, waving her hand, trying to catch Evie's attention.

'How could I possibly have waited?' said Mary, when they met on the quay. 'As soon as I knew you were coming, I began counting the days.' She turned to Jasmine, took a step back, then moved forward and flung her arms around the young woman. 'And Jasmine! What can I say?'

'I'm so happy to see you, Miss Helston,' said Jasmine, her eyes shining. 'I mean Mrs Hyde-Underwood.'

'You're not in my class anymore, Jasmine, so why don't you call me Mary.' She hugged her again.

'Let's make it Aunty Mary,' said Evie. 'You're still only sixteen, Jasmine.'

Mary gave Jasmine a conspiratorial smile, winked and wrinkled her nose.

There was an artificial cough behind them. Evie turned round and found Howard Baxter standing there. His eyes darted between Mary and Evie, his expression expectant.

Evie, irritated at the intrusion, said, 'Mary, this is Howard Baxter. He's going to be an assistant manager at Batu Lembah for Guthrie's. Howard, this is Mrs Hyde-Underwood, my dearest friend.'

Mary shook hands with the young man.

Jasmine had turned away, before she could be drawn into the conversation. She stepped aside from their group as Evie made the introductions, in order to say goodbye to Mrs Clark, who was continuing her journey to Kuala Lumpur by rail. Evie knew her daughter was deliberately avoiding Howard, as she had barely spoken to Mrs Clark when they were on the ship.

'I have a plan.' Mary linked her arm through Evie's. 'As today is a rare day of freedom for me – I'm not teaching and our *amah* is looking after Frances – I thought we could have lunch and a swim over at Tanjong Bungah.' She pointed at a motorcar parked at the dockside. 'Bintang will drop us over at the Penang Swimming Club and come back here to pick up your luggage and take it to the E&O. Later, he'll drop you back at the hotel and drive me home.' She touched Evie's arm. 'I hope you don't mind me organising you? After this afternoon I'll leave you two alone to enjoy yourselves until you come up to Bella Vista next week. We thought – Reggie and I – that you could have your last night with us before you sail home, Evie.'

Evie hugged her friend. 'How perfect. What do you think, Jasmine?'

Jasmine was beaming happily. 'I think it's a marvellous plan. I can't think of anything better than spending our first afternoon at the Penang Swimming Club.'

Another cough from Howard Baxter. 'I have to get on that truck over there.' As he spoke, the horn tooted and the young men who were crowded into the open back catcalled and whistled at him. Howard waved them away with an impatient gesture. He turned first to Evie. 'Mrs Leighton, it has been an absolute pleasure. I hope this is the beginning of a long and lasting friendship.' He tilted his head slightly in the direction of Jasmine. 'As you know, I intend to spend as much time as possible getting to know Jasmine better.' He turned to Mary. 'Mrs Hyde-Underwood, is there anywhere in George Town or Butterworth where one can buy gramophone records?'

Mary looked nonplussed. 'I'm sure there must be. I imagine you can buy them at Whiteaway's.'

'And do you have a gramophone that Jasmine can use?'

'Yes, we do. Of course.' She looked puzzled.

Jasmine looked pained. Evie sent a silent message to her friend that she'd explain later.

Howard looked over his shoulder as the parked truck sounded its horn again. 'Goodbye.' He looked at Jasmine. 'I'll be working on not being corny. But judging by the expression on your face I have a long way to go.' He turned and walked briskly to the waiting truck.

Jasmine rolled her eyes and gave a long sigh. 'Thank

goodness he's gone. Now let's get away from these crowds. I can't wait to have a swim.'

EVIE AND MARY sipped watermelon juice, sitting under sun umbrellas by the side of the pool as Jasmine swam up and down. A soft cooling breeze off the Straits wafted over them, easing the sticky heat. Evie sighed with contentment as she looked at her daughter, cutting through the water, swimming like a dolphin up and down the otherwise empty pool.

'She's burning off her excess energy.' Evie smiled at her old friend. 'The pool on the ship was barely big enough to get wet in.' She looked around at the well-clipped lawns and the neat plantings of scarlet zinnias. 'This place hasn't changed at all.'

'You should have seen it after the war. The gardens were ruined. Tank tracks all over the lawns. Anti-aircraft guns on the roof of the clubhouse. But they've done a good job bringing it back to its former state.' Mary dipped her head in Jasmine's direction. 'Are you going to tell me who that extremely handsome young man was and why he wants to buy gramophone records for Jasmine.'

'I haven't a clue about the gramophone records, but the poor fellow believes he has met the love of his life in Jasmine.' Evie raised her eyebrows. 'Unfortunately – or possibly fortunately – she doesn't happen to agree.'

'Ah! I thought that might be the case.'

'I have to admit to being relieved. She's still so young, and I hate to think of her growing up and our growing apart.'

'You won't ever grow apart, Evie. Jasmine adores you.' Mary turned her head in Jasmine's direction. 'I wonder why she's taken against him. He seems a nice enough fellow –

and he's certainly got the film star good looks.' She smiled. 'Not that looks are what counts.'

Evie stretched her legs out. 'He's a charming man. Polite, respectful, full of energy. I do think he's too old for her though. At Jasmine's age nine years is quite a gap. But I've no idea why she's taken against him, but it's her affair and I'm certainly not going to plead his case.'

'He'll no doubt forget all about her as soon as he starts work. He won't know what's hit him once he gets to Batu Lembah.' Mary swatted at a fly.

'You're probably right. Shall we take a walk on the beach?' Evie bobbed down by the side of the pool to tell her daughter to come and find them when she was ready, then she and Mary scrambled over the rocks and onto the beach below.

They walked along, side-by-side, comfortable with each other. Evie was happy that there was no strain in their relationship despite their very different wartime experiences. She knew the war was a closed subject to Mary and hated to imagine what her friend must have gone through during the long years she had been held as a prisoner of the Japanese.

It was quiet on the sandy beach, away from the voices and laughter around the swimming pool. It had been on this same stretch of sand that Arthur Leighton had kissed her for the first time, and she'd realised that she had fallen in love with him. A love that, at the time, she believed had no future as they were both married.

'I'd forgotten how beautiful it is,' said Evie at last, when they were sitting on towels under the trees. 'It's so calm, peaceful. Look at that view, the sunlight on the water, the hazy clouds drifting over the hills on the peninsula.' She took a deep breath. 'And the scent of the casuarina trees.' She lay back on her towel and gazed up into the feathery fronds above them. 'Beautiful,' she said at last.

'I wish you were living here.' Mary's voice was soft, wistful. 'Is Africa beastly?'

Evie turned over on her side, and propped herself on an elbow so she could see her friend's face. 'No! Not at all. It's very different from here, but I absolutely love it. Yes, I miss all this.' She waved her arm in front of her to take in the blue waters of the Straits and the distant hills. 'I do love the sea. But there's something majestic and moving about Kenya. The sounds you hear on the plains at night and early morning. The wild animals. The enormous skies.' She wiped her brow. 'And it's a dry heat with cool nights. Not this awful humidity.'

'So, you won't be coming back?' Mary's eyes were sad.

'I doubt it. Arthur is happy. So is Hugh. And so too, apart from missing you, am I.' She raised herself up to a sitting position. 'Oh, Mary, I am going to miss Jasmine so much.'

Mary touched her arm with a comforting gesture.

'Am I doing the right thing, letting her come here? I agonised over it. But she wasn't thriving in Nairobi. Seeing my girl so unhappy was worse than the idea of being parted from her. Can you understand that?'

Mary nodded but said nothing.

'And I could only do it knowing she's going to be with you.' She flung her arms around Mary. 'There's no one else in the world I'd trust to care for her. I realise it's a huge imposition on you, but––'

'It's no imposition. It will be a joy.' Mary looked thoughtful for a moment. 'But I need to make you aware of the situation here. Things aren't the same as they were before the war.'

Her fingers plucked at the towel she was sitting on. 'The

British Miltary Administration made a right old mess of things after the war to be honest. There was a lot of corruption in the BMA. Of course, the Japs introduced all that kind of skulduggery in the first place. It never existed in the old days. Can you imagine men like Arthur accepting bribes? It's unthinkable, but these days it goes on and some of the army men were part of it. A surveyor we know was imprisoned in Changi during the occupation. He went back to his bungalow on the day of liberation. Everything was there exactly as he'd left it when the war started. The servants greeted him with delight and told him they'd guarded the place for him throughout the war. He had to return for a night to get his things from Changi and say goodbye to his fellow inmates. The next day he got back home to be met again by the servants, who were now weeping. A British army truck had passed by and looted the whole house.

Evie gasped, horrified. 'The British army?' Then she thought of Ellis on the ship. She could well imagine him doing something like that.

Mary looked apologetic. 'I don't mean everyone in government is corrupt. There are some decent enough men – but most are more concerned with lining their own pockets than doing the right thing for the country. Reggie's always saying that the BMA was staffed with bus conductors and junior clerks sent out here and given the title of Colonel. No wonder they were drunk with power.'

Mary sighed. 'And then Harold MacMichael made matters worse by strong-arming the sultans into agreeing to cede power to the Malayan Union. That caused a lot of resentment.'

'How did he do that?'

'Threatened to expose them as collaborators with the Japanese. Some of them were, but certainly not all. Let's hope that now we have the Malayan Federation, things will improve, but somehow I doubt it. It's one big, fat muddle. The ethnic Malays are angry that the sultans have become powerless. The people respect them as their leaders whether we like that or not. It's history. Who are we to uproot all that? Also, the government contradicted everything they said about granting citizenship to the Chinese and so the Chinese Malays resent that too.' She sifted sand through her fingers. 'And many workers are fed up that they've worked like stink to get tin and rubber production back to how it was and yet many of them are now earning less than they did before the war. Some of the owners are taking advantage.'

'That's dreadful.'

'It's obviously not the case at Bella Vista. Our workers are happy. Reggie pays a fair wage. Their housing is good. They're well fed. We've built the school. But some of the other planters think that because the majority of the workforce are glad to be working for the British again and getting paid, rather than under the Japanese who treated them as slaves and did terrible things to people at the slightest provocation, that gives them carte blanche to underpay them.'

Further along the beach Jasmine was scrambling down the rocks from the Swimming Club. She dropped her towel onto the sand and ran straight into the sea.

'Look at her!' said Mary. 'She's a regular mermaid.'

'Making up for lost time. But go on, tell me more about the situation here.'

Mary explained how British trade unionists and Chinese communists had been encouraging unrest among the workforce across the country. 'There are numerous Chinese guerrilla fighters who took on the Japs. A lot of the British, including apparently the High Commissioner, are grateful for what these men did during the war and it's blinding them to what's happening now. They don't see that some of these former heroes are now working to undermine everything we've built here.'

Evie was surprised. Not by what she was hearing, but at the fact that it was Mary who was saying it. Last time she had seen her friend, before she married Reggie, Mary had been vocal in her belief that Malaya must become independent.

'I thought you were pro-independence?'

'I am. Absolutely. But this country is made up of many nationalities. Chinese people outnumber ethnic Malays. There are still many British. I want to see a country free from colonial rule, where everyone can play a part.' She sighed. 'I don't like thinking about politics too much, but I think about it enough to believe that there's a place for us all, no matter what our skin colour or religion or language. Some of the communists, all they want is to send the white man packing and turn us into another China.'

Evie frowned. 'But why are you worried particularly now? Has something happened?'

'Oh, it's just that one hears things. About growing pockets of trouble. Small dangerous groups intent on expelling us all and creating a communist state on Chinese lines. And they're being aided and abetted by Mao and others. Last October a planter near Johore was robbed and killed.'

'How shocking. Did you know him?'

'Reggie met him once. Chap called Nicholson.'

'You don't think it will lead to a rebellion, do you?'

'I certainly hope not.' But her face telegraphed her fear.

Evie sighed. 'We've had murmurings of problems in

Kenya too. The Kikuyu tribe have rebelled and withdrawn labour in the past and recently. But they're also divided amongst themselves. The war changed everything, didn't it? Arthur says Britain can no longer afford an empire. We're saddled with war debt. And all those men from the colonies who fought and died for us deserve to be rewarded for that sacrifice.' She raked her fingers through the sand, creating patterns. 'It's simply a matter of time until we can ensure an orderly transition.'

'That's it. It takes time for an orderly transition. Look at the mess they made in India by rushing it through. But some of these men aren't prepared to wait.' Mary stretched her arms out in front of her. 'I truly love the Malayan people and the last thing they deserve is for their country to be plunged back into conflict. We all want to get on with rebuilding our lives and raising our families.'

Jasmine had come ashore much further along the beach and was now a small spot in the distance.

'When Jasmine comes back, we'll go back up to the Swimming Club for lunch.' Mary squeezed Evie's arm gently. 'You can't imagine how pleased I am to be with you.'

'Me too. I know a lot of people in Nairobi but there's no one I'm as close to as you.' She glanced in Jasmine's direction. 'Maybe we'd better go and fetch her. She's talking to someone down there.'

Mary got to her feet. 'That's the *syce*, Bintang. He also works as a kind of general factotum for Reggie, running errands, helping out in the office. As well as sorting your bags he's been collecting some tools for Reggie from the chandler. He must have decided to come to the beach afterwards while he waits for us.'

Evie stood up too, brushing sand off her legs. The women began waving, trying to catch Jasmine's attention, but she appeared absorbed in conversation with the young driver. It was Bintang who saw them and pointed in their direction. Jasmine finished talking and began to run along the sand towards them. As they waited for her, Bintang disappeared behind the casuarinas where the shoreline curved away.

When Jasmine arrived, Evie asked what they'd been talking about.

'Oh, nothing really. We realised his sister was in my class at school.'

'Of course,' said Mary. 'I'd forgotten you were around the same age.' She turned to Evie. 'Bintang's sister, Siti, was one of my brightest pupils. She died during the war. Bintang and his family suffered a lot. His parents disappeared during the Japanese occupation, probably dead, so the war put an end to Bintang's education. When Reggie was looking for a *syce*, we decided to give him a chance.'

Evie glanced at her daughter, who said, 'Come on then, let's get some lunch. I'm starving.' Evie couldn't put her finger on exactly what, but something about what had just happened made her feel inexplicably anxious.

8

The door closed as Jasmine left the room, and Mary looked across at her husband, who put down his copy of the *Straits Times* and moved to join her on the sofa. He was a tall man, who before the war had carried too many pounds, but his years of near- starvation in Changi had melted away the weight and he hadn't regained it. While no one would describe him as handsome, unlike his late RAF pilot brother, Reggie had an interesting face, characterful, kind. He was the sort of man you didn't notice – until you did.

'Is the lass going to be all right?' he asked. 'You don't think she's regretting all this, do you? She was very quiet over dinner.'

'It's been a long day for her and it was obviously painful saying goodbye to Evie this morning. But I'm sure she'll settle soon enough. Coming here was her own decision.'

'I know, but mightn't a short holiday have been better?'

'If she wants to go home sooner than planned, then obviously she can. But I don't think she will.' Mary rested her head against Reggie's shoulder. 'And I was sad today too. It was awful standing on Swettenham Quay watching Evie's ship disappear into the distance.'

'It will be good for you to have some female company and Jasmine is a sweet girl. I only hope she won't get dreadfully homesick.'

Mary moved her head back so she could look up at Reggie's face. 'Jasmine thinks of Penang as home. Evie told me the poor girl's been utterly miserable in Kenya. Absconding from school, not eating properly. At least spending some time here will either work out for her or she'll get Penang out of her system and will be able to settle into life in Nairobi – or even go to London.' She reached for his hand and squeezed it. 'Evie says Jasmine's a talented artist and may want to go to art school eventually.'

'Art school?' Reggie looked dubious. 'Really?'

'If she's talented, it will help her get even better. Maybe she could become a famous painter one day. Have exhibitions and things.'

Reggie laughed. 'What's the point of that? She's a pretty girl. She'll probably get married.'

Mary pulled away from him in surprise. 'You might as well ask what was the point of me training to be a teacher.'

'That's different.'

'How?'

'I suppose because teaching is useful. Essential even. But art is a waste of time, in my opinion. And more suited to men. Men who aren't good at doing anything else.'

Mary stared at him. 'I can't believe you're saying that, Reggie. Don't you like art at all? And why shouldn't women be as good as men at it?'

He shrugged. 'I've never really thought about it to be honest.'

'I'm shocked. I hope Jasmine will be able to change your

point of view, which quite frankly strikes me as being an extremely narrow one.'

'Look, I've nothing against art. It's just that I've never really seen the point of it. Why bother to stare at pictures? Much better to read a book or listen to the wireless.'

'If I'd known you were such a Philistine I'd never have married you.'

Reggie pulled her back into his arms. 'Then it's a damn good job the subject never came up, isn't it? Think what you'd have missed out on.'

Mary laughed. 'I suppose you're right. But how odd that we've never spoken about it before.'

'I certainly had no idea that you were a great art connoisseur, my darling. If I'd known, I'd have found something else to hang on the walls of this place.' He swept an arm around the room, where a series of large, dark, Victorian portraits hung. 'Who are these people? Do you know, Mary, I don't think I've ever looked at them properly before.'

'I imagine they're Douglas Barrington's ancestors.'

Reggie got up and walked across the room to stand in front of a picture of a stern man with a handlebar moustache. 'He looks a bit of a tyrant. Must be the chap who built this place. I wouldn't fancy crossing swords with him if the rubber quotas were missed.'

Mary moved across the room to join him and studied the portrait hanging beside it – a regal woman in a ruby-red gown. 'She looks more fun. She isn't smiling but you can see a spark of amusement in her eyes. As if she's only going through with the ordeal of having her portrait painted because it's expected of her, and she's been having a chuckle with the painter.'

'Really?' Reggie stepped closer and studied the picture.

'Maybe you're right. She does seem to be suppressing her amusement.'

'I hope Old Handlebar Moustache treated her well. Mind you, she looks as though she could give him as good as she got if he didn't.'

'They must be Jasmine's great grandparents. Can you see any likeness?' Reggie peered more closely at the two paintings. 'I can't believe I've never really looked at them before.'

Mary linked her arm through Reggie's as they gazed at the portraits.

'I suppose there's something of Doug about the old boy. Both of them look pretty scary.' He gave a chuckle. 'But old Doug was a damn handsome fellow. And Jasmine is far better looking than either of these two. Mind you, her mother was a pretty woman too.' He frowned before saying, with satisfaction, 'Felicity. That was her name, wasn't it?' He shook his head, his face now solemn. 'Good man, Doug. Always knew where you were with him. Even though he sometimes had a short fuse. Died far too young.'

Mary stiffened.

Reggie looked sheepish. 'Sorry, Mary, he's one of many who went too soon, as we both know only too well.'

Mary felt the familiar wave of sadness engulf her as, despite her happiness with Reggie, it sometimes did when she thought of the war and her experience as a prisoner of the Japanese. Then she told herself that she owed it to her mother, her father, and to all the others who had died, not to dwell on the past. As a survivor it was her duty to look forward not back, to make her life worthwhile and justify the fact that she had been spared when so many others had not.

Reggie put an arm around her shoulder. 'Shall we turn in? It's past ten.'

She never needed to explain to Reggie. While she knew none of the details about his wartime experiences as he too chose not to speak of them, she was certain he must have suffered too and seen things he'd rather forget. At least he no longer experienced night terrors and most of her own dreams were now devoid of the images that had haunted her in the year after she was freed from the camps.

Perhaps it was the gift of Frances. Every time Mary looked at her baby daughter she was filled with a fierce surge of love and a desire to protect her. Like a tiger with her cubs. She'd take on anyone or anything that threatened the wellbeing of the child.

Mary went into her daughter's bedroom and stood beside the cot, looking down at the sleeping baby, her face like a cherub's, all soft puffy cheeks and tiny rosebud lips. The child made a snuffling sound like a small animal. There was a movement beside her and Mary turned her head as Reggie approached. They stood silently together, hand-in-hand, for several minutes watching their daughter sleep. Then they moved, as one, to the door and their own bedroom.

9

W
alking with Mary in the early morning through the fringe of uncultivated jungle beyond the plantation, Jasmine's heart lightened with every step. Her sense of liberation grew. Those last weeks in Nairobi had been like wading through a sea of sludge, every day dragging her down, threatening to submerge and suffocate her.

It was not because of her family. She loved them all dearly. Her adored little brother, Hugh, her only living blood relative, Mummy, whom she loved more than anyone else in her life, and Arthur, who had become a steady presence in a world in which Jasmine felt increasingly disorientated. No, it was not any failing in her family. Jasmine knew she was loved and she loved them in return, all too aware she was fortunate. Yet she still had an uncomfortable feeling of being an outsider, a misfit, a cuckoo in the nest.

The time they'd spent together on the voyage out to Penang had brought Jasmine closer to Evie, enhancing her guilt about the decision to leave Kenya. Saying goodbye in

George Town yesterday had been painful. More painful than she had ever imagined. They had never been separated since Mummy had come to Penang and married Daddy when Jasmine was a small child. They had gone through the war years in Australia, cut off from everything they'd known – even though for Jasmine those four years in Perth, swimming in the Indian Ocean every day, going to school, making new friends, had been a carefree, happy time.

She hadn't enjoyed Mummy dragging her and Hugh to London, even though she'd understood why her mother had done it. She'd never complained, and had tried to be as supportive as possible to Evie. Her mother had been so brave then, coping alone with two children after Daddy had died, trying to build a new life for them all. Now, walking in the cool of the early morning air, Jasmine shivered at the memory of England. Those ugly, dirty, litter-strewn streets. The bomb sites on every corner, the choking smog, the dreary suburban house they'd rented in Surrey. It had all been so unremittingly dull and grey.

Kenya was different. Maybe it was because as soon as they joined Arthur, Mummy and Hugh immediately and obviously were enchanted by the country. But the vastness of Africa overwhelmed Jasmine, making her feel insignificant. There was also the air of self-satisfied smugness among the girls at school and their parents. Their sense of superiority and entitlement. The way they looked down on the indigenous Kenyan people.

Of course, the expats in Malaya all had servants but it didn't feel the same. Take Mary – she even dressed like a Malayan woman, wearing the *baju kurung* or the Chinese *cheongsam*. Imagine in Nairobi a white woman wearing a *kitenge*, the vibrantly colourful sarong worn throughout east

Africa. It was unthinkable. Here in Penang, the white people got along well with the Malays and Chinese for the most part, whereas in Africa there was a chasm between the whites and the indigenous tribes. The girls at school were all white and British, and all of them behaved as though they were God's chosen people and black people uncivilised savages. Only Katie had been different and felt the same as Jasmine.

On the ship, Mummy had suggested that perhaps Jasmine's feelings were less about dislike of these other girls specifically, and more about the changes she was going through growing up. Jasmine hated that idea. She hated the thought of growing up anyway. It was impossible to understand why the other girls were always giggling and talking about boys. They were all desperate to get married and have babies. Jasmine could think of nothing worse. It would be exchanging the prison of school for the prison of marriage.

She had nothing against marriage itself. After all, Mummy and Arthur were happy together and clearly Mary and Reggie were devoted to each other. But she couldn't imagine that for herself. Being stuck in a house all day. Having to live forever with one man. Having to sleep in the same bed with him and do the thing you had to do to have babies.

The two women walked on, Mary carrying her sleeping baby in a cloth sling, tied across her breast. The forest floor beneath their feet was soft and springy, carpeted with layers of damp leaves. Dramatic, dark grey clouds hung low among the treetops, resembling smoke. The cloudscape, together with damp vegetation hanging down from the branches like casually discarded green cloaks, gave the rain forest an ethereal ghostly air. Jasmine looked up at the tall thin trees stretching skywards, the trunks bare until the highest sections near the light, where the foliage was delicate, like fronds of parsley. Through the gloom all around them they could hear choruses of whooping and whistling, chirping and tweeting. She wondered what the birdsong was about. It had to be a conversation. What were these birds saying? They sounded happy. Could birds think? Were their lives as complicated as humans' were?

'I feel so alive here,' Jasmine whispered. 'It's a magic forest.'

Mary adjusted the sleeping Frances as she nuzzled against her shoulder. 'Magic? Perhaps. It does sometimes feel full of ghosts and spirits.'

Jasmine detected a note of sadness in the voice of her former teacher. 'Yes. That's exactly how it feels. As if we're not alone.' She paused. 'But it's not scary. Not at all.'

Mary glanced at her but said nothing.

'How far is the *kampong*?'

'We're almost there.' Mary pointed ahead. 'See where the sunlight is? That's the end of this part of the forest. About another quarter mile. The whole trip is only a mile and a half. It's twice the distance by the road.'

'How long has the school been going?'

'A couple of years. Reggie built it as soon as he returned to Bella Vista after the war. There was no teacher then. I tease him that he only married me because he couldn't persuade another teacher to move up here.' She smiled – it was a smile that lit up her whole face. 'But honestly, Jasmine, I think something made Reggie build it. He didn't have to. He told me it was a compulsion. Something made him believe that it was the right thing to do. Even though at the time there seemed little point.'

Jasmine frowned. 'Do you think it was God?' Then quickly she added, 'I mean maybe God guided him to build it knowing that you would come along in the end. Maybe God sent you to him.'

'I'm not sure I believe in God, Jasmine.'

Jasmine's eyes widened. 'Really? You don't believe in God?'

'I said I wasn't sure.'

Jasmine thought about that for a moment. 'I'm not sure either.'

'Then that must make us both agnostics.' Mary gave her another of her sad smiles.

'What does that mean exactly? What was the word again?'

'An agnostic is someone who is uncertain about the existence of God. Not to the point of not believing at all, as that would make you an atheist. But more someone who believes that it is impossible to ever know that God exists. That there's simply no means of proving whether He does, or He doesn't.'

'Agnostic.' Jasmine repeated the word, testing it on her tongue and liking the sound of it. 'Yes, that's what I am. An agnostic. Do you think you can be agnostic about other things as well as religion?'

'Like what?' Mary tilted her head, her expression quizzical.

'Life, everything.'

'I suppose so,' she said doubtfully. 'Although there's plenty of concrete evidence around us to indicate that we exist.'

'I don't mean the world, people, nature, that kind of thing. I mean believing in things in life that are expected of you. Like falling in love and getting married. That kind of stuff.'

'I see.' Mary nodded, thought for a moment then said, 'I

think that's different. An agnostic might want to prove the existence of God but can't, whereas what you're talking about is surely a matter of choices or circumstances. I mean many people do fall in love, others don't. As to marriage, some choose it, others don't. Some seek love but don't find it. Others find it but don't believe in it.'

Jasmine frowned. She wasn't sure what Mary was trying to say.

'I didn't believe in love when it found me. I'd turned my back on it.' Mary's lips tightened. 'It's thanks to your mother that I finally admitted to myself that I loved Reggie.'

'Really?' Jasmine's eyes widened. 'Mummy brought you two together?'

Mary nodded. 'I used to think love was too painful. Everything and everyone I ever loved was taken from me, so I tried to push it away so I couldn't get hurt again. It felt like standing on top of a cliff but being too terrified to jump. Instead, I clung to the edge in a state of abject fear and misery. Once Evie convinced me to let go, it was like flying. That dive off the cliff was one of the scariest things I've ever done but believe me, Jasmine, soaring through the air is so much better than cowering in fear. It's about letting go and believing.'

Jasmine was about to reply, but they had now reached an open space, beyond the jungle. Ahead of them was a line of wooden huts with thatched *attap* roofs. Mary pointed to the largest building, a few yards away from the others: a wooden hut with a wide veranda. A group of Tamil women were sitting on the steps, feeding babies and watching over their children, while others, clearly Malays, sat on the veranda doing the same. 'That's the school. Come on, Jasmine. I'll introduce you to the children.'

They moved between the two separate groups, each

group chatting in their own language. All of them broke off their chatter to greet Mary and smile in welcome to Jasmine. Mary unstrapped the still-sleeping Frances and handed the baby to one of the mothers. Turning to Jasmine, she said, 'The ladies take it in turns to look after Frances. I didn't want to leave her at home all the time with the *amah*. Poor Jinjiang would never get any work done. This arrangement works really well as I'm on hand when she needs me. She's weaned now but it meant I used to be able to feed her.' Lowering her voice, she said conspiratorially, 'And it means there's no risk of her getting more attached to her *amah* than me.'

The interior of the schoolroom was cool. Shafts of light came in from tall windows at the rear, the shade of trees protecting them from the extremes of the sun. There were neat rows of desks facing towards a blackboard at one end and, at the other end, a cluster of smaller chairs grouped in a circle. A little girl was standing on a stool writing the date on the top of the board in chalk. Three or four other children had already taken up positions at the desks. All of them chorused their good mornings and all were wearing crisp white shirts over their shorts or skirts.

'I'll introduce you once everyone's here.' Mary indicated the circle of chairs at the rear of the class. 'I wonder if you might read to the children while I teach their mums? Some of them are keen to learn to read and write too. Then later on you can help the older children with their reading.' She looked around. 'The classroom's rather basic but it does us well enough. We have a mixture of Tamil children from the rubber estate, and local Malays from this *kampong*.'

'What about Chinese?'

'Only two. A brother and sister from a small farm nearby. But the Chinese tend to go to the Chinese schools in

George Town.' Mary straightened up a chair. 'In most of the village schools, children are taught in their own language and go to separate schools. Here, we want to give them all a chance to be taught in English too. So, I teach in English three days a week and then on the other two days local teachers take classes in their own languages. Otherwise the children would be disadvantaged compared to those from wealthier families who can go to the English-language schools in George Town.'

'Like St Margaret's.' Jasmine referred to the school she had attended herself before the war, where Mary had been her class teacher.

'Exactly. The Malay children, whose parents tend to live hand-to-mouth from fishing and working in the rice paddies, would otherwise have only the most basic of education. It's the same throughout Malaya. The Tamils are educated on the rubber estates, the Chinese have their own schools and the more affluent attend the British schools. But the poor Malays tend to get a very basic education and many of the girls none at all.'

'It's like that in Kenya. Many African children miss out altogether. My school was entirely white girls.' Jasmine felt a sudden rush of guilt at her own absconding from school. She'd had the opportunities for a privileged education and had shunned them.

Mary nodded. 'Of course, the government does sponsor local schools, and there are still mission schools, but they all tend to teach a narrow, British-oriented view of the world.'

Jasmine grimaced. 'Same at my old school. I never did understand the point of learning so much about English history and so little about the rest of the world.'

'Well, we do what we can here, but not as much as I'd like. School is only in the mornings and we have very little money. I work here unpaid, otherwise it wouldn't be possible at all. What little money we get from the government is barely enough to cover stationery and a few books. The rest comes from Bella Vista's profits.' She rolled her eyes. 'So not very much!'

The desks were filling up, and with a last glance at Jasmine, Mary clapped her hands. 'Good morning, children.'

This was met with a sing-song response. 'Good morning, Mrs Hyde-Underwood.' It sounded more like High-Onyud.

'We have a new teacher joining us today. This is Miss Barrington.'

'Good morning, Missee Bang-ton,' the children chorused.

JASMINE WAS surprised how quickly the morning passed. As well as story-telling and listening to the children read, she supervised them in a game of rounders while Mary was occupied teaching their mums and then it was time to head back to Bella Vista.

She grinned widely as Mary strapped the baby back into her sling. 'I enjoyed today so much. The children were such darlings. So well-behaved and eager to learn.'

'Yes, that's what makes it rewarding.' Mary smiled. 'I'm going to speak to Reggie and see if he can spare a bit of extra cash to order some paper and paints so you can teach an art class. It would free up more time for me to help the mothers. What do you think?'

'Really?' Jasmine's eyes widened. 'I'd love that.'

'Now, I don't know about you, but I'm rather hungry and this little one will soon be hungry too, so let's head for home.'

They walked across the open ground and into the gloom of the jungle, following the path back to the estate.

Jasmine was tired, but exhilarated. For the first time in longer than she could remember, she felt useful, needed and with a sense of purpose.

10

Today, Friday, was one of those weekdays when Mary didn't teach. After breakfast, when Reggie had left on his rounds of the estate, Mary announced that she was leaving the baby with Jinjiang, the *amah*, and she and Jasmine were to go into George Town.

'I managed to get Reggie to cough up some lolly for art materials,' she said with a grin.

'Really? How marvellous.' Jasmine clasped her hands together in delight. 'It will make such a difference to the children.'

The few days she had spent in George Town with her mother had been mainly within the grounds of the E&O and at the Swimming Club at Tanjung Bungah, so Jasmine was looking forward to rediscovering the streets of George Town. She decided to wear a daisy-patterned, Indian cotton dress her mother had bought for her in Colombo. She knew it suited her and she felt confident wearing it. It was also deliciously cool, thanks to the full skirt.

Bintang drove them down the winding roads from Bella Vista. 'Go past the racecourse, along Macalister Road, please, Bintang.' Mary turned to Jasmine and said. 'You may not remember, but as it's April the angsana trees will be blossoming.'

Jasmine frowned. 'No, I don't remember them.'

'Treat in store then.'

Bintang steered the motorcar as directed and, after a few minutes, Jasmine gave a cry of pleasure. As the racecourse appeared on their right, ahead of them, the wide road, verges and pavements were a bright yellow carpet, The trees were heavy with more blossom, the branches drooping under the weight of the flowers.

'Can we stop for a moment, please? I'd love to make a very quick sketch. To capture the shape of the trees. I'm going to paint this as soon as I get home.'

The *syce* eased the vehicle to a stop and Jasmine jumped out. She bent down and gathered up a handful of blossoms, pushing them into her pocket. 'I want to get the colour exactly right,' she said. 'I wonder why I don't remember seeing this when I was a child.'

'Every April.' Mary, still inside the car, had opened the door wide to let more air in. 'Each blossom only lasts a day. It's magnificent, isn't it?' She swung her legs out of the car but remained seated. Meanwhile, Bintang got out of the driver's seat, walked across to sit on the low fence separating the road from the racecourse, and lit a cigarette.

Jasmine knelt down on the yellow-carpeted grass verge and took her sketchbook and pencil out of the satchel she carried with her everywhere. She could feel Bintang's eyes on her from the other side of the road, but when she looked up, he turned away to look over the racecourse.

In a few minutes, Jasmine had what she wanted, and the driver had finished his cigarette. They resumed their journey into the centre of George Town.

'We'll go to Whiteaway's for the art materials and what we can't get there I'm sure we'll find in one of the Chinese calligraphy stores or in the market.' Mary turned to the *syce*. 'We'll be having lunch, so could you please pick us up from the Penang Club, Bintang. Shall we say, three o'clock?' She looked at Jasmine who nodded, secretly disappointed that they weren't to stay in George Town longer. She told herself there'd be other opportunities.

'I'm not terribly keen on the Club and we women are only allowed in The Grill Room anyway, but since the Runnymede is closed, I thought The Grill would be a change from the E&O,' Mary explained.

Jasmine was delighted by Mary's including her as 'we women' as it made her feel grown-up. She was also relieved not to be going to the E&O as it would make her sad that Evie wasn't there with them. Her memories of the Penang Club were entirely based on her one and only visit for a huge party thrown by the parents of her best friend at school, Penny. Jasmine still remembered how thrilling it had been to be sitting with the other children cross-legged on the lawn, watching a magician do conjuring tricks, only for Daddy to decide all of a sudden they were going home. Funny how the memory of being broken-hearted at being dragged away was more vivid than any recollection of the Club itself, its grounds or the other children present.

Whiteaway, Laidlaw & Co was on Bishop Street at the corner with Beach Street, near the Fort, and Jasmine felt a rush of nostalgia as they entered the department store. She remembered Mummy bringing her here for new frocks and school uniforms. That was before the terrible morning when the Japanese bombers flew over the island, strafing and bombing, forcing the entire European population to flee.

Inside the store, Mary bought up all the available stock of poster paints, cheap paintbrushes and everyday art paper, but the shop promised to order more and deliver it to Bella Vista within the next few days.

Satisfied with their purchases, they made their way from the bustle of Beach Street, past Fort Cornwallis and along The Esplanade where small children were playing tag on the *padang* with the sea beyond it. There were more angsana trees on the roadside and the blindingly bright blossoms had covered a parked motorcar.

They walked on, arm-in-arm, beyond the green expanse of the *padang* and the long stretch of the E&O, facing the sea. Out in the Straits, numerous sampans and small boats moved out into the wider channel where larger vessels made their way past the Fort to the harbour. Jasmine could have burst with happiness as she listened to the ship's horns, the clamour of seabirds and the gentle rush of waves lapping the shore. She could never feel this way about Africa. Where they lived was close to the vast and empty plains, the rightful domain of the animals. Penang was very much a place for people. All around, they were going about their business, on land and sea. Yes, there were people in the villages in Africa, and Nairobi was a big bustling city, but it wasn't the same. Here was a perfect communion of man and nature, a buzzing melée of life, from sea and sky, to the little boats, the heavily-laden ox carts, the colourful street markets and Chinese temples, the elegant white colonial buildings and the tumble of shop-houses crammed together, lining the busy streets.

They drew near the former Runnymede Hotel, another white colonial building, built on the site of the single-storey house Stamford Raffles built for himself and his wife when he was a junior administrator in Penang. Raffles' house had burned down long ago and been replaced by The Runnymede, with its magnificent ballroom and orchestra. The hotel had been popular among the expatriate community before the war, for dinner-dances.

'Is it shut down?'

'As a hotel, yes,' replied Mary. 'Since the war it's been used by the military. As far as I know it's an officers' mess and maybe accommodation too.'

'What a pity.' Jasmine peered through the wire fencing at the building behind and the military vehicles parked in the driveway.

'It was beautiful. They used to serve dinner on the lawns looking out over the Straits. The hotel had its own post office and a railway ticket office, a big fleet of chauffeured cars, even a bookshop and a hairdresser.'

'Do you think it will ever be a hotel again?'

Mary shook her head. 'I very much doubt it. There isn't the demand anymore. Not since the war. I doubt there ever will be again. The E&O finds it hard enough and it's still a shabby shadow of what it used to be. Before the war, the planters, the tin mine managers, civil servants, RAF officers, everyone who was anyone, would all come over to Penang for weekends. People came up from Kuala Lumpur and Singapore as well as the mainland estates for a spot of relaxation.'

'Don't they still?'

'I suppose so, but it's not the same. They're mostly different people and they have a different view on life. And so many didn't make it through the war.'

Jasmine looked sideways at Mary, who sounded distant, faraway, as though she were somewhere else. Maybe she was remembering how it was then and feeling nostalgic. Jasmine's mother had told her neither of Mary's parents had survived the war and Reggie's RAF brother, Mary's fiancé, had been shot down over the Straits and killed during the first attacks on Penang by the Japanese. She was trying to think of something to say to change the subject, but Mary lifted her head up and smiled. It was that smile she so often made, that wasn't a real smile at all, just her mouth turning up at the corners.

'Here we are. Let's hope it's not too busy as I haven't booked a table.' Mary indicated the sweeping driveway between two large angsana trees. The women stepped through the petal carpet and up to the pink-brick, Victorian clubhouse.

Inside, they were led past the portrait of a fierce-looking Queen Victoria and into The Grill, where they were placed at a small table in the corner, near the entrance to the kitchen.

'This is one of the many reasons I don't like the Club,' said Mary as they sat down. 'On the rare occasions when I've been here with Reggie, we're given a table by the window. Women without their husbands are only allowed in here on sufferance and are hidden away in a corner. I find that extremely annoying.' She glared at the waiter as he handed her the menu. Then breathing slowly, she brightened. 'But the food here is excellent, I will say that.'

It was two-thirty when they finished their lunch, and Mary suggested they walk down onto the beach until it was time to meet the driver. They took the steps from the veranda that faced the sea and started to walk across the lawn to the beach.

'I say!' A familiar voice called out to them. Jasmine instinctively sped up, but Mary stopped, so she had no choice but to stop too.

Howard Baxter bounded down the veranda steps and was running towards them over the lawn.

'Mr Baxter.' A smiling Mary held out her hand to greet the young man. 'What brings you to the Club on a Friday? I thought you were working over at Batu Lembah.'

Jasmine stood sullenly to one side, inwardly cursing that she hadn't spotted Howard, so they could have taken a more circuitous route out of his sight.

'Yes, that's right. I had a training meeting in George Town this morning at the Guthrie's office so I'm making a weekend of it. Wasn't worth heading back to the estate for what's left of today. There's a skittle alley here and some of the chaps have invited me to have a game. We're warming up with a couple of beers.' He beamed at Mary before fixing his eyes on Jasmine. 'What terrific luck to run into you. And I must say, that's a very pretty frock, Jasmine.'

'We're about to go,' said Jasmine, ignoring the compliment and deciding she'd gone off her new dress. 'The driver's meeting us here in a minute.'

'Twenty-five minutes, actually,' said Mary. 'We're going to have a stroll on the beach while we're waiting.'

Jasmine seethed. Why was Mary doing this?

'Mind if I join you then? We don't get on for our game till three.' He indicated the long narrow building that housed the skittle alley, attached to the clubhouse.

'I thought you were having a drink with friends.' Jasmine knew she was being ungracious but she was annoyed at Baxter's persistence. Hadn't Mummy said it was highly unlikely she'd ever run into him in Penang?

'Oh, they won't mind at all.' He turned to Mary. 'Did you have tiffin here?'

'Yes. We didn't see you in The Grill.'

'No. I ate in the dining room at the office. Dreary affair it was too.'

By now they had reached the beach. The three of them strolled along close to the water's edge as the white-fringed waves lapped the shore. Jasmine maintained a sullen silence as Mary chatted to Howard.

'How are you enjoying the new job, Mr Baxter?'

'Oh, please call me Howard, Mrs Hyde-Underwood.'

'Then you must call me Mary.'

Jasmine groaned audibly, but Mary, on the other side of Howard who had inserted himself between the two of them, didn't appear to hear and Howard ignored it.

'I absolutely love it, Mary. Jolly hard work, but extremely interesting. Although, as I'm the lowest of the low, I get to do all the worst jobs. Apparently as the new boy I get to be called "the creeper". They tell me it's because all the juniors creep around pretending to know what they're doing and hoping nobody will notice that we don't.'

Mary laughed. 'I suppose you get to do the check rolls?'

'How did you know?' His eyebrows shot up.

'I'm married to a planter. On every estate, the junior assistant is responsible for tallying them up.' Mary leaned forward to look beyond Howard to Jasmine, who was still maintaining a resolute silence. 'The check roll is the list of every estate worker and the hours they work each day and a record of any absences. Keeping the records and making sure they match is an essential job, but apparently frightfully tedious.'

'My father was a planter so I know that.' Actually she didn't. But she wasn't going to give either Baxter or Mary the satisfaction of admitting it.

'Of course, you do.' Mary looked hurt and Jasmine felt guilty; it was unfair to blame Howard's intrusion on Mary.

Deciding she needed to get away from Howard, Jasmine said, 'Look, why don't you two walk on while I go and sit over there and do a quick sketch.'

Mary and Howard exchanged glances but kept on walking and Jasmine made her escape. She knew she was behaving badly but she really didn't like Howard Baxter. He was far too full of himself. Just because he was good looking, he seemed to expect her to fall at his feet in adoration, but she wasn't going to. Not ever. Besides, he was boring. Who wanted to hear all about his stupid job anyway? Not her.

Jasmine sat down on the sand, took out her sketchbook but didn't even open it. She hugged her knees with her arms. He'd spoilt a beautiful day. And now, not only Mummy, but Mary too, was falling under his spell. It was too annoying. She stared out at the Strait, but any desire to draw the bobbing sampans and junks and the Kedah Peak veiled by clouds, had deserted her. He'd ruined it.

She glanced at her watch. It was already five to three. Howard and Mary had turned around and were heading back towards her. She fiddled with the straps of her satchel, pretending to be putting away her sketchbook, and got to her feet, brushing the sand off her dress.

To her annoyance, Howard walked with them back to the car. Jasmine mumbled a goodbye, avoiding all eye contact and got into the back of the car, as Bintang held the door open for her. Mary continued to stand conversing with Howard, even though Bintang was waiting patiently with the other passenger door open ready for her.

With a cheery wave, Mary finally clambered in beside Jasmine. 'Your mother's right. He is a very charming young man.'

Jasmine groaned. 'Not you too!'

'And Evie is probably right about something else.'

'What's that?'

'That as you are so incredibly rude to the poor chap the only possible conclusion is that you're nursing a crush on him.'

Jasmine's gasp was explosive. 'What? That's completely ridiculous!' It was as if Mary had punched her in the stomach. 'You and Mummy were talking about me?'

'Of course, we were. I am after all *in loco parentis* while you're staying here. It's only natural that we should have talked about you.'

Jasmine was aware of Bintang's eyes in the driver's rearview mirror. She felt a rush of humiliation.

Ignoring Jasmine's indignation, Mary went on. 'I've invited Howard up to Bella Vista for supper tomorrow. In fact, I've asked him to stay overnight. Much nicer than the scruffy old Station Hotel in Butterworth, where he's been staying.' She smiled at Jasmine. 'It will give you a chance to make up for your childish behaviour towards him today. And since he doesn't have to meet his lift until Sunday evening, you may want to think about exploring some of the sights of George Town with him on Sunday.'

Jasmine was ready to express that she'd rather be dead, but remembered that she was, after all, Mary's house guest. And she had been rude to Mary as well as to Baxter. Ashamed and annoyed, she realised she had brought all this upon herself.

11

After breakfast on Saturday morning, still nursing a sense of grievance about Howard Baxter, Jasmine decided to head off alone. Carrying her satchel of art materials, she went to explore the Bella Vista estate. Jasmine didn't know the plantation, even though it had been her father's and she had lived here for a while as a baby. Later, her family had gone to live on the peninsula at Batu Lembah, but Jasmine had been sent off to board with the nuns at a convent school near there when only five, so she had little memory of Batu Lembah either. Most of her childhood had been spent in the family home in the centre of George Town. Mummy still owned it, but it was now let out to tenants.

Jasmine started off down one of the mown grass alleys between the serried ranks of rubber trees. The tall brown trunks were mottled and bare. Higher up, gaps in the leaf canopy allowed narrow rays of sunlight to filter down and dapple the grass beneath. The trunks bore the scars of the rubber tapping – diagonal stripes, snaking down to meet the little metal cups attached by wire. The air was thick with the smell of latex and it caught in Jasmine's throat.

She walked up to one of the trees and peered inside the metal collection cup, watching the constant, hypnotic drip of the thick, white sap as it filled the cup, running down the edge of the cut strip in the trunk, like lava. It was as if the trees were bleeding milk. She dipped a finger into the cup, touching the sticky, viscous liquid, then wiped her finger dry on the bark of the tree.

It was relatively cool up here in the plantation, thanks to the elevation and the shade afforded by the tree cover. Jasmine looked about, wondering what to draw. Capturing the stippled light, the dark and shade between the trunks, would make an interesting abstract study. But, after hesitating a few moments, she moved on.

As she walked, she couldn't help rehashing the events of the previous afternoon. She dreaded the prospect of meeting Howard Baxter again, particularly after the comment Mary had made about her secretly nursing a crush on him. It was such a betrayal by Mummy. And so unfair. Untrue as well. Wasn't it?

She cringed, remembering how she had caught Bintang's eye watching her in the rear-view mirror. What must he think of her? The utter humiliation. He would consider her a complete idiot. It was extremely frustrating, as she liked Bintang and would like to get to know him better. One of her hopes about coming back to Penang was that she might meet Malayans rather than lots of other white people, and Bintang was intelligent and interesting. Now, he'd think she was like all the other British girls – wanting nothing more than to bag a planter and settle into life as a *mem*, when that was the last thing she wanted.

Everything had been so simple and uncomplicated until

Howard Baxter had come along and messed it all up. Was there something wrong with her? Was she incapable of fitting in anywhere? Why did life get harder, the older you got?

Eventually, she reached the end of a division where the land opened up and fell away down a steep slope, the rubber trees sweeping down towards the plain below and the sea beyond. Perfect. She found a spot under a hardwood tree which stood alone, apart from the rows of rubber, and set herself up in the shade beneath it. As the ground was damp, she sat on a small folding stool Mary had found for her.

As always when she was painting or drawing, Jasmine became so absorbed in her work that she lost track of time, and the thoughts that had been weighing her down vanished. In her focus and concentration, she didn't notice him until he was a few feet away.

'Bintang!' she cried. 'Where did you pop up from?'

'I visit grandmother. In *kampong*, down in valley.' He pointed towards a distant collection of buildings on the plain below. 'I disturb you?'

'No, not at all. I'm only doing some sketching.'

Unlike Howard Baxter, who hadn't even bothered to inquire if he was intruding on her when she'd been painting on the ship, Bintang was polite. He showed no curiosity about what she was drawing, or even the fact that she was doing it at all. How refreshing! Yet, at the same time, it was rather unflattering.

The driver leaned against a rubber tree opposite her and lit a cigarette. He looked out over the plain below and said nothing.

Eventually, Jasmine broke the silence. 'How was your grandmother?'

'She well,' he said.

'Do you visit her often?'

'When I can. She only family I have left.'

'It must be nice to have a grandmother. My grandparents died before I was born. My parents are dead too. Although I have my stepmother and my little brother. Well, half-brother. And I have a step-grandmother in America but nobody hears from her, not even Mummy.' She wondered if she was babbling.

'I know. Your father used to be *tuan besar*. Big boss. New *tuan* worked for him.' By new *tuan*, he was referring to Reggie, who had been the estate manager here while Daddy was alive and had bought the estate from Mummy after the war.

Jasmine put down her pencil. 'What happened to the rest of your family? When we were at the beach you told me Siti died in the war. I've been thinking about that and wondering what happened. We never got to finish our talk.'

Bintang turned to look at her, his eyes narrowing. He was tall for a Malayan, his nose long and straight, his brows dark and frowning over brown eyes. 'One day we are in fields working. Siti, me, and mother. Japanese come to take my mother.' He drew on his cigarette. 'To be comfort lady. She say them she cannot go with them as she need to care for Siti. So, they shoot my sister dead.' He mimed a gunshot with his fingers. 'In front of us.'

His eyes fixed on Jasmine's as he spoke. She wanted to look away yet couldn't.

'They drag my mother off into lorry, screaming and crying.' He stared at Jasmine. She felt as though he were challenging her, maybe even accusing her. 'I never see my mother again. Grandmother and me, we bury my little sister.' He threw away the butt of his cigarette into the long wet grass. 'Siti only nine. You were same age. You left Penang. You went on train to Singapore with all the white people.'

Jasmine started to speak, wanting to explain that, as a child, she'd had no choice, but Bintang fixed his eyes on her and she became tongue-tied, her eyes brimming.

'My father come home that night and when we say him mother gone with Japanese and Siti is dead, he is angry and go to join jungle fighters. He go to kill Japanese. I want to go too. I was thirteen. But he say me I must care for grandmother. He never come home again. Even when war over. Perhaps he died too.'

'I'm so sorry, Bintang. That's terrible. What a tragic story. Your whole family gone.'

He looked at her coldly, and Jasmine felt for a moment as though he were blaming her for their deaths. At last his expression changed and his eyes lit up. 'I have grandmother. We care for each other. She is very kind lady.'

'Did you ever find out what happened to your mother?'

'You know what comfort lady is?'

Jasmine felt the blood rush to her face. 'I think so.'

'If she alive, she too shame to come home after war.'

'Have you ever tried to find her?'

Bintang, his eyes still fixed on the valley below, said, 'When someone not want to be found, hard to find them.'

There was something about the expression on the young man's face that made her wonder if he might not want to find his mother. She felt a chill, despite the warmth of the afternoon.

They lapsed into silence and after a few minutes Bintang lit another cigarette. 'So, you like the man who comes here tonight? *Tuan* Baxter? He talk to you and the *mem*s when you come off ship. He is your boyfriend?'

Jasmine's stomach lurched. She'd put her anxieties about Howard Baxter aside and now they resurfaced in a rush. 'No. Of course he's not. Mrs Hyde-Underwood was teasing me. I barely know him. And I have no interest in him whatsoever.' She knew she was blushing again and felt the driver's eyes on her. She turned away to scrabble in her satchel for a pencil sharpener to cover her embarrassment.

'I go to George Town to pick him up and bring him here. *Mem* say tomorrow I drive you and *Tuan* Baxter round the island, where you want to go.'

She felt his eyes on her again and wondered if he was laughing at her, but his face was serious. It was always serious. She didn't think she'd seen him smile in the time she'd been in Penang. 'I think it would be better if you took him around the island without me.'

'Don't you want to see island? *Mem* say I take you to Penang Hill and Botanic Gardens. See places you know when you child before war.'

'I can always go another time.' She tried to look as if the whole idea was a big bore.

Bintang shrugged. 'Same to me if you come or just your boyfriend.'

'He's not my boyfriend.' She spoke in a rush, indignation rising.

Bintang pushed himself off the tree. 'Soon time for me to go get him and I must wash car first. *Tuan* want car cleaned every Saturday.' Was there a hint of contempt in the curl of his mouth? 'Goodbye, Missee Barrington.'

As he started to walk away, she called after him. 'Please call me Jasmine. After all, Siti was a schoolfriend of mine. I'd like to be friends with you too.' She gave him a smile.

He frowned, but then nodded. 'Goodbye, Missee

Jasmine.' And then he was gone, walking quickly back through the lines of rubber trees toward the house.

After he had disappeared from view, Jasmine thought about the fate of her schoolfriend. The savagery of those Japanese soldiers in killing a little girl because she was an inconvenience made her shudder. Siti had been a pretty child, bright, warm, always smiling. At the moment her life had been snuffed out, Jasmine would have been sleeping on a crowded train to Singapore or on a ship for Australia. How had they been dealt such different fates? Bintang seemed to be reining in his anger. Suppressing his feelings beneath a veneer of politeness. Little wonder.

12

J asmine examined her reflection critically in the mirror. She was wearing a beige cotton dress that had been part of her school uniform in Nairobi. Her intent was to make herself look as unattractive as possible, in an effort to put off Howard Baxter. It also might help underline their age difference and cause him to think again about chasing after her.

But as she looked at the sun-faded cotton, she knew it was not a look she wanted for herself. Why on earth would she choose to look ugly? It was also insulting to her hosts, who were laying on a special meal and would be dressed formally themselves. No, Jasmine had to acknowledge she was being childish. She'd let that bigheaded planter get under her skin. It was ridiculous to let him rule her life like this.

He'd mentioned that he was known at Batu Lembah as 'the creeper'. She smiled to herself – creeper was the perfect name for someone she had already decided was a complete creep. Yet perhaps admitting that he was known by that name was an indication that he wasn't actually that bigheaded after all.

Jasmine frowned at the mirror and reached behind her to unfasten the buttons at the back of her dress. She would wear her new, blue silk frock and the ring Mummy had given her. Better to look and feel confident as she faced the enemy.

Taking the dress from its hanger, she remembered Mummy helping her choose it on that shopping spree in Colombo. She pulled it over her head and ran her hands over the soft lustrous fabric. It was shot silk, and as she twirled in front of the mirror, the full skirt caught the light and shimmered, the blue changing to a deeper hue, closer to purple then back to blue again. She felt better already.

There was a tap on the door and Mary entered the bedroom.

Jasmine gasped. 'Oh, Mary! You look so beautiful.' A flood of relief ran through her as she realised how dreadful she would have felt if she'd kept that old school frock on.

Mary was in a cream, bias-cut, evening gown with a deep V-neck. It hugged her slight figure tightly. 'So do you, dear girl. That dress is absolutely stunning. Look how it shimmers when you move.'

'Thank you. Yours is too. You usually wear Malayan styles.'

'This is from years ago. Reggie saw it in the back of the wardrobe and convinced me to put it on. Not really my thing, but he insisted.'

'He has good taste. You look absolutely gorgeous.'

'I wanted to let you know that our guest has arrived and is having a sharpener on the veranda with Reggie, so come through as soon as you're ready.'

Deciding there was no point in delaying the inevitable,

Jasmine told her she was ready now and the two women went out to join the men for drinks.

Reggie and Howard jumped to their feet as soon as they appeared.

'What a feast for tired eyes,' said Reggie, smiling broadly, his eyes darting between the two women before settling on Mary, as he reached for her hand.

Jasmine had readied herself to bat away the attentions of Howard but, to her chagrin, he paid her no attention at all. It was as if she were invisible. He focused his attention on his hostess then the conversation moved on to rubber, as Reggie quizzed the younger man. Mary excused herself to consult with the cook in the kitchen and Jasmine felt like a spare part as the men discussed latex yields and Reggie inquired about people he knew at Batu Lembah.

'Worked there myself once,' said Reggie. 'I was a Dunlop man and worked on the estate next to BL. Jasmine's father lured me away from Dunlop's and gave me a job when he bought BL back in '31. The place was in a terrible state and he eventually moved over there himself and got me to take over Bella Vista. Of course this is an altogether smaller enterprise, but it suits me well. My first wife hated BL – couldn't stand the heat so Bella Vista was preferable. But it turned out she hated Malaya in general. Left me after the war.' He took a swig of his *stengah*, draining the glass. 'Good thing too, as it happens. Otherwise I'd never have ended up with Mary.' He smiled. 'She and the baby are the best things that ever happened to me.' He held his hand out for Howard's glass. 'Let me freshen that up for you, old chap.'

Howard relinquished his whisky tumbler and leaned back in his chair. 'You're a lucky man, sir.' He was still ignoring Jasmine.

She wasn't sure which was worse – being pestered by

him or treated as though she were invisible. She decided to try a new tack and be distantly friendly. After all he seemed to have got over his infatuation. 'What did you do in George Town last night?'

Howard turned and looked at her for the first time, his eyes revealing nothing. 'Some of us went along to a thrash at the Sports Club.'

Mary reappeared. 'What was that in aid of?'

'Twenty-first birthday party for the daughter of one of the Guthrie's estate managers. Apparently everyone who's anyone was there, and I must say it was chock full of very pretty girls. I don't think I stopped dancing all evening.'

Jasmine seethed – then asked herself why. This was actually good news. Howard Baxter had evidently moved past his stupid crush on her, as Mummy had predicted. It was what she'd been hoping for...wasn't it?

Mary looked at Jasmine, her lips stretched tight and frowning slightly. 'That's the kind of thing you're missing out on, Jasmine, being stuck up here in the hills. I do hope you aren't going to get bored and lonely.'

Reggie passed Howard his *stengah*. 'Any time Jasmine wants to go into George Town we can get the *syce* to run her in and pick her up later.'

'But how's she going to get to know people in the first place? Maybe we ought to throw a little party at the Club or the E&O to introduce her to some young people.' Mary addressed Reggie but glanced at Howard.

Jasmine felt humiliated again, terrified Howard was going to volunteer to take her out. 'Don't worry about me,' she said, embarrassed. 'I hate all that kind of thing. I'm perfectly happy up here. I can think of nothing worse than going to a dance.'

Before anyone could respond, the *amah* appeared and announced that dinner was ready and they moved through to the dining room.

To Jasmine's relief, the topic of her going out and meeting people was not returned to. They sat down to enjoy the meal, the highlight of which was an enormous joint of roast beef. Reggie and Howard tucked in with relish and Jasmine observed that, as usual, Mary ate like a sparrow and what she did manage to consume was mostly vegetables. Unlike Mummy, who enjoyed her gin, Mary barely drank at all.

The conversation was almost entirely between the two men, and soon moved on to the political situation.

'The damn commies are everywhere,' said Reggie. 'Trade unionists crawling all over the country. You had any strikes?'

'Not at Batu Lembah. We have a pretty happy workforce. But there have been strikes threatened at some of the other Guthrie's estates. It was one of the things talked about at the meeting I went to yesterday.'

'It's all the Maoists. The blighters were on our side against the Japs but the darn government failing to grant citizenship to the Chinese has screwed things up for everybody. And not a peep from Government House about granting independence, so that's upset the Malays as well. No wonder the commies find fertile ground for their propaganda. Mark my words, there'll be bloody civil war here if we're not careful.'

'Reggie!' Mary looked at Jasmine with alarm. 'You'll frighten the poor girl.'

He turned to Jasmine. 'Sorry, my dear. I get a bit hot under the collar when I think what a mess some of our countrymen have made of things.'

'How so? I'm still trying to figure out Malayan politics.' Howard put down his knife and fork and focused his attention on Reggie. 'I've been so caught up with trying to learn the ropes and spending late nights poring over the check rolls. And to be honest, I don't like to ask too many questions. Being the new boy.'

'Ah, the creeper, eh? Yes, probably best to keep your head down and get on with it until you know the lie of the land.' Reggie paused to chew a piece of beef. 'But to answer your question, the army made a hash of things when the BMA was running the country immediately after the war. Lost the trust of the locals. High-handed and stupid. And I think some of the jungle fighters got a taste for battle and don't want to stop. Having finished off the Japs they want to get shot of us too.'

'But surely there can't be many of them still out there in the jungle?'

'You'd be surprised. They reckon about five thousand. You heard of Chin Peng?'

Howard shook his head.

Jasmine listened, finding, to her surprise, she was interested.

'He's a Chinese communist who worked with the British during the war, behind the lines. After the Japs surrendered, we pinned a medal on him, but if you ask me, we should have thrown the blighter out of the country or locked him up. Trouble with some of my countrymen is they assume everyone plays by the rules. Does the decent thing. Believe their former comrades in arms would never turn on 'em.' He stabbed the air with his knife. 'But let me tell you, Baxter, our boys dropped a ton of weaponry into the jungle by parachute and barely any of it was returned after the war.

'Force 136. You heard of them? A small band of British

secret intelligence and army types who worked against the Japs. They got into bed with the Chinese led by Chin Peng and another chap. What was his name, Mary?' Reggie frowned in concentration. 'After the war the fellow was overthrown by Chin Peng but he double-crossed him and ran off with all the party funds.' He slapped the table. 'Lai Tek, that was his name.' Reggie grinned in satisfaction. 'Rumour was he was a Special Branch agent. In the pay of the British. Probably disappeared over the border into Thailand. Never heard of since. Story is Chin Peng had him murdered in Bangkok and I wouldn't be at all surprised. Anyway, there was enough weaponry airdropped in for an army. Apparently, Chin Peng and his boys buried it underground deep in the jungle, so we could end up being attacked with our own weapons.' He turned to look at Jasmine. 'Your stepfather was in Force 136, I've heard. He ever talk about it? He must have known Lai Tek and Chin Peng.'

'Arthur? Was he really?' Jasmine struggled to imagine her civil servant stepfather as a guerrilla fighter.

'That's what I heard but I don't know the details.'

'Arthur never talks about the war. Maybe he does to Mummy but certainly not to me.'

'Brave lot those Force 136 boys. All that time living in the jungle, risking being turned in to the Japanese. Hard to hide when you're a white man, sticking out like the proverbial sore thumb. I suppose it's no wonder that the top military don't want to turn on Chin Peng and his like. They were a band of brothers.' Reggie shook his head. 'But the war's over and it's obvious he and his pals want to turn Malaya into a Chinese communist state.'

Mary spoke at last. 'I think we've had enough war and politics for one evening.'

Reggie looked stricken. 'Forgive me. I have rather gone

on a bit, haven't I? Sorry, ladies.'

'I thought it was jolly interesting,' said Jasmine. 'Specially the bit about Arthur.' She grinned. 'I can't imagine him as a jungle fighter.'

Reggie looked as though he was about to respond but thought better of it. 'So, Baxter, Mary tells me you're going to be shown round the island by our delightful house guest tomorrow.'

Jasmine felt herself blushing. She had hoped that might have been forgotten and wondered how she could get out of it. Glancing at Howard, she couldn't tell what he was thinking as he was still avoiding her eyes. What was the matter with the man? One minute declaring he was nuts about her and now acting as if she were invisible.

Mary said, 'As you probably know, Howard, Jasmine left the island when she was only nine, so she's keen to rediscover it. I'm afraid we've been rather negligent since she's been staying with us.'

'No, you haven't at all.' Jasmine was vehement. 'It's paradise up here. I love the quiet and as long as I have my sketchbook, I don't need any other entertainment.'

Reggie cut in again. 'Anyway, my driver is at your disposal for the day tomorrow.'

'I thought you could show Howard the Botanical Gardens – you used to love the waterfalls and the monkeys when you were a little girl,' said Mary.

Jasmine bit her tongue before she could retort that she wasn't a child anymore.

'You like monkeys?' Howard Baxter addressed Jasmine for the first time that evening. 'I'd never have expected that.' He looked amused.

How patronising. The man was insufferable. How was she going to get through a whole day with him tomorrow? And with Bintang to witness it all. She prayed that once they were away from Mary and Reggie, Howard wouldn't start all that nonsense he had subjected her to on the ship again.

13

After looking in on her sleeping daughter, Mary returned to the bedroom.

'I think that went rather well.' Reggie was already sitting up in bed, waiting for her. 'Frances all right?'

'Fast asleep. And yes, everyone enjoyed the meal. I was relieved Jasmine wasn't in a huff. And maybe Evie was exaggerating when she said Howard was smitten.'

'He seems a decent chap.'

'He is. And very charming. I was dreading Jasmine being as rude to him as she was yesterday, but she was perfectly civil. And he didn't actually appear to be interested in her at all.'

Reggie tilted his head in a smile. 'I may well have had something to do with that.'

Mary paused, hairbrush in hand. 'And exactly how?'

'We had a bit of a chinwag before you two joined us. He's a surprisingly frank young man. Told me he has a thing for the lass. Absolutely besotted. I did point out that she was still very young but he doesn't believe that should be a barrier. So, I told him nothing gets a gal more interested than giving her the impression you're not interested in her.'

'Reggie Hyde-Underwood! What a devious chap you are. I wouldn't have expected that of you.'

'Well, it worked with you didn't it?'

'What are you talking about?'

'When you sent me away with a flea in my ear.'

'I didn't!'

'Of course you did, darling girl. You know jolly well you did. It was in your garden. And I can't tell you how low I felt after that and how many times I had to stop myself jumping in the car and driving back down to George Town to try to change your mind. But I stayed away and in the end you came to me, and thank God you did.'

'It's completely different. There was the little matter of me being pregnant.'

'Do you mean you only married me because of Frances?' Reggie looked crestfallen but Mary knew he was following a ritual they often went through.

She put on her nightgown and climbed into the bed beside him.

Reggie leaned towards her and kissed her slowly.

'Same goes for you,' Mary said. 'If I hadn't come up here that afternoon, you might never have asked me again.'

'I most certainly would. I'd have had to crack eventually. But would you have said yes the next time?'

'I probably would have said yes five minutes after I said no the first time.'

They kissed again.

'I do rather like Howard. Jasmine could do a lot worse,' said Mary. 'But she's very young. Probably too young to know what she wants yet. In some respects she's awfully mature, but then at times she's a little girl who doesn't want to grow up.'

'I agree. Look at me and Susan. Childhood sweethearts. We'd have got married at seventeen if it hadn't been for Guthrie's not allowing juniors to marry. We had to wait until I was an Assistant Manager. By then we'd been apart for five years with me out here and her back in England and being engaged was a habit.' He reached for Mary's hand. 'I'm absolutely sure if Susan and I had met for the first time when we were in our late twenties, she and I would never have got together.'

'It will be interesting to see if Howard Baxter is prepared to wait around for Jasmine to grow up a bit.' Mary smoothed the sheet with her hand. 'Especially if he goes to a lot of parties and joins all the sports and social clubs. There'll be young women lining up to snaffle a handsome chap like him.'

'Maybe. But if I were a betting man I'd lay my money on Jasmine. His heart's set on her.'

'Who knows? Time will tell.' Mary reached for the light and switched it off. 'Anyway, we've talked enough about them now.' She moved into his waiting arms.

JASMINE LAY IN BED, unable to sleep, all too aware that Howard Baxter was a few feet away on the other side of the wall, in the adjacent bedroom. Uncomfortable at the thought, she tried to divert her mind to something else. Something that would send her off to sleep.

Had he been playing games with her on the ship? Was he just a great big flirt, and she happened to be the only available target on the *Rosebery*? And, more importantly, would she be disappointed if that were the case?

No, Jasmine, don't go down that road. Don't even think about him anymore, she told herself. She absolutely one hundred percent didn't want a boyfriend. It had been embarrassing when he'd said all those stupid, corny things to her. It was vain and silly of her to be feeling a bit disappointed that he'd ignored her for most of the evening. Maybe she should continue behaving towards him the way she'd done tonight. Open and friendly but keeping him at a distance. Like friends. Nothing more than that.

From the way Howard had been this evening it was probably all he wanted too. She was sure. There was even a word for it that she tried to remember from school. Some kind of friendship the ancient Greeks had that was not romantic. She remembered doing it in History. Yes. A non-romantic friendship would be the best solution.

As she mulled this over, feeling pleased with herself, she heard a sliding noise. She sat bolt upright in bed. What was that?

A shaft of moonlight ran across the bedroom floor from a narrow gap in the bamboo chicks and illuminated a dark square shape on the floor in front of the door. She fumbled to find the switch on her bedside lamp.

Someone had pushed a thin package through the gap underneath the bedroom door. Puzzled, Jasmine got out of bed and padded barefoot across the room. She picked up the object, realisation dawning. It was a gramophone record. Through the large circular hole in the centre of the brown paper disc cover, she saw the words RCA Victor, under a picture of a dog listening to the sound of his master's voice coming from a gramophone horn. The promised recording of *When You Were Sweet Sixteen* by Perry Como.

Shivering, she put the disc on top of the chest of drawers and scuttled back into bed. Did this mean Howard was still interested in her? Her throat constricted. She would have to find an excuse to get out of this trip around the island. How could she possibly face him now? Unless she could persuade Mary to come too. But Mary and Reggie had little enough time to spend together and that wouldn't be fair.

Why was life so complicated? Why couldn't she be left alone to get on with her painting, helping at the school and doing her studies? Why had this man come pushing his way into her life and why did he make her feel so utterly miserable?

THE FOLLOWING MORNING, Jasmine went into breakfast with a sense of dread. To her relief, only Mary was at the table, with Frances in her lap. Mary was trying to feed her rusks soaked in milk, but the baby was getting more on her face than in her mouth as she wriggled about so much.

'Morning,' Mary said brightly. 'Giving Frances a bath before breakfast was a mistake. The little terror has soggy rusk all over her newly washed hair.'

After pulling faces at Frances to make her laugh, which rendered Mary's attempts to feed the child even more difficult, Jasmine sat down and reached for the toast rack.

'Don't have that. It'll be cold and rubbery. JinJiang is making some more.'

As Mary spoke, the *amah* came into the room with another rack of toast and a fresh pot of tea.

'Am I frightfully late?' Jasmine buttered her toast. 'Only I had trouble sleeping.'

'Poor thing. And no you're not. Reggie's taken Howard on a tour of the estate. Talking shop.' Mary rolled her eyes. 'I've asked Bintang to have the motor ready to take you both in about forty minutes. Hope that suits you.'

Jasmine mumbled something in reply. The sick hollow feeling she'd had since finding the record, made her realise she wasn't hungry. She let the piece of toast drop back onto the plate.

'Are you all right, Jasmine? You look a bit pale.'

'Just tired. I'll be fine.' She closed her eyes for a moment then decided to confide in Mary. 'I don't really want to go with Howard. You remember when we docked, he asked you about whether you had a gramophone player? Only he pushed a record under my door last night.'

'A record? What record?'

'It's a Perry Como song called When You Were Sweet Sixteen.'

'Ah.' Mary's tone was knowing. 'I see. You think he has designs on you?'

Jasmine nodded, miserable.

'And you don't like him?'

'It's not that...it's ... oh Mary, I don't know. I wish I'd never met him.'

'It's my fault. I shouldn't have invited him here without asking you first. In my keenness to find some friends for you, I've organised you too much. I thought he seemed such a nice chap.'

'He is nice. Well, I suppose he is. It's ...you know... I don't want to...all that.'

'I understand. You want to be friends and nothing more?'

'Yes! Exactly.'

'Would you like me to tell him you're unwell?'

'He'll know that's not true. And it's not fair to get you to lie for me.'

Mary adjusted the baby in her lap and wiped her chin

with her bib. 'I could explain to him that you want to be just friends. Has he ever tried––?'

'No! Never. Nothing like that.' Jasmine poured herself a cup of tea. 'He goes on and on about how much he likes me. It's embarrassing. I think there must be something wrong with me. I don't feel that way at all about him.'

'And why should you? Just because he's a handsome fellow doesn't mean you have to be attracted to him. Besides, you hardly know him.'

'I feel awkward and stupid when he talks to me that way. It gives me the creeps.'

'Would you like me to speak to him? Ask him to tone it down a bit?'

'Gosh, no! That would be even worse.' Yet, Mary's sympathy and understanding made Jasmine feel calmer. 'I need to do it myself. If he starts talking that way again, I'll make it clear that I have no interest in anything other than a Socratic friendship.' She decided she was hungry after all and took a bite of her toast.

'A Socratic friendship?' Mary smiled. 'That sounds interesting. What does that involve?'

'It comes from Socrates, the famous Greek philosopher. It means unromantic friendships.'

'I see.' Mary busied herself with Frances, clearly trying to disguise her amusement.

Jasmine had a horrible feeling she might have got Plato and Socrates muddled up. She would need to look the term up before she used it again.

'I can give him the choice.' Jasmine sipped her tea, feeling stronger and more determined. 'Either an unromantic friendship or none at all. Thank you, Mary.' She spread butter and marmalade on a second piece of toast.

'I haven't done anything.'

'You helped me get it straight in my mind.'

'What about Perry Como?'

'I won't even mention it.' Jasmine nodded her head. 'Yes, best not to bring it up as it might embarrass him. I'll act as if it never happened.'

'I see. It sounds like you have it all worked out then?'

'Yes.' Jasmine grinned. 'And it would be such a pity to miss a chance to see the monkeys.'

14

They sat in the back of the car as far apart as Jasmine could manage without opening the door. She stared ahead, eyes fixed on the back of Bintang's head, while the driver's eyes remained on the road. Beside her, Howard gazed out of the car window but said nothing. He had reverted to giving her the cold shoulder and Jasmine didn't like it at all. While she didn't want to talk to him, the tense silence was making her nervous that he might suddenly break it and say something outrageous in front of Bintang.

She studied the back of Bintang's neck: glossy black hair meeting taut muscles. Since he'd told her about the horrible way his little sister had been so brutally murdered in front of the family at only nine years old, she hadn't been able to stop thinking about it. How had Bintang found the strength to carry on, having witnessed such an act of senseless savagery? At nine, Siti had been less than a year older than Jasmine's brother was now. What if someone blew Hugh's brains out in front of her? It was too horrible to contemplate. The revelation had given Bintang a near heroic status in her mind. Since then, she had stopped thinking of him as the *syce* but as an individual, worthy of her compassion and respect.

Observing the back of his head, Jasmine decided he'd make an interesting subject to draw. Dare she ask him to pose for her some time? Would that be inappropriate? What might the Hyde-Underwoods think? More to the point what might Bintang think? On the other hand, sketching him when he was unaware and off guard might be more interesting than asking him to hold a pose. Every Saturday he washed the car, so Jasmine could find a spot where she could observe him at work and do some rapid sketches, then use them as the basis for a portrait later. It was tempting to take her drawing pad out now and sketch him as he drove, but that would mean Howard the Creep seeing what she was doing, and she wasn't going to let that happen.

The ominous silence was increasingly unsettling. Better to make some casual conversation. But Jasmine wasn't comfortable with the concept of small talk, as Mummy called it. Evie could walk into any room and sustain a conversation with anyone. When Jasmine had asked her how she did it, she'd said it was part of being married to someone whose job required him to entertain visiting dignitaries. She had to mix and mingle with all manner of people from high-ranking officials to local tribesmen and missionaries. Everyone has something that they truly care about, Mummy had told her. It's simply a question of discovering what that is and letting them tell you about it. Trouble was, the only things Howard Baxter appeared to be interested in were her, and rubber cultivation. Jasmine didn't want to talk about either.

They pulled into the Botanic Gardens and parked.

Leaving Bintang with the motor, Howard and Jasmine got out and started walking.

'Is there something between you and that chap?' Howard looked at her sideways.

'What chap?' She turned to look at him in surprise. 'Oh, my goodness, do you mean Bintang? Of course not. There's nothing between me and *anybody*. I wish you'd leave me alone, Howard.'

Howard had the grace to look ashamed. 'I apologise. As usual I've put my foot in it and offended you. I honestly didn't mean to, Jasmine, only...' He looked away into the distance. 'It's possibly because I'm jealous.'

'What?'

'The way he looks at you when you're not aware. The fact that he gets to drive you around and see you all the time, when I'm stuck over on the peninsula.' His eyes fixed on hers. 'And yet again, I've messed up by blurting all this out and making you mad at me. When all I want is for you to be mad *for* me.'

'That's never going to happen.'

He looked hurt and she felt bad.

'You haven't even mentioned the Perry Como record.'

'What do you expect me to say?'

He looked nonplussed. Shrugging, he said, 'Nothing I suppose.'

'Look, it was kind of you to bring me a gift, but as I told you before, Howard, I am not interested.' She knew she sounded cold, cruel even, so added, 'I mean, I'm not interested in anyone. Not like that. Nothing against you personally.' Remembering her conversation with Mary over breakfast she wished she'd had time to look up Plato and Socrates in the encyclopaedia. Too late now. 'I am very happy to be friends in the manner of the Ancient Greek philosopher.' She cringed, realising how pompous she sounded.

'Gosh. Not sure I can manage philosophy. I'm not feeling too philosophical right now.' He looked crestfallen. Then his mouth stretched into a resigned smile. 'But I'll do my best. Now, let's go and find your monkeys.'

'There are waterfalls as well.'

'Right. Waterfalls and monkeys it is.' He smiled again, but the smile didn't reach his eyes.

Jasmine felt an overwhelming sadness. The day was not turning out the way she'd hoped. Even the gardens were a disappointment. There was an air of neglect about them since their pre-war splendour and her childhood memories. Even the monkeys failed to move her. Perhaps the charm of primates had eroded somewhat. They were two-a-penny back in Kenya, driving Gichinga mad when they ate the vegetables in the kitchen garden he tended behind their bungalow.

Howard didn't appear that impressed by the monkeys either. He must also have grown up with them all around him in Ceylon. This was not the pleasant tour Mary had planned for them.

'Let's take the funicular up to Penang Hill,' Jasmine said.

'Do you think we'll see anything up there? There's a lot of cloud about.'

'What would you rather do?' she asked sharply, realising she'd rather be anywhere than stuck in a small train cabin with Howard Baxter.

'No. Penang Hill sounds perfect. I've never ridden on a funicular railway before.'

They returned to the car where Bintang was leaning against the bonnet, smoking.

'Haven't you told him it's a filthy habit, yet?' Howard said to her as they approached.

'Of course I haven't. It's none of my business.'

Howard's face broke into a broad smile. 'I will take hope from that. I'm telling myself that it means your zeal for reforming character failings extends only to me.' He opened his arms in an expansive gesture. 'Plenty of raw material for you to work on here. I could ask the Parentals to draw up a list of my many defects.'

Jasmine rolled her eyes but found herself smiling.

THE FUNICULAR WAS CROWDED, and the seats were narrow, so they had to squash closely together. Jasmine, self-consciously aware of Howard's thigh against hers, was glad he wasn't wearing shorts and she didn't have to see those tanned legs with the fine dark hairs.

The hills above them were wreathed in mist, the trees like spectres breaking through the swirling haze. It began to rain. Heavily. They looked at each other. The umbrellas were in the car. Above their heads the rain made a drumbeat on the cabin roof. Jasmine hoped that it would be over quickly.

The railway passed over a stone viaduct then cut into the hillside for the steep climb up to Middle Station. There the line went into a short passing loop, crossing the downward train on the opposite track. Jasmine watched the rain run down the windows and felt even glummer. Meanwhile Howard was deep in conversation with a middle-aged man who was explaining the feats of engineering involved in the creation of a funicular and the principles of its operation. She suppressed a yawn and wished she'd stayed at Bella Vista.

As soon as they stepped out at the top of the track, the rain stopped. That's how it was in Penang – frequent showers that were often over as fast as they started. To her delight, the sun broke through the clouds, which were moving away rapidly over the Straits. All around them was a dense canopy of lush green vegetation, the sound of birds, the flash of their plumage and the delicate bright wings of butterflies.

They walked up to the vantage point. 'What a view!' Howard said, looking down to George Town and beyond it, the Straits with the distant dots of boats. 'There's the ferry to Butterworth.' He pointed. 'I'm so glad you brought me up here, Jasmine. It's a magical place.'

His enthusiasm was reflected in his broad grin and she couldn't help but be infected by it, pointing out places of interest below them. 'See that big pagoda over there? With the buildings beside it? A Chinese temple. It's Ayer Itam. We can visit that next if you like.'

'Some time. But not now. Let's have some tiffin then go for a swim,' he said. 'We have our things. We can find a quiet beach somewhere.'

Jasmine wasn't sure she wanted Howard Baxter to see her in her bathing costume, but the thought of swimming was too delicious a prospect to resist. 'Shall we go to the Penang Club first for lunch?'

'No need. It's all planned. Mary offered to give us a picnic and I took the liberty of accepting on your behalf. There's a hamper in the boot of the car.'

'She didn't tell me.'

'You weren't there, lazy bones.' He winked at her.

At least now they were communicating. Jasmine didn't mind him when he was friendly and cheerful. It was the long silences or the declarations of his feelings for her that got her down. She decided to behave as if everything that had passed between them before hadn't happened.

'Where shall we go? The Penang Swimming Club?' she said.

'No. The sea. Mary suggested a place and told that sullen driver. I haven't a clue what it was called. But she promised it would be quiet.'

'But where can I get changed? We could go to the Penang Swimming Club and then go down onto the beach from there. At least then I can use the changing rooms.'

'It's Sunday, and Mary said the Swimming Club would be awash with people. I'm sure there'll be some trees to hide behind where we're going. And I promise not to peek.'

Reluctantly, she followed him to the funicular. They took the trip back down and found Bintang waiting near the parked motorcar, smoking and talking to a small group of fellow Malays. He said something to his companions then headed back to the car.

'Sorry, Bintang. We've changed our plans. We'd like to go to the beach now.'

Bintang shrugged and opened the car door for Jasmine.

The drive took about forty minutes, over the hills on a steep winding road, which then doubled back and headed to the north west of the island.

'Apparently many of the most beautiful beaches are only accessible by sea or if you trek for hours through dense jungle,' said Howard. 'Maybe one day we can hire a boat and visit one. There are small islands too.'

'I know,' said Jasmine. 'I was born here.'

'Of course, you were.' He smiled, adding, 'There I go again.'

She turned away to look out of the window. There was little traffic on the road, just the odd buffalo cart or rickshaw near settlements. They drove with the windows open, enjoying the cooling breeze, passing rice paddies and areas where local families grew subsistence vegetables. Everywhere was lush and green and vibrant under the sun.

Passing through small *kampongs,* they saw children working alongside their parents in the fields and vegetable plots. Washing hung on long wooden poles, like bunting. Chickens clucked around in the spaces underneath the stilted wooden houses and armies of ducks paraded everywhere. Men and women, wearing straw coolie hats, carried panniers filled with rice or freshly picked vegetables on wooden yokes over their shoulders. In the Chinese villages there were small enclosures with pigs. Everywhere was a hive of industry.

'I love this country. Everywhere is so green and fresh,' she said, her annoyance at Howard now dissipated by her surroundings. 'Africa is so dry and dusty.'

'I've never been. Maybe you can show me one day.'

There he went again, spoiling everything by trying to insinuate that they had some kind of shared future.

'I won't be living there anymore. I've left for good.' She turned away to look out of the window.

'But you'll go back to visit. After all, your family is there.' He was not easily discouraged.

Irritated, Jasmine said nothing else, and the rest of the journey passed in silence.

When they arrived at their destination, Howard lifted the picnic basket out of the boot of the car, as well as the bags containing their swimming gear. Jasmine went to take hers, but he shook his head. 'I've got it.'

Meanwhile, Bintang lit up a cigarette and sat on a fallen tree trunk between the road and the beach. It appeared he planned to stay within sight of them while they had their picnic and swam.

Howard turned to the driver. 'I say, we're going to be here for the rest of the afternoon, so why don't you take some time off and you can come back for us at four o'clock.'

Bintang scowled, folded his arms and said, 'I stay near Missee.'

Fearing a confrontation, Jasmine gave him what she hoped was a reassuring smile. 'Don't worry about me, Bintang. I'll be safe with Mr Baxter. Why don't you take the motor and visit your grandmother?'

'This is *tuan*'s car. I not use for me.'

'The *tuan* won't even know. If he did find out and wasn't happy then I'd tell him it was my idea.'

Bintang hesitated, then threw another scowl in Howard's direction, nodded, got back in the car and drove away.

'Thank goodness we're shot of him. Well done.'

Irritated by the grin on Howard's face she said, 'I only did it to avoid a scene and I don't want you getting any ideas now he's out of the picture.'

Howard lifted both hands, palms facing her. 'I won't lay a finger on you, dearest girl. You have my word. Come on, let's see what Jinjiang has prepared for our picnic.'

The sandy beach was lined with coconut palms; some of them bent over towards the sea as though they were trying to dip their fronds in the water. There were a couple of small islets not far from the shore: rocky humps with vegetation clinging to them. Further along the beach a small cluster of huts with *attap* roofs was nestled between the palms. In the shallow waters in front of the huts, a couple of colourful fishing boats were roped to stakes in the sand, rising and dipping on the gentle waves. No one was about.

Jasmine looked around, wondering where she was going

to get changed. She didn't like the idea of trying to do it discreetly under her towel in case she let it slip. Nothing would be more embarrassing.

Sensing her discomfort, Howard offered to find a suitable spot and ran off along the beach, in the opposite direction to the fishing boats. A few moments later he ran back. 'There's a huge rock down there. It's not overlooked from the road or the beach. 'You can squeeze behind it and slip your cozzie on.'

Grateful, she grabbed her swimming things and headed for the boulder. Behind it was an area of dense mangroves, their roots spreading over the edges of the shore. Quickly, she took off her dress and underwear and put on her swimsuit. Yet another gift from Mummy – this time bought from one of the shops at the E&O.

Aware she was alone with Howard, and feeling self-conscious, she hoped the swimsuit wasn't too revealing. Thank goodness her monthly period had finished three days ago. How would she have felt having to make excuses for not swimming? It was so hard growing up. Jasmine often wished she was still a child and didn't have to worry about all these unpleasant things.

When she got back, she was relieved to see Howard hadn't changed into his swimming trunks but was wearing a pair of shorts. He looked up at her as he was unpacking the picnic hamper, but fortunately said nothing about her swimming costume. Not that he could see much of it as she was clutching a towel in front of her.

'What a feast. I hope you're hungry,' he said. 'I'm famished. There's ham, salad, sausage rolls, little battered patty-cake things.' He took a bite of one. 'Mmm, I think it has prawns in. And ginger. Spicy. Delicious. Come on, before I scoff the lot.'

As she ate, Jasmine realised she did have an appetite. Sitting cross-legged on the cotton blanket, she began to relax.

'There's beer as well. And what looks like homemade lemonade.' Howard reached inside the basket.

'I'll have some lemonade, thanks.'

A soft breeze was coming off the Straits, but it was still very hot and the lemonade cooled her parched throat.

'I liked Colombo,' she said. 'It reminded me of Penang in so many ways.'

'You need to see the rest of Ceylon. It's beautiful. Deserted beaches like this. Temples, mountains, jungle, enormous stone statues. We even have monkeys. And better still, elephants.'

'Why did you want to leave then?'

'I didn't want to leave Ceylon. But I needed to get away from the old boy. One day I will return to live there.'

'Really? So, you're not staying on in Malaya?'

'Oh yes, I'm staying. At least for the foreseeable future. But when the old boy shuffles off this mortal coil I'll inherit the family business and then I'll have to go back to run it.'

'Mummy told me you didn't like tea and wanted to work in the rubber business.'

He shrugged. 'Nothing against tea. I just can't stand the constant pressure to be someone I'm not.'

Jasmine was curious now. 'What do you mean?'

'I had an older brother. Bill. He was killed in the Normandy landings. Dad's never got over him dying and the fact that he won't be coming back to run the business.' He turned his head to look out to sea.

'I'm sorry. That's awfully sad. How old was Bill when he died?'

'Twenty-nine. There was a big gap between us.'

'Do you have any other siblings?'

'A sister. Married. Lives in England. She's the eldest. Sixteen years older than me. I barely know her. Ellen was at boarding school in England when I was born. I saw her in the school holidays, then she got married at twenty to some chap in the insurance business. As far as I can gather, she spends her life playing golf and bridge. They don't have any children.'

'I often wonder what it would have been like to have an older brother or sister.'

'Are you an only-child then?'

She told him about her half-brother, Hugh. 'He's eight. Bursting with energy. I miss him dreadfully. I absolutely adore the little horror.' Her face broke into a smile. Then remembering that Howard had been telling her about his brother's death, she rearranged her expression.

'Bill was the best. Clever, brave, reliable, funny. Dad worshipped him. Mum too, but she was better at disguising any favouritism.' Howard's voice was hollow, slightly shaky. 'And I looked up to him and wanted to be like him. When they got the telegram to say he'd been killed I was away at university in England.' He took a swig of beer from the bottle. 'I couldn't believe it. But to the Parentals it was the end of their world. If Bill was the favoured son while he was alive, it was nothing to how they revered him once he was dead. And, in comparison, I was a shadow of my cleverer, braver, worthier brother. A living reminder of what they'd lost. Dad makes no bones about the fact that the runt of the litter survived. You've no idea, Jasmine, what it's like to be constantly compared to someone else and found wanting. Especially when you yourself hero-worshipped the person you are compared to.'

Jasmine felt a rush of compassion for him. He wasn't bigheaded at all. Quite the contrary. She gave him a weak smile that she hoped might convey her sympathy. For once she was lost for words.

Howard shook his shoulders and sprang to his feet. 'Let's go for a swim.'

She was about to protest that it was too soon after lunch for swimming, then told herself that was an old wives' tale. He held out a hand to her and pulled her to her feet and together they ran into the sea.

oward kept to his word and made no attempt to touch Jasmine. They spent a delightful afternoon, running in and out of the sea to swim, finishing off the remains of the picnic, and chatting under the palm trees on the beach. Jasmine no longer felt awkward with him. She found him relaxing and congenial company now she had got to know him better. His admissions about his family and his feelings about his dead brother had warmed her towards him. It was hard to think of him as bigheaded anymore. Yes, he did occasionally indulge in a spot of bragging about his work, but it was more in a spirit of enthusiasm for the job than outright boasting. He told her that his boss had hinted that, if he kept up the good work, he might be chosen to drive Sir John Hay around the estate when the Chairman of Guthrie's came for his regular tour of inspection to Malaya later in the year. Where just hours earlier she would have dismissed this as arrogant, now she admired his ambition and dedication to succeed at his work.

All too soon it was time to leave. Bintang had returned

promptly and was already waiting by the car, as usual with a cigarette in his mouth. This time, she and Howard talked constantly all the way to the quay where he was to take the ferry and meet his friends in Butterworth for a lift back to Batu Lembah.

Howard told her he was saving up for a car. 'I don't know when I'll be over here again. I'm working my socks off so I can progress as fast as I can. That means I don't have a lot of time – or cash. But I do hope I'll see you again before too long, Jasmine.' He looked at her with an expression that made her want to look away, embarrassed. There was no mistaking it. His feelings for her were clearly still as strong. She wanted him to go. To disappear into the crowds boarding the ferry before he said anything else. So much for her hopes it was now just friendship.

'You'd better hurry or you'll miss the boat,' she said, trying to inject some *froideur* into her voice. Then she held out her hand to shake his and said, 'Thank you for an enjoyable afternoon. Goodbye.'

Howard stared at the proffered hand as though she had slapped his face but didn't take it. He gave her a curt goodbye and strode away to board the ferry.

Back at Bella Vista, as she was getting ready for bed that night, she noticed the gramophone record where she'd left it on top of the chest of drawers. She certainly had no intention of playing it now – or indeed, ever.

JASMINE WAS ALONE in the classroom, cleaning paintbrushes, emptying glass water jars and putting away pots of paint. She was delighted by the enthusiasm of her pupils for the art classes and the walls of the schoolroom were adorned with an ever-changing display of the children's work:

simple stick paintings of the family units, stilted huts with smoke emerging from the roofs, bright boats bobbing on a deep blue sea and all manner of birds, trees and blazing sunsets. Standing back, she surveyed the work with a rush of pride.

Sensing something, she spun round. Bintang was leaning against the doorpost. How long had he been standing there? Silently watching her.

She hadn't seen him since the afternoon with Howard more than a month ago. Had he been avoiding her?

'How nice to see you, Bintang,' she said. 'What do you think of the children's work?' She swept her arm in a wide gesture.

The driver raised his eyebrows and she realised he hadn't noticed the artwork. He moved across and stood beside her, his long limbs moving languidly. He reminded her of a leopard or a panther – graceful, silent, aloof, and definitely to be respected. He glanced at the display, but showed little interest in the art. 'So that's what you teach them here. How to draw? What good will that do them?'

She was startled by his response and unsure how to reply. 'We teach them all kinds of things. Reading, writing, arithmetic, nature study, history.'

'History? You mean British History. Kings and queens and maps where most of the world is coloured pink. Why do Malayan children need to be taught about your history? It is not ours.'

The blood rushed to her face. Why was he being so hostile? She started to say that she herself didn't actually do any of the teaching except for art, merely helping out with the children's reading, but Bintang turned away and moved across the room to sit on top of one of the desks.

'I used to like going to school. I had a scholarship to St

Xavier's.' He sounded wistful, his anger gone. 'Top of class until Japanese come.'

'Have you ever thought of finishing off your education? I'm sure–'

'Not interested in education now. Not your British colonial education.'

'But with qualifications you could do something more interesting than being a driver.'

'Work in lowly position for your colonial government? No, thank you.' He took a cigarette from his pocket and lit it, giving her a rare smile.

Jasmine reflected that the only time he didn't smoke was when he was driving the car. She wrinkled her nose as the aroma of the tobacco smoke wafted towards her. She'd never dare to say to him what she had said about smoking to Howard.

'You not see boyfriend?' His eyes fixed on hers.

'I don't have a boyfriend.'

He made another little snort of derision.

'If you're referring to Howard Baxter, then he is a friend of the family. I was merely being friendly and hospitable, showing him around.' She knew she sounded pompous. Rather lamely, she added, 'Anyway, he works on the peninsula in Province Wellesley.'

'I know where he works. He must come to Penang often. They all do.'

'All?' She busied herself stacking the trays of paints back into a cardboard box and putting the box away in the cupboard.

'Junior planters. Pour off ferry at weekends. Come to play cricket and rugger.' He spoke the last word with an exaggerated British drawl, rolling the R. 'I surprised you not go cheer him on.'

'I told you, he's not my boyfriend.'

She could feel the blood burning her cheeks and she turned away, needlessly wiping the blackboard. Had Howard been back to Penang? If so, why had he not been in touch? Was it because she'd been cold to him when they said goodbye? Had he found a girlfriend? A proper girlfriend. Just as she had decided she liked him. Not in that way, of course, but as a friend. As someone she enjoyed spending time with. If only it were possible for a boy and girl to be friends without lovey-dovey stuff getting in the way. As long as Howard wasn't going on about all that romantic nonsense, she quite liked him. No, *really* liked him. And, if truth were told, she'd been disappointed he hadn't been in touch with her since she'd watched him board the ferry. He'd warned her that he was saving to buy a car but maybe that had been an excuse.

It was her own fault. She'd pushed him away. After that delightful afternoon at the beach, she'd made it clear at the ferry quay that she had no interest in him romantically. Was it any wonder that he'd given up on her? Maybe Mummy was right and when a chap got to a certain age, he set his sights on settling down, so it was quite possible he was now being chased by some girl who was also eager to settle down. Jasmine would have to forget about him. Up here at Bella Vista at least there was no risk of running into him and she had more than enough to keep her occupied, with her painting, helping at the school and – last in line – her studies.

'I thought you might want to know he here.' Bintang bounced forward onto his feet from his perch on the desk and moved towards the doorway.

'Here? What are you talking about?'

'In *tuan*'s office.'

'What?'

'I take *tuan* to George Town today and he meet your friend and invite him here tonight. Tomorrow your friend play cricket.'

Howard was here? On the estate? Now? Her stomach lurched. How could she go through all that again? Was he here for dinner? To stay? What kind of mood would he be in? Would he be the Howard who ignored her all evening? The Howard who declared he was besotted with her? Or the Howard who had opened up about his family to her on the beach? Whichever it was, she didn't think she could cope with it right now. Why did he make her feel happy one minute, the next angry, and always rather afraid and confused?

'Where are you going?' she asked Bintang, who was about to leave the classroom.

'Back to my quarters.'

'Don't go!' she said, impulsively. 'I'd like to draw you. It won't take long.'

'Draw me? Why?'

'Because you'll make a good subject. And I need more practice at drawing faces. Please.'

He looked doubtful but shrugged his assent. 'Where you want me stand?'

'Outside. On the veranda.' She grabbed a chair for herself and carried it out of the room. 'There. You can lean against the railing.' She indicated a spot. 'The light will hit one side of your face and the rest will be in shadow.'

'Why not want all light?'

'Shadows make it more interesting.'

He settled into position and she picked up her sketch-book and pencil. She began to draw, her eyes darting up and down between the marks she was making on the paper and the man she was trying to portray. Once Jasmine began a drawing, she was pulled into it. Nothing else existed except for the image taking form on the page and the object or person she was drawing. It made no difference whether it was a mountain, a flower or a human being. As she strove to capture its essence, it became for her light and shade, curves and lines. A creation where the addition of a small mark with the pencil to reflect the curve of a nostril could suddenly catch the spirit of her subject and hold it fixed on the paper.

Something broke her concentration for a moment. Looking up, she said, 'I'd like to paint you one day. I've been experimenting with oil paints and I'd love to try painting you.'

He narrowed his eyes. 'Why?'

'You have an interesting face. I've already painted the mother of one of the children. And Jinjiang.'

Bintang pushed himself away from the railing. 'Enough. What you doing? Painting the natives? Like we your toys. For show your British friends? No.'

'I don't know what you mean. I'm not only painting Malayan people. I've promised to do a portrait of the Hyde-Underwoods' little girl.' She stretched her hands out in front of her. 'Please, Bintang, I'm not patronising you at all. I thought you were my friend?'

'Your friend? How I be friends with you?'

She gave him a nervous smile. 'Because I like you. I'd like to get to know you better. I'd like to hear more about your life.'

'Why you care about my life?'

He was so touchy.

'It's interesting. And sad. Losing your family like that.' She hesitated. 'I barely remember my own mother. And

Daddy died when I was eight. He had an accident and died of blood poisoning. Fell down an old mine shaft. I didn't even get to visit him in the hospital or say goodbye. It all happened so quickly.'

'I know about your father. He was *tuan besar*.'

'Of course. I forgot you would have known him.'

'Now this *tuan* and *mem* your parents.' He said it as fact, not as a question.

'No, Mummy is married to Mr Arthur Leighton. They are now my parents. They live with my little brother in Africa. *Tuan* and *Mem* Hyde-Underwood are like an aunt and uncle to me. Terribly kind. I love them dearly.' She paused, waiting for him to resume his pose, and breathed in relief when he settled against the railings.

'Your parents not want you? Why they send you live here?'

'No!' She smiled. He saw everything in such simple terms. 'Of course not. I chose to come here because I love Penang. I didn't like living in Africa. I wanted to spend more time here. I had happy memories of the island.'

'British people run away when Japanese come. Leave us to die.' His voice was cold. 'Now they come back and want to have my country again. It is Malayan people country. Not white man's. Men like my father who fought with British against Japanese now betrayed by British. They act like comrades then when we get rid of Japanese they don't give independence.'

'I'm sure they will. It's just a matter of time.'

His face was sceptical.

Jasmine felt stupid. She didn't know what to say. She wondered whether the Hyde-Underwoods were aware of the strength of his feelings and his evident animosity towards anyone British.

Eventually she asked, 'Was it terrible here under the Japanese? I remember the planes flying overhead and the bombs. Our amah, Aunty Mimi, lost her husband. He was killed in the street in George Town. Machine-gun fire from an aircraft. And both *Tuan* and *Mem* Hyde-Underwood were prisoners of the Japanese. They don't talk about it.'

'Japanese very bad people. All along road near *kampong*, heads on posts. Japanese cut off heads and put there to make people afraid. Very afraid.'

Jasmine didn't want to think about something so horrible. 'I'm sorry about your parents and Siti.' She drew her mouth into a tight smile of regret.

Bintang looked up at the sky. 'Time you go back before dark.'

'Goodness me. I lost track of time. That's what happens when I get absorbed in a drawing. Thanks very much, Bintang. And do please think about letting me paint your portrait. You could give it to your grandmother as a present.'

He nodded, his face solemn, but she saw the spark of interest in his eyes.

'I walk back to bungalow with you. Get dark soon.'

Jasmine stuffed her pencils and sketchbook into her satchel and replaced the chair in the classroom, then followed him onto the path into the jungle that bordered the rubber estate.

He walked in front of her and once again reminded her of a cat – lithe, slender, and moving quietly. Jasmine fixed her eyes on the back of his head, as she had when they were in the motorcar. His hair had a glossy sheen in the dappled light filtering down through the trees. It looked soft, silky and she wondered what it would feel like to run her fingers through it. She had to hurry to keep up with his long stride. Impossible to tell if he liked or disliked her. He was inscrutable, arrogant, difficult. To be fair, she wasn't sure if she liked or disliked him and concluded she was both fascinated and afraid of him. His aloofness and distance made him interesting. There was nothing obsequious or servile about him. Yet she was all too aware of a coldness and hardness in him that she knew must trace to his terrible wartime experience.

It was only when they reached the muster area – the large grassy *padang* where the roll call of rubber workers took place early each morning – that Jasmine remembered Howard Baxter was here at Bella Vista.

16

W hen Jasmine walked onto the veranda to join the Hyde-Underwoods for their customary sundowners, Howard Baxter jumped to his feet to greet her. Jasmine felt a rush of nerves at being in his company again and was grateful to Bintang that she'd had forewarning of his presence. But why hadn't Howard been in touch with her? Navigating adult relationships was so hard. And Jasmine hadn't a clue how to read the signals where Howard was concerned.

'What a piece of luck that I ran into Reggie,' Howard said to her. 'I'm playing in a cricket match tomorrow and we bumped into each other as we came off the ferry.'

'I was over in Butterworth to meet with suppliers.' Reggie sounded almost apologetic. 'When I saw the awful digs the poor chap was planning to stay in tonight, I had to persuade him to come and bunk in with us at Bella Vista.' He raised his glass to Howard. 'And remember, you're always welcome here.'

'Do you come across to Penang every weekend?' Jasmine asked, pointedly. 'I imagine there are a lot of cricket games.'

'Actually, it's the first time I've been on the island since I stayed with you before. I'm not on the cricket team. No time for that. I managed to wangle this weekend off as they were a man down and I agreed to step into the breach. The *tuan* only let me have the time off because the club captain, who's a pal of his, was desperate.'

'Don't you get every weekend off?' Jasmine was genuinely surprised.

He blew out a little puff of air. 'You must be joking, Jasmine. I'm the lowest of the low and, as such, I'm always at the back of the queue for time off. Batu Lembah is a large estate and was horribly neglected during the war.' He turned to Reggie. 'Whole place was overrun with lalang and you know what a devil of a job it is to clear.'

'Don't I just?' Reggie chuckled. 'We still have some here. Hope to have the last of it under control soon, but it's taken me more than two years.'

'What's lalang?' Jasmine asked.

'I thought you claimed to know all about rubber estates.' Howard winked at her and she decided she hated him. 'It's a type of grass. Gets everywhere. Absolute nightmare to eradicate.'

'Because of the roots,' said Reggie, helpfully. 'They spread everywhere and go down deep. An absolute devil to dig them out.'

Jasmine nodded and sipped her bitter lemon as the conversation about eradication methods droned on around her. She took the opportunity to study Howard. His hair looked as though it was overdue for a cut, but she rather liked it like that, as it tended to flop heavily over his brow, making him appear artistic – which she was sure he was not. It was a light golden brown, so different from the jet black, spun silk of Bintang's.

Howard leaned forward, elbows on knees as he listened to Reggie speaking. He barely glanced at her. So, she was going to get the cold shoulder treatment again. She yawned. He was such a child, even though he was nearly ten years her senior.

As if reading her thoughts, Howard turned to her. 'Have you listened to the gramophone record I gave you yet?'

Before she could stammer out an answer, Reggie butted in. 'You gave Jasmine a record? Then let's all hear it.'

'It's in my bedroom,' she said quietly. It was still on top of the chest of drawers where she'd put it after he pushed it under the door.

'So you haven't played it at all?' Howard tilted his head to one side and frowned.

'Not yet. I hadn't had a chance to ask Reggie if he minded me using the gramophone player.' She knew she was blushing and was mortified. Why was he bringing this up in front of the Hyde-Underwoods?

'Of course, you can use the gramophone. You don't even need to ask. Let's hear it now. Jinjiang!' Reggie called to the *amah*, who immediately appeared. 'Miss Barrington has left a gramophone recording in her bedroom. Would you bring it here, please?' As the housekeeper left, he grinned at Jasmine. 'It'll be nice to hear a new tune. We really ought to listen to music more often, eh, Mary?'

'Perhaps Jasmine would rather listen to it on her own,' said Mary tactfully.

'Ah!' Reggie grinned again. 'Special significance, eh?' He winked at Howard and Jasmine died a thousand deaths.

She wanted to run away and hide. All the while, she was aware of Howard's eyes on her and she squirmed, feeling a mixture of embarrassment and shame.

Jinjiang returned with the record. Howard got up and

took it from her. 'I thought Jasmine might enjoy it. It's by Perry Como and was very popular last year. She said she'd never heard it so I bought it for her as a present.'

'How thoughtful. But we should wait until after dinner as Jinjiang is ready to serve now.' Mary to the rescue again. Jasmine hoped by the time they'd finished eating, the record would be forgotten.

Talk over dinner was all about politics and rubber. While the latter bored her, Jasmine found herself interested in the political discussion, particularly after talking that afternoon with Bintang.

'Things are definitely hotting up with the MNLA. You were right that Chin Peng should have been booted out of Malaya.' Howard took the salad bowl from Jasmine, helped himself, and passed the bowl on to Reggie.

'Exactly.' Reggie nodded. 'The man's a menace. Never should have got the OBE.'

'What he's doing now has nothing to do with why he got an OBE.' Mary put down her knife and fork. 'He was incredibly brave fighting the Japanese. Men like your stepfather, Jasmine, depended on Chin Peng and his ilk.'

Reggie nodded. Jasmine had noticed how rarely he disagreed outright with Mary. 'True. But that counts for nothing as far as he's concerned now. He's laughing at us behind our backs. Anyway, you were saying, Baxter, how exactly are things hotting up?'

'Nothing concrete yet. More union agitators hanging around, trying to stir up trouble. They're putting a lot of pressure on the Chinese tappers to call for strikes. The poor chaps get bullied into it. Their families get threatened. The *tuan,* Gordon O'Keefe spends his life trying to calm things down. But lately, there have been all kinds of strange things happening.'

'Like what?' Jasmine asked.

'Strange people hanging about the estate. Odd noises in the middle of the night. Money stolen. Rice supplies too.'

Mary looked at her husband, frowning. 'Nothing like that here, is there, Reggie?'

Reggie shook his head. 'Fortunately Batu Lembah is close to the main road so they're probably safe there, but some of the other estates are pretty isolated,' said Howard. 'No one goes anywhere without a gun these days.'

'You carry a gun?' Jasmine's eyes widened.

'Not one that works.' Howard gave her a tight-lipped smile. 'It's a clapped-out old Japanese carbine missing its bolt. Completely useless. But O'Keefe reckons it's better than nothing and might scare off someone who doesn't know better before I'd need to fire it.'

Mary shook her head and looked worried. 'But if these MNLA chaps are armed you won't stand a chance if it won't fire.' She kept exchanging glances with Reggie.

'There's talk of sending the gurkhas in to guard the estates, if things really hot up. But High Commissioner Gent has cloth ears.'

'Let's hope it doesn't come to violence.' Mary closed her eyes.

'I'm afraid it probably will.' Reggie put his hand over hers. 'At least over on the peninsula. Please God, we'll be all right here. One of the benefits of being a small island.'

Jasmine decided to speak up. 'Why do these MNLA people want to cause trouble?'

Reggie answered. 'Because they're a bunch of commies and want to create a Chinese communist state here in Malaya.'

'Why not campaign for that openly then?'

Reggie snorted. 'For a start the communist party is

banned. And anyway the Chinese were denied the vote when the Federation was set up. We offered it, but the Sultans didn't want it. They like to keep the Chinese down. And some of those chaps developed a taste for armed conflict. Jungle warfare. All that stuff. No one else wants communism. Most of the Malayan people want to get on with their lives. And that includes the majority of the Chinese Malays. That right, Baxter?'

Howard nodded. 'Many of the Chinese tappers hate communism with a passion. And not just the ones who supported Chiang Kai Shek and the Kuomintang. I've been spending as much time as I can trying to get to know some of our Chinese tappers. Most of them seem to be decent fellows. They simply want to earn a fair wage and feed their families.'

'And then there's the triads.' Reggie leaned back in his chair. 'They used to be a big deal over here in Penang. Probably still are, but more underground these days, since Ang Bin Hoey was disbanded.'

'What's that? What's a triad?' Jasmine asked.

'Chinese secret societies,' said Mary. 'They used to control everything in Penang, including everything going in and out of the harbour.'

'But they were caught between the reds and the Kuomintang too.' Reggie gave his head a little shake. 'The police rounded up the leaders and the whole structure was dismantled. I imagine some of them headed off to join the communists and others set up smaller groups. The Chinese love to gamble and where there's gambling, there are opportunities to extort money. And make illegal profits.'

Reggie stopped talking while Jinjiang cleared the main course away and served the pudding. Once she'd left, he took a sip of beer and continued. 'Once upon a time the triads were all rich merchants, now they're low level crooks. Pickpockets, rickshaw riders and black marketeers.'

Mary chipped in. 'They do have the most delightful gang names though. Things like Red Flower Society and the Skeleton Gang.'

'And are these triads causing the strikes and violence?' Jasmine was starting to feel lost by the turn in the conversation.

'No, no. They're all about money, not politics. Gosh, that sherry trifle is rather good.' Reggie put down his dessert spoon. 'But who knows what they could get up to in future. The communists must need money to fund their political campaigns, so my view is never trust any of the blighters, eh, Baxter?'

Before Howard could answer, Jasmine spoke up. 'Don't you think we ought to stop interfering in politics and let Malaya be run by the Malayan people? After all, this is their country, not ours.' Jasmine felt all eyes turn to look at her. Howard sniffed derisively. Remembering the passion and anger with which Bintang had castigated her this afternoon, she sat up taller.

'It most certainly is their country.' Mary touched Jasmine's wrist softly with her hand. 'But it's not that simple. The original Malayan people are now outnumbered by Chinese, Indians and others. Malaya for Malayans is no longer a straightforward concept.'

'But it was we who brought all the Chinese here to work in the tin mines and brought in the Indians to tap the rubber. Maybe if we left, they could sort it out amongst themselves.' Jasmine could feel her cheeks turning red. It had sounded so compelling when Bintang had spoken. From her own mouth, she was less sure. Three faces turned to look at her, surprise registered on each of them.

'You're saying we British should leave?' Howard looked at her as if she'd lost her mind. 'Do you realise how much Malaya contributes to the British Treasury? Do you understand how hard people have worked to rebuild the rubber and tin industries after the Japanese destroyed them?'

Jasmine looked down at her half-eaten sherry trifle. Why had she interrupted? She knew nothing of politics and it was all terribly complicated. The more she discovered, the less she understood. She determined never to try to discuss the subject again. Feeling small and rather stupid, she got up from the table. 'Do you mind awfully if I turn in? I have a frightful headache.'

Brushing aside Mary's offers of aspirin, she hurried out of the dining room to the safe haven of her bedroom. There she flung herself on her bed and drew her knees up to her chin. Why hadn't she kept quiet and listened to the conversation instead of trying to show off?

THE FOLLOWING MORNING, Jasmine stayed in bed. Facing Howard Baxter was not something she was ready to do. And she certainly didn't want anyone to suggest she go along to watch him play cricket.

Last night, she'd felt like an interloper among the adults. For the first time since she'd left Africa, she missed sitting around the table with Mummy, Hugh and Arthur. She could be herself with them. Here she was in a constant state of confusion. When she'd listened to Bintang it seemed he had a strong and logical case. But her suggestion that the British leave Malaya had been greeted with an open mouth from Reggie and a self-satisfied smirk and a mini lecture from Mr Know-It-All Baxter. And the truth was, she didn't want the British to leave, as that would mean leaving herself.

Why was everything so incredibly difficult, the older you got and the more grown-up you tried to be?

When she heard Reggie and Howard talking outside, followed by the car starting up and driving away, Jasmine got out of bed, washed and ventured forth.

Mary and Frances were on the veranda, the baby crawling about on a large cotton blanket. Jasmine got down on all fours to play with the child, who squealed with delight. Jasmine held Frances up by the hands as the little girl tried to balance on her wobbly legs.

'You've made a remarkable recovery.' Mary gave her a wry smile. 'Is it anything to do with the departure of our friend, Mr Baxter?'

'It was only a headache, but I had trouble sleeping and then managed to oversleep this morning.'

'That's a pity. Reggie's gone to watch Howard play. You could have gone with them.'

'I don't like cricket.'

Mary was doing some embroidery. She looked up. 'Are you upset about something, Jasmine? Was it all the politics last night? I never think it's good to talk about these things too much. I'm always telling Reggie it's not good to dwell on it. He gets so steamed up.'

'I felt stupid. Everyone was laughing at me.'

'No one was laughing. Come and sit down.' Mary patted the rattan sofa beside her. 'We were a little surprised when you came out with the British Go Home line. But I have to admit, I have a lot of sympathy for that view. Well, maybe not that we should go home, as I consider Penang to be my home, but that Malaya should be governed by Malayans. Of whatever ethnicity.'

'That's what I meant. But Howard was so patronising. He

made me feel stupid. All that stuff about the British economy.'

'Actually, he was mortified.' Mary looked at her with a kind expression. 'After you'd gone to bed he was full of remorse. Said he's always putting his foot in it with you.'

'We don't get on. We're simply not on the same wavelength. When I'm cross with him, he's nice to me. When I'm nice to him, he's rude or ignores me. It's like being on a seesaw.' She moved her arms up and down in a seesawing motion. 'I feel confused every time I'm with him as I don't know whether I'm coming or going. And as for him bringing up that record...' She covered her face with her hands.

'Yes, I sensed the last thing you wanted was for Reggie to put it on.'

'Thank you for rescuing me.'

'What's the song called?'

'*When You Were Sweet Sixteen*.' Jasmine felt her face burning.

'Ah, I see. Have you listened to it?'

Jasmine shook her head.

'Would you like me to take Frances for a walk so you can listen to it in private?'

'I don't really want to hear it at all, but if I do, I'd rather you were with me. But not in front of Reggie and certainly not in front of Howard.'

'Then let's put it on now. Frances loves it when there's music on the gramophone and she won't understand a word of it.'

Jasmine went over to the gramophone player, which stood just inside the drawing room adjoining the veranda where they were sitting. The disc was where Howard had left it last night. She slipped it out of the paper cover and found a folded note inside it. She was sure that hadn't been there before. Stuffing the note into her pocket before Mary noticed, she placed the record on the turntable, wound up the handle, lifted the arm, blew the fluff off the end of the needle and lowered the arm over the record. With a hiss of static it started to play. She stood motionless in front of the machine as the music poured out of it. First the sweeping melody of the orchestral accompaniment, then the tender voice of Como. She felt her face burning as he sang of first seeing the light of love shining in his lover's eyes. Other voices joined in like a heavenly choir. Jasmine leaned over and jerked the arm off the record. The needle scratched in strident protest.

She felt Mary's hand touch her and she turned around and buried her head in her former teacher's shoulder. Mary's arms went around her, holding her. Behind them Frances was wailing at the cessation of the music.

'Jinjiang!' Mary called out. 'Bring us some coffee on the veranda, please.' She led Jasmine back to the settee and picked up the baby.

'Why did he do that? He knew what an utter embarrassment it would be. I hate him.' Jasmine burst into tears.

'You don't hate him. Otherwise you wouldn't be so upset. But I agree he was unwise to make his feelings for you so apparent so soon, and then to embarrass you in front of us.' She sighed, then gave a little laugh. 'But, to be honest, Jasmine, most men are clueless about these things.' She bounced Frances up and down on her knee. 'Especially when they're head over heels in love.'

'Don't! He's not!'

'I'm afraid he is. Like it or not, my dear girl. He's got it bad. I'm sure he'll have been burning Reggie's ears all the way to George Town this morning, asking for advice about how to win you over.'

'No!' She buried her face in her hands.

'Maybe it would be a good idea if you weren't to see him for a while. Take some time to sort out your true feelings. You're young. Your whole life is in front of you. There are plenty of other nice young men as soon as you feel ready to meet some. Just because Howard Baxter is crazy about you doesn't mean you have to like him. If you find him odious, then you don't have to have anything to do with him. I'm sorry if Reggie and I seemed to be trying to throw you together. I can promise you, Jasmine, that was not the intent at all. We wanted you to have some younger company and we both rather like Howard, but if you don't—'

'I do!' The words were out before she could stop them. 'Well... sometimes I do.' She bent her head back and looked up towards the ceiling. 'But mostly, I don't.' She twisted her hands around as though she were washing them. 'I mean, I don't know what I really think. I'm so confused.'

Mary gave her a sad smile. 'He seems to have got under your skin. As I said, darling, give it time. Don't see him. He's not exactly on the doorstep anyway. Forget about him.'

'Yes.' Jasmine took a deep breath. 'Yes. Yes. I'll forget all about him.'

She smiled at Mary, gave a long sigh, and told herself that was the right decision.

17

R eggie had offered Jasmine a wooden hut on the far side of the padang to use as a studio. Open on one side, it got plenty of light. Overjoyed, for the first time in her life she had the time and space to experiment freely with her art without anyone looking over her shoulder or telling her to clear her materials away. There was even running water and a small tin sink where she could clean her brushes, as well as plenty of light, but away from the glare of direct sunshine.

She received a small monthly allowance from the sum of money left in trust for her by her father, so she had saved up and ordered an easel and some good quality oil paints. Malaya's climate was not conducive to oil painting, as the high humidity made paintings slow to dry, but Reggie had suggested she try putting them in the rubber-drying sheds. Instead of canvases, he had cut up some pieces of hardboard in varying sizes for her. Jasmine looked around her, a quiet sense of satisfaction mixed with anticipation. Her materials were laid out neatly on shelves. No untidy messes for her –

Jasmine liked order. A place for everything and everything in its place.

Now that the arranging of the space was completed to her satisfaction Jasmine felt a strange paralysis. Usually she worked rapidly, knowing exactly what she was going to work on and how, but now with the luxury of time and space, she was uncertain what to do next. She went to the pile of prepared boards. Maybe she could use her preliminary sketches to begin her painting of Frances. It was impossible to get the baby to pose – unless sleeping – and so she'd executed a series of quick pencil and charcoal studies and could use these to begin a painted portrait of the child. Yet, she hesitated. Thanks to Reggie's kindness, she could paint undisturbed, and yet she felt a curious reluctance to do anything.

She decided to go for a walk instead and look for inspiration. She could take her sketch book and gather some ideas then play with them when she got back. If she went for just an hour, she'd have the rest of the afternoon to work on what she'd found. Maybe she'd start small – gather some leaves, patterns of tree bark, the shapes of shadows on the ground, the splash of colour from orchids in the forest, or the receding perspective of endless ranks of rubber trees. Packing her satchel with a pad, some pencils, her portable tin water holder and a tiny palette of watercolours, she turned to leave the studio.

There in the doorway was the dark outline of Bintang. He seemed to take pleasure in creeping up on her.

'You say you want paint me. Now is good time?'

Surprised, she put down her satchel. 'Yes, of course. If you're not needed elsewhere.'

He didn't reply, but came into the room, looking around him. 'This was place for last *Mem*'s gardening equipment.'

'Last *Mem*?' For a moment she thought he must mean her own mother, then she reminded herself that, before the war, Reggie had been married to the woman she had called Aunty Susan, who during the war had shared a house with her, Mummy and Hugh while they were in Australia. Jasmine had forgotten Susan had been Mrs Hyde-Underwood, before the war changed everything. Susan's little boy, Stanford, used to be Hugh's best friend. Jasmine hadn't known Reggie then. He'd had to stay behind in Singapore and was imprisoned by the Japanese. It was hard to imagine Reggie with Susan. Such a different person from Mary. But then Mary had been a prisoner too. Jasmine imagined an experience like that must change people.

'Last *Mem* grow many orchid.'

'Really?' Jasmine couldn't picture Aunty Susan as a gardener. In Australia the former Mrs Hyde-Underwood had been more interested in getting her hair done and spending time with her friends at the hospital where she volunteered. Susan had had a rather strident laugh, as though trying to convince herself she was happy when she wasn't really. It was odd that Jasmine hadn't given Susan a thought in all this time. Mary and Reggie were such a devoted couple.

Changing the subject, she said, 'I think I'll do your head and shoulders only. A close portrait of your face.' She pulled a canvas chair over to the centre of the room and asked him to sit.

Once again, Jasmine noticed the fluidity of his cat-like movements: he glided rather than walked. Capturing that sense of motion could not be done with a static pose. The sketches she planned to make while he was cleaning the car would be essential. Should she tell him what she intended to do? She didn't want him to be self-conscious and hence behave in an artificial way, so she probably wouldn't. But sketching him as he went about his work, without telling him she was doing it, could be construed as a form of theft. How might he react if he found out – or if she showed him afterwards? She'd worry about that when the time came. Right now, she wanted to capture his face, his velvet-dark eyes, his aquiline nose.

Jasmine adjusted her easel, then took a fine brush, squeezed a tiny amount of burnt sienna into a saucer of turpentine, mixed it to a thin solution and used the brush to form the outline of his head. Using the diluted paint, she drew the basic framework of his skull until she'd settled on the correct proportions. Absorbed in her task, Jasmine moved rapidly, working now with larger brushes and directly in oils. The smell of the paint, cut through with the sharp tangy aroma of the turpentine, filled the air in the shed.

She lost track of time as she applied the paint, building up patterns of dark and light, forming the sharp contours of Bintang's face with the oil paint. Her challenge was balancing the sculpted angles of his face with his smooth complexion and the dark richness of his hair.

Bintang sat, motionless, and she marvelled at his self-containment. Most sitters by now would be fidgeting, impatient.

'You're a good subject. You've not moved a muscle. You make it easy for me.'

He said nothing, continuing to stare into space. She wondered what he was thinking about. Usually this kind of self-possession and tranquility in a sitter would be welcome, but Jasmine gradually began feeling uncomfortable and wanting to fill the silence. There was an intensity in him, a pent-up anger that both scared and fascinated her.

Eventually, she decided to force him to break his silence. 'Tell me more about how it was here during the war. I'm really curious. I was so young, but my memories of the Japanese planes are still vivid. I'd ask the Hyde-Underwoods, only my mother told me they wouldn't want to talk about it. Same with Arthur, my step-father.'

'So why you think I tell you?' His voice was neutral. 'Why I talk about it?'

'I don't know. I suppose because you've already told me about your parents and Siti. And you weren't a prisoner, so I thought you could tell me about everyday life here. How it was for you and your grandmother. I mean after the invasion, during the years of occupation.'

He looked at her with narrowed eyes. 'Everyone in Penang a prisoner. You say everyday life. Like it easy. You think because *Tuan* and *Mem* are in camp they suffer worst.'

'I didn't mean that at all.'

'You think see your sister have head blown off is everyday life?'

'Of course not.' She wished she had never embarked on this. 'That must have been utterly hateful. I can't imagine how it must have felt. But that was at the beginning of the war. The Japs were here for more than four years.'

'You think I got used to them being here? You think after while I forget what they do to my mother and sister?'

'No. I suppose not.'

His face contorted. 'Every time I see Japanese soldier I want to kill him. Cut throat from ear to ear. Every time I see Japanese soldier I see sister die again. I see again my mother screaming. See her pushed into lorry and taken away. See myself digging hole in ground for sister's grave. See a bloody hole in her head where her face used to be.'

Jasmine put down her paintbrush and covered her face with her hands.

'Every day I want to go into jungle to find my father and help him kill Japanese soldiers. But I must stay here like a girl with grandmother. I must stay and watch my cousin taken away to police station and never come out again.' He spoke the words with a contemptuous snarl.

'They imprisoned your cousin?'

'When go to police station in George Town no one come out. They torture for days, then they kill.'

'What had your cousin done?'

'Nothing.'

'Why did they take him then?'

'They say he spy. Take messages to MPAJA.'

The Malayan People's Anti-Japanese Army was, she remembered, the guerrilla fighters Reggie said Arthur had fought with. The fighting force that were supposed to have disbanded after the war but had morphed into the MNLA. 'And was he a spy?'

'My cousin not right in head. Never grow up. Like little boy. Too stupid to be spy. But they take him to police station in George Town and torture him and then they cut his head off. Put it on post on Weld Quay.'

A wave of nausea swept over her. 'I'm so sorry, Bintang. How old was your cousin and what was his name?'

He grunted and for the first time moved out of his pose, looking her straight in the eye. 'Ayyash. Name mean long life. He nineteen when die.' Bintang rose from the chair. 'I go now. Drive *Tuan* to George Town.'

Jasmine was relieved. She was desperate to be alone. 'Goodness, is that the time?' she said quickly, trying to cover her confusion. 'I've almost finished,' she lied. 'Perhaps we can have another session one day when you have more free time.' She turned away and dipped a brush in the jar of turpentine, then wiped it with a rag.

'Excuse me for barging in on you.' Mary stepped over the threshold, doing a double-take when she saw Bintang. 'Frances is having a nap, so I thought we could have a look at those French irregular verbs that are giving you so much trouble.' She looked again at Bintang and frowned slightly. 'But if this isn't a good time?'

Bintang said, 'We done.' He slipped outside and hurried away.

'You've been painting his portrait? Am I allowed to have a look?'

'Of course. But it isn't finished.' Jasmine felt herself blushing. Mary was clearly wondering why she was spending her time painting one of the servants. Jasmine hadn't even asked him if he was off duty. She hoped she hadn't got him into trouble.

Mary moved behind the easel. She looked at the portrait for several moments, while Jasmine busied herself cleaning the brushes.

'You're very talented, Jasmine. You've really captured Bintang. The rather arrogant expression, his guarded nature, those dark soulful eyes. It's unmistakably him. You must show Reggie. Not that he knows a lot about art, but he will definitely see the likeness.'

'I hope you don't mind me painting him. He has an interesting face, especially in profile and he said he had some free time.'

'He's driving Reggie into town this evening so, yes, he's free this afternoon. Reggie's got something on at the Club and I don't like him driving back up here at night with all those hairpin bends after he's had the inevitable number of *stengahs*.' She smiled indulgently. 'So, it'll be just us at supper tonight.'

Mary moved to a table at the back of the studio where Jasmine had gathered a collection of objects – oddly-shaped pebbles, pieces of bark, shells from the beach.

'This reminds me of the nature table we used to have at school,' said Mary. 'Do you remember? We should set one up at the school in the *kampong* – we could ask the children to bring in any interesting objects.' She picked up a brightly coloured feather and stroked it across the back of her hand before replacing it on the table. 'French verbs, then?'

Jasmine gave a resigned nod.

'Only I did promise your mother I'd make sure you were ready for the examinations.'

Jasmine smiled. 'I hate French. But it's a jolly sight more bearable with you than it was with the nuns in Nairobi.'

AFTER THEY HAD EATEN that evening, Mary and Jasmine sat together on the veranda, as the cicadas buzzed and the sounds of nightbirds and other creatures drifted towards them from the copse of hardwood trees behind the plantation bungalow.

'I rather put my foot in it with Bintang today,' Jasmine said. 'I made the mistake of asking him what it was like here under the Japs.'

She sensed Mary stiffen.

'Did he tell you?'

'Not much. But what he did tell me, I wish I hadn't heard.'

'Then forget about it.' Mary's tone was unusually curt. 'Best not to dig over these things.'

'I hope you don't mind that I was painting him?'

'Why should I mind?'

'I suppose with him being one of the servants.'

'That makes no difference to me. Reggie too. You can paint whom you please. I was rather surprised Bintang was willing to sit for you though.'

'I don't think Howard likes him.'

'Really? Why's that?'

Jasmine had the impression that Mary wasn't all that interested in the answer, so she shrugged – she didn't want to admit that Howard had told her he was jealous of Bintang. Too embarrassing. 'No reason that I could understand.'

'So, that's why you decided to paint him?' There was the shadow of a smile on Mary's face.

'I'm painting him because he has an interesting face. In fact, I find him a thoroughly interesting person. He reminds me of a cat. Maybe because I never hear him coming. I turn round and he's there.'

'Are you frightened of him?' Mary looked alarmed.

'No! Not at all. It was an observation not a criticism. I like him very much; even though I may have offended him by asking him so many questions.'

'I doubt that. If he'd been offended, he wouldn't have answered them.'

Jasmine nodded. 'I suppose that's true.' She gave a rueful smile. 'I can't imagine Bintang would ever do anything he didn't want to do.'

Mary got up from her chair. 'School tomorrow. An early night for me.'

'That's a jolly good idea.'

Jasmine was grateful for the chance to get to her room where she could mull over what had happened today.

Understanding other human beings was even more complicated than French irregular verbs.

She noticed that someone, Jinjiang possibly, had
returned the Perry Como record to where it had been on top
of the tallboy. She should have thought to do that herself.
Imagine if Reggie had decided to play it one evening. She
picked the record up, put it inside a drawer and covered it
with her underwear.

It was only then that she remembered she'd never read
the note she'd found inside the sleeve. She'd slipped it into
the pocket of the dress she'd been wearing that day. She
located the right frock in the wardrobe and retrieved the
paper. Crumpling it into a tight ball, she decided she
wouldn't read it and flung it into the litter basket.

Curiosity got the better of her after a few minutes, so she
fished it out again, uncurled it and flattened the creases. She
sat down on the edge of the bed and started to read.

'Dear Jasmine,

*Yet again I have managed to upset you. Please forgive me. I
always open my mouth before I've put my brain in gear. You
must think me a pompous twit for going on about the political
situation when I've only been in Malaya five minutes. I'm trying
desperately hard to understand the country and, if I'm honest,
trying too hard to impress you. You must think me a shallow
show off.*

Jasmine found herself smiling, imagining him writing it.
She read on.

*And I know my bringing up that Perry Como recording must
have embarrassed you. If I could wind the clock back, I would.
The last thing I want to do is upset you or hurt you. I'd rather
hoped you'd have come along to the cricket this morning. It would
have given me a chance to make amends.*

I don't know when we will get a chance to meet again. Every day until then I'll be fuelled by hope that you will have managed to forgive me. I have no right to expect it but I can't help but hope.

It was signed only with his initial. She was glad he hadn't signed it 'with love'. He had rather nice handwriting, bold and confident. She read the note again, then went across the room and placed it underneath the record in her drawer.

18

A few days later, Jasmine and Mary had returned from the school and were about to go in to lunch, when Reggie burst into the house and onto the side veranda to find them.

'Not like you to be late for tiffin, darling.' Mary smiled.

'We need to talk.' Reggie's face was ashen.

'Then we can talk over lunch. Jinjiang is about to serve.' She saw his face and frowned. 'Here, sit down and get your breath back. You look white as a sheet.'

'No. It can't wait.' Reggie's expression was grim. 'This is serious.' Exchanging glances, Mary and Jasmine perched on the edges of their chairs. Reggie's tone shocked Jasmine. Normally such a genial man, he was almost barking at them.

Mary looked up at her husband. 'What's happened? What on earth's wrong, Reggie? You're frightening Jasmine.'

'I've had a phone call in the office. There's been an incident.'

'An incident?'

He lowered his voice but Jasmine could still hear what

he was saying. 'More than an incident. The commies have shot three planters dead.'

Jasmine's hand shot up to her mouth. A spike of fear rushed through her. Not Howard. Please not Howard. The force of her terror surprised her.

Mary spoke calmly, 'Who? When? Where?'

'In Sungei Siput. This morning. They've been ringing round everyone but we're at the end of the chain since we're over here on the island. This is it, Mary. This is war.' Reggie's expression was grim and he was speaking faster than usual. 'Dear God, we've barely recovered from the last one.' His face looked haggard, his eyes wild.

Mary got up and placed her hands on his arms. 'Calm down, Reggie.' She then addressed Jasmine without turning to look at her. 'Go in and ask Jinjiang to make tea. Strong with plenty of sugar.'

Jasmine was about to go, when Jinjiang, as if telepathic, appeared at the entrance to the veranda. Mary issued her instructions again.

'It's not tea, I need, it's a damn stiff scotch.'

'Well you can't have one, darling. It sounds as though you'll need to keep a clear head.'

Reggie ignored her and went inside to the cocktail cabinet in the sitting room beyond. He swigged down a gulp of whisky and settled himself in one of the veranda chairs with the tumbler. 'I was at Sungei Siput only a couple of weeks ago. There was a meeting to discuss holding the line against the strikers.' He glanced at Jasmine, then looked at Mary, who immediately said, 'She's nearly seventeen. She needs to understand what's happening.'

Reggie looked down. 'Soon after nine this morning. Three men on bicycles arrived at Elphil's Estate. All Chinese. Walker was in the office and they went in, greeted him with a friendly "*Tabek, Tuan!*". Walker returned the greeting and they shot him twice, there at his desk in front of the Indian clerk. Straight through the heart.'

'Oh my God! That's horrible. Wally Walker! Is Verna all right?'

'Verna's fine. Well, she's obviously in shock at losing her husband like that, poor woman. She'd gone into Kuala Kangsar early that morning to do some shopping so wasn't there when it happened. She and Wally were due to go on home leave. Bloody awful timing.' Reggie took another gulp of scotch. 'The poor clerk was scared out of his skin but they didn't touch him. Looked him right in the eye, then one of them spat at him. Must have wanted a witness. That's the kind of men they are. Cold-blooded killers. They want to put the fear of God in people. They walked away and escaped on their bikes as if nothing had happened. There was money in the safe but they didn't touch it.'

'So, who else was killed? You said three men are dead.' Mary sounded impatient.

'Round about the same time, a gang of about a dozen men turned up at the Phin Soon estate down the road from Ephil's. John Allison and his assistant, a young chap called Ian Christian, had their hands tied behind their backs and marched at gunpoint to Allison's bungalow. They wanted his gun which was in the house. Then they took them back to the office and onto the veranda. They tied them to chairs and shot them both dead with tommy guns.'

Mary and Jasmine gasped.

'Then they torched the drying sheds and the rubber stores.'

'You think the two attacks were coordinated?'

'Must have been. You know how much trouble there's been

over at Sungei Siput among the Chinese tappers. They'd been on strike. Only been back at work two days. Posters all over the place about killing the "running dogs". According to the police there was a big meeting of all the communist leaders in the town a few weeks ago. Must have been plotting this then.'

'If they knew they were all in town why on earth didn't the police round them all up?' asked Mary.

Reggie shook his head. 'Not allowed to. The police reckon every top communist in Malaya was there that night and they couldn't do a damn thing about it. It was only a matter of time until something like this happened. Bloody useless government.'

'Did something specific trigger it?'

Reggie shrugged. 'The endless demands for higher wages. Allison took a hard line with them. Always was a difficult bugger.' He pursed his lips. 'But it looks like standing up to them cost him his life, poor bastard.' Reggie shook his head.

Jinjiang was hovering in the doorway, waiting to announce lunch. 'Bring me another *stengah*, JJ, and make it a stiff one.'

This time Mary didn't object.

Jasmine was struggling to take in the import of this news. 'Where is Sungei Siput?' She couldn't help wondering how close it was to Batu Lembah.

'In Perak. North of Ipoh.'

'Is it near Batu Lembah?'

'About an hour's drive.' Reggie polished off his second whisky and Mary coaxed him into the dining room and made him eat something.

Jasmine didn't feel hungry and picked at her food. The cold-blooded murder of three planters was much too close to home for her to absorb. That assistant could have been Howard.

'I need to call Verna Walker and pass on our condolences,' said Mary. 'Was Allison's assistant married?'

Jasmine marvelled at the teacher's calm.

'Christian? No. He was just a lad. Twenty-one apparently. Been out here less than a year. He'd been due to start his first manager's job in a couple of days, poor devil.'

Jasmine felt as though a shard of ice had been plunged into her. Only four or five years older than her. She tried to imagine how she'd feel if it had been Howard. A wave of nausea washed over her and she made it to the bathroom just in time to throw up. After splashing cold water over her face, she returned to join the others. 'Excuse me.' She slipped back into her seat, but couldn't eat another morsel.

'Are you all right, Jasmine?' Mary's eyes were full of concern.

'Absolutely.'

'I need to go over to Perak.' Reggie's face was still contorted with suppressed anger. They'll be burying the men tonight. It's only right I show up. And there's a meeting of the planters. We can't let the bastards get away with this.' He gave a groan and shook his head. 'Walker was imprisoned in Changi with me. He survived that only to be butchered in his own office.

Mary placed her hand on his arm. 'I think you should leave it to those on the peninsula. Things are different over here. You don't need to be involved.'

'We're all involved. We planters stand together. This is war, Mary.'

'It might not come to that. It could have been a couple of isolated incidents.'

'Why in God's name would it be isolated incidents? They

got away with it. Those devils will have disappeared back to their jungle camps to start planning the next attack. If we don't crush this now they could come after all of us.'

'Stop it, Reggie, you're scaring Jasmine.'

'I'm not scared,' she lied.

'But you planters shouldn't be playing soldiers.' Mary was still the voice of calm. 'It's up to the government. They'll have to act now. Three British planters dead. They have no alternative.'

Reggie harrumphed. 'I wish I shared your confidence, darling, but the High Commissioner couldn't run a piss up in a brewery. Pardon my language, Jasmine.' He got to his feet. 'I've no idea when I'll be back. Don't wait up for me. I need to get moving.'

Mary tried to stay him with a hand on his arm. 'Are you taking Ronny and Kevin?' She was referring to the Assistant Manager and the junior.

'No. I'm going on my own. They need to keep things going here. And I'm not leaving you girls and Frances unprotected.'

'Then you'll have Bintang drive you?'

'No. I want to leave as many men here as possible. I'll be fine. Main roads all the way. Those bandits rely on stealth and being able to melt back into the jungle. They won't risk the main roads. Anyway, there'll be police crawling about everywhere.'

Jinjiang came in to clear away the lunch. 'Tiffin not good?'

'It's perfect, Jinjiang. But none of us has much of an appetite today. Has Frances had hers?'

The *amah* nodded solemnly. 'She very hungry. Good baby.'

'I'll come and get her in a moment. We can sit in the

shade on the veranda.' As Jinjiang left the room, Mary
turned to her husband again. 'You're determined to go
alone?'

He nodded. 'I'll take the jeep.'

'Then I won't try to stop you. But be very careful. No silly
risks. And stay overnight. Better than driving in the dark.
Promise me.' She held onto his arm.

Reggie bent down and kissed the top of his wife's head.
'I'll be back as soon as I can tomorrow. I'll get a room in
Ipoh. Or stay with the Hembrys at Kamuning. He runs his
estate like Fort Knox. I'll be safe there.' Then with a wave to
both of them, he bounded down the steps and strode away.

It was only once he was gone that Mary showed any
emotion. Then it was only a small sob that she managed to
choke off before it turned to tears. 'What's going to happen?
I should have been stronger in what I told your mother,
Jasmine. I should have told her that civil war here was
inevitable.' Her expression was wretched. 'We'll have to
arrange to send you home.'

'No!' Jasmine was surprised at her own vehemence. 'I
don't want to go back to Kenya. Not yet.' She actually hoped
never to have to go back. 'Anyway, as you said, this might be
an isolated incident. And we're safe here on Penang. If
there's trouble, it's going to be on the peninsula.' She folded
her arms. 'I don't want you to tell Mummy what's happened.'

'Oh, darling, it's going to be all over the news everywhere. Three British men murdered in one morning. Evie's
going to find out. She may know by now anyway with
Arthur being in the Colonial Office. It will have come
through on the wires.'

Jasmine frowned. 'Then we need to reassure her if she's
worried. It's going to be fine here. I know it is. Why on earth
would the communists come across here to Penang on the

ferry? Bella Vista is small in comparison with most of the other estates across the water. As Howard Baxter was all too keen to point out when he was boring me to death about his job.' She felt a twinge of guilt at speaking ill of Howard when she had felt genuine fear for him when Reggie brought them the news. She brushed the thought aside. 'That's why Daddy bought Batu Lembah in the first place when he wanted to expand.'

Mary said, 'You're probably right, but it's not up to me to make that decision. I'm not your mother and imagine how I'd feel if something happened to you. How could I face Evie?'

Jasmine gave her a wry smile. 'If something happened to me it would probably happen to you too, so you wouldn't be around to worry about it.'

Mary narrowed her eyes. 'You're too clever for your own good, young lady.'

But Jasmine knew she'd won the argument. She wasn't going to raise the subject of Frances but Mary wouldn't put her own baby at risk. And Mary would never leave Reggie's side. If they were staying here then so would she.

'You didn't eat any lunch. Maybe you should ask Jinjiang to make you a sandwich.'

'I'm not hungry. I'm going over to the studio. I'll take some fruit with me.' It was the first time she'd called the wooden shed by that name and she liked the sound of it.

'Stay in your studio then. Don't go wandering off around the estate. Not until Reggie gets back and we know exactly what's going on.'

BINTANG MUST HAVE SEEN her going into the studio, as he appeared on the threshold moments later.

Jasmine was pleased and relieved to see him. She had worried their last conversation may have marked the end of their understanding. 'Have you come to sit for me again?'

'You say not finished.' He shrugged. 'But if you doing something else–' He turned to leave.

'No! Now is perfect. If you don't mind. And if you aren't busy?'

'*Tuan* tell me to stay near house. Watch you and *Mem* and baby.'

She placed the unfinished portrait on the easel, and he took up his seat again in the centre of the room.

'You heard what happened, then? Three planters murdered.'

'Yes.'

She looked up at him, surprised at the monosyllabic response. 'Don't you find it shocking?'

'No.'

At a loss for words, Jasmine's hand trembled as she unscrewed the tube of paint and squeezed some onto her palette. 'Three innocent men, shot in cold blood.'

'Innocent?'

'Of course they were innocent. And defenceless. Mr Hyde-Underwood said two of them were tied to a chair. That's an execution.'

'And you think British people don't do executions too? You have death penalty.'

'Only when someone has been tried in court and found guilty.'

'Maybe these men try in court too. Not your British court.'

She put down the brush and moved round from behind the easel to look at him. He continued to stare ahead, maintaining his pose. 'You think those communists were right, don't you? Why?'

'After war we work to rebuild our country when Japanese try to destroy it. Now tin and rubber production up but wages stay low. British are greedy. It's our rubber, our tin, our timber, our land, but British steal it and send rubber and tin to America and England. Better we drive them out and run our country ourselves.'

Jasmine's mouth was wide open, but she couldn't help but follow the logic of his argument. 'Those men who killed the planters aren't even workers. They're bandits who live in the jungle. Chinese communists. Not Malayans. They don't even have Malayan citizenship.' She hoped she was correct in what she was saying, trying to remember past conversations between the Hyde-Underwoods on the subject.

'They promised citizenship to Chinese but British and sultans betray them.'

'But the sultans are Malay. You are Malay, Bintang. Why do you care so much about the Chinese Malayans?'

He looked at her with cold, hard eyes. 'Chinese people are in Malaya because British bring them here to work in tin mines. Like Indian people in rubber estates. British want us work to make money for them. Nothing for us.'

She shivered involuntarily. Yet she wasn't afraid. Rather, she was fascinated. His perspective was so different from any other she'd heard. Jasmine had always believed there were two sides to most arguments. Yet to hear the British spoken of this way was deeply shocking to her. Bintang was brazen. Fearless. She felt a surge of admiration.

'Does the *tuan* know you feel this way?'

Bintang gave a sardonic laugh. '*Tuan* know nothing. I not say these things to *Tuan*. Only to you because you school-friend of Siti.'

Jasmine was shocked, but strangely touched. She had liked Siti at school but barely knew her and didn't feel she had ever regarded her as a proper friend.

Hiding herself behind her easel, out of his view, she thought about what Bintang had said. She realised it was not because Siti was an unlikeable girl. It was simply because she was Malay. While they had been friendly enough in class and on the playground, the idea of inviting Siti to her home would never have entered her head. Inside the four walls of the school they were all equals but that equality never extended beyond. Jasmine thought of all the friends she had visited, all the parties she had attended. Siti and the handful of other Malay girls had never been included. A sense of shame filled her.

'Siti speak often of you. She like you best. You had other friend, Penny.'

'Yes. Penny lived next door to Mrs Hyde-Underwood before the war.' She was about to add that Penny had been her best friend, but then decided it was better not to. Instead she said, 'She was a prisoner of the Japanese with Mrs Hyde-Underwood. She lives in Australia now.'

But Bintang was staring into the middle distance again, uninterested in hearing about Penny.

19

The following day, Jasmine and Mary remained in the bungalow, waiting for Reggie's return. It poured all morning in a heavy deluge and Jasmine felt like a caged tiger, pacing up and down the veranda, unable to concentrate on her schoolwork, wishing she could escape to her studio but conscious she'd promised Mary to work on her Latin vocabulary for a test. She held the primer open in front of her but the words swam out of focus and she looked past the book to the downpour. She was supposed to be revising prepositions and conjunctions and couldn't remember which prepositions went with the accusative and which with the ablative. In fact she couldn't even understand the difference between these. And as for the ablative absolute – she'd been close to tears trying to master that one and still hadn't managed.

Translation was just about bearable when it was Ovid. The Metamorphoses were actually quite interesting with all those stories of killing serpents, burying the teeth and warriors springing up out of the soil. But when it came to endless Gallic and Punic wars, she was bored to death. It was patently clear she was going to fail the exam, so she felt a rising resentment at having to waste time swotting for it. Even those ghastly French irregular verbs were preferable.

What was the point of it all? Latin was a dead language for dead people. It existed now for the sole purpose of driving living people round the bend. Back in Nairobi she'd begged to be allowed to give it up but Arthur had convinced Mummy that an education was incomplete without mastery of the Classics. The one concession Jasmine had managed to win was giving up Ancient Greek. All her efforts to convince her parents that the only reason to study Latin was to meet the entrance requirements for university, and she didn't want to go anyway, fell on fallow ground.

Jinjiang brought in the post and newspaper and handed the bundle to Mary, who set aside the mail and pored over *The Straits Times*. The headlines were stark: 'Five estate murders in one day. Three Europeans killed: Gurkhas rushed to scene.'

Jasmine, looking over Mary's shoulder, asked, 'Five?'

Mary looked up from the paper. 'Two Chinese killed as well. A contractor in Taiping and a Kuomintang member down in Johore. The Kuomintang chap was ambushed, apparently. There was a strike on the estate where he worked which had just ended. She folded the paper. 'Here, you can read it. I need to check on Frances.'

Jasmine, grateful for the reprieve from Latin, pulled the newspaper towards her and started to read. She'd never bothered with it before but she was determined that from now on she'd read the news every day. It was important to keep pace with what was going on. It would lessen the chance of making an utter fool of herself in future in front of obnoxious Howard Baxter.

The paper was full of the estate killings and the consequent announcement of a state of emergency in parts of Perak and Johore. Jasmine couldn't help noticing that while the report of the deaths of Allison, Christian and Walker dominated the front page, the details of the other killings were scanty. She pointed this out to Mary, who had come back to join her.

'That's because, alas, the murder of Chinese has become all too common. A daily occurrence. Since the end of the war the communists have been exacting revenge on anyone suspected of collaborating with the Japanese. During the war they allied with the Kuomintang but as soon as the Japs were defeated they turned on the Chinese nationalists. Now they include anyone they see as strike breakers. And not only the individuals concerned, but their families too – and the local villagers. The communists work on striking terror into people so they'll have no choice but to support them and withdraw their labour from the tin mines and rubber estates.'

Jasmine debated whether to ask the question that was on her mind. She felt so ill-informed. But Mary was no supercilious Howard. 'I know I ought to know...' she said, hesitantly, 'but what's the *Kuomintang*?'

There was no implied criticism in Mary's response. 'It's the Chinese nationalist party, under Chiang Kai Shek. Sworn enemies of the communists.'

A sudden high-pitched wailing. 'Her ladyship has woken up.' Mary rolled her eyes. 'Teething has turned my little angel into a howling devil, poor wee soul.' She went to attend to her daughter.

JASMINE AND MARY had just sat down to tiffin when they heard the sound of Reggie's motorcar. As soon as he entered the dining room he went straight to the cabinet and poured himself a scotch.

'How did you get on? Was it beastly?' Mary's eyes were filled with concern.

She got up from the table and went to Reggie, putting her arms around him and resting her head on his chest. He dropped a kiss on the top of her head.

'I hope I don't ever have to go through something like that again.' Reggie shook his head, his eyes sad. 'Bloody awful. Poor Verna was distraught. The estate workers are in fear of their lives. There was a miserable little ceremony to bury the three chaps. All far too young. Allison was the oldest and he was only fifty-five. And that poor Christian fellow still in his twenties with his whole life ahead of him.' Reggie looked away, shaking his head.

Jasmine bit her lip. She felt conflicted. Bintang's words were fresh in her mind, but he surely couldn't condone the cold-blooded butchering of planters? Tying them up and blasting them with tommy-guns was a cowardly act.

'And that useless excuse for a High Commissioner still thinks this is all exaggerated and won't do a damn thing about it.'

'Surely he's going to do something?' Mary, as ever, was conciliatory.

'He's sent the Gurkhas in, but not enough troops to protect everyone. We planters are going to have to protect ourselves. That means we need to be armed and Gent is doing nothing on that score. I think he thinks if he keeps his head down it will go away.' He finished off his *stengah* and pulled out a chair at the table. 'Well it won't.'

Jasmine carried on eating her lunch while she listened intently.

Reggie helped himself to cold meat and salad, then called out to the *amah*, 'Bring me a beer will you, JJ?'

When Jinjiang returned with the bottle and a glass, he took a swig, then began to eat. 'I'm going to get the telephone put in here in the bungalow. It's not enough just to have it out in my office.'

'Nothing's going to happen. And there's no point as I never use the telephone.' Mary smiled fondly at her husband. 'If anyone wants to reach us they can get you at the office. And if you're not there, the clerk always knows where you are. Honestly, Reggie, please don't bother. Save the expense.'

He looked up at her. 'No arguing, darling. Decision already made. They're coming to fix it next week. I want you to be able to get hold of me if anything happens or you're worried for any reason. And the other way round – if I think something's afoot I can call you so you can either get away or hide.'

Mary opened her mouth to respond but must have thought better of it. Jasmine wondered if her presence at the table was, as she had learned in her French lesson the previous week, *de trop* and whether she should excuse herself so they could talk freely.

Before she could decide, Mary spoke again. 'Who was at the funeral then?'

'Everyone within driving distance. Usual suspects. Afterwards we all repaired to the FMS Bar in Ipoh. The talk was around how we're going to keep safe from these devils and how we're going to get the damn government to take this seriously.'

'What do they want to do?'

'First thing is self defence. All the estates over there have

run barbed wire everywhere and put a guard on the gates –
we're going to have to do that here too.'

Mary looked stricken. 'Surely that's not necessary here
on the island. I can't bear the thought of being hemmed in
by barbed wire as if we were in a prison camp.'

Reggie leaned across the table and took her hand. 'I
know, my darling. I don't like it either. Better that though
than putting ourselves in danger. And if those idiots in
Whitehall and the useless waste of space sitting in Government House in Kuala Lumpur pulled their fingers out, this
could be all over by Christmas. But as they likely won't, we
need to get used to being constantly alert.'

Jasmine was desperate to ask Reggie if he'd seen Howard
Baxter at the funeral but didn't want the Hyde-Underwoods
to think she was interested in him, when she wasn't,
was she?

But her curiosity was answered when Reggie said, 'Our
friend Baxter was there too. Asked after you, Jasmine.'

She felt her face turning red.

'How was he?' asked Mary. 'I don't imagine he expected
to walk into this when he decided to come to Malaya.'

'None of us did.' Reggie's face was grim. 'But yes, he
seems a resilient chap. If he's half as good with a sten gun in
his hands as he is with a cricket bat, he'll be safe enough at
Batu Lembah.'

'A sten gun? I thought he said he only had an old gun
that didn't work.' Jasmine didn't like the sound of this at all.

'O'Keefe managed to get hold of some sten guns. Only
problem is they haven't got the ammunition for them yet. A
delegation of planters has gone down to KL to see the High
Commissioner. Intend to read the man the riot act. I think
things may start to move in the next few days. He can't keep
pretending there's nothing happening. Old fool.'

A fully functioning sten gun with no bullets or a broken Japanese castoff. Neither would be much use to Howard if the terrorists came calling. He'd be better off with his cricket bat.

Mary got up from the table and went to fetch *The Straits Times*. 'Did you have time to read the editorial today?' she asked Reggie.

'I read the front page on the ferry.' He took the paper from her, turned to the editorial and started to read. He gave a long whistle. 'They haven't pulled their punches, have they? "Govern or get out!". Maybe that will convince Gent that he can't sit any longer in his ivory tower with his head up his–'

'That's enough, Reggie.' Mary's voice was quiet but authoritative. 'With the newspaper spelling it out like that I don't think he has any choice but to act now.'

Reggie nodded. 'Let's hope so.'

THE NEWSPAPER EDITORIAL had the required effect and the following morning the High Commissioner, Sir Edward Gent, extended the state of emergency nationwide. Over the following days, terrorist incidents continued, as planters took to driving in armoured vehicles. Barbed wire surrounded plantations and mines, traffic police wore guns, even in the cities, and there were soldiers and special constables everywhere. This was not enough to stop the communists, who could slip in and out of the jungle at will without detection.

One evening as they ate supper, Reggie said, 'Next week we have a guest. He will be staying with us overnight.'

Mary looked up sharply. 'Who? Why?'

'Some chap from the military. Anti-terror division. He's

coming to undertake a security assessment and help us prepare our defences.'

'What?' Mary put down her knife and fork. 'You're not serious, Reggie. What defences?'

Reggie coughed and looked down. 'That's the point. We don't actually have any. That's what he'll be doing here. Assessing what we need to do. How we prepare ourselves so nothing untoward happens.'

'Nothing untoward? What exactly do you mean by that? Are you telling me we're in danger? We're under threat?' Mary looked quickly at Jasmine who was listening intently.

'Goodness, no! I certainly hope not. We're a long way from the communist terrorists over here. It's more of a precaution. And a reassurance. Making sure the place looks like a stronghold will help to keep any CTs away. If we look entirely unprepared it's an invitation. All cosmetic really. And a case of being ready, should things break out over here on Penang.' His eyes darted between the two women. 'Which of course they won't.'

Jasmine looked sideways at Mary and saw her jaw was set tight and hard.

'You're right of course, Reggie.' Mary reached across the table and took his hand. 'We need to be ready for anything. And we will be. We've been through worse. We'll get through this. But we can't forget we are responsible for you, Jasmine, and we're going to have to let your parents know exactly how the land lies.'

'I'm not going back. If Mummy and Arthur say I'm to come home I won't go.' Though she spoke the words defiantly, she realised she couldn't stay at Bella Vista if the Hyde-Underwoods refused to allow her. 'If you won't let me stay here, I'll stay somewhere else. I'll ask our old *amah*,

Aunty Mimi, if I can stay with her in George Town. Please don't scare Mummy into insisting I go back.'

Another glance passed between the Hyde-Underwoods.

Reggie stretched his mouth into a grim line. 'Here's what I think. We should wait and see what this army chap has to say. Once we get a proper assessment of the situation, we can decide what to do.'

'When is this man coming? And what's his name?'

'He'll let us know but it's likely to be the middle of next week as he's working his way through and I imagine we're near the bottom of the list. He said his name was Harris. Don't know which regiment.'

Mary smiled. 'It wouldn't mean much to me if you did. I'm not exactly well-versed in the construction of the British army, darling.'

Jasmine wasn't looking forward to meeting another stranger and having to make polite conversation over the dinner table. She had come here to Penang expecting the calm and tranquillity of her idyllic childhood home, and now here she was in a country on the brink of what looked like becoming a civil war. After the suffocating atmosphere of her convent school and the tedium of the rote learning she was expected to do in order to pass her school certificate, being in the middle of a war was a very different prospect. Whatever it was, Jasmine was ready for it.

20

Jasmine had been putting off doing something she considered her duty – going to visit her father's grave. Before the Japanese invasion she and Mummy had regularly gone to tend it and she was feeling guilty that she hadn't yet fulfilled her promise to Evie to stop by there every now and again.

Her memories of Douglas Barrington were perhaps filtered through a rose-coloured, childhood lens. To be honest, she had to admit she hadn't known Daddy all that well. There had always been a distance between them – imposed by him not her. For a start, he'd spent most of his time at Batu Lembah and only weekends with her and Mummy in George Town. He'd always been kind to Jasmine, but it would be stretching things to say he had been affectionate. He wasn't that type of man. But she had nonetheless loved him with an intense devotion.

'Would you like me to come with you?' Mary asked her over breakfast. 'I could leave Frances with Jinjiang.'

'No. I'll manage. It's something I have to do. And it's

probably better that I do it on my own. Bintang will make sure I'm safe.'

In truth, Jasmine was looking forward to spending some more time with the driver. There was so much she wanted to talk to him about.

THEY SET off at around nine, Jasmine as usual in the back seat, Bintang silent, his eyes fixed on the road ahead. Trying to talk to the back of his head when she couldn't read his facial expression was awkward, so she settled back against the leather upholstery and stared out of the window as they descended to George Town, wishing she could be seated beside him in the front where conversation would be easier.

The cemetery was on Western Road, at the foot of Penang Hill. The graveyard had been the Christian burial place since it superseded the Old Protestant Cemetery in the late nineteenth century. Diseases such as cholera and malaria meant early European settlers had died in large numbers and the old graveyard had rapidly filled.

Bintang parked outside the gates and Jasmine walked under the tile-roofed entrance porch and into the grounds. She looked over her shoulder and saw he was following her at a distance. Probably Reggie's instructions.

The cemetery was a quiet and shady sanctuary, full of trees, peaceful apart from the omnipresence of mosquitoes. She stopped, as she had done as a child, by the grave to Andrew Duncan, a man who had died in the previous decade, before the war. His simple slab tombstone was made distinctive by the addition of a large white marble dog who was lying across the grave as though pining for his master. According to the inscription, he had been only forty-three when his wife Evelyn had dedicated the memorial. The same age as her father when he'd died. And Evelyn was Evie's name. When Jasmine had seen the tomb as a child these thoughts had not occurred to her, so taken had she been with the large, white, grieving dog. Daddy had had a beloved mastiff too, Badger, overlarge, black and not a little intimidating. After her father's death, Reggie Hyde-Underwood had taken care of Badger, who had survived the war, the Japanese occupation, and Reggie's imprisonment, only to die a few weeks before Jasmine had arrived at Bella Vista.

She walked on, uncertain of the way to her father's plot. After more than ten minutes in which she was starting to think she'd never remember where the grave was, there it was in front of her. Moss and lichen speckled the surface of the stone but the inscription was still clear. She had brought pagoda flowers, wanting something native to Malaya – a mass of delicate clusters of red, white and orange blossoms. Jasmine arranged them in a tall stone jar, which she filled from a nearby tap, adding two sprigs of foliage from a rubber tree. Her father had been passionate about growing rubber. He had lived and breathed it and was never so happy as when striding along the serried ranks of rubber trees with Badger at his heels. But rubber and Badger had been the cause of his premature death – he had fallen down a disused tin mine shaft while looking for the dog who had run off into the jungle on the edge of the estate at Batu Lembah, and Doug had died as a result of his injuries.

Jasmine supposed she ought to say a prayer for him, but she wasn't in the habit of praying and, to the best of her knowledge, Douglas Barrington had not been a religious man. She cleared away some encroaching creepers and pulled up some weeds, then sat back on her haunches and surveyed the grave.

How would her life have been had her father lived?

Would they still be living in the house here in George Town, while he spent his weekdays at Batu Lembah? Would he have survived the war? Would he have been one of those men who stayed behind during the war, like Arthur, or might he have died anyway doing hard labour on the Siam railway, or starving to death in Changi prison? Mummy would have been still with him, instead of living with Arthur in Africa. Wishing Daddy to be alive would be the same as wishing Mummy to be unhappy. For, whatever she thought of Africa herself, Jasmine couldn't deny that Evie was happy with Arthur and she couldn't begrudge her that.

Her reverie was interrupted by the arrival of Bintang, who had evidently been lurking out of sight while he smoked one of his blessed cigarettes. He came to stand beside her and looked at her father's headstone.

'Good you have place to come to remember dead.'

'I'm sorry, Bintang. I know you have no grave to visit for your parents.'

'Maybe they not dead.' He gave a shrug. 'I have place for Siti, but it bad. Not peaceful place like this.'

'What do you mean?'

'We bury Siti where Japanese men kill her on edge of field. Grandmother put wooden sign but it wash away in rains. There is jackfruit tree. After Siti die, no more jack fruit grow.'

'Gosh.' Jasmine didn't know what to say. Bintang always appeared unhappy, filled with repressed anger and resentment. But it was little wonder, given the terrible events he had witnessed. 'That's awful, Bintang. I'm so sorry.'

He nodded towards the flower arrangement she had constructed. 'Flowers for the *tuan besar*.'

'I'd like to place some flowers for Siti. Would you take

me to her grave some time?' She hoped he wouldn't be offended. 'Perhaps I could meet your grandmother too?'

His face clouded. 'Grandmother speak no English.'

Somehow, she didn't think that was a genuine objection. If it were even true. Yet the expression on his face made it clear a visit from Jasmine would not be welcome. How she wished she could win his trust.

She scrambled to her feet.

'I don't want to go back to Bella Vista yet. Will you take me somewhere else? Penang Hill?'

He frowned, his dark brows dipping over his brown eyes. '*Tuan* say I must stay with you all time. If you go in train I must go too.' He looked uncomfortable.

'That's all right. We can go up together.'

'You not want to go in train with servant.'

Jasmine laughed. 'Don't be silly, Bintang. What difference does that make?'

His face was expressionless but he drove the car in the direction of the funicular, clearly uncomfortable about riding in the rail car with her.

Once they were on the train, he tried to stand, but she told him to sit down beside her. 'If you stand up, you'll block the view.'

He sat beside her and stared in silence out of the window.

Jasmine remembered the last time she had been here, when Howard had talked nonstop to the man in the car who was explaining how the railway worked. Today, they were the only people in the carriage and the silence was deafening.

When they reached the top Bintang followed behind her, as he had done in the cemetery.

Jasmine turned round and stopped. 'For goodness sake,

Bintang, please walk with me. I feel very odd walking along with you trailing behind me as if you don't know me.'

Scowling, he complied and they walked on in silence.

When they reached the panoramic view point, where she had stopped with Howard, Jasmine sat down on a bench and signalled to Bintang to join her.

'Visiting Daddy's grave always makes me sad.' She stared out over the island below her. 'He shouldn't have died. But he was lying in agony for hours at the bottom of an old mineshaft in the jungle until they found him. By then his injuries were so badly infected that the doctors couldn't save him. I wasn't allowed to see him as he was so poorly. I wrote him a letter and Mummy read it out to him.'

Bintang said nothing. He was staring down at his feet. Jasmine noticed how shabby and scuffed his shoes were.

'When I was little I was brought up by the nuns. They used to say that when you died there were four possible places you could go. Hell if you were really bad, Heaven if you were exceptionally good, Limbo if you were good but not a Christian or died as a baby before you had a chance to be baptised, and then Purgatory.'

Bintang turned to look at her, curious.

'Purgatory is a kind of waiting room for heaven where you go and suffer until your sins are washed away and God decides to let you into Heaven. I was frightened of Purgatory. They described it as almost as bad as Hell but with a chance to get out if God takes pity on you. When I was little, I didn't think I was naughty enough to go to Hell but I was scared that God would be counting up all the times I was naughty and would put me in Purgatory for a very long time. When Daddy died I had nightmares thinking he would be suffering terribly in Purgatory. But I told Mummy and she said he would definitely be in Heaven as he'd already suffered so much that God wouldn't make him wait anymore.'

'You think because I am not a Christian I go to other place?'

'Limbo. *I* don't think any of it. I'm not even a Catholic. I think nuns speak a load of rubbish. If there is a God, I'm sure he would let innocent babies and good Mohammedans into heaven too.'

'I do not want your Christian God. Malay people say Allah is the one God and Mohammed is his prophet.'

'You believe in Allah then?'

'No. I do not follow any religion.'

'I don't either. I am an agnostic.' She said the word experimentally, hoping she'd remembered how to pronounce it correctly.

Bintang shrugged, got up from the bench and walked over to stand leaning against a tree while he smoked another of his cigarettes.

'I meant what I said about wanting to put flowers on Siti's grave. Will you take me?'

He said nothing for a few moments, drawing on his cigarette. He tossed the butt into the wet grass. 'All right. We go now.'

THEY TURNED off the road they would normally take up to Bella Vista, following a narrow track that Jasmine had never noticed before. After about ten minutes Bintang pulled the car up and turned to her. 'We walk from here.'

In the distance she could see a collection of straw-roofed wooden huts, but instead of following the track towards the *kampong*, Bintang led her along a narrow path that skirted a paddy field.

Eventually the paddy ended and there was a small cluster of trees and beyond that, what looked like a market garden with vegetables growing in strips.

Under the trees was a patch of bare uncultivated land. 'Here is Siti grave.'

Jasmine clutched the handful of hibiscus she had gathered on Penang Hill. 'I'll have to lay them here without water,' she said, wishing she'd thought to bring a jam jar.

Bintang watched in silence as she placed the flowers on the damp earth. It was such a paltry token. Her eyes welled with tears as she thought of her schoolfriend. Siti's resting place was a miserable spot, gloomy, unloved. 'Why don't you make another marker for her grave?'

'Why? No one come here. Only Grandmother and she know where it is.'

Jasmine turned to look at him, at the hard lines around his mouth, at his expressionless eyes. Sometimes he appeared almost cruel. She decided she would make something to mark the grave herself. It was the least she could do. She wouldn't tell Bintang until it was done, but she was determined her young former schoolmate should have something to record the passing of her brief life.

WHEN JASMINE RETURNED to Bella Vista a letter was waiting for her. Not, as usual, with a Nairobi postmark, but with a local stamp. She recognised the handwriting from the note Howard Baxter had left her before he'd gone to his cricket match.

With a sinking feeling she slit open the envelope.

Dear Jasmine

I've tried. I've really tried. But it's no good. I have to get in touch. I'm going to be in George Town next week. We have a meeting at the Guthrie's office and I can't bear the idea of being on the island and not seeing you. There's some dreary function I have to go to on the Friday evening but I'll be free on Saturday and I am hoping you might be able to come down and meet up. If the H-Us can spare their driver we could go for a swim. Or to that place you suggested last time. The one with the pagoda. I have to be back at BL that evening – we need all hands to man the defences. But it would be terrific if you could get away and join me for the day – or even part of it.

The car savings fund is going well. Before long I'll be able to drive over on the car ferry and take you around without us having to rely on that driver chap.

Please say yes. I miss you.

H

JASMINE SCREWED the letter into a ball and flung it into the waste basket.

As a result of the state of emergency, Reggie insisted that Bintang or, if he were otherwise engaged, one of the house servants, accompany Jasmine and Mary when they walked to the school. The following morning, the three set off in blazing sunshine and entered the gloom of the forest.

The two women walked in front and Bintang followed behind. Sunshine broke through the dense canopy of trees and formed pools of light on the forest floor. Butterflies danced in the shafts of sunlight, their iridescent wings shimmering like bright jewels: emeralds, rubies and sapphires.

Jasmine breathed in the air – clear and light up here at the top of the island, but with an underlying smell of decaying leaves and dampness that was not unpleasant.

After a few minutes, Mary broke the silence. 'I wonder what this Harris chap is going to tell us. I hate the thought of Bella Vista being surrounded by barbed wire.' She shuddered. Not for the first time, Jasmine wondered what the teacher had gone through during the war.

'Let's hope he doesn't suggest that then.'

'Reggie says if he does, it's more about protecting the tappers than us. They're the most vulnerable in all this. Everyone gets frightfully shocked about planters being murdered but there are far more Malays, Tamils and Chinese being killed and threatened, so I suppose I should shut up and put up with it.'

'Let's hope it's over before Christmas.' Jasmine held up crossed fingers.

'I fear it won't be.' Mary's brows narrowed and she looked down at the baby in her cloth sling. They walked on, silent again. 'The British underestimated the Japanese and now it's likely they are doing the same with the CTs.

Jasmine wished she had a chance to talk to Bintang, but she didn't want to speak to him in front of Mary, doubting the driver would be as open with his employer's wife there. She looked over her shoulder at the *syce*, but he avoided her gaze, instead sweeping his eyes over the jungle around them. There was something about the way he was doing it that made Jasmine think he was playing a part for her benefit. Going through the motions, when he knew there was actually no risk to them on this well-worn path.

That morning, a small girl of about six was attending her first day at school. As Jasmine and Mary entered the padang, the child was clinging in desperation to her mother's skirts and weeping copiously.

'Oh dear, someone doesn't want to come to school. Will you take care of her, Jasmine?'

Jasmine nervously greeted the child and her mother. The little girl turned away, burying her head in her mother's skirt and wrapping her arms like a vine around the woman's legs.

Instinctively, Jasmine squatted down beside her. 'Hello, what's your name?'

The question produced a louder wail.

Remembering she had a tin of barley sugar in her satchel, Jasmine fished it out and offered a sweet to the little girl. 'Please don't be frightened. Everyone here is very friendly and we'll take care of you.'

The child looked at the sweets suspiciously, then picked one out and put it in her mouth and her tears subsided.

'Her name Amina.'

'Hello, Amina, I'm Missee Barrington. Would you like to sit with me?'

The child, sucking her barley sugar, nodded her head solemnly and to the relief of both Jasmine and the grateful mother, she took Jasmine's proffered hand and followed her into the school building.

Jasmine led the little girl to the back of the classroom where they could sit quietly and the child was less likely to feel intimidated by the other children.

Mary usually began the lessons with a short singsong. This always captured the children's interest and bonded them together, readying them for the more arduous tasks of learning their spellings and reciting their times tables. Little Amina's face lit up with pleasure at the singing and she relinquished her tight handhold and happily entered into the lessons for the rest of the morning. At playtime she looked as though she were about to start crying again. Jasmine was poised to go to her rescue, when two small girls approached the child and led her off to join their skipping game.

By the time the lessons finished and Bintang appeared at the edge of the *padang* to escort them back to the bungalow at Bella Vista, Jasmine was tired. She thoroughly enjoyed the classes, particularly when she took the children individually to hear their reading, and most of all her weekly art class. Yet she couldn't imagine dedicating herself to teaching as a profession in the way that Mary had done. For Jasmine, nothing compared to being alone or with a subject, losing herself in bringing a work to life on paper or canvas. If she had ever been uncertain about her wish to spend her life as a painter, these months in Penang had dispelled all doubts.

As THE TWO women ascended the steps of the bungalow, they heard voices. The military guest wasn't due until some time the following week, yet evidently someone was on the side verandah with Reggie. They made their way round and found Reggie and his guest drinking beers.

Mary stepped forward to be introduced to the uniformed man, but Jasmine felt herself shrinking back, distancing herself. It was not Harris, but Ellis, Lieutenant SlimeBall from the *Rosebery*.

The men got to their feet. Ellis was shaking hands with Mary when he noticed Jasmine lurking in the background. He dropped Mary's hand and moved towards Jasmine, arm extended. 'Well, well, well, we meet again, Miss Barrington. What an unexpected pleasure.'

Jasmine shuddered as his clammy hand gripped hers. His time in Malaya had done nothing to improve his breath which now had overtones of the Tiger beer he was drinking, mixed in with pipe smoke, but neither were enough to counter the rottenness of his underlying halitosis.

'I didn't expect to see you, Lieutenant. Mr Hyde-Under-wood said the officer was called Harris. And wouldn't be here until next week. Quite a surprise.'

'A pleasant one I hope.' His smile was more akin to a leer, revealing the ugly teeth that were presumably the source of his sewer breath. It made her think of an angry dog, curling back its lips in a snarl.

Jasmine didn't answer and was glad when Reggie started talking about his blindspot in remembering names, and Jinjiang appeared on the threshold to announce that tiffin was served.

Over lunch, Jasmine tried to be as inconspicuous as possible, avoiding joining in the conversation, which centred on the political situation and the continuing escalation of attacks by communist insurgents.

'All the planters over on the peninsula are driving armoured cars now,' said Ellis.

'Really?' Mary looked horrified.

'Armour plating everywhere. They look like tin boxes. Driver has a small peephole to look though. Not a lot of fun to travel in with the sun beating down on all that metal plating. It's like being inside a blast furnace. And the weight of the metal slows them right down. But without that kind of protection, planters would be sitting ducks.'

'How horrible.' Mary glanced at Reggie anxiously. 'I hope you're not suggesting we do that here?'

'I'm hoping it won't be necessary. But you are rather isolated up here. Anyway, I'll have a better idea after I've inspected the estate.' Ellis gave another of his smiles. Creepy. An unpleasant mixture of contempt, obsequiousness and bad teeth. Jasmine didn't trust the man and hoped Reggie would feel the same.

Reggie folded his arms. 'There's no evidence of any CT activity over here on Penang island.'

'So far.' Ellis frowned. 'You have the advantage of being separated from the peninsula by the Straits. We've instituted security checks on the ferries and the CTs would anyway be cut off from their main jungle hideaways over here on the island, so I believe it's unlikely. There's easier prey for them on the peninsula. Plenty of isolated rubber estates and tin mines. Lots of quiet stretches of road for ambushes, and dense jungle running the entire length of the country for them to disappear into.'

'Then why are you bothering with us?' Mary clearly hadn't warmed to the man either. It sounded as if she really wanted to say bothering us, omitting the 'with'.

'There are other threats over here.'

'Yes?' Mary folded her arms. 'What exactly?'

'The *Min Yuen*.' The officer looked smug.

'What's that?' Jasmine addressed Mary rather than Ellis.

Before Mary could answer, Ellis did so. 'The hidden army. Not fighters. But just as dangerous as we can't see them. The CTs can only survive if they get cash to pay their men and food to eat. That's where the *Min Yuen* come in. They also act as spies giving the commies intelligence about troop movements and suchlike.'

'And you think there are *Min Yuen* on Penang?'

Ellis gave a dry laugh. 'They're everywhere. And the trouble is it's impossible to tell who most of them are. Some are ignorant peasants who give rice to the CTs under threat of death. But there are others. Often respectable people who sympathise with the Reds. Doctors, waiters, rubber tappers, bank clerks, teachers. My sources say Penang is rife with them. And my aim is to stamp them out.' His mouth curled in a sneer. 'Filthy vermin. I'd like to crush them all under my boots.'

Mary and Reggie exchanged glances. Jasmine's dislike of Lieutenant Ellis had increased and she now found him utterly loathsome.

'I'm going to get the blighters though. I'm building files

on them, gathering intelligence. There'll be a reckoning before too long.'

Reggie got to his feet. 'Come on then, Lieutenant, it's time I showed you around the estate.'

After they'd gone, Mary leaned back in her chair. 'What a thoroughly unpleasant man. Is he by any chance the chap your mother told me tried to paw you on the dance floor when you were on the ship?'

Jasmine felt her face turn scarlet. Had Mummy told Mary all of her secrets? 'Yes. I call him Lieutenant Slimeball. He's really creepy.' As she spoke the words, she remembered she had once described Howard Baxter to herself as creepy too, but there was absolutely no comparison. Howard annoyed her at times, but he didn't make her skin crawl.

'I wish we could somehow get out of him staying here tonight. The thought of having to entertain him at dinner is not appealing.' Mary crumpled her napkin in her hands before dropping it onto the table. 'The way he talked of Malayan people as vermin. Whether you agree with some of their political convictions or not, there's no excuse to speak that way. They are human beings and this is their country.' Mary's voice was full of suppressed anger. 'Who does Ellis think he is? He's only been in the Straits for five minutes and he acts like he has more rights than people who were born here. Men like him make me sick.' She looked at Jasmine and shook her head slowly. 'And as for him trying to put his hands all over you, it's too horrible to think about.' She closed her eyes momentarily. 'Changing the subject, what are you going to do this afternoon? How's the Latin going?'

Jasmine pulled a face. 'I think I'm going to go to my room for a while and I promise to take my Latin primer with me. Then later, when it's a bit cooler, I'm going to the studio to work.'

'Righto! Don't forget we're doing a test paper tomorrow morning, so swotting up on your grammar is definitely a good idea.' She put a hand on Jasmine's shoulder. 'You don't have to excel in the exams. As long as you do yourself justice. You're intelligent enough to put in a credible performance and I don't want Evie and Arthur blaming me if you don't.'

'Of course not. I promise. I won't let you down, Mary. You and Reggie are so incredibly kind to me, I owe it to you to do my absolute best.'

'You owe it to yourself, darling.' Mary left the room, heading for the kitchen to find Jinjiang and reclaim her daughter.

It was almost four by the time Jasmine had dispensed with her Latin grammar book, her head throbbing from her efforts to grapple with declensions and cases, and her eyes glazing over with the sheer pointlessness of knowing words for bards, altars, and sacrifices.

The studio was cool. The *attap* roof was shaded by tall hardwood trees and the open side-elevation allowed the cooler hilltop air and the breezes off the Straits to circulate. She looked around. The unfinished portrait of Bintang stood on the easel but she decided she would start work on the memorial marker for Siti.

She picked up a sketch pad and began to draw shapes and ideas. Wanting something to reflect the natural beauty of the island and the innocence of a little girl robbed of life before she'd completed her first decade, Jasmine racked her brains. Perhaps she could use some seashells and incorporate them into her design. The idea of flowers and fruit was appealing – something that would be there rain or shine, a symbolic offering to Siti. She could make a collage effect on a piece of timber, a mixture of natural objects and heavily layered paint and varnish. Her pencil worked fast as it flew over the paper, experimenting with different ideas. She'd need some wood. Something solid – hardwood or mahogany. Not a cross as that was for Christians and she didn't want to offend Bintang or his grandmother. Better to stick with a rectangle. Reggie might be willing to find her a suitable piece.

So absorbed in her task was she that she didn't notice Lieutenant Ellis approaching until he was striding across the threshold.

'So, this is your little hidey-hole is it, Miss Barrington? Don't you get lonely sitting in here all on your own?' He looked about him. 'You'd be better off down in George Town than stuck up here in the back of beyond with only a married couple for company. Not exactly the life an attractive young woman dreams of.'

Jasmine shuddered and wondered what kind of life he thought she dreamt of. The only thing she was sure about was that her dreams didn't have him in.

He moved about, lifting objects from her collection, turning them over in his hands and looking at them with a kind of contempt, before replacing them. 'A bit of a squirrel, are you? Collecting all this rubbish.' He swept his hand broadly towards the collection of natural objects as though he were about to bark an order for it to be taken away and burnt, then he turned and walked over to the easel.

Ellis stood for several moments in front of the half-finished portrait of Bintang. He had his back to her so Jasmine couldn't see his expression but, based on what he had been saying over tiffin, he was hardly likely to approve of her choice of subject.

He turned to face her. 'You're a talented artist. Why waste your time painting a native? Bunch of ugly mugs the lot of them, if you ask me. The world would be a better place if people stuck to their own species. Men like this are only fit to be servants. It's a waste of time and paint for you to draw one of them. And it might give the fellow ideas above his station. A sense of importance.' His mouth was curled in that habitual sneer. He noticed the chair where Bintang had sat for the portrait. 'Did you actually have that native sitting here in the room with you, while you painted him? I must say, Miss Barrington, I think that's extremely foolish of you. Some of these men are little more than savages.'

Before Jasmine could reply, Reggie's voice interrupted them. 'There you are, Ellis. I thought we'd look at the drying sheds now and then walk down to the entrance gates.'

Ellis moved towards the open veranda. 'Take my advice, Miss Barrington. I mean what I say. These natives are not to be trusted.' Then he strode away in Reggie's wake.

THAT EVENING JASMINE did wear her old beige school dress. While she may have had second thoughts about doing so in Howard's company, she had no such compunctions in Ellis's.

It seemed Mary felt likewise, as she too had made little effort for their guest, wearing one of the everyday baju kurungs she often wore to school. 'You must take us as you find us I'm afraid, Lieutenant Ellis. We don't stand on ceremony here at Bella Vista.'

'You wear native clothing, Mrs Hyde-Underwood?' Ellis's expression was incredulous. He glanced at Reggie, evidently surprised that the planter permitted his wife to indulge in such folly.

'I have lived almost all my life in Malaya,' said Mary.

'There's good reason that the indigenous people choose to wear these clothes. I'm sure if I were in London I would dress quite differently. But I'm mostly concerned about comfort these days. Not about some tired British convention as to the done thing.' Her tone was cutting.

Ellis gaped, mouth open, and Jasmine raised a silent cheer.

But Lieutenant Slimeball was not to be deterred. 'I must say, Hyde-Underwood, it's probably time for you to give these ladies a stiff talking to.'

'Oh yes?' Reggie raised one eyebrow. 'And why exactly should I do that?'

Ellis gave a smirking laugh, but looked embarrassed, as both Mary and Jasmine stared at him, waiting for enlightenment. He cleared his throat and said, 'We Brits should be flying the flag for the Empire, for King and country, common decency and for the values of the white man. Standards must be kept up. We must lead by example. Never been more important than now.'

Jasmine opened her mouth to reply but then decided it was better to leave him to get on with it and let Reggie deal with him. If she rose to the bait it would mean engaging in an argument and Slimeball wasn't worth the effort. She looked at him with undisguised contempt.

'I have to say, Hyde-Underwood, I may be here to report and recommend on security measures but part of that is running a tight ship and keeping up standards. If you give natives an inch, they'll take a mile. As the superior race we need to give the blighters something to aspire to and look up to. I must say I was shocked that you permit Miss Barrington to spend time alone with your servants, painting their portraits. Not appropriate at all. And a man at that. What would her mother think?'

Unable to contain herself any longer, Jasmine said, 'My mother would be delighted to know I was getting to know Malayan people. She would be proud of me and has never had time for snobbery or people who look down on other human beings.'

'Hear hear!' Reggie boomed across the table. 'Who have you been painting, Jasmine? I must come along and have a look.'

Mary spoke. 'She's painting Bintang and a jolly good likeness it is too.'

'You approve?' Ellis spluttered.

'Jasmine is an accomplished artist.' Mary leaned forward and patted Jasmine's hand. 'Both Reggie and I are proud of her. And Bintang is one of our most trusted employees. Jasmine is doing his portrait as a gift for his grandmother. Bintang's parents were killed during the war.' She smiled at Ellis. 'Where are you from Lieutenant Ellis? And where were you posted before Malaya?' It was a clear dismissal of his line of questioning.

Ellis narrowed his eyes, his bushy brows almost meeting, evidently annoyed at the sudden change in conversation. 'I come from Essex originally. During the war I was in North Africa. I've been in Palestine since the end of the war. As you can imagine, my experience with the civil unrest there will stand me in good stead in Malaya.'

'Are you from a military family?' Mary asked.

'Not as such. Although my father fought in the First War.'

The group lapsed into silence. Normally Jasmine and the Hyde-Underwoods would have had a relaxed conversation over dinner, comfortable in each other's presence, but none of them wanted to have that kind of intimate familial banter with Ellis in the room. It was apparent that both

Reggie and Mary felt the same way about the officer as Jasmine did.

The tension was broken by Jinjiang bringing in the pudding.

'That was delicious, JJ,' said Reggie. 'First class. The pork was cooked perfectly.'

Mary and Jasmine were equally effusive and Jinjiang looked taken aback at the sudden outflow of compliments.

'Same usual, *Tuan*. Nothing special.'

'Your cooking is always special,' Reggie added, clearly relishing the discomfort of Lieutenant Ellis.

When the *amah* had returned to the kitchen, Ellis spoke again. 'I won't be staying tomorrow night after all, Hyde-Underwood. The estate's a lot smaller than I expected and I think I've gathered enough information to make my report. I'll leave after breakfast and you'll have my report and recommendations in a couple of days.'

The relief was almost audible around the table.

But Ellis wasn't done. 'I was thinking Miss Barrington might like to come to our regimental dance next Saturday. We're in need of a few more pretty faces.'

Jasmine almost choked on her tapioca.

Mary looked at her and smiled. 'What a pity, Lieutenant, but I'm afraid Reggie and I have bagged her for babysitting duty that night as we've been invited to friends for dinner.'

Jasmine reached under the table for Mary's hand and squeezed it in gratitude.

'Some other time then.' Ellis looked annoyed. 'I'll be in touch. Now if it's all right with you I'll turn in. I'd like to make a start on my report.'

'Good idea.' Reggie rubbed his hands together.

'Your bag is in your room,' said Mary. 'I'll show you the way.'

When they were gone, Reggie rolled his eyes. 'Let's have a swift nightcap on the veranda.'

Mary came back, shaking her head. 'What a thoroughly obnoxious man. Thank goodness he's leaving in the morning. I couldn't have faced another night.'

'Thank you so much for rescuing me, Mary. You are an absolute angel.'

'If my dear wife hadn't done it then I would have. I wouldn't like to think of you anywhere near that loathsome man.' Reggie finished pouring his *stengah*. 'He told me he's compiling a list of Most Wanted. Says he's going to round up every last member of the *Min Yuen*. How he imagines he'll accomplish that when he hasn't the first idea about the country or the people, is beyond me.'

'Money, I imagine.' Mary's tone was dry. 'People like him think the best way to accomplish anything is bribery. After all, who is ever going to be a willing informant to a man like him?'

22

There was no school the following morning, so Jasmine headed straight out to her studio after breakfast. She was relieved that she had missed Lieutenant Slimeball at breakfast and imagined he must have left the estate very early.

Her back was turned to the open verandah as she selected her brushes. This morning she would do some more work on Bintang's portrait until she had a chance to ask Reggie about finding her a suitable piece of wood for Siti's memorial marker. She might need another sitting from him but meanwhile she would work on the background.

At the sound of footsteps, she turned around in surprise, smiling, expecting to see Bintang. As he was always so quiet and catlike, she should have realised that the heavy tread could not have come from him. The source was the steel-tipped boots of Lieutenant Ellis.

'Oh, my goodness! You made me jump, Lieutenant!' she cried. He was standing there in front of her, too close. Why did some people feel the need to get right up into one's personal space? Especially when their poisonous breath was almost overpowering. Hadn't anyone ever told him? He must surely notice when people flinched from him.

Ellis twisted his lips into his characteristic smile, like a dog's snarl, revealing the crooked stained teeth under the little moustache. He leaned closer to her and she pulled away, almost bending backwards, blocked by the chest of drawers where she stored her art materials.

'I was disappointed you can't come to the dance on Saturday. I was looking forward to sweeping you round the dance floor again and getting you in a clinch without your mother to interrupt us.'

Before she could take evasive action, he had grabbed hold of her and pulled her against him as if they were dancing. 'Like this,' he said.

Ellis spun around, holding her as if they were about to waltz, and she struggled to break free of his grip. His hands were damp with sweat. One hand tracked down her spine to her bottom, his palm squeezing her buttock as he pushed his body up against hers. She brought her own hands up to his shoulders, trying to hold him away from her, but his head was moving down to try to kiss her. The urge to be sick was powerful.

'Stop it!' she cried. 'Get off me!' She tried to shove him away but he was too strong.

'You'll love it. Relax. Don't be such a tease. Girls like you are always gagging for it once they try.'

No! The only way to break free was to bite him, and she dipped her head but he was dragged off her. The sudden release from his hold caused her to trip over and land on the bare wood floor and she struggled quickly back to her feet.

'Leave her!' Bintang's voice was louder than she had ever heard it. 'I get *Tuan* now throw you out. You go away. Don't come back.'

Jasmine brushed the dirt off her skirt and wiped her hands on her apron, trembling and breathing heavily. Bintang and Ellis were standing a few feet apart. The driver's arms were folded, signalling that he had no plans to initiate a fight, but was ready to respond if required.

Ellis's face was choleric – his anger visible in red cheeks and narrowed eyes, as he looked from one to another. 'I'll make mincemeat of you, you upstart blighter.' His voice dripped contempt. Turning to Jasmine, he said, 'So that's how it is, is it? That's why you've been painting him.' He looked at her with loathing. 'You're unnatural. Going with a filthy, common native. If that's what you want, you're welcome to him.' He raised his fist in threat to Bintang. 'And you haven't heard the last of this!'

He turned towards the veranda just as Reggie appeared.

'What the devil's going on?' Reggie looked angry. Jasmine had never seen him that way before. 'Ellis? What the hell are you doing here? I thought you'd left half an hour ago.'

'I didn't but I'm going now. If the CTs come and slit all your throats in the middle of the night it'll be no more than you deserve, Hyde-Underwood.' Ellis pushed Reggie out of the way and strode towards his jeep, parked on the other side of the *padang*.

Reggie let him go. 'Thank goodness we've seen the back of him. The most obnoxious man I've ever met. Are you all right, Jasmine? What on earth was going on?'

Jasmine brushed tears of rage away with the back of her hand. 'It was horrible. He was horrible.' She turned to the *syce*. 'Thank you, Bintang, I don't know what would have happened if you hadn't turned up when you did.'

'I do,' Bintang said quietly, then walked away. As he passed Reggie, he said, 'He very bad man, *Tuan*.'

'Looks like Bintang got here in the nick of time. I'm so sorry, Jasmine. I can't believe the fellow behaved like that. He's supposed to be an officer. And he's a guest in our house. Absolute bounder. I've a mind to report him.'

'No, don't.' Jasmine was quick to respond. 'He'll only make more trouble. Let's forget it ever happened.'

Reggie stretched an arm around Jasmine's shoulder. 'I thought he'd already left, then I saw his jeep was still here. I had a feeling he was up to no good. Let's get you back to the bungalow and get some strong coffee down you. Maybe even a tot of something in it. That should sort you out.'

Mary was standing, Frances in her arms, on the steps of the bungalow when Jasmine and Reggie walked up. 'What's happened?'

'You were dead right about that Ellis chap. Scum of the earth. If it weren't for Bintang...'

Mary gave a gasp of horror. 'Oh no!' She rushed down the steps and flung one arm around Jasmine, holding the baby with the other. 'Did he hurt you? Did he–?'

'I'm perfectly all right. Bintang rescued me before he could do anything.' She looked at Mary, her face burning in shame. 'He tried to kiss me. He said the most horrible things about me. About Bintang too.'

Mary hugged her again. 'My poor darling. Come on, let's get you a nice cold drink. You need to sit down.' She looked at Reggie. 'Why don't I leave Frances with Jinjiang and Jasmine and I can spend the day at the Swimming Club? You wouldn't mind, would you, Reggie?'

'Splendid idea.' Reggie nodded. 'Just the ticket.'

'You won't mind having tiffin on your own?' said Jasmine.

'I'll cope, ladies.'

·   ·   ·

IT WAS A PERFECT PENANG DAY. Hot, sunny but the heat tempered by a cool breeze off the Straits. The Swimming Club was busy, so the two women scrambled over the rocks at the end of the lawn, down onto the beach and went for a swim in the sea.

Afterwards, Mary said, 'Are you going to tell me exactly what happened? Do I need to tell Evie about it?'

'No! Please don't. I don't want to make a fuss. It was scary but Bintang must have seen where Ellis was going and followed him because he arrived so quickly. The man grabbed me and he was squeezing my bottom but Bintang pulled him off.' She smiled. 'Actually, Bintang must be jolly strong.'

'Or jolly angry.' Mary looked thoughtful. 'He will never be a guest at Bella Vista again. Last night Reggie told me the whole inspection was completely pointless. Ellis already had a map of the estate anyway and showed absolutely no interest in any of the rubber operations. Apart from saying we need barbed wire round the perimeter and an armed man at the entrance gate, he had nothing else to offer. And Reggie said that was obvious.'

'Why did he come and plan to stay so long originally?'

Mary's lips tightened. 'I've no idea. Unless of course he knew you'd be here.'

'I never told him where I was staying. I danced with him the first night but then I went out of my way to avoid him and made sure I didn't sit next to him again at dinner.' Jasmine stretched her legs out in front of her. The sun had already dried the sea water from them, leaving a faint tracery of salt. She brushed her leg with her palm. 'He was terribly boring anyway. We ran out of conversation the first night on board. He just droned on about himself and what a hero he was.'

'I doubt he was a hero. The man's a permanent soldier and in his thirties. A lieutenant is a fairly junior officer. If he were any good, he'd be at least a captain by now.'

'Bintang was absolutely brilliant. He dragged him off me then stood up to him. I think Slimeball was quite shocked. I bet he's actually a bit of a coward.'

'A coward and a bully. I know his type. He won't be welcome at Bella Vista anymore and I'm sure Reggie will make others aware that he's not to be trusted.' Mary hugged her knees. 'Now that's enough about him. We need to talk about you. It's two months until the exams and then what? Have you had any thoughts?'

'You want me to leave?' Jasmine felt a cold chill grip her.

'No! That's the last thing I want. Reggie and I love having you with us. Frances adores you. You're a huge help to me at the school. It's super having someone to talk to when Reggie's working – and to do things like we're doing now. As far as I'm concerned, you can stay forever.' Mary took Jasmine's hand and gave it a gentle squeeze. 'But living on top of a hill, with no young company and nothing to do, isn't good for you. You're nearly seventeen and should be enjoying yourself with friends your own age. And thinking about your future.'

'You sound like Mummy now.'

'That's because we both have your best interests at heart. Seriously, Jasmine, have you any ideas about the future. University? Teacher-training college?'

'Art school. But I hate London.'

'Who says it has to be London? You could always go to Paris. Of course you'd have to make a lot of effort with your French studies.' Mary gave her a teasing look. 'There's also Glasgow. My best friend at school went there.'

Jasmine looked horrified. 'Ooh no. Glasgow's in Scotland, isn't it? Far too cold and gloomy up there.'

Mary shrugged. 'Yes, and I think it was heavily bombed in the war. That's the benefit of Paris. The German occupation meant they didn't bomb it to bits like England.'

'I hadn't thought of Paris. That might be interesting.' Jasmine stared towards the horizon. 'It's so far away. But it wouldn't be forever. And apart from the nonsense the nuns spouted in school I've never actually been taught art properly.'

'That certainly hasn't held you back. You are extremely talented, Jasmine, and it's only right you should nurture that talent. Maybe we could make some enquiries and write off to find out whether you might be accepted as a student.'

'Imagine! Being able to paint in the city of light. Following in the footsteps of the Impressionists.' Jasmine grinned. 'And being expected to paint all day long. What joy! I've so much to learn.'

'Well, don't get your hopes up until we have more information. They may not take on international students.'

THEY WALKED INTO THE CLUBHOUSE, changing quickly before going into the dining room for lunch. Inside there was a buzz of conversation, more than usual. A portly woman passed by their table and stopped to greet Mary, who introduced her to Jasmine as Mrs Crawley.

'So lovely to see you here, dear Mary. You are a rare visitor to the club lately.'

'The baby doesn't allow me a lot of time.'

'Of course. How is the little thing?'

'Frances is doing very well, thank you.'

The woman shook her head, a solemn expression on her

face. 'I suppose you've heard about the High Commissioner?'

'What about him?'

Mrs Crawley replied by almost mouthing the words silently. 'Dead. They called him back to London. Presumably to give him the heave-ho. The aeroplane he was on was in a collision with another as it was coming in to land. Poor Sir Edward was killed.'

'Good gracious!'

'A lot of people said he was absolutely hopeless at dealing with the situation here and had been summoned to Whitehall for the chop, but no one would wish that on the poor chap.' Mrs Crawley pursed her lips. 'Let's hope someone who knows what they're doing replaces him.'

Mary nodded but appeared unwilling to be drawn further into conversation, so Mrs Crawley bade them goodbye and returned to join her table.

'Let's hope they don't spend too long in London trying to find someone to replace him.' Mary picked up the menu and glanced at it. 'Not that having nobody will be a whole lot different from having Gent. But if we don't want the Emergency to get out of hand or drag on, we need some rapid decisive action.'

'What do you think they should do?' Jasmine was trying to decide between cheese and onion pie or grilled chicken and the cheese was winning.

'I haven't a clue. I've no idea about military tactics, but I imagine rooting those fighters out of their jungle hideouts is a far from easy task. But it strikes me that anything they do has to put the protection of the Malayan people – Chinese as well as Malays – at its heart. If we lose the goodwill of the population we've had it.'

'Most people don't support the communists, do they?'

'No. But they want to stay alive. The insurgents use threats to force them into helping them. Remember what that awful Ellis said about the *Min Yuen*? I don't mean his nasty colour prejudice, but the part about the CTs striking terror into local villagers. They need to see us as their allies and the communists as the bad men.'

The mention of Ellis brought back the horror of the lieutenant's behaviour that morning. The prospect of the cheese and onion pie was less enticing. The waiter appeared and Jasmine, like Mary, just chose a salad.

'Why do you think men pick on me, Mary?' she asked when the waiter disappeared. 'Do you think I send the wrong signals? Only I'm really not interested in any of that kind of thing.'

'I expect it's because you're uncommonly pretty, dear girl. Although why on earth a man like Ellis should entertain the possibility you might return his interest I can't imagine.'

Jasmine stared through the window. Beyond the lawns and the swimming pool the water in the Strait was shimmering in the sunlight. She wished they hadn't bothered with lunch but had stayed down on the beach.

'Sometimes I think there must be something wrong with me.'

'Wrong?' Mary jerked her head back in surprise. 'What do you mean?'

'Other girls... when I was at school... you know...the only thing they ever thought about was boys. But I'm not interested in boys at all.' She fiddled with her napkin. 'Does that mean I'm abnormal?'

Mary didn't laugh at her. She looked sad and gave her a thoughtful smile. 'You're sixteen. I'm pretty sure I didn't think about boys at all until I was about eighteen. And I didn't actually have a boyfriend until I was in my twenties.'

Jasmine tightened her lips. 'Mummy said the same thing. But why then can't they understand that and leave me alone?' She stopped talking for a few moments while the waiter brought their salads. 'I just don't have feelings that way. Why can't they get that?'

'They?'

'Not only Slimeball. I mean Howard too. Although he's completely different from Ellis, I don't want to think of him in that way. I want to be left alone.' She toyed with a lettuce leaf. 'It's what scares me about going to art school. What if there are lots of boys there and they expect me to go out with them?'

'If you like them and want to see them then you say yes. If you don't you say no.'

'Oh, Mary, you make it sound so simple.'

'At art school the other students will be a similar age to you and that may make it more relaxed. I know when I was a student we used to go around together in large groups. Most of us were just friends. Of course, there were one or two who had serious relationships, but the vast majority merely wanted to have a jolly good time.' Mary wriggled her brow. 'Your problem is that you're deprived of friends your own age. You spend all your time with me and Reggie. Two old crocks.'

Jasmine shook her head fiercely. 'No. Don't say that. I love spending time with you both. You talk about more interesting things and you don't treat me as a child.'

23

O ver the coming months, the Emergency continued, with constant attacks on rubber estates, police stations, tin mines and other colonial outposts. The communist insurgents derailed trains and torched buildings and buses, as well as whole villages where the population was unwilling to support them with supplies or where they believed villagers to be collaborating with the colonial powers. The colonial government responded with curfews and detention without trial of suspected CTs – or bandits as they were commonly known. The planters and their families became accustomed to living under siege conditions, walking their estates with pistols in their belts and going to bed at night with armed guards posted outside.

At Bella Vista there was now a permanently manned gate, and a barbed wire fence surrounded the property. Reggie kept a loaded pistol on his person, but otherwise life on the estate continued much as before.

September 1948 brought a new High Commissioner to Malaya to replace Sir Edward Gent. The new man, Sir Henry Gurney, had been Chief Secretary in Palestine, dealing with the Jewish insurgency there. Gurney's approach was immediately more effective than his predecessor's, recognising the vital importance of close collaboration with the military and the need to cut off the supply chain to the communist insurgents – very different from the more cerebral Gent, who had doggedly focused on long term plans for independence, even as such plans were rendered unactionable while the insurgency was happening.

That month, Jasmine took her school certificate. She was required to sit the exams in George Town in an invigilated examination room in the Town Hall. In the month leading up to this ordeal, reluctantly forsaking her little wooden studio, she had knuckled down and spent hours on the bungalow veranda bent over Latin and French grammar books, doing tedious mathematical exercises and reading set texts. This was not a Damascene conversion to the importance of study, but was out of duty and gratitude to her hosts and a desire not to disappoint.

On exam days, Bintang was to drive her into George Town, returning at the appointed hour to transport her back to Bella Vista. Since the incident with Lieutenant Ellis, the driver had withdrawn from Jasmine's company, and had not returned to the studio to sit again for his portrait. The only time she saw him now was on the walk to the school in the kampong, when Mary was also present and Bintang maintained a respectful distance behind them on the narrow pathway. So, when the day loomed for the exams to start, Jasmine's nerves about the tests were intensified, or indeed overshadowed, by her nervousness about finally being alone with the driver whom she longed to call her friend.

Bintang held the rear door of the car open for her. Jasmine obediently climbed into the back as Mary stood on the veranda to wish her luck and wave goodbye. After the car had passed through the estate gates and was proceeding downhill, Jasmine leaned forward. 'I'd like to ride in the front with you, Bintang. Can you stop the car?'

He gave his head a little shake and kept his eyes fixed on the road ahead. 'Not good for white lady to drive in front with *syce*.'

She flung herself back in her seat and gave a long sigh. 'That's ridiculous. Anyway, I don't think of you as the *syce* but as my friend.'

He continued to stare ahead and said nothing.

'Are you angry with me, Bintang?'

'Not angry, Missee Barrington.'

Jasmine was perplexed. Why had he reverted to such formality? 'Is this anything to do with Lieutenant Ellis? Has he threatened you?'

She thought at first he wasn't going to answer then he said, 'Bad man. You stay away from him.'

'I have every intention of staying as far away as possible from him. And I didn't thank you properly for rescuing me from him.'

'I do my job.'

His tone was curt, clipped. Jasmine leaned back against the leather upholstery and wondered what she could say to restore things to how they had been before. Bintang had never been an easy conversationalist, although he had opened up to her on several occasions. But a trap door had slammed shut and she was stuck on the other side.

When they reached George Town he drove straight to the town hall, a grand palace-like structure next to the municipal offices, opposite Fort Cornwallis. As Jasmine got out of the motorcar, her nerves returned. Today she faced two exams, back to back. Looking up at the white Palladian building her stomach flipped.

'How long, Missee?'

'I have two two-hour papers today with an hour's break in the middle.'

'I be outside when you finish. Three o'clock.'

Clutching her leather pencil case, she stepped under the elegant arched portico and into the building. Her first exam was her hated Latin. She hoped the translations would not be too taxing. At least after today she could say goodbye to Latin forever. With relish, she imagined a ritual textbook burning.

Jasmine looked around her and hesitated on the threshold of the designated room. Two neat rows of three desks each were placed wide distances apart to prevent any possibility of cheating. At the end of the room on a raised dais, a stern looking woman was sorting through papers. A few people were already seated at desks. Jasmine was relieved to see she was not the only person taking the examination outside of school.

Another girl approached as she stood on the threshold. The girl had a halo of blonde curls and was tall and leggy. 'Hello. Is this your first exam?'

'Yes. I have six more to come.'

'Me too. But I've a mind to bunk off some of them.'

'Bunk off?' Jasmine had never heard the expression but guessed what the girl meant.

'What's the point of the stupid old school certificate? Mummy and Daddy plan for me to be presented next year and I plan to bag a husband, so who needs a school leaving certificate?'

'Presented?'

'At court, silly. I'm to be a debutante. And we all know so long as you don't look like the back of a bus it's a jolly sure way to get married off.' She winked at Jasmine. 'I'm rather hoping to land myself someone with a big fat castle.' She gave a little giggle. 'A duke or a fabulously rich landowner. Or even an American. Now that would be exciting! How come you're not doing this at school?'

'I left.'

The girl laughed. 'Me too. Well, got expelled actually.'

'Expelled?'

'Are you an echo or something?' The girl rolled her eyes but went on. 'I was caught smoking on three separate occasions and then the last straw was when they found a copy of *Lady Chatterley's Lover* under my pillow.'

'You mean a book?' Jasmine had never heard of it.

'It's banned in England. So, it is here too. But I have a cousin who lives in France and she sent me a copy from there. I'd let you read it only they confiscated it. It's incredibly boring actually, apart from the rude bits but they're absolutely filthy!' She gave Jasmine a nudge with her elbow.

Before they could continue, the woman on the raised dais rang a bell. 'Take your seats. The examination will begin in three minutes. Complete silence now, please.'

Jasmine read through the questions. The prose translation was a tedious description by Livy of some ancient battle. With relief she recognised it as one she had revised a few days ago. The poetry was from Ovid but she didn't know it. Meanings were given for two of the more obscure words. Whilst she recognised most of the other words, she struggled to put them together in any logical way. Taking several deep breaths, she read it through again and decided it was about a woman pining for her lover, so she cobbled together the words she knew with guesses at the rest and moved on to the next question, which was to scan and mark the stresses and caesuras in the first four lines of the poem. As she wrestled with this task, the time flew by and she had to race to finish the paper in time. Fortunately, the last two questions involved describing the lives of notable Greek and Roman figures in English and writing a brief description of a Roman villa and she was able to dash them off without too much trouble.

The bell jingled and they all put down their pens and waited for the papers to be collected. Jasmine hoped she had done enough to scrape a pass.

'Quick lunch at the E&O? My treat. I'm Barbara Appleton by the way.' Before Jasmine could respond, Barbara linked an arm through hers. 'Don't worry, Daddy's stinking rich and has an account at the E&O so we'll put lunch on that.' She patted Jasmine's arm. 'He's such a sweetie. Mummy can be a bit of a dragon, but Daddy can't deny me anything. Besides, we have to celebrate. One down and six to go.' She propelled Jasmine along the road towards the hotel, keeping up a constant flow of words that left Jasmine exhausted. 'Wasn't that paper quite the most hideous bore?'

'I thought it was rather hard. Especially the Ovid.'

'Goodness. You didn't actually try to answer the questions, did you?'

'Of course. Didn't you?'

'I did the short ones at the end in English but I couldn't remember whether Jason was the one with the Argonauts or the one who was tied to the rock. So I took a guess and made the rest up.'

Jasmine looked at her in awe. 'But won't you get into trouble if you completely flunk the exam?'

'Who cares? Not me.' Barbara steered Jasmine into the hotel, and towards a table. All the waiters appeared to know her. 'Don't tell me you're a swot! You're far too pretty to be one of them.'

'I'm certainly not a swot, but I don't want to disappoint my parents.'

Barbara made a derisive pout. 'You have to live your own life. They've already lived theirs. We're young and need to make the most of it.' She looked up at the waiter, 'Bring me the Welsh rarebit, Walter.' Turning to Jasmine she said, 'It's my absolute favourite thing.'

'I'll have that too then.'

'Now, I want to know everything about you. And you'd better start with your name as we didn't actually get to that did we?'

'It's Jasmine Barrington.'

'Jasmine! What a wondrously exotic name. I hate being Barbara. In fact I'm thinking of acting like an American and calling myself Barb or Barbie. What do you think?' Without waiting for an answer, she ploughed on. 'But then that extremely rich Woolworth's heiress is called Barbara and she was a deb too. You know. The one who was married to Cary Grant then married that Russian prince this year. Her fourth husband. I see her as someone to aspire to. I love the idea of casting off husbands like last season's coat and getting yourself a new one.' She called to the waiter. 'Do tell the kitchen to hurry up as we are sitting an exam and have to be back at the Town Hall at one. How old are you, Jasmine?'

'Sixteen. Nearly seventeen.'

'A mere babe. I'm already eighteen but I'm a complete dunce. And bone idle apparently. Daddy had to pay for all kinds of tutors for me after I got booted out of school and they kept saying I wasn't ready.'

The waiter returned a minute later bearing the plates.

'Bring us each a glass of champagne will you, Walter.'

'Not for me!' Jasmine was shocked. They had the English paper this afternoon.

'Miss Appleton, your father has left us strict instructions that you are not to be served with alcohol if he is not present.'

'Oh, come on, Walter! He'll never find out. You could put it down on the bill as something else.'

The waiter consulted the maitre d' who shook his head.

'Sorry, Miss Appleton.'

Barbara rolled her eyes again. 'I'm going to have to work on Daddy. How annoying.'

'Surely it's better to keep a clear head. Otherwise you might fall asleep over the paper.'

Barbara feigned a yawn. 'I'll do that anyway. Unless there's a question on the rude bits in Lady Chatterly I'm doomed, as I haven't read any of the set texts. Can't even remember what they are. I shall have to make it up. Use my imagination. More fun anyway. Now, tell me about you and why you're sitting the exams externally. Did you get booted out of school too?'

'Yes. I didn't fit in. I hated it.' Jasmine gave her a brief explanation of her time in Africa and how she had wanted to come back to Penang.

'Africa, eh? How thrilling. Will you be doing the season too? Oh, do say you will! It would be frightfully good to have a kindred spirit when I get to London.'

Jasmine was tempted to ask how she had decided they must be kindred spirits. She herself felt they were anything but. 'Actually, I'm hoping to go to Paris to study art.'

'You really are exotic, aren't you?' Barbara clasped her hands together. 'I can picture you, in a garret overlooking the rooftops, with the dome of Montmartre in the distance, lying naked on a bed while your artist lover paints your portrait. How wonderfully Bohemian!'

Jasmine laughed. 'I have no intention of being anyone's lover, let alone posing naked. I'm going there to improve my own painting technique, not to be someone else's model.'

'You're quite right. You are a modern woman.' Barbara pointed a finger at her. 'Even better. Your handsome lover will be lying naked on the sheets as you paint him. I can see it now. You've been making mad, passionate love and he's lying among tangled sheets. Oh, if only I could paint. I'd be tempted to join you. It would be far more interesting than going to lots of balls. Paris is full of such fascinating people. Artists, jazz musicians, writers, poets.' She smiled. 'Once I've bagged my duke, I shall tell him to buy a house in the Bois de Boulogne and we can come and visit you and your handsome lover and pay lots of money for your paintings.'

'You might not like them.'

'Oh, darling, I'm sure I won't. But what does that matter?'

Jasmine looked up at the large wall clock. 'We need to get back. It's nearly one.'

Barbara flung her napkin on the table and got to her feet. 'You old bossy boots, you! Very well. Back into the jaws of the giant whale.'

As they hurried back to the Town Hall, Barbara linked arms again. 'I am so glad we met, Jasmine. I know we're going to be such great friends. Mummy and Daddy have told me I'm not allowed out at night until the exams are finished, but once they are, I shall throw a fabulous party and you will be my guest of honour.'

24

Four days later, after the final exam finished, Barbara Appleton took Jasmine's arm as they left the Town Hall and steered her along the street towards the *padang* and the waterfront.

'My driver's waiting for me,' Jasmine protested, seeing Bintang leaning against the car, smoking.

'Then tell him to wait. I told our *syce* that the exam didn't finish until four, so we have an hour to walk by the sea and talk.' Barbara Appleton was clearly unused to being gainsaid.

Jasmine apologised to Bintang and told him the plan. He nodded and followed them at a distance.

'Why is your man following us?'

'Ever since the Emergency began, he's been under instructions to stay close to me. The Hyde-Underwoods whom I'm staying with are extra protective because of my parents not being here.'

Barbara rolled her eyes. 'How tedious to have him trailing around everywhere with you.'

'Not at all. I like him. He's more of a friend really.'

Barbara's eyebrows shot up. 'Good Lord! He's a native. And a servant. How can he be a friend?'

'I went to school with his sister. And I'm painting his portrait.' As she spoke she wondered why she was trying to justify herself.

'Gosh. It gets worse!' Barbara gaped at her. 'It's not the done thing to be friends with natives. Really! I'm going to have to take you in hand.' She looked over her shoulder to where Bintang was following them at a distance. 'And it must be awful to be followed everywhere.'

'He's giving us privacy.' Suddenly defiant she added, 'And if you weren't here he'd be walking with me. I like talking with him actually. He's very interesting.' Annoyed, she wondered why she was having to defend Bintang again. Howard had been the same. Not about her talking to a native but rather more about mistrusting Bintang. Why did they have to take against him? It made her all the more determined to like him. 'I don't want to discuss this anymore. I can choose who I like to be friends with. I don't need help with that.'

Barbara put her hands up in front of her, palms out. 'All right. Message read and understood.'

Attempting to smooth things over, Jasmine asked, 'How did you get on with the paper? I thought the questions were hard. I did the one on The East India Company and the one about Thomas Cromwell's statesmanship. What about you?'

'I wrote a short paragraph on each of the three questions and then used the rest of the time to write to my best friend at school. But that old witch collected the letter up with the answer papers so it was a complete waste of time. Here, let's sit under that tree in the shade and I'll tell you what I'm planning for my party. Two weeks from tomorrow. I'll be sending out the invitations next week.'

They settled down on the sand, backs against the wall and Jasmine felt drowsy in the late afternoon sun. After all that concentration she could feel the threat of a headache coming on. At least she didn't have to worry about finding something to say to Barbara, as her new friend needed no prompting and was happy to sustain a monologue that was akin to a stream of consciousness.

'So you will come won't you?' Barbara paused for breath.

'I won't know anyone. Apart from you.'

'That's the whole point. I shall introduce you. I know everyone who's worth knowing in Penang. In the whole of the Settlements, for that matter. And I love having a new person to introduce. Everyone is going to adore you, darling! We'll have such fun. I knew at once I'd like you. I can always tell by looking at people. Particularly at what they wear. And that dress is so heavenly.'

Jasmine was wearing the daisy-patterned dress Evie had bought her. 'I got it in Colombo.'

'So pretty. You have good taste. Few people do.' She smoothed down the fabric of her own dress, a full-skirted confection in vibrant pink. 'This came from Paris. One thing you can look forward to when you're living there. I can tell you all the best places to shop. Not that you'll be wearing clothes too often as I definitely see you as the talented mistress of the most handsome man in Paris. A musician I think. I am picturing you together in your love nest, only venturing out late at night to go dancing in darkened basement bars in the Quartier Latin. Gosh! I'm actually making myself envious of you. Of course you will have to read Lady Chat before you go, so you'll know exactly what to expect.'

Jasmine tilted her head on one side. 'You have a very vivid imagination, Barbara. Maybe you should write books. I can assure you though, if I'm lucky enough to get into art school in Paris, I have no plans to do any of those things. And certainly not to be anyone's mistress.' She gave a little shudder. 'No, thank you.'

'Don't you have a boyfriend?'

'No – and I don't want one.'

'I don't have one either. Well, not at the moment. But I certainly intend to have as many as possible before I settle down with my duke and push out the heir and the spare.'

Out of the corner of her eye, Jasmine could see Bintang leaning against the sea wall about a hundred yards away. Beyond him was the white bulk of the former Runnymede Hotel, now surrounded with high barbed wire fencing and warning signs.

Barbara broke off her monologue and nudged Jasmine in the ribs. 'Smiles on. Pout those lips. Our boys are coming.'

Approaching from the direction of the fort was a platoon of army recruits, parading along the sand, evidently returning to their barracks in the Runnymede. A sick feeling washed over Jasmine as she spotted Lieutenant Ellis standing close to the water's edge awaiting their arrival.

'I think I should go.' Jasmine scrambled to her feet.

Barbara reached up a hand and pulled her down beside her again. 'What's the hurry? Let's have a look at the talent first. I know they're only squaddies, but no harm in admiring the goods.'

Jasmine jerked her arm away. 'Let me go. I'm leaving.' She spoke with force and this time Barbara got to her feet too.

Bintang started to move towards them and as he did, Jasmine realised Ellis had seen him and was following. The soldiers were clearly new recruits, who looked fresh out of school, pale spotty faces not yet burnt by the Malayan sun, crisp uniforms unsullied by expeditions through the jungle.

'National Service. All ugly conscripts.' Barbara nonetheless smiled flirtatiously as the young men marched past.

Jasmine barely looked at the soldiers. Her eyes were
tracking Bintang and Ellis. Bintang, seeing that Jasmine and
Barbara hadn't actually moved off, was hesitating. He
stepped back towards the wall as the soldiers approached,
and he looked to see if Jasmine was leaving. He was clearly
trying to both protect her and remain unobtrusive.

Ellis barked out an order to the sergeant who was
escorting the squaddies. Jasmine couldn't make out what he
had said as the wind carried his words out of earshot.

Then everything happened quickly. The men broke
ranks and encircled Bintang. Jasmine could no longer see
him. Voices were raised and she could make out one of them
as Bintang. Protesting.

'What are they doing to him?' She turned to Barbara in
alarm.

Barbara was frowning. 'Looks like they're about to arrest
your driver.'

'No!' Jasmine began running up the beach, Barbara
behind her.

'I do nothing wrong. I am driver. Just waiting.'

Two of the soldiers were restraining an angry and frightened Bintang, while another put his wrists in handcuffs.

Jasmine pushed through the soldiers to where Ellis was
standing, a look of contemptuous triumph on his face.

'Let him go,' she cried. 'You know perfectly well he's
done nothing wrong. You know he's my driver and is telling
the truth.' She turned to address the sergeant, but it was
hopeless, as he was not in a position to countermand an officer. 'Lieutenant Ellis is well aware who we are and knows
perfectly well my driver was waiting for us. He has instructions to keep me in sight at all times. He's just doing his job.'

The sergeant glanced at Ellis, who barked, 'Take his picture. Check it against the wanted list. If he's on there lock him up. If he's not he can go.' He turned on his heels and headed back to the barracks, after giving Jasmine a look of disgust.

The sergeant turned to Jasmine. 'Sorry about this, Miss, but we can't be too careful. There's a lot of suspicious characters around at the moment. I couldn't see what it was that caused the lieutenant to be suspicious but he's only acting to protect you and your friend. We'll deal with this as quickly as possible and then you can be on your way.'

He had a kindly look and Jasmine nodded. 'Please let him go as quickly as you can. I'm already late.'

Bintang, head down, humiliated, was pushed into the middle of the platoon and marched through a gateway, inside the wired fence and out of sight.

25

It was more than an hour before Bintang was released from the barracks. Jasmine was grateful to Barbara Appleton for waiting with her on the shore, even though she was late for her rendezvous with her own driver.

When Bintang eventually emerged from behind the wire fencing, he looked dishevelled, his shirt pulled out from the back of his trousers and a nasty bruise forming under his left eye.

'They've hurt you!' Jasmine rushed to greet him.

The driver looked away, avoiding her gaze.

'We need to make a complaint. They can't be allowed to get away with that. You did nothing. They've hit you. Tell me exactly what happened, Bintang.

The *syce* looked down, 'Nothing happen, *Missee*. We go back to estate now.'

Jasmine turned to appeal to Barbara, but her new friend was uncharacteristically quiet.

The three headed in silence along Farquhar Street. Outside the E&O a large black limousine was parked. 'My driver,' said Barbara. 'I'll see you at the party.' She flung her arms around Jasmine. 'Don't let what's happened get you down. Your driver will be fine. And if you don't come to my party I'll never speak to you again.' Blowing a kiss, she climbed into the back of the motorcar.

Bintang held open the rear door for Jasmine. Not wanting to draw attention in the busy street, she got in, saying nothing, and he turned the key in the ignition. He negotiated the streets of George Town, expertly steering between people carrying straw panniers on long yokes over their shoulders, handcarts piled high with boxes, trishaws, bicycles, street food stalls, and men and women hurrying by, going about their business. As usual, Jasmine stared at the back of his head. His normally immaculately groomed hair was sticking up on one side and she wanted to reach a hand up and smooth it down.

She waited for him to tell her what had happened, but he remained silent, driving as though he were alone in the car. When they pulled up at a junction to wait for a wooden hand cart, laden with water chestnuts, to be moved away from where it was blocking the road, without stopping to think, Jasmine hitched up her skirt and scrambled over the back of the front passenger seat, landing beside him.

A small almost indiscernible shadow of a smile fleeted across Bintang's face, gone so quickly, Jasmine couldn't be sure it was ever there. She adjusted her skirt over her knees.

'Now will you tell me what happened?' she asked, as the car pulled away from the junction.

'Nothing to tell, *Missee*.'

'Don't lie to me, Bintang. You have a black eye.'

He looked up at the rear-view mirror and winced. 'Must have tripped over.'

'You were hit.'

'I told you. Ellis very bad man.'

'I'm going to talk to Reggie. He'll take it up with the commanding officer at the barracks. Ellis can't go about beating up innocent men like that.'

Bintang looked at her. 'He say I am *min yuen*.'

'That's preposterous!'

'Is it?'

'What do you mean? Of course, it is!'

'Easy for him say I am. Now he has photograph of me. He will put it on wanted list. Can arrest without trial. No proof needed.'

'I'm going to talk to the *tuan* as soon as we get home. He'll put a stop to this.'

'No, *Missee*. He hurt grandmother.'

'Reggie?' Jasmine twisted around in the seat to face him. 'Of course, he won't!'

'Not *tuan*. Soldier. Bad man.'

'But how does he even know about your grandmother?'

Bintang shrugged. 'He know everything.'

'Why on earth would Ellis hurt your grandmother? She's an innocent old lady.'

'He say she *min yuen* too. Age not important.'

'But what are we going to do? We can't let him get away with this.'

'I leave here. Go where he can't find me.'

Jasmine felt a sudden chill, despite the balmy warmth of the early evening. 'Where? What are you going to do?'

'I leave island. Go to jungle.'

She was sitting sideways on the seat, one leg tucked under her, trying to read his face, but he stared ahead, his face expressionless as he negotiated the bends in the steep road.

'You're going to join the communists?' Her throat closed in fear.

He turned his head and looked at her steadily. 'You tell no one. Not even *tuan*. I go find my father.'

'But you told me your father is dead. That he was killed in the war.'

'No, I said he did not come back from war. I think he is in jungle.'

Jasmine experienced a rush of emotion. What was happening? She was out of her depth. 'You're going to be a communist? You're going to join the terrorists. Why?'

'Why you think? Now I have no choice.'

'Of course, you have a choice! Just because Ellis is a bad person it doesn't mean you have to become one. The communists murder innocent people. They kill people like the *tuan*, people like me.' Tears welled up in her eyes, unexpectedly. A mix of fear, anger and shock. 'Please, Bintang. Don't do this. I beg you, please don't. You can't join the terrorists. Stop the car now.'

'We late. It's dark. *Tuan* and *mem* worried if you not home. Please, say nothing about what happen.'

'I can't talk like this. I want you to look at me. Stop the car!' She was almost shouting.

He did as she asked, drifting the vehicle to the side of the road under some trees. Where the road curved, Jasmine glimpsed a silver trail of moonlight lighting a pathway over the distant sea.

Switching the ignition off, Bintang turned at last to face her. Seeing her tear-stained face, his own registered surprise. 'Don't cry. Missee Jasmine. Please don't cry.'

'I don't want you to go. Do you understand? Don't go, Bintang. I wouldn't be able to bear it. It will be all my fault.'

'Not your fault. Why you say that?' His eyes were full of concern.

'Ellis is angry with you because you helped me. He prob-

ably feels you humiliated him when you stopped him trying
to kiss me. Now I wish you hadn't. I'd rather have put up
with that than lose you. Oh, Bintang, I will do anything if it
means you'll stay. I'll even go and apologise to Ellis.'

'You not apologise. You do nothing wrong.' His voice
verged on anger.

'Neither have you! That's my point!' But she could see no
solution. Short of going to Ellis and offering her body to him
– and that was unthinkable and anyway probably wouldn't
make any difference. She had to get Bintang to talk to the
Hyde-Underwoods. She had to make him stay.

She looked up at his sad brown eyes. 'Don't leave me,
Bintang,' she said.

This time he held her gaze. Instinctively, she moved
closer. She put her hand against the smooth skin of his
cheek and touched his lips with her own.

At first, she felt him hesitate, his hands gripping her
arms as though about to push her away, then he began
kissing her back, slowly, tentatively. His lips were soft and
the kiss was tender. It had come from nowhere and Jasmine
surprised even herself. It had never occurred to her to think
of Bintang this way, but now it felt right, natural, inevitable.
As the kiss intensified, her body was filled with a warm glow
and she felt a charge of happiness, despite the conversation
they had just had. He couldn't possibly leave her now. This
would make all the difference.

But Bintang broke away first, and abruptly started the
engine. Leaving it running he got out, opened the front
passenger door and said, 'You need to get in back now.'

She nodded and did as he said.

As they drove the rest of the way to Bella Vista, Jasmine
was certain that everything was going to be all right. He
wouldn't leave now. How could he? Not now he knew she

cared for him. They'd talk to Reggie about Ellis. Reggie would make sure the lieutenant could not persecute Bintang. In fact, Ellis would probably be reprimanded for his conduct – including his attempt to kiss her. She shuddered, remembering her disgust at his advances. How different from the welcome warmth of Bintang's kiss.

Her tears were gone, her spirits rose. Everything would work out somehow. She leaned her arms on the back of the front seat so she could watch Bintang as he drove. His face was a mask of concentration, negotiating the steep climb and the hairpin bends. She had never fully recognised how beautiful he was until now. The straight line of his nose, the sensual curve of his mouth, that lustrous black hair. She reached up a hand and touched the top of his head, letting her fingers run down that dark silk, smoothing down the part that was mussed up. He raised one hand and gently pushed hers away. 'Stop please, Missee, we almost there.'

She longed to kiss him again but it would have to wait until they could be alone again. Perhaps in the studio. Tomorrow. It couldn't come fast enough. All her doubts about ever having feelings for any man had vanished in those few stolen moments in the dark interior of this car.

'I will talk to the *tuan* about Ellis tonight. At dinner. I'll tell him what happened. He'll know what to do.'

Bintang said nothing but nodded. His face was solemn – but then that was one of his most notable characteristics. He rarely smiled. Jasmine's heart swelled. Was this what love felt like? Did it always creep up on you like that? Unexpectedly. Out of nowhere, changing everything utterly, completely. All Jasmine knew was that in those few moments her entire world had been transformed.

The guard on duty opened the gates to Bella Vista as their vehicle approached. They swung through the gates,

drove past the *padang* and pulled up in front of the bungalow. As she got out of the car Jasmine brushed Bintang's
fingers with her own when he held the door open for her.
She remembered the sensation of his mouth on her hers,
the soft texture of his lips. A warm tingle spread through her
body, banishing her fear. 'Tomorrow. Come to the studio.
We can talk there. Goodnight, Bintang. Everything will be
all right.' She smiled up at him, wanting him to gather her
up and hold her. Instead, he looked at her with that same
sad expression. Then he nodded and walked away in the
direction of his quarters.

'You HAVE TO DO SOMETHING. Please, Reggie.' Jasmine said,
as she finished recounting what had happened on the shore.
'The man is a monster. Wait till you see Bintang's eye. By
morning it will be black and blue and swollen.'

'I'll ask Jinjiang to go over and clean it up for him,' said
Mary.

Jasmine felt a stab of jealousy. She should have offered
to do that herself – regardless of the fact she hadn't a clue
about first aid.

Reggie was frowning. 'I need to have a think about this.
It will require careful handling. Trouble is most of these
army wallahs are new in the country. I don't even know
who Ellis's CO is. But I'll make some enquiries. Maybe
drop into the club and find out if anyone there has any
contacts with them and can give me some pointers.
Problem is, we should have raised a formal complaint
about his appalling conduct when he tried it on with you
in the first place, but weeks have gone by. And the military
tends to stick together. Band of brothers and all that.' His
mouth formed a hard line. 'Since the Emergency laws were

passed, they have a pretty free rein where law and order are concerned when there's even a hint of terrorist activity.'

Jasmine was outraged. 'There was not even the tiniest hint. Bintang was doing exactly what you told him to do. He was keeping an eye on me while I went for a brief walk with Barbara. He did nothing wrong. Nothing.' She turned to appeal to Mary. 'Ellis beat him up only because it was Bintang who had pulled him off me. And now Bintang's sure he's going to mark him out as being in the *min yuen*.'

'That's ridiculous. He can't do that.' Mary looked at Reggie. 'Can he?'

Reggie had a grim expression. 'Look,' he said. 'Here's what I think we should do. I'll call the barracks and ask to speak to the CO and tell him I want to make a complaint about what happened to Bintang. I may need to make it sound as though there was some kind of misunderstanding to avoid them digging their heels in. Let Ellis save some face.'

'There was no misunderstanding!' Jasmine was seething with anger. 'I told the sergeant as well as Ellis that Bintang was our driver and had been minding his own business waiting for me. And Barbara can corroborate that.'

'I know. But these army types can be tricky. They don't like to back down. We don't want to make more trouble for Bintang and certainly not for you either, Jasmine.' Reggie leaned forward to reach for his pre-dinner *stengah*, beside him on a side table. Now your exams are over it's best to stay away from town for a while, until this quietens down. And I'm going to make some enquiries. Makes no sense for that cad to be here in George Town anyway when the commies are on the other side of the Strait. Maybe I can arrange for some strings to be pulled to get the blighter sent off on jungle patrols. The leeches will soon teach him a thing or two. Nasty little man. He's a cowardly pen-pusher.'

Mary looked at Jasmine. 'He's right you know. Better to work things out without making a fuss. Give them room to back down rather than maintain an entrenched position. I know you want Ellis to be punished but we have to find the best way to protect Bintang.'

'I'll have a chat with Bintang first thing in the morning and make it clear he has our full support,' Reggie added.

Jasmine was far from mollified but decided to see what happened next day.

'You haven't even told us how the exams went. You must be relieved they're over. Reggie and I were thinking we could all go and have a slap-up lunch and an afternoon at the Swimming Club to celebrate.' Mary looked at Jasmine expectantly.

'Today was hard, but I think I did enough to pass.' Her voice was flat. She had no interest at all in any of this. She wanted to be away from everyone and alone with only her thoughts of Bintang. Despite the awfulness of the afternoon, those moments of joy in the dark leather interior of the motorcar with him had made her see everything differently and now she couldn't wait to feel his arms around her again, his mouth on hers.

JASMINE WOKE next morning to the clatter of dishes in the kitchen below. She reached for her wristwatch on the bedside table and saw it was nearly nine. She'd overslept.

After quickly washing, she pulled her clothes on and hurried downstairs. Reggie would have been up for hours and must have already talked to Bintang and probably tele-phoned the barracks. She cursed the tiredness the past week's exams had brought on her and wished she'd asked Mary to wake her. Last night had been one of those nights where she'd struggled to drift off and then had fallen into the sleep of the dead. Her last thoughts had been of Bintang, replaying their beautiful kiss over and over in her head. Now, in the cold light of day, she also remembered his threat to leave to join the communists. Yesterday, she had been certain he couldn't possibly leave her – not now he knew her feelings for him. Today, that conviction was less strong. But she told herself not to be silly. Bintang would never be capable of killing people. He would never leave his grandmother. And most of all, in her heart she was sure he wouldn't leave her.

She hurried into the dining room, where her place setting remained on an otherwise empty table. Realising she was starving hungry, she made her way to the kitchen to find out what was left. Mary and Jinjiang were standing at the table preparing vegetables. Jasmine had been surprised when she first came to Bella Vista at how often Mary assisted the *amah* in meal preparation. Not behaviour typical of most *mem*s. She'd once asked her about it but Mary had merely said that she used to enjoy helping her mother and there was a lot for Jinjiang to do – something that Jasmine doubted. Bella Vista was unusual in that Jinjiang was the only house servant, when most *mem*s would have had a whole squad of servants at their disposal, never lifting a finger themselves.

The baby was sitting in her high chair, chewing on small slices of raw carrot. Frances gurgled with delight as Jasmine entered the room. But today, Jasmine had no inclination to play with her, merely kissing the top of the little girl's head.

'I'm so sorry I overslept.'

'That's because you needed to sleep. You've had an

exhausting week with all those examinations and then with that horrible experience yesterday. Let's go into the dining room and get some breakfast into you. Jinjiang will bring you some bacon and eggs.' Ignoring Jasmine's protests that she didn't want to interrupt the vegetable chopping, Mary bustled her out of the kitchen.

They sat down at the dining table.

'Did Bintang say anything to you last night about exactly what happened to him? What they did to him in the barracks?' Mary asked, frowning.

'No. Only that they had taken his photograph. He didn't want to talk about it. He tried to say he'd hurt his eye when he fell over but I told him I knew that wasn't true.' Seeing Mary's frown, she added, 'Why? Why are you asking me that?'

'Because he appears to have gone.'

A chill of fear coursed through her body. 'Gone? What do you mean? Gone where?'

'I don't know. Jinjiang treated his bruise last night before we had dinner. No one has seen him since. Reggie looked in his quarters this morning when he didn't appear as usual at the estate office. His bed hadn't been slept in and his clothes and belongings, not that he had a lot, were gone.'

Jasmine tasted bile. She gave a choked sob. 'No! Oh God, no!'

Mary reached across the table and touched Jasmine's wrist. 'You're not telling me everything, are you? Something's happened, hasn't it? If you want to help Bintang you need to tell me everything.'

26

—————

Jasmine crumbled. Everything that had happened the day before crowded in on her. The fear over what Ellis might do to Bintang. The shock when he'd told her he intended to join the communists. The sudden unexpected joy of the kiss they had shared. And above all, her overwhelming conviction that she loved him, but that she was the one to blame for what had happened to him.

Mary moved around the table and put an arm round Jasmine's shoulder. 'You have to trust me. If you know where Bintang has gone you need to tell me. Do you think he's been arrested?'

'No,' Jasmine wailed. 'He hasn't been arrested. Not if his things have gone.' She swiped the back of her hand across her eyes to brush away the tears.

'Then why has he left? Where has he gone?'

'I think he's gone to the jungle.'

'The jungle? You mean to his *kampong*?'

'No. On the peninsula.'

Comprehension dawned on Mary's face. 'Are you saying you think he's joined the CTs?'

Jasmine nodded mutely

'But why in heaven's name would he do that? He's not even Chinese. As far as we know there are no CTs recruiting here. There's been no trouble.' Her face registered anxiety. 'Reggie's sure there's absolutely no hint of unrest at Bella Vista.'

'Bintang's family were destroyed by the Japanese.'

'I know. His sister's murder was horrible and his mother was taken away from the family. I completely understand why he'd hate the Japanese as a result, but why would that make him want to fight the British?' She leaned forward. 'We've treated him well here at Bella Vista. Reggie is terribly fond of him. He was only saying the other day he wants to persuade Bintang to take classes in George Town so he can take on more responsibility here. He's a clever man, wasted as the *syce*. When the clerk goes back to India next year Reggie wants to give the job to Bintang.' Her face was puzzled.

'He doesn't hate the British because of you and Reggie. I think it's because of his father.'

'But isn't his father dead? I'd understood he died fighting the Japanese.' Mary tightened her lips, paused a moment, then nodded. 'I see. You think the father didn't die but stayed in the jungle? You think he's with Chin Peng?'

Jasmine nodded. 'Bintang hates the British. Not you and Reggie, but the British in general. He wants Malaya to be governed by Malays. He doesn't trust the government.'

Mary frowned. 'I had no idea. He hid that well. And you think this is why Ellis beat him up? You think Ellis knows he's in the *min yuen*?'

'He's not in the *min yuen*.' Jasmine spoke with force, then added, 'At least he wasn't. But he thinks Ellis will say he is. So, he might as well be. Ellis took his photograph. Bintang says he'll put him on the wanted list. Then they can pick him up off the street or come here and take him away.' Jasmine started to sob again. 'But I thought I'd persuaded him to stay. I thought he'd agreed to talk to you and Reggie. I thought you'd be able to sort it all out. I promised him.' The sobbing engulfed her, making her breathing jerky. 'Oh, Mary, what am I going to do? It's all my fault.'

'It's not your fault, Jasmine.' Mary's voice became harsh. There was an edge to it that Jasmine had never heard before. 'Get that out of your head, right now. If anyone's to blame – apart from that nasty Lieutenant Ellis – it's Reggie and me, for not overruling you and insisting a complaint was lodged immediately about Ellis assaulting you.'

'But he didn't get a chance to do anything. Thanks to Bintang. I didn't want Bintang to get into trouble. But I've made it worse. If only I hadn't agreed to go for a walk with Barbara.' Her voice was ragged and the tears wouldn't stop.

Mary got up and took a clean napkin from the sideboard drawer. 'Here, dry your eyes.' She smiled at Jasmine. 'Nothing is ever as bad as it seems. Believe me. We'll talk to Reggie when he comes in for tiffin.'

But Jasmine was inconsolable.

'Are you sure you've told me everything, my darling?' Mary sat down again beside the girl.

Another huge gulping sob escaped from Jasmine and she buried her head in Mary's shoulder. 'Oh Mary, what am I going to do? I'll never see him again. I can't bear it.'

Mary held her as she wept. Eventually, when the sobbing levelled off, she fixed her eyes on Jasmine. Her voice was that of the school teacher, calm, controlled, competent. 'Now, I think you need to tell me exactly what's been going on. Are you trying to say there's something romantic between you and Bintang?'

Wretched, Jasmine looked at her, tears still rolling unchecked down her cheeks. 'I love him.'

If Mary was shocked or surprised, she did a good job at disguising it. 'And does he feel the same way about you?'

More tears. 'I thought he did. But if he did, how could he leave me? How could he go away and not even say goodbye.' Her words were coming in breathless gasps.

'How long has this been going on?' Mary spoke quietly.

'It only happened yesterday. After Ellis took him. On the way back here. In the car. I didn't even know I felt that way about him. But something inside made me kiss him. And then he kissed me back and everything changed. I knew right away I love him. Now all I want is to be with him. Oh, Mary, what am I going to do?'

Mary smoothed a hand over Jasmine's hair. 'You poor dear girl.'

'You're not angry with me?'

'Of course not. How could I be angry with you?'

'Because he's Malayan. Because he's one of the servants.' Then Jasmine remembered something. 'You won't tell Mummy about this?'

'I won't tell her, but I hope you will.'

'Do you think she'll be angry?'

'Why would she be angry? She will certainly be concerned. Concerned that you are so unhappy.'

Mary stroked the girl's hair again. 'You'll hate me for saying this. But Bintang won't be the only person you'll love. Believe me.'

'Yes he will.' Jasmine was absolutely certain of that. 'I know you think I'm too young to fall in love but I never ever believed I'd feel like this about anyone.' She groaned. 'I thought I might even be abnormal. That I didn't like boys. But now, I feel so differently. I really love him. Oh, Mary! Is it always so painful? I don't think I've ever felt so unhappy. And yesterday I had never been as happy as I was when we kissed.'

Mary said nothing for few moments, still holding Jasmine against her. 'When two people truly love each other they stop feeling alone and lonely. They stop worrying what the other person might think or feel. They become as one. Not as in being the same person – but as thinking always of the other person first. I cared for the two men I was involved with before I met Reggie, but only after I met him did I know beyond doubt that whatever happens Reggie will always be standing beside me.' She paused. 'And I think it's the same for Evie and Arthur.' We can love other people but if and when you meet the right person, nothing you can do can make each other unhappy.'

'That's not true!' Jasmine was indignant. 'I know Mummy was terribly unhappy in London when she found Arthur again and he left her standing in the street. She cried all the way home on the train. Hugh was asleep and I pretended not to notice. But she was really sad.'

Mary sighed. 'You're right. I was unhappy too after Reggie and I first got together. But once we were honest about our feelings for each other it was inconceivable we could ever be apart from each other. I think that's the case for your mother too.'

'Well that's how I feel about Bintang.'

Mary gulped, then smiled and reached for Jasmine's hand. 'And if he feels that way about you too, he will come back. If he truly loves you, he can't possibly want to cause you pain.'

'You don't think he does?' Jasmine wasn't sure whether to be angry at Mary or feel sorry for herself.

Mary looked at Jasmine, her expression compassionate. 'I am going to be completely honest. I'm not going to patronise you. I hope Bintang does love you. It's no more than you deserve. I find it hard to imagine how anyone who knows you wouldn't love you.' She paused and took a breath. 'But is Bintang the man you are going to love more than anyone else and spend your life with? I have to say I don't believe he is. You won't want to hear that, but eventually you'll acknowledge it's true.' She gave a quick smile. 'Of course, that's no comfort whatsoever right now. I am truly sorry, my darling.'

MARY DIDN'T WAIT for Reggie to come in for tiffin. As soon as Jasmine had calmed herself, Mary left the bungalow and went to the estate office to find him.

'We have a problem.' Mary told her husband everything Jasmine had revealed about Ellis, Bintang and the latter's disappearance. She avoided revealing the depth of Jasmine's feelings for the driver. One step at a time.

'Let me get this straight. You're saying old Bintang's run off to join the commies?'

'And Jasmine is blaming herself.'

'But what on earth would make the fellow do that?'

'Jasmine thinks Ellis has it in for him and is planning to frame him and arrest him for being *min yuen*.'

'You have to be Chinese. Doesn't that fool Ellis know the difference?'

'Probably not. And apparently Bintang told Jasmine his father is with the communists. I had no idea but apparently he was with the MPAJA in the war and Bintang thinks he stayed with them. With Chin Peng.'

'Bintang told you that?' Reggie was astonished.

'No. He told Jasmine. You remember I mentioned she'd been painting his portrait. They must have become quite close.'

'Good grief! You're not saying–'

'It seems in the heat of the moment last night after what happened with Ellis, they exchanged a kiss.'

'What the devil? He pounced on her?' Reggie jumped up from behind his desk and began pacing up and down the small office.

'Quite the reverse. I rather think Jasmine pounced on him. And now the poor child has convinced herself she's head over heels in love with him.'

'What a godawful mess, Mary. Why didn't we see that coming? I know I'm a bit slow on the uptake but didn't *you* notice anything?'

Mary shook her head. 'Not a thing. Yes, I knew she was painting him, but I didn't think there was anything wrong with that. She painted Jinjiang too – and one of the mothers at the school.'

'Did she ever talk about him?'

'Never.'

Reggie sat down again and put his head in his hands. 'I wish I'd spoken out when Evie asked us to put her up. I should have expressed my misgivings. The child's only fifteen.'

'She's sixteen. Nearly seventeen. She's a young woman. And it's not your fault. It's mine. You have the estate to run. I should have kept a closer eye.'

'Damn it but I told the lad to stay with her wherever she

went. If I hadn't said that he'd never have been on the beach in the first place.'

'It might have happened eventually anyway.' Mary moved behind her husband and put her arms around him. 'There must have been an attraction there.'

'But the silly girl couldn't possibly have thought there was a future in it. He's a Malay and a servant to boot. She's Doug Barrington's daughter.' He looked up at Mary, spinning round in the chair. 'You're not implying that was why, are you? That Bintang saw her as a means of improving his lot? Because I can tell you that's not him at all. I trust the fellow implicitly.'

'Of course I'm not. I know he's not like that.' She sighed then perched on the edge of the desk. Here's what I think happened. Jasmine was swept up by her own emotions and Bintang's plight. He responded in the heat of the moment. He is a sensible young man. He would have known there's no future so he's gone away. Whether it was fears about Ellis or the realisation that he'd probably overstepped the mark, he didn't wait to find out.'

'And you really think he's gone to join those bastards in the jungle?'

Mary nodded.

'It will take him hours to get into town. Probably five. Maybe if I leave now I could catch him.'

'No point. He has a bicycle so, assuming he left some time last night, he'll have disappeared across the Strait hours ago.'

'Where's Jasmine now?'

'In her studio.'

Reggie got up. 'Let's go and have a word then. She might have some more details as to exactly where he was heading.'

'I think she'd have told me if she had. She was shocked

and upset he'd gone after all. She thought after their romantic interlude he couldn't possibly leave her.'

'The poor creature.' He shook his head sadly. 'She's such a sweet little thing. I hate to think of her being disillusioned. I'd like to wring Bintang's neck. And him being a secret commie.' He shook his head again. 'She's not the only one who's disillusioned.'

When they reached the studio there was no sign of Jasmine.

27

From the top of the hill, where she had once talked under the trees with Bintang, the *kampong* where his grandmother lived appeared to be quite close by, and the route down to it straightforward.

But once Jasmine started to descend the hillside, she could no longer see her destination clearly. There was no obvious footpath at all in places, as well as merging and diverging paths. The lower down she got, the hotter it became, particularly in the stretches without much tree cover and sweat poured down her back. The large bag she was carrying on her back was heavy, slowing her progress further. Her only consolation was that she had decided to leave her satchel behind. That had been an easy decision as she had no intention of sketching this morning. In fact she couldn't imagine ever wanting to pick up a pencil or a paintbrush again.

She was smarting from what Mary had said to her. Mary's intention was to be kind but that didn't help at all. Jasmine didn't want sympathy and she didn't want someone trying to tell her that the intense feelings she had for

Bintang weren't real. Mary had implied she wasn't properly in love.

How she hated the way grownups treated her – as though they knew everything and she knew nothing. Just because she wasn't yet seventeen didn't mean she was incapable of feeling real love. Juliet Capulet had been even younger and for hundreds of years people had held her and Romeo up as the ideal of true love. A lump formed in her throat. If he joined the communists it would only be a matter of time before he was dead. Or worse, responsible for the deaths of others. How could she bear to go on living?

Distraught, contemplating these horrible eventualities, Jasmine passed through a dense clump of trees and found herself in the native village. She spoke no Malay; how was she to track down Bintang's grandmother? Would anyone here speak English? They were all presumably uneducated subsistence farmers she imagined. Yet Bintang and Siti had been well educated. His English was good – she suspected he pretended it was more broken than it really was.

Several people appeared in open doorways and stared at her in surprise, some smiling, but most looking concerned. It must be unusual, to say the least, for an unaccompanied young white woman to come crashing out of the forest. Some small children ran up and surrounded her, chattering away incomprehensibly. She looked about. Who could she ask? And how?

'Bintang?' she said, tentatively, to no one in particular. 'Bintang grandmother?'

A young woman approached. She was wearing a head covering and had enormous, beautiful eyes. 'Come,' she said. 'Come with me. I take you.'

Relieved, Jasmine followed the woman between the rows

of wooden *attap*-roofed huts. They reached one at the edge of the settlement, next to open fields.

'This is place.' The young woman smiled, before turning and walking away.

Nervously, Jasmine called out a greeting at the open doorway. 'Hello!' She had no idea how she should address Bintang's grandmother. He had never mentioned her name.

A diminutive old woman, wearing a black *baju kurung*, her head covered by a black scarf, her face lined and wrinkled, emerged from the door of the hut.

'Bintang Grandmother?'

The woman said nothing, frowning.

'Is Bintang here?'

'Bintang gone.' She turned to walk back inside the hut.

'Wait please. I am his friend. My name is Jasmine. I've brought something for you.' She jerked the heavy bag off her shoulder and pulled out the portrait of Bintang. 'I painted this for him to give to you. A gift from him. It's not quite finished–'

Her voice stumbled at the thought that it would never be finished now. She held it up, resting the top under her chin. It was unframed but then she didn't imagine there was anywhere for the old lady to hang it, as the interior of the hut would be dark. Maybe coming here had been a mistake. Then she remembered how the prospect of giving this painting to his grandmother had caused Bintang to agree to sit for her in the first place.

The old woman stepped forward and took the picture from Jasmine. She propped it against the outside of the hut and stepped back to inspect it.

Jasmine waited nervously for her reaction. As she studied the picture now, the sunlight falling across it, she acknowledged to herself that she had captured the essence of him. She choked back incipient tears.

'Bintang,' said the woman at last. She turned to face Jasmine, joined her hands together and bowed her head in thanks.

'There's something else.' Jasmine reached inside the bag and carefully drew out the heavy piece of hardwood. It was intricately decorated with shells, dried fruits, spices and casuarina cones, which she had varnished and stuck to the wood. At the top she had painted the name, Siti. She had planned to do it in Malay characters but had not had the chance to ask what they were and had hastily added the name this morning. 'Siti was at school with me. I was sad there is no marker for her grave.'

'You put flowers there?'

'Yes. That was me.'

The old lady said nothing. Perhaps she didn't like the marker – or that it might be inappropriate to her faith or custom. Wishing she had been able to show it to Bintang, Jasmine regretted the decision to bring it today.

She was about to put it back in the bag, when the woman said, 'Come.' She started to walk along a path at the edge of the adjoining field. Jasmine could see the clump of trees where Siti was buried on the far side.

Together they made a hole, using their hands and some stout sticks. The ground was damp from overnight rain and the earth easily handled. They inserted the memorial and filled in the soil around the base, then stood back to see how it looked.

The grandmother smiled and closed her eyes. 'I thank you, Missee. You kind lady. Now Siti has good grave. Siti with Allah and she smile today.'

'Oh, I hope so.'

'Come. I give you fruit and water.'

Realising she was parched with thirst after her long hot walk and their exertions erecting the grave post, Jasmine nodded gratefully.

They sat on low wooden chairs under a tree close to the hut and Jasmine drank the water and ate sweet and refreshing strips of mango. She imagined Bintang sitting here beside his beloved grandmother and felt close to him.

'Do you know where he is?' she asked. 'Where Bintang has gone.'

Knowing it was futile didn't stop her hoping that the old woman would tell her he was here in the *kampong*.

'Gone to jungle. He go to my son.'

'Bintang's father is still alive? He didn't die in the war? Have you seen him?'

'After Japanese war he visit. But not come back for long time. Not since war against British begin. Too much danger.'

'Does Bintang know where he is?' She bit her lip, wanting to ask where exactly he was so she could try to find him, but the old woman would be unlikely to know and even if she did, she wouldn't tell.

'He find him. He know.' The woman's eyes welled up with tears.

Jasmine wanted to put her arms around the frail old lady but didn't wish to cause offence. Instead she reached for her bony hand and clasped it between hers.

As she was about to confess her feelings for Bintang the sound of a motorcar cut through the quiet. Jasmine could see between the neighbouring huts that it was a jeep. A stab of terror ran through her. Ellis. In search of Bintang. Grateful he wasn't here to be dragged away into the jeep and locked away in prison, she didn't want Ellis to see her either.

She wondered whether to run into the jungle or hide in the grandmother's hut.

But the woman didn't share her concern. Turning to Jasmine, she said, '*Tuan* come to find you.'

Relief surged through Jasmine as Reggie jumped out of the jeep and she heard his voice asking questions in Malay. Several people pointed in her direction. She thanked the old woman for her hospitality and said, 'I will pray Bintang is safe.'

The woman smiled. It was the same rarely offered fleeting smile Jasmine recognised from her grandson. Then the woman went back inside her hut and shut the door.

Jasmine ran to greet Reggie. At least she wouldn't have that steep climb back up the hillside in the midday sun.

28

Her pilgrimage to meet Bintang's grandmother, and the acceptance and kindness of the elderly woman, had made Jasmine feel calmer. She still longed for Bintang to return and was riven with guilt at being the cause of his defection, but the near hysteria she'd suffered when she found out he had left was gone. What remained was a hollow ache, an abiding sadness and a desperate longing to be in his arms.

When she and Reggie returned from Bintang's *kampong*, Mary greeted her with relief, and made no criticism of her visit there, accepting that she'd wished to pay her respects to Bintang's grandmother.

'When you didn't appear for tiffin I went to look for you in the studio,' Mary said. 'I noticed the portrait of Bintang was missing and guessed where you might have gone.'

'He agreed to me painting him so he could give the picture to his grandmother. It was the least I could do to let her have it. Particularly as I don't know how long it will be until she sees him again.' Her voice trembled and she looked away, reluctant to let the Hyde-Underwoods see her grief.

Jasmine didn't mention the memorial marker for Siti. No one, not even Bintang had known she had made it. Now it would remain a secret between herself and Bintang's grandmother.

Although neither Mary nor Reggie had said anything critical about her feelings for their driver, Jasmine sensed their unspoken disapproval. Mary looked at her with a sad expression and Reggie avoided looking at her at all.

Now that the exams were over and the native school was closed for a week for the end of the second term holiday, Jasmine found herself with time on her hands. Normally she would have exulted in being able to spend hours on end wandering around with her sketch pad or standing painting at her easel in the studio, but instead she spent hours lying on her bed with the shutters closed, thinking about Bintang.

Her feelings for him had been so unexpected. They had crept up on her and surprised her with their sudden force. Until she had been swept up in her emotions for him, Jasmine had found the very idea of a romantic relationship with anyone distasteful. It had seemed furtive, dirty, unpleasant. But now she knew that was just what her experiences in Nairobi had made it.

Memories of seeing the mother of her Nairobi schoolfriend, Katy, cavorting around the pool with young men, had convinced her that intimacy was something crude and shameful that she herself would never want to do. The fact that there were positive examples to the contrary in her stepparents and the Hyde-Underwoods had failed to eradicate the shock of wandering back to the ladies' changing room at the Nairobi Sports Club to collect a forgotten towel and witnessing Mrs Granville with the pool boy.

Katy's mother had been groaning, and at first Jasmine had thought the young man was attacking her. Then hearing his grunts and seeing the rapid thrusts of his buttocks, the realisation dawned. Jasmine had been frozen to the spot, the lovers too preoccupied to see her. She'd run back outside. The near-violence and angry movements of the copulating couple had frightened her. It had been ugly, primitive, undignified, like animals. She'd never want to do that herself.

But now she found herself imagining doing it with Bintang. Not in that angry violent way, but slowly, gently, tenderly, like their kiss. Lieutenant Ellis and her own stupidity had intervened to ensure that would now never happen. She shuddered at the thought of Bintang's face adorning wanted posters, him being dragged off, handcuffed and thrown into a prison cell, shot dead, or worst of all, captured and sentenced to death. The punishment for anyone found in possession of weapons was a mandatory death sentence. Jasmine's fists pounded the pillows.

If she couldn't be with Bintang, then she would be alone forever. There could be no one else for her now. For the first time since arriving in Penang, she wondered whether she ought to return to Africa. Right now, she desperately wanted to be with Mummy; to fling her arms around Evie and let herself cry her troubles out. But how could she possibly run away when the man she loved was in danger? He may not be with her but he was here in Malaya, so that was where she must be too.

Jasmine made her mind up. She would go back to the studio. She had the sketch she'd made of Bintang at the school. That could be the basis for another painting. This time for her only. She couldn't have him, but she must have something to help her feel close to him.

. . .

THE INVITATION to Barbara Appleton's party arrived. Jasmine racked her brains for an excuse not to accept. But she had promised Barbara, and Jasmine hated the idea of breaking a promise. Besides, it would be nice to have someone to confide in – someone her own age to tell how she was feeling.

She mentioned the invitation to Mary who grinned like the Cheshire Cat.

'That's wonderful, Jasmine. Exactly what you need. A chance to meet some other people your own age.' She cocked her head on one side and lifted her eyes, thinking. 'Appleton? Is she the daughter of Sir Percy? The canned fruit king?'

'Gosh, I've no idea. Only that her family is frightfully rich. She's going to be presented at court and she has an account at the E&O and can spend whatever she likes. She says her father spoils her.'

'It must be him. Reggie, you know Sir Percy, don't you?'

Reggie looked up from the *Straits Times*. 'Do I?'

'Yes. Sir Percy and Lady Appleton. They live in Kuala Lumpur but they have a place up here too. Can't remember exactly where. Friends of Dorothy and Clifford Rogers. At least they were before the war.'

'What of him?'

'Jasmine has become friendly with the daughter. And she's been invited to a party there.'

'Good show.'

Mary frowned. 'We still don't have a *syce* to replace Bintang. We'll need to come and collect you ourselves. I don't like driving up and down at night. Maybe we could stay in town, Reggie? Or in Butterworth? We could drop Jasmine off then book into a hotel and drive back here in the morning.'

Reggie grunted.

'Actually, Barbara has invited me to stay. She'd like me to come on the afternoon of the party and stay until late Sunday afternoon. And she says they will send a car for me and bring me home on Sunday.'

Mary raised her eyebrows. 'Well, well. You're the honoured guest. That solves that one then. Now what are you going to wear?' With a big smile she added, 'It must be that beautiful blue shot-silk dress. You look stunning in it, Jasmine.'

SITTING in the back of Sir Percy's sleek black Rolls Royce, Jasmine felt like royalty. The driver was a turbaned Indian so there was no comparison with all the times she had been driven with her eyes on Bintang's hair. She leaned back against the leather upholstery and tried to put all thoughts of Bintang out of her head.

Even though she didn't relish the prospect of a party with guests she didn't know, Jasmine was glad to be away from Bella Vista and the constant anxiety about the man she was certain she loved. A party would be a distraction and much as she was fond of the Hyde-Underwoods, it would be a refreshing change to be with people her own age.

The driver drove in silence and reached the car ferry just in time to board. It was a long time since she had taken the ferry across to Butterworth. The last time had been the night they fled Penang for the crowded train to Singapore to escape the advancing Japanese army. Hugh had been a baby and they travelled with Mary and her parents, and Susan Hyde-Underwood with her and Reggie's baby son, Stanford. The details of that journey were hazy, but Jasmine remembered all too well the fear of everyone in that crowded compartment and the shock that they were having to flee their homes. It made her think again of Bintang – he and his family, like all the non-Europeans, were left behind to fend for themselves, at the mercy of the Japanese invaders.

THE GROUNDS OF THE APPLETONS' grand residence, Orchard House, were encircled by barbed wire fencing, reminding Jasmine of the realities of life on the peninsula since the beginning of the Emergency – although Orchard House was close to a major thoroughfare. The Rolls Royce passed through the metal gates, operated by two armed guards, and crunched over the gravel of the long driveway. They drove almost a mile, between avenues of palm trees, until she saw the imposing white house, its porticoed frontage in the classic colonial style. Barbara Appleton was waiting on the steps as the car pulled up. She rushed over and flung her arms around Jasmine as she got out of the Rolls.

'I'm so glad you were able to come early. My parents agreed not to visit the scene of the crime and they've stayed in KL, so we have the run of the place. I thought you and I would have some celebratory fizz by the pool then we can get our frocks on and have an early light supper before the guests arrive. There will be a buffet later and Daddy's arranged for the chef from the Penang Club to prepare it. Had to pull a lot of strings as Saturday nights are always so popular at the PC. But Daddy always manages to get what he wants.' She grabbed Jasmine's hand. 'Come on! I want to know everything you've been up to since we last met.'

At the rear of the mansion, there was a large swimming pool surrounded by a paved terrace, with lawns beyond that swept away to meet a river, beyond which was the jungle.

Barbara flung herself into a cushioned rattan armchair. 'I'm so excited about tonight.'

Another turbaned servant approached, wearing a colourful uniform. 'Daddy used to be in India and he says they make much better servants than Malays or Chinese,' Barbara said breezily as, without being asked, the man took a bottle from an ice bucket and poured them each a glass of champagne.

'I don't drink alcohol.' Jasmine decided it was better to confess now.

'Don't be silly, Jazz, everyone drinks. I hope you don't mind but I've decided to call you Jazz.'

'My stepfather sometimes does.'

'What, drink?'

Jasmine giggled. 'No! Well yes, of course he does. But I meant he calls me Jazz.'

Barbara looked slightly peeved as though her thunder had been stolen, but she raised her glass and chinked it against Jasmine's. 'Why don't you drink?'

'I don't think I'd like it.'

Barbara rolled her eyes. 'You timid creature! You won't know until you've tried. And I promise you're going to love it. Bottoms up!'

Jasmine took a tentative sip and felt the bubbles burst on her tongue and a surprisingly sweet taste in her mouth. She took another sip. For the next hour she listened as Barbara kept up her usual monologue. Today it revolved around the identities of the invited guests, none of whom meant anything to Jasmine.

'I plan to have a smooch with someone tonight. Some heavy petting and maybe even go all the way.'

She giggled and Jasmine wondered how much of her talk was bluster.

'I intend to make the most of my freedom before I have to do all that debutante stuff when I get to London and be on my best behaviour until I'm engaged. Over here, no one is ever going to know. Make hay while the sun shines – that's my motto. I have several candidates in mind. Godfrey Fairchild is top of my list – but if you take a fancy to him, I'll let you have first dibs, darling. We absolutely have to get you a boyfriend.'

'I told you before, I don't want one.'

'Nothing to stop you having a bit of fun. Most of the boys here are more than happy to keep it light-hearted. They're not looking to find a wife yet, so you've no worries on that score.'

'No! I mean it. I don't want any of that.' Jasmine was now almost at the end of what she thought must be a second glass of champagne. The turban-wearing servant had a way of topping the glass up so discreetly that she couldn't actually keep track of how much she had drunk. It was a relief when Barbara suggested they go upstairs to her bedroom to get ready for the party.

Walking up the sweeping curve of the marble stairway, Jasmine felt unsteady on her feet. She told her friend she was beginning to get a headache.

'Never mind, there's plenty of time. You're probably a bit dehydrated.' Barbara poured a glass of iced water from a glass on a side table and handed it to Jasmine who drank it greedily and immediately felt better.

'Now, let's get to the bottom of why you don't want a boyfriend or even a bit of a pash. Come on, Jazz, spill the beans. There's already somebody, isn't there?' She flung herself dramatically onto the bed, propped herself up against the piled-up pillows and fixed her eyes on Jasmine.

The champagne had loosened Jasmine's tongue. It

would be a relief to tell Barbara everything. 'Yes, there is. Well, there was. But he's gone.' She hesitated, then decided that Barbara was unshockable. 'It's Bintang.' Her voice was barely a whisper.

'Who on earth is Bintang? Surely not a native?' Barbara's eyes widened.

Jasmine nodded. 'Actually you've met him. He's the Hyde-Underwoods' driver.'

Barbara clasped her hands together. 'Good grief, girl, you're a dark horse. I suppose I should have realised when I saw how distressed you were when that horrid little soldier arrested him. How frightfully exciting. Do you know, I've never tried that. Having a thing with one of the servants. It would drive Daddy absolutely nuts if I were to do it.' She started to giggle. 'Very tempting for that reason alone...' She pouted. 'But all our servants are decidedly unattractive. Unlike your handsome driver.' She gave a long sigh. 'So, what have you done with him? Did you, you know...?' She gave Jasmine a salacious look.

'Of course not! But that night...after we were with you... we kissed. In the car.'

'The cheeky devil. How did he come to kiss you? Did you give him a good slap round the chops then melt into his arms like butter?' Barbara clutched a hand to her breast in an exaggerated gesture.

'No! It wasn't like that at all. *I* kissed *him*.'

Barbara clapped her hands. 'You little devil, you, Jazz Barrington! And there was you being all coy when I suggested taking handsome French lovers in Paris. Was he shocked? Did he kiss you back?'

'Yes.' Jasmine was starting to wish she hadn't revealed any of this.

'Did you let him touch your breasts? Was it nice? Do

Malays kiss the same as white boys? I bet they're better. Was it full tongues?'

A beautiful romantic moment was transforming into something sleazy under Barbara's questioning. Jasmine decided to say nothing more. Why had she drunk all that champagne? It had dulled her judgement.

'Awfully clever of you to choose a local, as there's no risk of falling in love with them when they're servants. Come on. What happened next?'

'Nothing. And you're quite wrong.' Jasmine felt defiant. She didn't want the love of her life described as a furtive fumble and herself as a predatory female. 'Bintang and I are in love.' There. It was out.

Barbara gasped. 'Did he tell you that? Did he actually say he's in love with you? And what does he propose to do about it? Marry you and have you live in his poky old hut in a native village bearing a tribe of little Malayan children with him? Don't be daft, Jasmine.'

Tears pricked the back of Jasmine's eyes. She took another gulp of water. Barbara had made it all sound foolish. And for the first time it occurred to her that the idea of living in a windowless hut in the *kampong* where his grandmother lived was nonsensical. How would she fulfil her dream of becoming a serious painter?

'He could have got a different job.' Her argument sounded feeble, even to herself. 'He could have gone to college to get qualifications. He's a clever man. He could have worked for the government.' Then she remembered how he had derided her when she'd suggested that. But that was before The Kiss.

'You're talking about him in the past tense. Has he dumped you already? Or did the Hyde-Underwoods find out and send him packing?'

'He had to go. He had to leave Penang. Because of Lieutenant Ellis.' She was determined she wasn't going to tell Barbara about his intention to join the CTs. 'Ellis hates him because Bintang stopped him trying to kiss me. He was trying to make out Bintang was in the *min yuen*.'

'What's that?' Barbara yawned, already bored.

'Spies for the communists.'

'Well he probably is. Look, Jazz. If you take my advice, you'll forget all about him. He was obviously taking advantage. And why wouldn't he, when a beautiful girl like you throws herself at him? You're well rid of him. Imagine if he'd stuck around! You'd soon have gone off him and then you'd have had him staring at you with those big beautiful brown eyes and following you round like a lost dog.'

'Bintang would never have done that. And I would never go off him. I wish I hadn't told you.' Jasmine wanted to get away. Out of the palatial mansion. Out of the extremely pink bedroom and back in her own one at Bella Vista. But she was stuck here with no means of getting back to Penang tonight. She would have to grin and bear it.

The two girls changed into their outfits for the party, Jasmine wearing the blue shot silk dress and Barbara in a plunge-necked, blood red gown with voluminous under-skirts that made her look as though she'd invaded a dress-ing-up box. She looked Jasmine up and down, eying the simple blue silk dress critically. 'Where did you get that dress?'

'In Columbo. Our ship stopped there on the way here. Do you like it?' Jasmine did a twirl.

'No, no. That simply won't do. You look like a country bumpkin. I'm going to lend you something of mine.' Barbara marched up to her enormous lacquered wardrobe and shuf-fled between the garments on the rack. Eventually she found what she was looking for. She pulled out a vivid pink satin gown and told Jasmine to try it on.

'It's not really my colour, Barbara. And it's very bright.' She was feeling wounded by the country bumpkin comment.

'Nonsense! It's a genuine Schiaparelli. Shocking pink is her signature colour. You'll look wonderful. Trust me.' She whipped the garment off its hanger and flung it on the bed. 'Come on. Slip it on. I have the perfect lipstick to match it.'

Beyond caring, Jasmine put on the dress and stood like a mannequin in a shop window while Barbara fiddled about, adjusting the layers of fabric and smoothing down the enormous bow that sat low on her back and from which folds of fabric cascaded down into a train. She looked at her reflection in the full-length mirror. The bodice was sculpted over the bust and was strapless. She didn't recognise the woman who stared back at her – a large pink lobster with an overlong tail.

'Barbara, I don't think this is me. It's far too grown up. I can't carry off a dress like this.'

'Don't be such a silly! You look stunning. Sophisticated. Elegant. A woman of the world!'

'But I'm not any of those things.'

'Well, no one will know that. Now hurry up. The guests will be here any minute.'

THE GUESTS all arrived in a rush, a constant stream of motorcars pulling up in front of the house to disgorge their passengers. Barbara kept a proprietorial arm through Jasmine's, wheeling her between groups, parading her around like the winning dog at Cruft's.

'This is my wonderful new friend, Jasmine, who is quite

the nicest, most lovely creature, and you're going to absolutely adore her.' Barbara spoke emphatically and unequivocally.

Jasmine felt self-conscious in the shocking-pink gown. Most of the other women were dressed to the nines, but her blue shot-silk would have not been as out of place as this over-elaborate construction. She kept glancing down nervously, terrified that the bodice might be gaping and revealing more than she cared to display. She was less well endowed than Barbara and the décolletage had been supplemented by deftly added padding which her hostess had inserted into Jasmine's brassiere.

Forcefully declining another glass of champagne, Jasmine accepted an orange juice instead. Barbara's grip on her elbow tightened. 'Here he is. Godfrey Fairchild. Mmm... and he has an even better-looking friend with him. I'm going to be spoilt for choice.' She nudged Jasmine in the ribs. 'But I did promise you first dibs, didn't I? Come on, let's find out who the handsome stranger is. What's wrong, Jasmine?'

But Jasmine was rooted to the spot, wishing she had never agreed to come. The young man accompanying Godfrey Fairchild was Howard Baxter. And he had seen her, so she had no chance to hide.

The two men crossed the room to greet their hostess. Barbara air-kissed Godfrey then turned her attention on Howard. 'Who are *you*?' she said, flirtatiously, 'and why have we never met before? Godfrey where have you been hiding this handsome hunk?' Remembering her guest of honour, she stretched an arm out and hooked Jasmine's, drawing her into the group. 'I suppose that makes us even, Godders, as I have someone utterly gorgeous to present to you. Meet Jazz!'

Then she pushed Jasmine towards Godfrey and grabbed Howard's arm and steered him away.

Howard looked back over his shoulder at Jasmine, his eyebrows raised, mouthing the word Jazz in silent query. She wished she could melt away and simply disappear. Godfrey Fairchild introduced himself and told her that he, like Howard, worked for Guthries and was the number two at Batu Lembah. Jasmine tried to look interested as, yet again, she was treated to an explanation of the workings of the rubber industry. Godfrey lacked Howard's enthusiasm though and seemed as bored as she was. In the end she put him out of his misery by telling him that she knew all about rubber cultivation as her late father was the previous owner of the Batu Lembah estate. Then she made her excuses and headed outside.

Several guests were dotted around the terrace and the surrounding lawns, so she wandered off towards a quiet spot under some trees where there was a stone bench, overlooking the river. Walking was something of a challenge in her couture gown, her movements more akin to scuttling, as the fishtail train dragged behind her. If it became grubby then it was Barbara's fault for pressurising her into wearing it. She wondered whether she might slip back upstairs and change into her blue dress, but she was wary of offending Barbara.

It was a beautiful evening, the heat of the day having dissipated, leaving a slight breeze in the air. The sky was dense black velvet, pierced by a million tiny stars, with a crescent moon casting a pale glow over the trees and the river. She looked across at the dark silhouette of jungle across the river and wondered if she might be near to wherever Bintang was. The noise of the revellers was evident still, yet softened into a background hum by the distance, and above it she could hear the soft strains of the dance band mingling with the sound of cicadas. The breeze carried the scent of gardenias and waxflowers. Jasmine breathed it in deeply.

What was Bintang doing now? She imagined him in the depths of the jungle, sitting with his comrades in a circle, eating tapioca or rice, while being indoctrinated with communist propaganda. Reggie had told her that the MLP were said to hold regular meetings where each CT was expected to publicly declare their personal shortcomings in the service of the cause and be criticised by his brethren. It was hard to imagine Bintang taking to this. He was too proud, too independent. That gave her a little spark of hope that perhaps he might quickly become disenchanted and return to Penang, to the grandmother who loved him and to her.

Leaning back against the stone bench she gazed up at the myriad stars and imagined him looking up at those same stars too. Although, in the dense heart of the jungle, the tree cover could well block out all view of the sky. Was he thinking of her too at this very moment? Was he also remembering the magical kiss they had shared?

'You never replied to my letter. You completely ignored my invitation to meet you when I was coming to the island.' Howard Baxter emerged from the shadows and sat down beside her on the bench.

Jasmine was glad it was dark and he couldn't see her embarrassment. 'Sorry. I couldn't have made it as I was swotting for my exams. In fact, I was so busy swotting I forgot to reply.'

'How did they go?'

'Not as bad as I expected, actually.' She wished he'd go and leave her in peace.

'So, you've escaped too?' He nodded in the direction of the house.

'I don't really like parties.'

He studied her closely, his eyes taking in the sculptured gown and its voluminous train. 'Don't like parties? I'd never guess it to look at you. Jazz, eh? Does the new name and the expensive frock mean you're about to embark on a new career as a torch singer?' He gave a chuckle. 'If you don't mind, I'll stick to Jasmine. It's a beautiful name and suits you much more.'

'I don't recall asking your opinion.'

'Well, you're getting it anyway.' He bent down and took a bit of the fabric between finger and thumb. 'I suppose you think you're the cat's whiskers in that. But it doesn't suit you at all. You're far too beautiful to need all this froth. I much preferred you in that blue dress you wore at Bella Vista. The one that shimmered when you moved.'

'In that case I'm jolly glad I decided not to wear it tonight.'

'But what possessed you to choose this? It makes you look like a well-cooked lobster.'

Jasmine spun round and slapped him across the face. Then promptly burst into tears.

Howard gathered her into his arms and let her weep into his shirt, her body shaking with the sudden release of tension. She felt his hand stroking her hair. 'What's wrong, lovely? What's made you so unhappy? It's me being tactless and bigmouthed again, isn't it?'

She pulled back from him. 'It's nothing to do with you. I'm just feeling emotional. Probably too much champagne earlier.'

He handed her a large linen handkerchief and she wiped her eyes and blew her nose.

'You're quite right. I do look like a lobster. And I never wanted to wear this in the first place. I was going to wear that blue dress you mentioned, but Barbara–'

'Ah! I might have guessed it would be Barbara. It's taken me an hour to find a way to escape from her. She's an extremely forceful young woman. How do you know her?'

'We sat the exams together and she sort of took me over.'

He grinned. 'I can imagine that. I suppose she wants to refashion you in her image. Well, don't let her. You don't need powder and paint and screaming pink dresses to make people look at you. I wouldn't be able to take my eyes off you if you were wearing a sack.'

'Do you like Barbara? I know she likes you. I could tell right away.'

'She's a nice enough girl, when she eventually lets you get a word in. And very attractive. Yes, I can see she has her charms. But she does nothing for me.'

'That's a pity. She may be a bit forceful at times,' she ran her finger over the pink satin of her gown, 'but she's been kind to me. You should get to know her.'

'You'd like me to?'

'Yes.'

'Then I will, for you. I am incapable of denying you anything, Jasmine.' He gave a long sigh and leaned back against the bench, his eyes lifting to gaze at the sky. 'What a beautiful night. Completely perfect. Apart from the fact that all those people are close by. I wish they'd disappear and leave me alone with you. You've no idea how much I've missed you. I think about you all the time.'

'Please don't talk like that, Howard. I've told you before. I'm not interested in that. I like you a lot and want you as a friend, but I don't think of you that way. Please, don't spoil things. Now go back and join the party. I'm going to go and get out of this ridiculous gown.' She smiled at him. 'I can see your friend Godfrey is on the terrace looking for you.'

'Looking for you, more like.' Howard looked glum.

'Then please go and head him off while I make my escape. I certainly don't want to spend any more time talking to him.' She smiled up at Howard. 'I may not want you as a boyfriend, Howard, but I'd far rather spend time with you than with him. See you in a while.' Then she hitched up her gown to clear her ankles and ran towards the house.

29

By the time she got to her bedroom, Jasmine was overcome with tiredness. Her earlier overindulgence in champagne had left a sour cloying taste in her mouth and made her drowsy. Taking the Schiaparelli gown off carefully and placing it on its padded hanger, she decided to lie down on the bed for a few minutes before changing into her blue dress and going back to join the throng.

She woke from a deep sleep, lying on top of the sheets. She'd been dreaming. A baby, tightly wrapped in a papoose and left in her studio, evidently starving. She picked it up to cradle. Pointy teeth. Glowing red eyes. She dropped it in alarm and it scuttled away on four legs into the undergrowth, sideways like a crab.

Someone was shaking her. 'Wake up, Jazz. Party's over but we have to talk. I can't possibly sleep yet. Where did you disappear to?'

Disorientated, Jasmine shuffled upright and tried to focus. 'What time is it?'

'Six. Come on. Let's go for a swim and cool off. We need to have a post-mortem.'

Jasmine gave a groan. 'Where do you get your energy from?'

'My little secret!' Barbara tapped the side of her nose.

'I was having a nightmare.'

'Then you should be jolly glad I rescued you from it.' Barbara took Jasmine's hand and tried to pull her up. 'You can have a sleep by the pool - there are comfortable loungers there. It's already hot so we can jump in whenever we want to cool off. And I've asked for coffee and orange juice and bacon sandwiches. I need to sober up.'

Knowing Barbara would not be gainsaid, Jasmine rubbed her eyes and swung her legs off the bed. 'I'll put on my swimsuit.'

'No need for one. It's only us. We'll skinny dip. Much nicer anyway. Come on.'

Ignoring the instruction, Jasmine quickly undressed and put on her swimming costume, slipping a cotton shift over the top. She wasn't swimming naked with servants hovering everywhere. She followed Barbara down the sweeping marble staircase, past the detritus of the party and out onto the terrace, where a *kebun* was sweeping away party streamers with a broom, while one of the other servants collected glasses abandoned on tables and along the stone balustrade. It was still dark but a roseate tinge was beginning to lighten the horizon beyond the trees.

They lay down on the cushioned wooden loungers and a servant, Chinese this time, arrived with the promised bacon sandwiches and a pot of coffee.

As she bit into her sandwich, Jasmine realised she was hungry. She hadn't partaken of the buffet last night and hadn't eaten since the cheese on toast she and Barbara had had before the party began. 'This is good,' she said, grateful.

'I adore bacon butties almost as much as Welsh rarebit and cheese on toast.' Barbara flourished her sandwich. 'Mummy and Daddy are always telling me I eat like poor people.'

Stunned by the casual snobbery, Jasmine said nothing.

'Where did you sneak off to last night and with whom?' Barbara gave her a knowing look.

'I didn't sneak off anywhere. I felt tired and decided to lie down for a few minutes and the next thing I knew you were waking me up.'

'Really? You mean you weren't French kissing Godders in a quiet corner?'

'Of course not.'

Barbara rolled her eyes. 'You're such a puritan. I was sure you'd hit it off with Godders. Didn't you like him?'

'He's nice enough. But I've told you a thousand times, Barbara, I'm not interested in anyone. Apart from Bintang, of course, and since he's out of reach that means no one.'

Barbara gave an exasperated sigh. 'You're no fun.' Then she dropped her voice conspiratorially. 'But I've rather fallen for that chap he brought with him, Howard Baxter. How come you never mentioned him before? He's an absolute dish.'

Jasmine put down her half-eaten sandwich. 'You're going after Howard?'

'I'm rather hoping to have *him* go after *me*!' Barbara pulled up her shoulders and contorted her face into a silly grimace. 'I have a plan to catch him in my net. But I need your help.'

Jasmine's mouth felt dry and she took a gulp of coffee.

'You really like him? You're serious about him? What about your wealthy duke?'

'The duke isn't here. He's next year's project. Until I meet him I'm having as much fun as I can. I have no intention of going into marriage blind.' She swept her arm out in an exaggerated gesture. 'I will be the mother of the duke's children and spender of his vast wealth, but everything I know about the British aristocracy tells me they are not likely to get the juices flowing. No, Jazz. I intend to learn as much as I can about the art of love before I settle down. My master-plan is to find my version of Mellors the gamekeeper and make as much mad passionate love as possible before I head for London. And Howard Baxter fits the bill perfectly.'

'But Howard isn't that kind of man.' Jasmine felt a proprietorial anger at her erstwhile suitor being described like a piece of meat.

'*Every* man is that kind of man, given half a chance.'

Barbara picked up a paper fan and began to flap it lazily. The sun had now risen and the swimming pool was dappled with pink. She turned and looked at Jasmine, her voice sharp. 'You're not interested in him yourself, are you?'

'I told you. No. But he's a friend. A good friend. I'm very fond of him and I don't feel comfortable talking about him like this.'

Barbara chuckled. 'Oh, Jazz. Always so principled and seeing only the good in people.' She batted her fan at an insect. 'I can promise you, your Howard will be all too capable of putting his principles behind him if there's a chance of no strings fucking.'

Jasmine gasped in shock. She had never heard that word before but she had absolutely no doubt what it meant. 'Barbara!'

'DH Lawrence uses it all the time in Lady Chatterley. It's

a perfectly good word that has been around since the Middle Ages. And I love it as it sounds so terribly naughty.'

Jasmine experienced a rush of anger. 'Stop it. Right now! I can't stop what you think and I can't stop your nasty little plans, but I will not listen to them. I've told you. Howard is a dear friend and I don't like it. I don't like it at all.' She sprung off the lounger, whipped her shift over her head and dived straight into the pool. The shock of the cold water revived her and she ploughed up and down, burning up her anger as she swam.

Howard was a grown man and didn't need her protection. Barbara was attractive. If he chose to succumb to her advances that was not Jasmine's concern. She didn't want him herself, so why begrudge someone else having him?

By the time she'd covered twenty lengths of the pool, her anger was gone. She pulled herself up the ladder and dripped her way back to the lounger.

'You could be a professional.' Barbara smiled a conciliatory smile.

'I'm sorry for snapping at you. It is, of course, entirely up to you and Howard what you get up to, but if you don't mind I'd rather not hear about it.'

'And you're absolutely sure you don't mind me having a fling with him and you don't want him for yourself?'

Jasmine rolled her eyes in response. She was tired of this already. And tired of listening to Barbara.

'So, you'll be willing to distract Godders today when they come to take us to show us round their rubber estate? Howard says he thought you might be interested in seeing it, as apparently you lived there when you were a little girl.'

'We're going to Batu Lembah? Today?'

'Sorry. I know I promised you all day by the pool, and one rubber estate looks like all the others but I thought you could easily get Godders out of the way by asking him to show you all the machinery and boring stuff like that, leaving me free to whisk hunky Howard into a shady corner. Godders can bore for Britain when it comes to taking about rubber.'

Jasmine had been manipulated. But now she had no choice. She was dependent on Barbara for a lift back to Bella Vista.

'You'll help me, Jazz? Please.'

Reluctantly, Jasmine nodded.

SOON AFTER NINE O'CLOCK, the two young men arrived. They cast longing looks at the pool but Barbara led them around to the front of the mansion, putting her arm through Godfrey Fairchild's. Her plan, as she had explained in detail to Jasmine, was to focus her attention on Godfrey then, once they were at Batu Lembah, switch to Howard. Jasmine was under instructions to walk ahead and ask Godfrey to show her how the latex was processed, leaving Howard and Barbara alone to walk through the lines of rubber trees.

Howard caught Jasmine's arm as they approached the area where the vehicle was parked. 'You never came back last night. I thought you were going to change clothes and come and find me.' His tone was accusatory. 'I wanted to see you in that blue dress. I wanted to dance with you.'

So, last night's rebuff hadn't deterred him. Jasmine sighed inwardly. 'I was tired. I fell asleep.'

'You weren't avoiding me?'

'No. Of course not. I told you, Howard. I like you. But only as a friend.'

'I got stuck with Barbara. She loves to dance, doesn't she? I kept looking around for you to rescue me as she and I were dancing to two completely different beats.' He smiled at her. 'Isn't that what friends are for? To help each other get out of sticky situations.'

'Don't you like her? She's very pretty. Good fun too.'

'I can't disagree on either count. Though it's hard to dance with a woman when she tries to lead.' He looked about to say something else but didn't.

'Word of warning, girls,' said Godfrey. 'It's hot as hell inside. Like a blast furnace. There are water bottles back there, so drink plenty and be ready for a lot of bumps. Fortunately, it's only about twenty minutes away and, apart from one brief stretch, it's all open road so unlikely to attract an ambush. We'd usually drive without the plates but we're not taking chances with such a precious cargo.'

They got into the vehicle, which was a large jeep but now looked like a tank, completely covered with armour plating with a small slit for the driver to see the road.

He was not exaggerating about the heat. Jasmine looked across at Barbara whose face was soon wet with perspiration. There were some small cloths, which they dowsed with water and used to try to cool themselves.

'Imagine what this is like in the full force of the midday sun.' Howard, who was driving, glanced back at them over his shoulder.

'The housekeeper is laying on a spot of tiffin, so we thought we'd give you the tour first then head back for that. After we've eaten, we can play cards and we'll run you back here about three,' said Godfrey.

As they bumped and rattled along, the two girls bounced up and down on the bone-shaking seats, banging their heads on the windowless metal sides when they went round corners. This was the most unpleasant Sunday Jasmine had spent since coming to Penang. She hoped Barbara appreciated the sacrifice she was making.

'This is absolutely thrilling,' said Barbara. 'Being in an armoured car. Do you think we might get attacked by bandits? Wouldn't that be a lark? As long as they didn't actually catch us.'

Jasmine thought she detected a look of scorn on Howard's face, but it was hard to tell in the gloom of the interior. She felt a little glow of satisfaction. Maybe it was mean of her, but she couldn't help hoping Barbara's plan would misfire. She didn't want to think of Howard as a pawn to be manipulated by Queen Barbara.

Once they arrived at Batu Lembah, Barbara threw her a meaningful look, so Jasmine engaged Godfrey in conversation and increased her walking speed, compelling him to keep pace with her. As Barbara had planned, the gap between the couples lengthened as Barbara reduced her own pace.

Jasmine turned to Godfrey and said, 'I don't remember much about my childhood here. Maybe you could show me the drying sheds and the place where the latex is processed. It might help me remember something.'

Godfrey was all too willing, and Jasmine hoped this little charade wouldn't lead him to think she had designs on him. While he was a reasonably good-looking chap, he spoke with a public-school drawl and reeled off facts as if he were being tested. She couldn't imagine why Barbara had even entertained the idea of kissing him. A cardboard cutout would stand a better chance of raising Jasmine's pulse. But she mustn't let herself think of kissing as it would only bring on the ache she felt for Bintang and she wanted to forget about that – at least until she was alone and could indulge her misery without witnesses.

There was nothing about the estate that revived any
memories for Jasmine. It was like any other rubber estate.
Much bigger than Bella Vista and with more modern equipment, but she was hardly a connoisseur. She'd been a small
child during the brief time they'd lived there – and it had
not been the happiest time of her life. It was all hazy –
vaguely remembered arguments between her late mother
and father and her mother's constant irritation and bad
temper.

Godfrey demonstrated the equipment in the small
factory, going into elaborate detail over the machinery and
how each piece functioned. She was tempted to tell him that
she was currently living on a rubber estate, but she'd
promised Barbara to play her part. Her eyes were glazing
over until, eventually, Godfrey looked at his watch and
suggested they make their way back to the bungalow he
shared with Howard, where lunch would be ready.

They left the factory and Godfrey pointed out the *tuan*'s
larger bungalow. 'Over there, that's where you would have
lived. It's O'Keefe's place now. He and Mrs O'Keefe have
three kids and another on the way.'

'What's that?' Jasmine pointed towards what looked like
a bunker in front of the property. Sandbags were piled in
front of it.

'It's a dugout. For the guards. There's always a couple of
armed men in there, day and night. Not that we've had any
trouble here at BL. Word gets out that we're heavily
defended and that probably puts the bandits off. It connects
to the cellar under the bungalow so Mrs O'Keefe and the
children can take refuge there if needs be.'

It was strange how quickly people adjusted to the need
for constant armed vigilance. Clearly the threat here was
more imminent than over on the island. Jasmine shuddered

at the thought of having to hide in a dark cellar with Mary, Frances and Jinjiang and hoped it would never come to that at Bella Vista.

Something made her glance back at the factory behind them. A sense of being watched. She halted. 'Did you see anyone just now? When we were at the factory?'

'No. It's Sunday. No one's working today. Probably one of the guards on his rounds.'

Satisfied, she fell into step behind Godfrey, then something caught her peripheral vision and she stopped dead. A figure moving through the rubber trees. She gave a little cry. It was the way the man moved that gave him away. Silently. Like a cat. Even though he disappeared, and she hadn't seen his face, Jasmine knew with absolute certainty who it was. Her heart raced and she gasped. How could it be? Why here? Had he seen her? Had he come because he knew she was here? But how could he have known?

Godfrey looked at her, frowning. 'What's wrong? What have you seen?'

'Nothing,' she said quickly and hurried after him. Her heart was beating fast against her ribs and she wished she could have run off into the trees after Bintang. He must have intended her to see him. Surely that meant he would find some way to speak to her before she left the estate. She wanted to shout for joy. That fleeting glimpse filled her with hope that maybe soon they would have a chance to speak. She imagined telling him of her visit to his grandmother and the gift of his portrait. Perhaps she could try to find him after tiffin. She would suggest another walk instead of the card game. It might be hard to give the others the slip, but she'd find some excuse.

Inside, the main room of the assistants' bungalow was cool, a large fan rotating above their heads and the chicks drawn to keep the sun out. The *amah*, a small woman in a purple cheongsam, was waiting with the luncheon.

When Godfrey and Jasmine walked into the room, Jasmine saw Barbara had a sullen look on her face and couldn't help a small moment of satisfaction. But now was no time to think badly of anyone else. She was on a cloud, barely able to stop her mind running away with the possibilities for how to engineer meeting Bintang.

Her thoughts were interrupted almost immediately. As soon as the housekeeper saw Jasmine, the woman became agitated and started speaking quickly and loudly in her own language. She clasped her hands together and bowed her head repeatedly to Jasmine, ignoring the three others.

Jasmine didn't know how to react. There was something vaguely familiar about the woman, but she couldn't place her. And she certainly couldn't understand what she was saying. Helpless, she turned to Howard and Godfrey. The woman continued to speak,

Godfrey spoke at last. 'Nayla says you are the former *tuan*'s daughter and she's very sorry that he died.' He glanced at Howard. 'She says she wants your help.' He spoke rapidly in Malay to the woman who replied, then bowed her head and left the room.

'I don't understand,' said Jasmine when the woman had gone. 'I barely know any Malay. How does she want me to help her?'

Howard spoke. 'I don't think she meant that. Nayla worked here before the war. She must have known you as a child. In those days she was the housekeeper at the main bungalow, for the *tuan*, for your father.'

That was it. It all flooded back. It had been a day out with Mummy and Mary and Jasmine's best friend, Penny, to the Jungle Pools at Taiping. On the way back, Jasmine had

had a desperate need to go to the lavatory. In the car she'd kicked up a fuss. Mummy and Mary, who was driving, had decided to make a quick stop here at Batu Lembah so she could use the bathroom. They walked into the bungalow and Daddy was sitting at the table with the housekeeper standing behind him. She remembered thinking it funny because Daddy was wearing a sarong and she'd never seen him dressed like that before. He always wore shorts. The Malayan lady had taken Jasmine to the bathroom. That was all she could remember except for Mummy telling her to go and wait in the car with Mary and Penny. Mummy had looked angry, but then had cried on the way back to George Town. After that, Evie had taken to her bed for days and days and Daddy didn't come home for ages. Jasmine's memory was hazy – after all she could only have been eight or nine. Mummy was expecting Hugh. But she did remember blaming herself – thinking that her sudden need to use the toilet had been the cause of all this upset – even though as a child she hadn't understood why or what had made Mummy so sad.

Now, looking back at this through her older eyes, the realisation dawned that the woman must have been her father's mistress. She felt sick to the pit of her stomach. Poor Mummy. 'I know who she is,' she said, simply, then pulled out a chair and sat at the table. She must put on a brave face. It was all in the past. From another world. Daddy had been dead for years. What did it matter now?

They ate the lunch and she was grateful that the *amah* didn't reappear.

Barbara was morose during lunch, barely speaking. Not at all her usual ebullient self. She avoided looking at Howard at all and Jasmine suspected that her friend would find an excuse to avoid the card game and ask to be taken home. Evidently her plan to ensnare Howard had failed to ignite. Jasmine felt vindicated. While she was sure he was no angel, she didn't like the idea of him so easily succumbing to Barbara's wiles. He had always struck her as being an honourable man and not someone who would jump in and out of bed with girls he wasn't serious about. One thing Barbara would have made abundantly clear was that she had firm plans for her own future. Jasmine glanced at her across the table. It must have been a blow to Barbara's pride to be rejected. It had probably never happened before.

They were halfway through the simple meal, with Jasmine still struggling to think of a way to leave the others and search for Bintang among the lines of rubber trees, when the sound of shouting reached them. Howard and Godfrey jumped up and ran to the open doorway onto the veranda. Jasmine and Barbara exchanged glances.

'It's the rubber sheds.' The muscles in Howard's neck visibly tightened. He nodded to Godfrey who patted the gun in his holster. Turning round, Godfrey told the young women to stay put and bolt all the doors. 'The guards will keep an eye on the place. Get down into the cellar. You'll be safe there. There are mattresses to sit on and a light switch next to the hatch. Wait until we're back,' barked Godfrey. 'Don't even think about coming out until we get back.' Then the two men began to run in the direction of the rubber stores.

Jasmine stood frozen in the doorway. She didn't want to be shut up inside the bungalow cellar unable to see what was going on. This was the opportunity she had been hoping for to find Bintang. 'There's smoke coming from those sheds. I'm going too. They'll need as much help as possible to put out the fire. Are you coming?'

Barbara was shaking. There was no sign of the bravado

that she had shown in the armoured jeep that morning. 'You must be joking. There may be bandits out there.' She was already tugging open the hatch in the floor that Godfrey had indicated. 'Come on!' Seeing her friend hesitate, Barbara screeched at her, 'Hurry up. I'm scared.' Her face was stricken.

'Get down there and I'll follow in a while. There are guards outside. You're safe here, Barbara. I'm going to see what's happening and I'll be right back.'

Trembling with fear, Barbara climbed down the wooden steps into the cellar. She flicked on the light.

Without waiting for her friend to argue further, Jasmine pushed the hatch into place and dragged a straw mat over it. Taking a deep breath, she ran towards the thick noxious clouds of smoke and the stench of burning rubber.

30

Jasmine could feel the heat as she crossed the *padang* and drew closer to the factory and stores. Through the acrid smoke she could see two or three white men organising the tappers into lines to form a human chain and pass along buckets of water. Presumably Godfrey and Howard were among them. Her vision was distorted and blurred by the intensity of the heat. She turned away to cough.

A hand grabbed her by the wrist and jerked her away. Stumbling, she looked up, expecting it to be Howard about to tell her to return to the safety of the bungalow.

Her heart stopped. It was Bintang.

She gave a little cry of surprise. 'I saw you,' she said. 'Earlier. Running through the trees. I knew you'd come to find me.'

He didn't answer. Holding her wrist in a painfully tight grip, he pulled her away from the buildings, running through the lines of rubber, moving on a diagonal, tacking slightly from left to right so the trees would block the sight lines of anyone who might be looking their way. But no one would be. All attention was focused on the fire.

She was starting to stumble, wearied by the heat, her lungs straining after breathing in the smoke. But Bintang ran on, until the estate buildings were completely out of sight. Eventually he stopped, releasing her wrist from his grip.

He looked haggard, thinner, after only two or three weeks, and his beautiful silky black hair was unkempt and matted. A gun was strapped to his waist.

'You set the fire, didn't you?'

He said nothing, staring at her, his eyes cold. The arrogant expression that had sometimes bordered on cruelty was all too evident now.

'What the hell do you think you're playing at, Bintang? Setting buildings on fire. Do you have any idea how much mindless damage you've caused? Those stores were full of rubber. Do you know how much it was worth?' After her recent lecture on the subject from Godfrey Fairchild she was only too well aware of the numbers involved. 'Do you realise how much work went into producing it? Hundreds of tappers and their families are dependent on this place for their livelihood and you've sent it up in flames.'

'Good. The running dogs must go. Leave my country.' His voice was cold, flat.

'You've been brainwashed by those people. What kind of rubbish are you talking? What do you mean by running dogs?' Exasperated, she tried another tack. 'You're worth much more than this, Bintang. Don't throw your life away. There are so many opportunities open to you. Please. Come back. The Hyde-Underwoods will help you.'

'Never go back.' His tone was angry, clipped. 'Never go back to imperialist running dogs.'

Jasmine stared at him in astonishment. 'But what about us? You and me? Is that why you've come here? Is it because of me? Because Batu Lembah used to belong to my father?' She hesitated then blurted, 'Or is it because Howard Baxter's here? Are you punishing him because you know he likes me? Because you're jealous of him? Because, Bintang, you mustn't be. You have no need to be jealous at all. I'm only here today because of my friend. You know, Barbara – she was there when Ellis arrested you.'

'You think everything is about you. You spoilt little white girl.' His words were laced with a sneer. 'Yes, I don't like your boyfriend. Not because he your boyfriend. Because he is a white man stealing our land, stealing my country's wealth. I don't care about you.'

'That's not true, Bintang. I know it isn't. You're just saying that. You don't mean it. I love you, Bintang. And I know you love me too.' She reached for him, certain that if he held her everything would be all right.

His expression was horrible, conveying utter contempt. 'Love you? I don't love you. I hate you.'

It was a punch in the stomach. Her mouth fell open and she looked at him in shock and horror, her eyes filling with tears. 'But you kissed me. And the way you kissed me... I loved you...' She felt less sure of herself and hesitated. His eyes continued to bore into her, making her doubt herself. 'But...'

'I kiss you because I want to know what like to kiss white girl. Curiosity. And you are pretty. Why not? You act cheap. You offer. Why not take? But I have admitted my shame to my comrades in the struggle. I tell them in Retrospection and Review meeting.'

The ground was pulled out from under her and she was falling, blindly, into nothingness. The tears rolled down her cheeks and she did nothing to stop them. Looking at him now, his contempt was all too evident.

'And all the times you talked with me.' She spread out her hands in a gesture of supplication. 'I thought we were friends.'

'Never friends. I servant. Do what told. Follow orders. Now not servant. Follow orders from my leaders in communist revolution. Soon Malaya will belong to my people. White men will be gone. And those who don't go will die.'

She gasped. 'What have they done to you, Bintang? They've brainwashed you. All this talk of running dogs and killing people. It's horrible.'

'Soon Malaya will be communist country. People live in peace and harmony. Now we must spill blood of white dogs to be free. I do my duty for fight.'

Desperate, Jasmine tried another tack. 'I met your grandmother,' she said, hoping to appeal to his strong sense of family. 'I gave her the portrait I painted of you. I liked her very much. We went together to visit Siti's grave.'

It backfired. His face set harder. 'Keep away from Grand-mother.' Then he drew out his gun. 'You think I won't kill you because you young girl and once I kiss you.' His laugh was more of snarl. 'You think I care for you? I never care for you. I will care only when your body lies here dead on ground for ants to eat. I go back to camp and say them not only burn rubber stores but kill white woman, *tuan besar*'s daughter, girl from Penang. My comrades very pleased. Now give me your watch and that ring. We sell for food. Worth much money.'

Jasmine's heart stopped. This wasn't happening. He doesn't mean it. He can't mean it. Not Bintang.

'You can have the watch but not the ring. It belonged to

my grandmother. It's a family heirloom.' She touched the pearl protectively.

'Take it off. Now!'

His voice was loud. Angry. She could no longer recognise the Bintang she knew.

'You not need heirloom when dead.'

Terrified, she handed him the watch and eased the ring over her finger. He snatched it from her. 'You turn away. I kind man. I give you few moments to get ready to die. More than Japanese gave my sister.'

Numb with shock that he intended to shoot her in the back of the head, Jasmine stood her ground. So, this was it. The end of her short life. Longer than Siti's had been, but shorter than was right or natural. A few minutes ago, she'd been so wretched she'd almost have welcomed it, but now she wanted nothing more than to live. She wouldn't turn and give him the easy way out. Her legs trembling, she made herself look at him. If he was going to kill her, she'd force him to do it as she watched him.

The rubber trees crowded in around her. Her own father might have planted some of these. Was he up there watching her now? What are you supposed to do when you're about to die? How do you prepare? Time stopped, even as she realised it was running out. She fixed her eyes on Bintang, staring into his large brown ones, taking in that beautiful face she had loved and believed to have loved her too. If she kept looking at him, unblinking, he wouldn't do it, couldn't do it. He raised his arm and took aim. Blind terror coursed through her and her legs were jelly. But she kept her eyes fixed on him through the blur of tears. 'I love you, Bintang,' she said.

He hesitated, the hand holding the gun shaking, before he lowered it.

Hope surged. He couldn't do it. Of course, he couldn't do it. She took a step towards him, breathing his name.

An angry voice cut through the silence. Jasmine turned.

A small man wearing a khaki military-style cap with a red star stood several feet away from them. He was screaming at Bintang. Jasmine couldn't understand the words he was saying but had no doubt that he was ordering Bintang to kill her. Around his waist was an impressive munitions belt and his outstretched arm held a pistol pointing straight at her. He continued to scream orders at Bintang.

Jasmine closed her eyes and the shot rang out.

But she felt nothing. No pain. She was in a heap on the ground. Had she fainted and the shot missed her? How else would she have heard it? There was an eerie silence. Time had frozen. Was she dead?

Then she saw Bintang. He was sprawled on his back on the ground. A small singed hole broke up the smooth contours of his forehead. His wide-open eyes stared up at her, unseeing. Seeping out from under his skull a sticky pool of blood formed a halo around his shock of black hair.

Jasmine lowered her head so she wouldn't see the terrorist take aim. No hope of mercy in his case. Nor did she want it.

The second shot rang out but the man crumpled and fell to the ground.

Jasmine didn't wait to find out if he was dead. She shuffled on her knees towards Bintang and lay across his still warm body, her head where his heart should be beating. She thought of that evening in the car on the way back to Bella Vista, when her head had lain in the same place, only for his hand to cradle her hair and his heart to beat strongly.

'Bintang, what did they do to you, my love?' She whispered before her words became incoherent and then turned to keening. Pain poured out of her. Shock. Disbelief. Sorrow. Grief. She sobbed and wailed. It was only when she felt herself being gently eased away from Bintang's body, that she remembered there was someone else there. Whoever had shot the terrorist.

Howard Baxter held her against his chest as she sobbed. He stood immobile, patient, holding her while the shock and grief drained out of her.

Her body calmed, but her thoughts continued to race. 'I loved him and he loved me.'

Howard tried to draw her back into his protective hold.

She pushed him away.

Howard's eyes flickered momentarily in pain, but his expression was one of compassion and sympathy. 'He was about to kill you, Jasmine.'

'He wasn't. He couldn't do it. That's why the bandit shot him.'

Then something occurred to her. 'If that other man hadn't appeared, you'd have shot Bintang, wouldn't you? Because he burned down your rubber stores.' She gave a little sob. 'And because I love him.'

'I couldn't give a damn about the rubber store. I'd have preferred him to be arrested and tried for arson. But no, I wouldn't have let him kill you. And yes, I was jealous of him and I still am, even though he's dead. Seeing you grieving over him hurts.' His jaw was set in a hard line. 'You need to be clear about something, though. No matter what your feelings for him might have been, whatever he felt for you wasn't love. No man who loved you could point a gun at you – even if he didn't fire it. And a man who does love you with every fibre of his being wasn't going to stand here and watch him do it.'

Howard's face was stricken. His last words were choked with emotion. He turned and walked away, back through the rubber trees towards the *padang*.

Jasmine dropped to her knees again, beside Bintang's body. The heat and humidity of Malaya and its jungle made it a paradise for all forms of wildlife, including insects. Already a swarm of ants was colonising his face. The body would be rapidly consumed if left alone – which of course it wouldn't be – she could already see a small group of men in the distance, making their way towards her.

Jasmine felt only sadness: for the way Bintang had been indoctrinated, for his sad, too brief life and the wasted possibilities for his future. Sad also for his grandmother, who had now outlived the last member of her family. And sad for herself. For the child she had been and the innocence she had lost forever.

With a last look at that beautiful face she began to walk back to the bungalow.

31

The rest of that day passed in a blur. Jasmine was as drained as if she had been put through a mangle, all the life and energy squeezed out of her. But she did remember an angry Barbara ranting at her for leaving her in the bungalow cellar.

'Anything could have happened. The bandits could have broken in and murdered me. I've never been so terrified in my life. And it was so gloomy down there. One naked light bulb. Disgusting. And nowhere proper to sit.' She folded her arms and glared at Jasmine. 'I had to sit on a mattress on the floor.'

'Shut up, Barbara.' Howard's voice was tense with anger. 'Stop moaning. Jasmine doesn't want to listen to it. And neither do I.'

Barbara turned to Jasmine. 'Did you hear what he said?' Eliciting no response, she resorted to Godfrey and said, 'I want to go home. Now. I don't want to spend any more time in this godforsaken dump.'

'I'll take them,' said Howard to Godfrey. 'I know you want to get on with assessing the damage.'

Godfrey, grateful, nodded. 'Thanks, pal. I think we got off quite lightly this time. But those guards are going to get a rocket up their backsides. See you later. Bye, Jasmine.' Without a glance at Barbara, he was gone.

Barbara looked as though she were about to burst into tears.

The three of them left the bungalow. As she was getting into the back of the jeep, Jasmine saw the Malayan house-keeper again. The woman was running across the *padang*, towards the jeep from the line of houses where the tappers lived, a young boy clutching her hand. Howard had evidently not noticed or deemed it unrelated to their depar-ture. He released the throttle as soon as Jasmine was inside, and the jeep moved quickly away.

The journey passed in total silence, Howard keeping his eyes on the narrow slit in the armour plating that covered the windscreen and Barbara still in a huff. Alone in the back seat, Jasmine wallowed in her own private misery.

As soon as they reached Orchard House, Barbara got out, slamming the door behind her, ignoring Jasmine and not even bothering to thank Howard for the lift.

'How are you getting back to Penang?' Howard turned to Jasmine.

'I've no idea. Barbara's driver picked me up from Bella Vista and was supposed to be dropping me back. But that's looking unlikely now. I'll have to ask her if I can telephone for Reggie to come and get me.'

'I'll run you home. Don't worry, I'll take the armour plating off. The main road between here and the ferry is safe.'

She tried to protest that it was out of his way, that it would mean he would be driving back in the dark, but he brushed that aside. 'Go and get your things while I get the panels off.'

Inside the house there was no sign of Barbara, so Jasmine hurried upstairs to fetch her bag. The shocking pink gown was still hanging on the outside of the wardrobe door, its fish tail trailing limply across the carpet. Was it only last night that she'd been wearing it? A lifetime ago and she had been a completely different person. Her reflection in the mirror stared back at her. How could she possibly look the same as she always did, when inside she felt so different?

It was more comfortable in the front of the vehicle, as Barbara had no doubt realised when she'd made sure she sat there. Jasmine leaned back and pretended to doze, grateful that Howard didn't try to talk to her, didn't dredge up what had happened. Without all the armour plating, now stacked in the back, it was much cooler and a relief to be able to see out of the windows.

The internal wounds from this afternoon would stay with her forever. How could she ever get over it? She tried to block out the memory of the contempt and loathing on Bintang's face. She shivered with remembered fear, despite the heat of the afternoon, at the image of him raising the gun and steadying his arm to take aim.

Howard was wrong. Bintang would never have gone through with killing her. The other CT had known that and that's why he'd shot him.

With a sudden cry of anguish the tension inside her broke, as she acknowledged how close to death she had been. A mere moment later it would have been her, alongside Bintang, lying on the ground with ants covering her face.

'I'm sorry,' she said, tears rolling down her face. 'I

shouldn't have said what I did. I didn't mean it. You saved my life, Howard. I'm sorry I was being insensitive and ungrateful.'

'You were in shock,' he said simply. 'You have no need to apologise.' He kept his eyes on the road, so she couldn't read his face.

'I do. And I need to explain. About Bintang.'

'There's nothing to explain. I'm sorry you went through all that. He doesn't deserve your tears. But there's no point me saying that, is there?'

She turned her head and looked out of the window. It had started raining heavily. A sudden tropical rainstorm. It suited her mood. Acres of dripping rubber and oil palm trees gave way to the buildings on the edge of Butterworth. They were almost at the ferry.

The woman she had seen at Batu Lembah, Nayla, drifted into her thoughts again and with her, the memory of that other drive from Batu Lembah to the ferry before the war, with her stepmother, Mary and Penny. Then it had been Mummy who was encased in misery. Utterly distraught. Even at such a tender age and tired from a long day, it had been evident that something terrible had happened to upset Evie. Now Jasmine understood what it was. That long-ago afternoon, and the days that followed it, her mother had plumbed the depths of despair and misery. Even a child could see that. Somehow remembering this made Jasmine feel better. Mummy had been badly let down by a man but had gone on to find happiness with Arthur. Even before that, she had managed to patch things up with Daddy until his death, another blow to Evie. If Mummy had been brought low by all that and yet remained strong, then she must be strong too.

She was fast asleep when they reached Bella Vista, the motion of the car lulling her off. Mary and Reggie were on the veranda when they pulled up. As she was getting out of the car, Howard reached over and squeezed her hand lightly.

For a moment she was disorientated, sleep having banished the events of the day temporarily.

Howard took her hand and put her watch and the pearl ring in it. 'I almost forgot. They found these in Bintang's pocket.'

'Thank you,' she whispered.

'Remember, Jasmine, if you ever need to talk, don't hesitate. Call me at BL or drop me a line and I'll come at once.'

'Thank you,' she said, her voice almost a whisper. 'And I'm sorry about everything, Howard. You didn't deserve to be treated that way.'

Exhausted, Jasmine went straight to bed, leaving Howard with the Hyde-Underwoods, to be fortified with a sandwich and a *stengah* before the long drive home.

THE FOLLOWING MORNING, Jasmine felt drained.

Mary had just started her breakfast when Jasmine walked into the room. She looked up and smiled. 'We tried to persuade Howard to stay the night and set off early this morning but he insisted he had to get back. He told us there was an arson attack at Batu Lembah.' She handed Jasmine a cup of tea. 'I got the impression there's more to the story than he was ready to tell me. He was very concerned for you. Told us to keep a close eye on you. Was it terrifying?'

'The fire? No. I got nowhere near it.'

Mary stretched her hand out and laid it on Jasmine's.

'What's happened, Jasmine? Why did Howard have to bring you back? Did you fall out with Barbara?'

She nodded.

'It's a pretty poor show on her part to drag you over there for a party with a promise of transport and then leave you to find your own way home. I had heard she was a bit of a handful. Spoilt rotten, apparently. I didn't want to put you off her but I wish I'd guessed something like this might happen.' She took a sip of her own tea. 'How was the party? Was that at least fun? Did you meet some nice people?'

'The party was fine.' Her voice was flat.

'There's something wrong, Jasmine. I can tell.'

'Bintang's dead.'

Mary gasped. 'How do you know?'

'Because I was there.'

'What on earth happened? Was it to do with the fire?'

'I suppose it was. He started it. Then he tried to kill me. He told me he hated me and pointed a gun at my head but he couldn't go through with it, Mary.' She took a gulp of air. 'So one of the communists shot him dead.'

Mary gasped. 'Oh, my poor darling.'

Jasmine shook her head when Jinjiang stuck her head round the door to ask what she wanted to eat. 'Thanks but I'm not hungry.'

She glanced up at Mary. 'When someone you care for tells you that rather than loving you back, he hates you enough to want you dead, it's the worst of all possible rejections.' Her own voice sounded hollow, flat.

Mary jumped up and came around the table to her and pulled her into a tight hug. 'You poor dear girl. What a terrible experience. I am so sorry.'

'I really believed I was in love with him, but I can't have

been, can I? You can't love someone when they threaten to kill you – can you?'

'But he didn't kill you, Jasmine. Isn't that the point?'

'Howard says if Bintang had loved me he wouldn't have been able to point a gun at me. Even if he didn't actually fire it. Mary, even if he didn't want to kill me, he said he hated me.'

'Bintang didn't hate you, my darling. I'm certain of that.'

'I don't want you to think badly of him. I know you and Reggie cared about him. But in the end he wasn't like the Bintang we knew. He said terrible things. About all of us. He called us all running dogs.'

'They indoctrinate people. It is a form of brainwashing. To put the party first. They do it in order to get men like Bintang to do terrible things. To kill people. To commit arson. They teach them how to hate. They punish those who don't obey. And they expect the men and women who work for them to commit atrocities. It's drummed into them all so fanatically that they lose all moral sense. I think that must have happened to Bintang.'

'So, he wasn't always like that and hiding it from us?'

'No. I am sure he was a good person. The Bintang we all knew wouldn't hate or kill. But who knows what the communists did to him in those jungle camps. What they threatened to do if he didn't obey. It's a form of mind control.' She took Jasmine's hand. 'And he must have known they'd shoot him if he refused to obey the order to kill you. That means that at the end the good man that he was came through.'

Jasmine took another deep breath and felt herself relax a little. 'Thank you, Mary. I feel better about it now. I don't want to think badly of him. Or of myself for caring about him. I will have to break the news to his grandmother.

Doing that while believing him to be a bad person would have been too hard for me.'

'But I don't understand what happened next. Why didn't the terrorist kill you after he'd shot Bintang?'

Jasmine gave a little sob. 'Howard saved my life. He shot the other bandit. And instead of being grateful I was angry.'

'Ah. I see.'

'Am I a terrible person, Mary?'

'No, my love. You are a kind and warm person who has undergone a terrible experience. The last thing you should do is blame yourself.'

LATER THAT DAY, Mary drove Jasmine to the *kampong* where Bintang's grandmother lived. Mary waited in the car while Jasmine went alone to the little hut at the edge of the village.

It was awful witnessing the old lady's distress. No weeping and wailing, but more of a silent crumpling up inside as though she had lost any reason for living.

Yet the woman appeared to have expected it. 'I know he never come home. I know it was the end.'

Together they went to Siti's grave and the old woman propped the painting of Bintang against the trunk of the jackfruit tree. 'Now I come each day and talk to both my grandchildren. They together in paradise.'

Jasmine reached for the old lady's hand, her eyes full of tears. 'I cared for Bintang very much. He was my friend.' Her voice broke.

The old woman put her arms around Jasmine and held her as she cried. 'Bintang talk always of you. He say you like Siti. Clever and beautiful. He like you very much.'

. . .

THREE DAYS LATER, Jasmine was in her studio painting. Since the shocking events of the weekend, she had flung herself into her work, finding consolation and peace in the silence of the little wooden studio. The act of painting helped her lose herself: the almost meditative process of creating the work, of moving her eyes between the object or scene and her translation of it onto the canvas. Locked in concentration, there was no room left for morbid thoughts to enter her head as they did whenever she tried to read a book or go to sleep.

In her art she was experimenting with a less figurative approach, more abstract, pushing at the boundaries of form and colour. It was liberating; this freeing up allowed her to see connections between the objects she was capturing and their place in space. She let her hand and her imagination run free. She wasn't confident about the end results, but the process was deeply satisfying. It was as if she were gently feeling her way in the dark and, eventually, she would reach the light and it would all make sense.

Jinjiang appeared in the doorway. It was the first time she had ever been near the studio and now she stood, hesitant, on the threshold, curling her nostrils, perhaps repelled by the smell of the oil paint. Her eyes ranged over the collection of works stacked around the room, leaning against the walls. '*Mem* say you come house now. Someone here to see you.' The housekeeper hurried away.

Puzzled, Jasmine, wiped a rag over her brush. She hated being interrupted when she'd found her flow. It was like floating gently down a stream only to crash into a boulder. She pulled off her apron and made her way back to the bungalow.

She'd expected to find Mary on the veranda. That was where she spent most days when she wasn't teaching –

reading a book or, more often, playing with Frances. But she wasn't there. Jasmine went into the cool dark interior of the house.

'In here, Jasmine. In the drawing room.'

Jasmine walked though the open doorway and pulled up short. Mary was sitting on the sofa with her back to the door. Opposite her was Nayla, the housekeeper from Batu Lembah. Jasmine gasped and took a half step back.

Mary patted the sofa beside her and Jasmine reluctantly sat down. The woman said something rapidly in Malay and Mary replied, before turning to Jasmine. 'I understand you met Nayla at Batu Lembah this weekend?'

'I know who she is. I remember that day. When we were with Mummy and Penny and I had to use the bathroom. And I've realised now why Mummy was so upset.' Jasmine avoided looking at the woman, who was sitting on the edge of the seat, her hands clasped in front of her. 'This woman was my father's mistress, wasn't she?'

'Did you know that then?' Mary looked startled.

'No. But as soon as I saw her this weekend I worked it out and I realise now why Mummy was so upset that day.' She glared at Mary, feeling angry and uncomfortable. 'Why has she come here? What does she want with me?' Jasmine glanced at the woman, still sitting patiently, although perched as if poised ready to move. She was wearing the same purple cheongsam. It was looking grubby. 'She must know my father is dead.'

'Nayla walked here. It took her more than two days. She brought her little boy with her.'

Jasmine remembered the small child holding Nayla's hand on the *padang*. 'Where is he?' She looked around her.

'In the kitchen. Jinjiang is giving him something to eat, poor child. You'll meet him shortly.' Mary reached for

Jasmine's hands and wrapped her own around them. 'After what happened all those years ago, your father dismissed Nayla. He gave her money and sent her away. She says it was a generous sum. She went to live in a *kampong* in Selangor where she had some relatives and subsequently married a man there. But he died during the war and his family stole what was left of the money Doug had given her. So, she returned to her own village. There were Japanese soldiers billeted at Batu Lembah and she got a job as a cook. She's been there ever since and now is housekeeper for the Assistant Manager and the assistants, including Howard.'

'What has all this to do with me?'

Before Mary could answer, the woman, evidently impatient at the time Mary was taking to explain her story, sprung up from her chair and fell to her knees in front of Jasmine, grasping the fabric of Jasmine's dress and gazing up at her with enormous almond-shaped eyes.

'My son. You help my son. Your brother. You help him.'

Until then, Jasmine hadn't realised the woman could speak English. 'What are you talking about?' She recoiled and Nayla sunk back onto her bottom on the floor.

'My brother is in Africa. Stop this now.' She looked at Mary. 'How can he be my brother? You've already told me she was in Selangor. Married. It must be that man's son.'

Nayla started weeping, and Jasmine felt ashamed.

Mary said, 'She discovered she was pregnant with your father's child so her family arranged for her to marry the man in Selangor. He was quite old man. He treated Nayla like a slave and often beat her. She only stayed because of Amir, her son.'

'He bad man. Very bad.'

'Just because he was a bad man doesn't mean he wasn't

the father of her child. She must be lying. Can't you see, Mary?'

Nayla spoke again rapidly in Malay to Mary who translated Jasmine's words. Then the woman knelt again, like a supplicant in front of Jasmine. 'They want kill my son. Your brother. They know I have child from white man. They know *Tuan Besar* Doug was father. They say kill me for go with white man, for work for Japanese. Then say kill Amir because he white boy.'

'I don't understand. *Who* wants to kill you and your son?'

Mary spoke again. 'The communists. Nayla received threats. They wanted her to steal rice supplies for them. Money too. From Batu Lembah. Look, Jasmine, you've read the papers. You know what happens to villagers who won't do as they ask. Last week, a man who refused to help them was made to watch as they beat his small child to death. When he said he'd changed his mind, it made no difference. They wouldn't stop. After the child was dead, they murdered him anyway as an example to the rest of his village.' She gazed intently at Jasmine. 'The day of the fire they stole her identity card. Without that the police will assume she's one of the communists.'

Nayla slipped her hand beneath the collar of her cheongsam and pulled out a folded piece of paper. 'British want kill me too.' She handed the paper to Jasmine. It was a handbill with three rows of mugshots. Nayla was pictured at the end of the top row. Jasmine's breath stopped when she saw Bintang's face, dead centre on the page. Over the top were the words, Wanted Dead or Alive. At the foot of the page was an instruction to report sightings to local police or members of the British army and the imprimatur of one Lieutenant Bernard Ellis.

Jasmine passed the paper to Mary who gave a groan. 'Him again. That cursed evil man.'

Nayla's gaze moved between the two women before resting on Jasmine, who felt cornered.

'I don't know how to help. I'm only sixteen. I'm a guest here in Malaya. I won't even be here for long.'

The dark brown eyes bored into her, full of fear and despair. 'You no help brother? Please, Missee.'

The door opened and the boy, Amir, appeared on the threshold. Close behind him, tottering on her barely stable legs was little Frances, stretching out her hands toward him. Behind them a harassed-looking Jinjiang scooped up Frances who began to bawl. The *amah* reached for Amir's hand to lead him back into the kitchen. 'Sorry *Mem*,' she said. 'I turn away one second and they go.'

'Leave them,' said Mary. 'They'll be all right with us now.' She stretched out her arms for Frances and the Chinese *amah* handed her over.

Amir stood, his face bewildered, gazing at each of the women in turn before moving to stand by his still-kneeling mother. He put one hand protectively on her shoulder.

Jasmine stared at the boy. At his shock of dark brown hair, his skin much paler than his mother's, and then at his eyes. He blinked at her and a lump formed in her throat. Her little brother Hugh did that, the same rapid flickering of his eyelids, as if he were either pulling in or pushing away what he was seeing while his brain processed the information.

Jasmine turned to look at Mary. 'He looks so like Hugh.' Her voice was barely a whisper. 'We have to help them.'

Mary nodded. 'We do.'

'But how?' Jasmine looked from Mary to the little boy and his mother. 'Can they stay here?'

'I've already suggested that to Nayla, but she is afraid either the British or the CTs will find her here. She wants to go to Bangkok.'

The young boy, still with his arm around his mother, was staring at Jasmine. He looked so vulnerable, so innocent. How could anyone possibly threaten his life?

Impulsively, Jasmine moved towards him and took his hand. The smell of him. The skinny limbs. He was so like Hugh, apart from his dark hair, the same wavy brown as her father's. 'Hello, Amir,' she said, 'I'm Jasmine.' She turned to look at the two women. 'Does he know?'

Nayla nodded.

'I'm your sister.' She pointed at herself. 'Jasmine.'

The little boy looked up at her with his mother's almond-shaped eyes. 'Jasmine,' he repeated.

Tears welled up. She had not expected to feel this way a few minutes ago. Yet now, she impulsively drew the child against her, feeling his breath warm on her neck and was overwhelmed with a rush of instinctive love for him.

Mary put Frances down on the rug, got up from the sofa and walked to the door where she called for Jinjiang to come. She spoke to her quietly, evidently giving her instructions.

As she did, Frances shuffled across to Amir and tugged at the bottom of his shirt. The boy looked down and grinned at her.

'Your son has a devoted fan.' Mary smiled at Nayla, then spoke to her once more in Malay. The woman nodded and took her son's hand and followed Jinjiang out of the room.

'What did you say? Where have they gone?' Jasmine was anxious.

'This has all been a big shock for everyone, particularly you. We need time to digest it and work out how to help them. I've asked them to stay here with us tonight.' Mary got up and began to pace around the room. 'You and I need to talk about it with Reggie.'

'But what can we do? Can we hide them here?'

'Nayla believes it's too risky. She wants to leave the boy here and go away and find work until she can safely send for him.' Mary bit her lip. 'But I have a horrible feeling about the kind of work she'd end up being sucked into in Bangkok.'

'Couldn't she get work as a housekeeper and keep him with her?'

'That's what I want to speak to Reggie about. There must be someone who could take them in where they'd be safely out of reach of the communists and the police.'

'I still don't understand why both the CTs and the British authorities should be after her.'

'I imagine it's as she said. The CTs got wind that her child is the son of a British planter. And working for the Japanese can't help. The communists view anyone who worked for them as collaborators. As to the British, who knows? Look at poor Bintang. If that nasty Lieutenant Ellis hadn't had him in his sights he would still be here at Bella Vista.'

A surge of anger rushed through Jasmine. 'I've lost Bintang to this horrible war. I don't want to lose my brother too.'

Mary hugged her. 'I know you don't. I was worried you'd be so angry about your father that you'd reject poor Amir.'

'Daddy's dead. There's no point being angry with him. Mummy forgave him. And how can I possibly blame Amir?' Jasmine had a sudden thought. 'Do you think Daddy knew Nayla was having a baby?'

'She says he didn't. She only found out herself after

she'd gone to Selangor. Hence her marriage. The poor woman seems to have gone through hell with her husband. She said he never accepted Amir. That was why she returned to Batu Lembah after he died. She had no idea then your father had died too.'

Jasmine sighed. 'What an awful mess.' She gave Mary a little smile. 'But I can't believe I have another brother.'

'He's a sweet boy.'

'Oh, he is, isn't he, Mary?'

32

Mary wanted to talk to Reggie alone rather than telling him about the unexpected arrival of Amir and his mother in front of Jasmine. He'd need time to take it all in and she didn't want him to say something he might later regret. Reggie often took a rather extreme initial position but after he'd had time to mull things over he usually modified his opinions.

Closing the inner door to Reggie's office, so that the Indian clerk in the adjoining room couldn't overhear their conversation, Mary perched on the edge of his desk and told him everything that had happened.

He took it more in his stride than she'd expected.

'So, old Doug was a naughty boy? I remember that housekeeper at BL. Rather a looker. Hair down to her bottom and great big eyes.'

'You have a remarkable memory, Reggie.' Mary's voice was slightly acerbic. This was no time for levity.

'Well, it was all that time him being out there on his own, before Evie came to Penang to marry him. Temptation in front of him every night I suppose. Hard to blame the old devil.'

'Is that the kind of thing you got up to here before you married me?' Mary raised her eyebrows as though she were affronted.

'Hardly. For one thing I'm not that kind of fellow. For another, Jinjiang, treasure that she is, was never going to set my pulse racing. But most of all, after that evening I spent with you, my darling girl, there was no other woman on this planet who stood a chance. I fell for you, Mary, hook, line and sinker.'

She smiled. 'Me for you too. It took me a bit longer to acknowledge it. But all this is beside the point, darling. We have a pressing problem. Nayla appears to have made enemies on both sides. She's convinced that her life and the child's are in danger. And based on what she's told me, I'm inclined to agree.'

Reggie leaned back in his chair, put his hands behind his head and looked up at her. 'You think Evie should take him in?'

Mary was horrified. 'Certainly not. This isn't anything to do with Evie. She's the injured party here and shouldn't be expected to clear up the long-term consequences of Doug's infidelity. For heaven's sake, Reggie – that child must have been conceived while Evie was expecting Hugh. Besides, how can she possibly take him in when she lives in Africa now? Amir is a Malay and needs to grow up here in Malaya. Sending him across the world to a completely different culture and country would be an indescribable cruelty. And he knows nothing of the Leightons.'

'But Hugh and Jasmine are his blood relatives.'

Mary sighed. 'What about his mother? You're speaking

as though she were dead. She clearly adores the boy and wants to do whatever will keep him safe.'

'What does Jasmine think?' he asked.

'She needs time to take it all in. She was angry at first. Disbelieving. Until she met the boy, then she took to him.' She pulled her lips into a tight smile. 'And Frances is absolutely besotted.'

'What are you trying to say, Mary?' Reggie let out a groan. 'You've made your mind up, haven't you? You want to take the boy in.'

Mary turned her gaze on him. 'No. The best thing for Amir is for him to stay with his mother. But she's terrified he'll be at risk if she doesn't manage to hide him. She wants to establish herself and then send for him when she's built a new life in a safe place. Can't we help her do that? I was thinking you might know of someone who would take them *both* in. Obviously, it would need to be out of the country.' She pleaded with her eyes. 'She mentioned Bangkok but that's not a good idea. Will you have a think. There must be something we can do to help them.'

'Of course, I will. But right now, I'm stumped.'

'You'll think of something, darling.'

'Your faith is touching, dear girl, but I fear it's greater than is merited.'

OVER DINNER THAT NIGHT, Reggie and Mary told Jasmine that they had decided, if she was in agreement, that they would help Amir and his mother to get to Singapore and meanwhile they could stay here at Bella Vista.'

'But will they be safe? How will they get to Singapore?'

Reggie and Mary exchanged a look. 'We think the train is too dangerous,' said Mary. 'Reggie's going to find out when we can get them a passage on a ship. They'll be out of the reach of the communists that way.'

'But the British?'

'They won't be looking for her on a passenger liner. Besides, we all know the hand of Ellis is behind this. Reggie's talked to a wealthy friend of his in Singapore who's in shipping. He thinks he can find some suitable work for Nayla.' She looked at her husband. 'Neither of us thinks Bangkok is a good idea.'

'I want to pay for their passage. I have my allowance from Daddy's will. It's only right.'

Reggie started to protest but Jasmine interrupted. 'Please. I want to. He's my brother. Let me do this.'

Already, she felt a strong connection to Amir. The fact that Hugh was Evie's birth-son had never made the slightest difference to the way Mummy had treated them both. Yet Jasmine had always felt slightly apart from the rest of the family, with only the haziest recollections of her own birth-mother, Felicity, and with her father dead. Now here was Amir, who had never even known their father and, now poor lamb, with his life in danger.

IT RAINED HEAVILY during the night, but now the sun shone brightly, reflecting off the pools of rainwater, making the dripping trees sparkle. Jasmine pulled up the chicks and let the light flood into the bedroom. Jinjiang always grumbled that it made the room heat up, so she'd have to remember to let the slatted blinds down again before going to breakfast. But first she wanted to witness the beauty of the morning, drink it all in and breathe the rain-freshened air.

While there was no indication that the Emergency was going to be short-lived, she couldn't imagine the commu-

nist insurgents holding out for ever. Once hostilities ended,
Nayla could return to Batu Lembah with Amir. Jasmine
would be able to see her brother from time to time.
Already she hated the thought of him going to Singapore
and out of her life. She was determined she would stay in
touch.

She leaned on the window ledge, gazing out over the
verdant garden to the *padang*, and beyond that to the endless
avenues of rubber trees, stretching towards the horizon.
Reggie was crossing the open sward, returning to the
bungalow for breakfast – he rose every morning at five for
the muster. Rubber tapping took place in the cool of the day,
before the heat slowed the flow of the latex, making it
coagulate.

The chugging sound of an approaching motor carried
through the trees from the main driveway into the estate,
invisible, behind the lines of rubber. Straining forward to
catch sight of the vehicle as it reached the open spread of
the *padang* – visitors to Bella Vista were a rare occurrence –
she saw it was a jeep. It must be Howard.

She quickly washed and dressed, choosing to wear the
frock with the daisy-patterns, and brushing her hair into
glossy submission. Today she would be able to apologise
properly and thank him again for saving her life. After one
last look in the mirror to make sure everything was in place,
she slipped out of the room, forgetting to lower the chicks,
and tried to walk as slowly and in as dignified a manner as
possible, downstairs for breakfast.

When she opened the door into the dining room, disappointment awaited. Lieutenant Ellis was sitting at the table
with Reggie and Mary, drinking a cup of tea. Jasmine froze
in the doorway. Impossible to retreat now. Why hadn't she
checked first?

Reggie signalled her to come in and join them so, exchanging glances with Mary, she pulled out a chair.

'Is this a social call?' Mary's tone was clipped. 'Only we're awfully busy today, Lieutenant, as the new term is about to start and Jasmine and I have a lot of preparations to make.'

'Wages day tomorrow,' added Reggie. 'Day before is always the busiest day of the week. Have to check the rolls, get the cash from the bank and make up the wages.' He looked at his watch. Jasmine knew he was lying as the clerk was more than capable of all these tasks.

Ellis narrowed his eyes but didn't respond to the unmistakeable brush-off he was receiving. He put a manilla folder on the table in front of him, pushing the sugar bowl aside to do so, managing to knock several lumps onto the tablecloth. He made no apology, but picked one up and put it in his mouth. Jasmine could barely stand to look at him.

Removing a sheet of paper from the folder, he held it towards them. 'Have you seen this?'

It was the wanted poster with Bintang's photo in the centre and Nayla's at the top.

'No,' said Reggie. 'Should we have done?'

Ellis shrugged. 'These posters are all over the peninsula. Maybe they haven't made it up here. I'll have to fix that. But it won't have escaped your notice that your former *syce* is one of the bandits pictured here. These men and women are communist terrorists or known members of the *min yuen*.' He paused while he drained his cup. 'But I have some good news for you.' He flashed a grin at them, revealing his discoloured rotten teeth, and stabbed his finger against the photograph of Bintang. 'He was shot dead last Sunday on the Batu Lembah estate in Province Wellesley. He was running away like the coward he was, after he had set fire to rubber storage facilities there and caused significant damage. Fortunately, the planters contained the fire before it had a chance to spread and shot your driver dead as he was trying to flee the scene of the crime.'

He looked up, drilling his eyes into Jasmine. She squirmed in her chair, wishing she'd stayed in her room.

'We already know about Bintang's death.' Reggie started to get up. 'Now if you'll excuse me, Lieutenant–'

'I haven't finished!' the officer barked. He swivelled in his chair and turned to address Reggie. 'Do you honestly think a man of my seniority would take the trouble to drive all the way up here just to let you know one of your servants has been killed? Even if the man was a known communist terrorist.'

Jasmine's anger erupted. 'If Bintang was a CT it's because you made him one. You beat him up and threatened him and took his picture and put it on your nasty wanted poster. All because he stopped you trying to force yourself on me.'

To her horror, Ellis started to laugh. 'Spirited little thing, aren't you? I was about to get to you. In fact, you're the reason I'm here, Miss Barrington. I understand you were present at Batu Lembah the day of the fire. Were you there to meet this man?' He stabbed his finger again at the photograph of Bintang. 'Was he your lover? Is that why he rushed to your aid?' He leaned back, tilting the chair to balance on the back legs only, before letting it bounce back under him as he leant forward towards Jasmine, pushing his face closer to hers. 'Women like you disgust me. You're a shame to the British empire and your race. Consorting with natives. Sleeping with the enemy. It isn't natural. It's against the order of things.'

Jasmine could take no more. She jumped up.

Reggie banged his fist on the table. 'Enough, Ellis! How

dare you come into our home and speak to Miss Barrington in this way.'

Ellis ignored him, fixing his gaze on Jasmine. 'Sit down!' he barked.

She complied, her body shaking with anger.

'Much as I find your behaviour reprehensible, I'm not here to give you a lecture on your lack of morals.' Ellis waved his hand dismissively in the direction of Reggie and Mary. 'I'll leave that to them as your guardians. 'I'm here to ask you questions about your time at Batu Lembah.'

'Look here, you can cut this out, Ellis. I told you. This is our home.'

Ellis gave him a withering look. 'And *this* is His Majesty's business.'

'Then damn well get to the point.' Reggie's face was flushed in anger.

'I've nothing to say.' Jasmine folded her arms. 'As you point out, Bintang is dead. I didn't see him. I was with my friend, Barbara Appleton in the cellar while they were fighting the fire.'

'I've already talked to Miss Appleton. She was extremely cooperative. She happened to tell me you were not with her in the cellar. Rather upset about that actually. Says you ran off and abandoned her. Presumably to meet your native.' He reached again for the wanted poster. 'Are you a communist sympathiser, Miss Barrington? Or do your sympathies extend only to that particular one? Were you having a sexual relationship with him?'

Reggie leapt to his feet. 'Look here, Ellis. I don't care whether you're a bloody officer, you are not a gentleman. I will not have you speaking to Miss Barrington in that manner. You can damn well apologise or get out!'

Ellis put his hands up in a gesture of apology. 'I'll try to choose my words more carefully.'

'You'd better. But it isn't going to stop me making a formal complaint to your superior officer. Something I should have done long ago when I found out what you tried on last time you were here. The reason I didn't was that Miss Barrington asked me not to. So, you owe her a debt of gratitude, you blackguard.'

'Now who's throwing around defamatory statements? Let's call it quits then, shall we, Underwood, and I'll carry on with my questions.'

'No. Let's not. You can leave now. If you want to interrogate us, you can get a court order for it. And the name's Hyde-Underwood.'

'I have all the authority I need to question you now. May I remind you, under the Emergency powers I can interrogate whoever I need if I believe it's necessary in the defence of the country.' He pushed the poster across the table to Jasmine. 'It's not actually the dead man I'm interested in. It's this woman. He stabbed his finger at the image of Nayla. 'You must have seen her when you were at Batu Lembah last Sunday. She's the housekeeper for the junior managers there. According to O'Keefe and Fairchild, she served lunch to you and your friends. That was the last anyone saw of her. You're not going to deny it are you, Miss Barrington?'

Jasmine avoided looking at Mary and Reggie. 'Why would I deny it? She served us lunch. I only saw her for a few minutes. It was before the fire. I don't understand what you want from me. She came in, served the meal and left.'

'According to your friend Miss Appleton, there was a bit of a commotion. She says the woman spoke to you directly and claimed to know you.' Ellis got up and began pacing up and down the room as though he owned the place.

'Yes, she did. But it was hardly a commotion. She mentioned that she remembered me from before the war when my father owned the estate. I didn't remember her. I was only a child. That was all.' She pushed the paper back.

'Only no one on the Batu Lembah estate has seen or heard from the woman since Sunday. She's vanished. Her identity card was found in the pocket of one of the dead bandits. It's clear she was a communist and has now fled to join her comrades.' The last word was spoken with contempt.

Mary spoke. 'Her disappearing doesn't make her a communist. You know only too well that's what the CTs are starting to do. They steal ID cards to make stupid people like you believe that anyone unable to provide them must automatically be a terrorist. We've read the reports in the *Straits Times*. Isn't that the new tactic? Holding up buses and collecting all the cards?'

'Funny that it's only hers that was found. Funny that she's the only one who disappeared on Sunday.'

'Is it? Doesn't seem funny to me at all.' Reggie was getting increasingly impatient. 'Look, this is all pointless. I think you should leave now. I told you today is not a good time for any of us. Miss Barrington has answered your questions.'

Ellis, who had turned to glance out of the window, lunged towards the door, flung it open and rushed out of the room.

'What the devil?' Reggie spluttered.

The three of them looked at each other as the same realisation dawned on them all simultaneously and they jumped to their feet.

'Nayla! He must have seen Nayla! My God! Reggie, do something!' screamed Mary.

Too late. The sound of a gunshot rang out.

Jasmine was the first to get there. A shell-shocked Amir was kneeling beside his mother's inert body. Jasmine flung her arms around him and held him tight against her. Ellis was standing several feet away, his pistol still in his hand, a smile on his face. 'Bullseye!' he said.

No sooner were the words out of his mouth than Reggie landed a blow, knocking Ellis backwards, sending him sprawling on the grass. 'You miserable coward. You've murdered an innocent woman in cold blood. And in front of her child.'

Ellis looked up at him, blood pouring from his nose. 'You'll pay for this, Underwood.' As he staggered to his feet he added, 'If she was innocent, why was she running away?'

'Because you were pointing a gun at her,' Jasmine screamed at him. 'Because you've plastered her face on wanted posters. She'd done nothing. The communists were threatening her because she wouldn't help them and now you've killed her. You're despicable.'

'Get out now!' Reggie yelled.

'All right I'm going. But I have to do one thing first.' He went to his jeep and fetched a camera from the front seat and took a photograph of the dead woman. Where he had shot her through the chest, her purple *cheongsam* was drenched dark with her blood. 'Have to have proof of the kill.' He wiped his bloody nose against his arm. 'It's like the game of bingo. We have the poster on the barracks wall and cross them off as we get them.'

'Unless you want me to make that nose bloodier, you'll get in that jeep and get the hell out of here. And, Ellis, if you ever set foot on my property again I won't answer for the consequences.'

Mary ran back to the house, fetched one of the throws

from the veranda and draped it over Nayla's body. As she covered the woman's face, the boy gave a low wail.

Jasmine held Amir against her, rocking him gently until his cries of grief lessened. He looked up at her, his beautiful eyes full of tears. 'Why man kill Ma?'

'He's a bad man.'

'Will he kill me too?'

'No. He's gone now. You're safe, Amir.' She turned to Mary, not knowing what else to do or say.

Mary reached for Amir's hand. The little boy began howling again. He jerked away from her and knelt beside his mother's inert body, trying to pull back the throw that covered her.

Mary eased him away. 'Ma's gone to Heaven, Amir. She's in paradise now. Later we will all say our prayers for her. And you can say goodbye. Come with me now. We'll go and find baby Frances. And Jinjiang will make you something nice for your breakfast.'

His thin body still jerking with tears and shock, he took Mary's outstretched hand and walked towards the house with her.

Jasmine let herself sink from her knees to a slump. Reggie held his hand out to her. He pulled her onto her feet. 'I'll get some of the men to dig a grave for the poor woman.'

He looked around. 'How about if we bury her over there, under that tall hardwood tree? We can have a little ceremony for her tonight.'

'I'll make a marker for the grave. I made one for Bintang's sister's grave. There was nothing to show where it was. I wanted her to have something to record her life. I'd like to do the same for Amir's mother. Could you find me a solid piece of wood, Reggie.'

'Pleased to do so.' He looked down at her. 'You're a good

girl, Jasmine. You have a big heart. Especially... you know... since she and your father...'

'Ancient history.' She shook her head. 'Ellis will get away with this, won't he?'

Reggie punched his fist into the palm of his hand. 'I tell you, Jasmine, I'd swing for that man. He deserves to be court-martialled.'

'He won't be, will he?'

'Almost certainly not.' Reggie's mouth was a hard line. 'Men like him are a disgrace to the uniform. But the army look after their own. And they'll use the powers of the Emergency.'

'But she was an unarmed woman.'

'He'll say she was running away. And that she was on the wanted list.'

Jasmine sneered. 'His concoction.' She sighed. 'It's my fault. If I'd let you make a complaint when he attacked me...'

'It would have made no difference. He'd have wriggled out of that too.'

'But two innocent people are dead. He didn't shoot Bintang, but he might as well have done.' She looked up at Reggie and he drew her into a hug.

'Don't let Ellis fill your heart with poison. Go and find the lad. Amir needs you. You need to be strong for the poor chap.'

'Thanks Reggie.'

'What for?'

'For understanding.'

JASMINE SPENT most of the day crafting the grave marker. Uncertain what decorations would be appropriate, she went in search of Amir and asked him to help her make the sign to honour his mother's memory. The boy was bemused, but followed her to the studio and was soon absorbed in helping her fix some of the natural objects in her collection to the wooden post Reggie had supplied. Afterwards, she gave Amir a brush and let him apply the varnish. Doing this together seemed to comfort him and the task was a temporary distraction from his grief.

That evening they buried Nayla under the hardwood tree. Jasmine's eyes brimmed with tears when all the estate workers appeared and stood in line, heads bowed as the woman was laid to rest. Reggie said a few words and prayers were offered by one of the Malays. Amir clutched Jasmine's hand tightly. He had stopped crying and seemed to be now in a state of shocked numbness.

THAT NIGHT, Mary turned to her husband as they were getting ready for bed. 'Are we going to talk about it?'

Reggie looked sheepish. 'About what?'

'About what happens to Amir.'

Reggie grunted.

'We can't let him go to an orphanage. It wouldn't be right, Reggie.'

'No, I suppose not.'

'After the terrible experience he's had, he needs love and attention.'

Another grunt.

'And he's Jasmine's half-brother.'

'You've made your mind up, haven't you, Mary? You want us to take the boy in permanently. I get the feeling you've already set your heart on it.'

'Unless you feel the same way about him, I will *not* be set on this.'

'It's only...'

'Only what, Reggie?'

'He's a native boy. You said it yourself, he belongs with Malayans.'

'We're Malayan.' She spoke with force.

'Don't be obtuse, Mary, you know what I mean.'

'But we're never leaving here, are we? This is our home. Our country. And anyway, he's as much white as Malayan. Don't forget we're talking about Doug's child, about Jasmine's brother. You must have seen how like Doug he is. And surely we owe it to his mother?'

'Don't you think this could be rubbing poor Jasmine's nose in it? In what her father did? She can't be feeling very proud of old Doug right now.'

'I'm sure she's not. It brought back a lot of memories of Evie going through hell at the time. But Jasmine's mature enough to acknowledge human frailty – God knows, she's certainly experienced plenty of that in the past few days – and she also knows her mother is blissfully happy with Arthur, so there's no point wasting time feeling bitter on Evie's behalf.'

'Let me think about it, my love. You need to as well. If we agree to take the boy in and it doesn't work out, what on earth do we do then? Does he even speak English?'

'Reggie! You haven't even talked to him! Otherwise you'd know he does. He's been going to the estate school at BL. He speaks as well or even better than the children I teach. He does appear to be a bright boy.' She leaned forward and kissed him softly on the lips. 'I think you should spend some time with him, Reggie. Just the two of you. See what you think. Unless you are one hundred percent sure, I won't put pressure on you. It's too important for all of us.'

'Frances does seem to have taken to him.'

'Utterly besotted.'

'And after what the doctors said when you had Frances... We accepted it, didn't we, old girl? That she would be the only one. We were disappointed, but we'd come to terms with it. She was the gift that brought us together. Now this.' He looked wistful. 'I'd always imagined Stanford would be here...but that's never going to happen if Susan gets her way.' He took a slow breath, mulling the idea in his mind.

Mary looked at her husband tenderly, reminding herself that she had once been ready to throw away the possibility of happiness with Reggie because of fear of the unknown, fear of happiness itself, of opening herself up to the possibility of loss again. She waited, watching, as he thought.

'He's awfully young,' he said eventually. 'But lots of time to learn. Why don't I take him with me tomorrow on my inspection rounds? It'll give me a chance to get know the boy. And him me.'

The following day, after lunch, Mary stood on the veranda, watching as her husband stepped out of the estate office and began to cross the *padang* towards the small rubber factory. Amir was walking beside him. Her heart leapt in her chest when she saw the boy say something to her husband, then put up his hand and Reggie's large paw wrapped around Amir's small one and the two walked together across the grassy space.

OVER DINNER, Reggie and Mary told Jasmine that they had decided, if she was in agreement, that Amir could stay on at Bella Vista.

'We're prepared to bring him up as if he were our own son.' Mary looked at Reggie for affirmation.

'Yes,' he said. 'It depends on the lad himself, and you too, but if things work out, maybe we can make it a formal adoption. Let's give it time. But if you think it's a good idea, Jasmine, we'd love to give it a go.'

Jasmine looked from Reggie to Mary. Both of them were smiling, holding hands under the table in a gesture of unity.

'We've both taken to him, Jasmine,' said Mary. 'As has Frances. Obviously, we have to give Amir time to grieve for his mother's death, but we both believe...' She glanced at Reggie for approval before continuing. 'We both believe that Amir could be the son we had hoped for but cannot have. Frances was our miracle. We never expected to be blessed again when the doctors told me I could never bear another child. So, Amir may prove to be our second miracle.' Mary was still holding Reggie's hand. 'One thing we want to make clear, Jasmine, you are his sister and his next of kin. We need your blessing. We won't do it without that.'

Tears welled in Jasmine's eyes. 'I've been hoping and praying for this. I don't even think I believe in God, but I wasn't taking any chances. You two mean as much to me as Mummy and Arthur do. Amir and Hugh are my only blood relatives. My blood brothers. Hugh is with Mummy and Arthur. What could be better than Amir being with you? That would make me so happy.' She held her hands out and clasped both of theirs.

ABOUT A FORTNIGHT after Nayla's funeral, instead of retiring to the veranda for his habitual pre-dinner *stengah* Reggie asked Jasmine if he could come and look at her studio. 'I've been meaning to look at all the great work Mary tells me you've been doing.'

Jasmine grinned. 'Really, Reggie? I'd no idea you were interested in art.'

He winked. 'I'm rather hoping you'll give me some clues so I can report back to Mary and convince her that I know what I'm talking about.'

She smiled and they went into the studio. It was growing dark. Reggie turned to look at her. 'I can't pretend.' He sucked his lips in. 'I've brought you here on false pretences, Jasmine. I want to know if you're still happy about Mary and me eventually adopting Amir?'

'I couldn't be happier. It's perfect. As long as you're happy, Reggie.' She hesitated then added, 'I know it was Mary's idea and I'd hate to think you were going along with it just to keep her happy.'

He shook his head, smiling. 'I'm the happiest man on earth. Mary and I are as one on this. I miss Stanford dreadfully, and I've had to come to terms with that. Knowing Mary and I couldn't have any more children was a bitter blow, but I'm more than grateful that we have each other and our darling Frances.' He paused, seeming embarrassed to be speaking so openly. 'Yes, it's hard to believe, but I fell in love with that little lad the moment I set eyes on him. I promise you, Jasmine, I will love and care for Amir as if he were my own son. Mary and I have come to see you as another daughter. When you eventually leave us, it will be hard to let you go. Having your brother here as part of our family, as our son, well...' His voice broke and he put his hand up to cover his eyes.

'Oh, dear Reggie,' she said and gave him a hug. 'You lovely man.'

33

Jasmine's examination results were in and she had done well enough to make Mary beam from ear to ear and jump up and down on the spot. 'You clever thing! I knew you wouldn't disappoint. Evie and Arthur will be so proud of you.'

'I couldn't have done it without you, Mary.'

'I did nothing. Merely tested you on those dratted irregular verbs.'

'It's not just that. It's everything else you've done for me. If I'd stayed in Nairobi I'd never have taken the exams, let alone done well in them. You opened your home to me, made me feel part of the family, put up with my moods and supported me through everything.'

'You *are* part of our family. And even more so since your brother is going to be our son. Reggie and I think of you as a daughter, even though it's an honour we share with Evie and Arthur.

Jasmine flung her arms around her dear friend.

'I think I've done well enough to apply for a place at the

Beaux Arts in Paris. Apparently, they accept the school leaving certificate results in lieu of the French Baccalaureate – just as well as I don't think I could face another set of exams.' She rolled her eyes. 'But they get loads more applicants than they have places and you have to present a portfolio and then a jury interviews the best candidates. I probably don't stand a chance but I'm going to have a jolly good try.'

'I have every faith in you, Jasmine.'

'If they won't take me, I'll carry on painting anyway.' She drummed her fingers on the wooden arm of her chair. 'The art schools in London are very good but I don't think I could bear London. It's so bleak.'

'New York?'

'Ooh no! Far too scary. I'd feel crowded in by all those skyscrapers. And it's simply too far away. No. It's Paris or nothing.'

'Then you'd better make sure it's Paris, hadn't you?'

Jasmine grinned. 'Yes. I need to make my portfolio so good they can't possibly refuse me.'

'When does the term begin?'

'Next year. September.'

'Have you told Evie and Arthur about it yet?'

'No. Well, they know I was thinking about art school, but I hadn't actually broached the subject of Paris.' She plucked at the fabric of her skirt. 'I was thinking of going to Nairobi for Christmas so I can tell them in person. It's been a long time.'

'It's gone too quickly for me. Reggie as well. We were only saying so yesterday.'

Jasmine hesitated. 'I thought I might stay there after Christmas. Spend my last months before art school with them. I feel as though I left them rather ungraciously. But if the Beaux Arts turn me down, I was wondering if you might agree to me coming back here.'

'Nothing would make us happier. We will always have a home for you here, Jasmine. Whenever you need it.'

The sound of Frances's laughter drifted towards them across the lawn. Jinjiang had hung sheets on the washing line and Amir was playing a game with Frances, wrapping himself in a sheet like a ghost then popping out and saying 'Boo!' to her endless amusement.

'Amir is so brave. He puts his sorrow aside to play with Frances.' Mary gave a wistful smile. 'I don't know how he manages to do it. I just hope Frances's love for him is helping him recover.'

'They adore each other. I can't believe how well Amir has settled. It's hard to believe he witnessed his mother being murdered.' Jasmine gazed at her brother across the lawn.

Mary frowned. 'Children are incredibly adaptable. But he wakes in the night crying for Nayla. I leave his bedroom door open so I can hear and go to him when it happens. It's becoming less often and not at all in the past week.'

'I'm so happy he has you and Reggie.' She thought for a moment. 'Would you mind if I took him to meet Bintang's grandmother? They are both going through grief and they might be able to help each other. The grandmother must be lonely.'

Mary smiled. 'That's a lovely idea, Jasmine. It's also important for Amir to keep his links with the Malayan language and people.'

'You don't mind?'

'Not at all. And I'm sure the old lady would love to meet him, Jasmine.'

Jasmine squeezed her hands together. 'Then I'll take him there this afternoon.'

'I was just thinking, Jasmine, since you have to work on your portfolio, I'd better let you off your teaching duties until you leave.'

'You'd better not! I love being at the school. Besides I plan to photograph the children's art with the camera Mummy and Arthur sent me and find a way to include something related to it in my portfolio. It would give me something interesting and a bit different to talk about if I get called to interview. How we introduced painting and collage to the children when they'd never done anything like that before. It's an essential part of my entire Penang painting project. I'm excited. I've got lots of ideas mulling about in my brain on how to bring it alive. I bet no one else will have anything similar. It's all about making the jury think you have something different to offer. Not just talent.'

'How will they ever be able to refuse you?'

'That's the idea.'

'So, you'll be leaving here before Christmas?' Mary's mouth turned down.

Jasmine nodded. 'If you won't mind me going. I was thinking in two weeks' time.'

'Of course, I'll mind – but I totally understand. It's the right thing to do.' Mary gave her a tight-lipped smile. Does Howard Baxter know you're leaving?'

Jasmine felt herself blushing. 'Not yet. Well...maybe I won't tell him at all.'

'That's rather cruel. He'll be hurt if he misses the chance to say goodbye to you. I know you didn't hit it off with him but he's awfully fond of you. Wouldn't you like me to invite him up here for a weekend – maybe next week?'

'No. Please don't.' A sudden rush of emotion hit Jasmine

and she bit her lip. 'I think if you did I might find it too hard to say goodbye.'

'Oh, my goodness, Jasmine! You do have feelings for him.'

The blood rushed again to Jasmine's face. 'I don't know. I really don't know what I feel. He saved my life and I was horrid to him. All I've ever been is horrid to him.' She sucked her lips in. 'I don't know what to think anymore. It's probably because I'm frightened. Really scared of feeling something for him.'

Mary took her hand. 'Loving someone can be a very scary thing. I do understand exactly what you're going through, my darling. With Reggie, the feeling was so unexpected and so strong that it terrified me and I hid myself away. I wouldn't acknowledge how I felt, even to myself. It took your mother to make me confront it.'

'Why did it make you afraid? There's nothing scary about Reggie.'

Mary smiled. 'There's nothing scary about Howard either. It's our emotions that scare us. The intensity. In my case it came from nowhere. I'd been engaged to be married twice before and had lost both men, one of them Reggie's brother. I'd made my mind up that I was cursed. Reggie was so completely not my idea of the man I'd spend my life with that I let my guard down when we met again after the war. My feelings for him overwhelmed me. I didn't see it coming. So, I shut him out. It was as if I curled myself into a tight ball like a hedgehog. Now, rather than believing that I was cursed, I realise that the right man hadn't come into my life until Reggie did.'

'What a beautiful story. Thank you for telling me that, Mary.'

'So, you will see Howard? You'll give him a chance?'

'I can't. Don't you see, Mary. I met Howard at the wrong time, just as you met Reggie at the right one. If I don't study painting now I never will. Whatever my feelings for Howard might turn out to be, if I see him and let him persuade me to stay, I will be letting myself down. I have to follow my dreams. And to be honest, Mary, they don't include being stuck in an ugly bungalow out at Batu Lembah, kicking my heels and having babies while my husband is out working all day. It's not like here. Up here on the island, it's beautiful. Over there, it's just a flat expanse of rubber trees.'

Mary nodded. 'Perhaps you're right. You are very young. And very talented. If Howard is the one for you, he'll wait for you.'

'That's why I can't say goodbye. I can't give him that hope. Who knows what will happen with me? He's older. He can't put his life on hold waiting for me to grow up and settle down. I couldn't do that to him.' She felt tears brimming in her eyes and sniffed them away. 'No. The way I feel now I'm sure if he were to come here for the weekend I'd crumble. And I don't want to crumble. I won't let myself crumble. I will go to Paris. I simply must.'

'Very well. I understand. Will you write to him?'

'Probably not. Though it will kill me not to. If I do, he might not get me out of his system and get on with his life.'

'You are such a strong person for one so young, Jasmine.'

Jasmine smiled. 'Not inside I'm not. I'm a great big pile of wobbly jelly.'

Mary got up. 'I'm going to go and see what those two are up too. Poor Jinjiang's probably run ragged. And it's time you were in that studio of yours. It sounds like you've a lot to do.'

34

J asmine knew saying goodbye to her Penang family was going to be hard, but it was even more painful than she imagined. They had all piled into the car together, having sent her luggage ahead to the ship.

Now that they were here on the quayside, Mary appeared anxious to get away. 'If you don't mind awfully, Jasmine, I think we'll say goodbye now. We promised the children we'd take them to the Swimming Club and you'll want time to settle into your cabin before you sail. I really hate goodbyes.'

'Me too.' Why was Mary so eager to get away? Had she already written her out of their lives and was anxious to get on with cementing Amir into his new family? She felt a little hurt. But then she hated goodbyes too. Better to get on with it. She wrapped her arms around her little brother one last time and tears streaming down her cheeks watched them climb into the car and drive away.

As she dried her eyes and turned to make her way onto the ship, Howard Baxter was standing in front of her.

Jasmine gasped. That must be why the Hyde-Underwoods had beat such a hasty retreat.

Howard moved towards her, looking uncomfortable, nervous even. He was wearing shorts and his long legs were tanned. He ran a hand through his hair. 'I was shocked when I got Mary's letter. I'd been hoping you were going to stay on here in Penang.' He looked at her intently. 'I can't believe you're actually going away.'

'Neither can I. It's all gone by so quickly. I love it here.'

'So why leave?' His eyes were sad, searching.

'I haven't seen my family in months.'

'Then go for Christmas and come back after New Year. I thought you didn't like Africa.'

'I don't, but I love my family and I left them rather too abruptly when I came here. This is the last significant amount of time I'll get to spend with them – possibly ever – so I want to make the most of it. And I may have mixed up my problems at school with my feelings about Nairobi in general. I may actually even get to like it. You never know.' She gave him what she hoped was a mischievous smile, intending to make light of the situation – when inside she felt anything but. 'That's the thing about me. I always get things mixed up.'

He looked at her sadly. 'I'm going to miss you, Jasmine. More than you can even begin to imagine. I'm hoping you're going to tire quickly of those dried-up plains and long for some lush green scenery. When you do, I'll be here waiting for you.'

'Don't say that, Howard. I hate to think of you waiting for something that may never happen.'

He grinned. 'May never happen? I'll take heart from the fact you didn't say *won't* ever happen. And I've told you before, I'm a patient man. And in my experience, all the very best things in life are worth waiting for.'

'It's likely to be a long wait. Possibly forever. Certainly for a good few years. I've applied for a place at the Beaux Arts in Paris to study painting. It's to do a foundation year and, assuming I get through that, the full Fine Arts course. Five years in total.'

His face fell. 'A long time. But don't most great artists just get on with painting? They don't study it. Shouldn't it be instinctive? You have a true talent, Jasmine. I'd hate to think they might teach that out of you.'

She smiled at him. 'You are such a nice man, Howard. You really mean that, don't you?'

'Of course, I mean it.'

'I have a lot to learn actually. I read somewhere that it's only once you've mastered technique that you can afford to develop an individual style. I've had no formal training. I need to dig the foundations deeply enough or my house might fall down.'

He stretched out his hand and held his palm against her cheek. 'Why are you so young and yet so wise?'

'Silly!' she laughed. 'Nothing wise about me. Changing the subject, did you hear about my brother?'

'Apart from the fact you're now off to see him, no.'

'Not that brother. My Malayan brother.'

Howard looked puzzled.

'Your housekeeper, Nayla. You knew she was dead?'

'Yes. Apparently, she was a communist. I'd never have guessed. Shows how much I know.'

'She wasn't a communist and she was shot in cold blood up at Bella Vista by Ellis. Remember him?

Howard nodded but he was frowning. 'Unfortunately, yes. But why were they up at Bella Vista?'

'It turns out her little boy, Amir, is my half-brother.' She looked at him, suddenly nervous. 'Nayla was my father's housekeeper and evidently she was his mistress too.'

To her relief, Howard showed no sign of shock or disapproval. 'I didn't know that,' he said.

'Reggie and Mary are adopting Amir.'

'Gosh. Really? How do you feel about that?'

'Incredibly happy. They love him – as I do. And he's growing to love them too. I was wondering... no, never mind.'

'What? Tell me.'

'It's just... I was wondering whether you might occasionally stop by there to visit them and see Amir. Maybe, if you have time, drop me a line to tell me how he's doing. Obviously, the Hyde-Underwoods will write, but they adore him and he may be afraid to tell them how he really feels. I thought if once in a while you happened to see him you could let me know how it looks to someone outside. I mean... I'd hate to think of him being sad...and being afraid to admit it. Missing his mother...you know what I mean.'

'I'll make it my personal mission.'

'But don't let Reggie and Mary know. I don't want them to think I'm checking up on them, because I'm not.'

Howard clasped her hands between his. 'Jasmine you don't need to explain. I'm glad that you've asked me. That you trust me that way. Think of me as Amir's honorary older brother.' He gave her an easy grin. 'And I'd be a liar if I didn't admit I'm delighted to have the perfect excuse to write to you.'

She bit her lip. 'You don't need an excuse.'

The foghorn sounded. 'I have to go,' she said, needlessly. 'You don't have to stay to wave me off. Goodbye Howard.' She began to walk towards the ship, then just before the gangway, turned and ran back to him, throwing her arms around him. He drew her in and held her against him. She could hear the beating of his heart through his thin cotton shirt. He bent down and kissed the top of her head. 'Good-bye, my sweet girl. Go and do great things. Send me a post-card occasionally and try not to forget me.'

'I could never forget you, Howard. I owe you my life.'

'And what a life it's going to be. Paris won't know what's hit it.' He eased her away. 'Now go, before they sail without you, or I try to make you change your mind.'

Her cheeks streaming with tears, Jasmine turned and ran up the gangway.

THE END

IF YOU ENJOYED A PAINTER IN PENANG

It would be fantastic if you could spare a few minutes to leave a review at the retailer where you bought the book.

Reviews make a massive difference to authors - they help books get discovered by other readers and make it easier for authors to get promotional support – some promotions require a minimum number of reviews in order for a book to be accepted. Your words can make a difference.

Thank you!

CLARE'S NEWSLETTER

Why not subscribe to Clare's monthly newsletter? Clare will update you on her work in progress, her travels, and you'll be the first to know when she does a cover reveal, shares an extract, or has news of special offers and promotions. She often asks for input from her subscribers on cover design, book titles and characters' names.

Don't worry - your email address will NEVER be shared with a third party and if you reply to any of the newsletters you will get a personal response from Clare. She LOVES hearing from readers.

As a special thank you, you'll get a free download of her short story collection, *A Fine Pair of Shoes and Other Stories*

Here's the link to sign up - Click below or go to clareflynn.co.uk to the sign-up form. (Privacy Policy on Clare's website)

https://www.subscribepage.com/r4wɪu5

AUTHOR'S NOTES AND ACKNOWLEDGEMENTS

I have used the spelling Sungei Siput for the location of the 16th June murders that kicked off the Emergency, rather than the spelling used today - Sungai Siput. All contemporary accounts use the Sungei spelling, including the newspaper reports. This may cause confusion as there is another town spelt with the 'e' in the south of Malaysia in Malacca. I considered using the current Sungai spelling to avoid such confusion, but prefer to be historically accurate. This also goes for other spellings such as kampong or kampung – I have used what I believe would have been the common colonial British usage at the time, based on contemporary accounts.

Apart from significant historic figures, including the murdered planters, Chin Peng and named members of the government, all characters are entirely products of my imagination. One exception is Kuttan, who makes a brief appearance as the waiter at the Galle Face Hotel in Colombo. This is the late Kottarapattu Chattu Kuttan, who was reputed to be the longest serving hotel employee in the world. He died in 2014, aged 94 while still working at the hotel as their iconic doorman, after seventy years' service there. At the time of Jasmine's and Evie's stay in the hotel he would have been a waiter in the restaurant.

I drew on various sources in the background research to this book. These include

The Malayan Emergency: Essays on a Small, Distant War (Nias Monographs 2016), Souchou Yao;

The War of the Running Dogs, (Orion 2004) Noel Barber, 1971;

Malayan Spymaster, Memoirs of a Rubber Planter, Bandit Catcher and Spy, (Monsoon, 2012), Bruce Hemby;

Out in the Midday Sun, (John Murray Ltd 2000, new edition 2015 Monsoon), Margaret Shennan,;

Growing Up in British Malaya and Singapore, (World Scientific, 2015) Maurice Baker.

The BBC 1998 documentary, *Malaya, The Undeclared War*, which included interviews with Chin Peng, was invaluable as were past editions of *The Straits Times*.

The Huntley Film Archives proved to be a superb source of original footage of life in Malaya before and during the period.

My thanks also to Jeffery Seow for answering questions and pointing me in the direction of several useful online resources on Penang during the Emergency. Also to the Facebook group *The Malayan Emergency 1948-1960* – the members' posts and photographs made the period feel immediate and tangible.

As always thanks to Jane Dixon-Smith for her beautiful cover and Debi Alper, my wonderful editor.

Thanks also to the fellow members of my local critique group, Margaret Kaine, Jay Dixon and Joanna Warrington, and to Clare O'Brien, Debbie Marmor, Liza Perrat, Victoria

Riley (who is also the fabulous narrator of the Penang audiobooks) and to Sharon Phelps, Judy Granit, Jane Willis, Lynn Osborne, Judy Cordiner and Jill Hiatt for their eagle eyes. And last but not least thanks to my readers across the world who make it all so worthwhile.

GLOSSARY

Amah - nursemaid or housekeeper

Attap - straw thatching for roofs

Baju kurung – Malayan traditional woman's dress

Cheongsam - traditional Chinese-style woman's dress

Chicks – wooden slatted blinds

Kampong - village or rural settlement

Kebun - gardener

Mem - term used for European women, like ma'am or madam

Missee - European girl

Padang - grassy space for recreation, used for the daily muster on rubber estates

Stengah - whisky and soda – the favoured drink of expat European men

Syce - driver, groom or chauffeur - word imported from India

Tiffin - lunch - word imported from India

Tuan - honorific for addressing European men - sir, lord, boss

Tuan besar - big boss - head of enterprise

BMA - British Military Administration - in force between 1945 and April 1946

CT - communist terrorist - also referred to at the time as bandits

MPAJA - Malayan Peoples' Anti-Japanese Army

MNLA - Malayan National Liberation Army (sometimes wrongly translated as the Malayan Races Liberation Army)

Force 136 - name used from 1944 for the British Special Operations Executive (SOE) in the Far East – a guerrilla force parachuted into the jungle behind enemy lines to support indigenous resistance groups. In the last few months of the Second World War this group dropped around 2000 weapons into the jungle for the MPAJA. Most of these were never returned after the war and were used by the MNLA against the British during the Emergency.

ABOUT THE AUTHOR

Clare Flynn is the author of twelve historical novels and a collection of short stories.

A former Marketing Director and strategy consultant, she was born in Liverpool and has lived in London, Newcastle, Paris, Milan, Brussels and Sydney and is now enjoying being in Eastbourne on the Sussex coast where she can see the sea and the Downs from her windows.

When not writing, she loves to travel (often for research purposes) and enjoys painting in oils and watercolours as well as making patchwork quilts and learning to play the piano again.

f 𝕏 ⊙

ALSO BY CLARE FLYNN

The Pearl of Penang

Winner of the 2020 BookBrunch Selfies Award for Adult Fiction; Discovering Diamonds Book of the Month

"Following the death of my wife, I am in need of support and companionship. I am prepared to make you an offer of marriage."

Flynn's tenth novel explores love, marriage, the impact of war and the challenges of displacement – this time in a tropical paradise as the threat of the Japanese empire looms closer.

ALSO AVAILABLE AS AN AUDIOBOOK

A Prisoner from Penang

After Penang is attacked by the Japanese at the end of 1941, Mary Helston believes Singapore will be a safe haven. But within weeks the supposedly invincible British stronghold is on the brink of collapse to the advancing enemy.

Mary and her mother are captured at sea as they try to escape and are interned on the islands of Sumatra. Imprisoned with them is Veronica Leighton, the one person on the planet Mary has reason to loathe with a passion.

As the motley band of women struggle to adapt to captivity, relationships and friendships are tested. When starvation, lack of medication and the spread of disease worsen, each woman must draw on every ounce of strength in their battle for survival.

A vivid and moving story of sacrifice, hope and humanity.

"In this testament to the strength of female friendship and endurance under the harshest of conditions, Flynn has imagined the unimaginable - a dazzling achievement." Linda Gillard, Author of *The Memory Tree* and *House of Silence*

ALSO AVAILABLE AS AN AUDIOBOOK

The Chalky Sea

Two troubled people in a turbulent world.

Gwen Collingwood is an English woman, and **Jim Armstrong**, a young Canadian soldier. Their stories entwine during World War Two in a small English seaside town.

" Flynn's novel is a vivid page-turner that depicts the destruction of war, but it is most notable for its portrayal of the effects it has on individual lives. *(BookLife, Publishers Weekly)*

ALSO AVAILABLE AS AN AUDIO BOOK

The Alien Corn

They faced up to the challenges of war – but can they deal with the troubles of peace?

The follow up to *The Chalky Sea*, *The Alien Corn* is set in rural Canada in the aftermath of World War 2. **Jim Armstrong** has returned to his farm in Ontario where he is joined by his English war bride, Joan. Jim suffers from the after-effects of the horrors he witnessed in the Italian campaign, while Joan struggles to adapt to her new life and family.

"Flynn's novel captures the obstacles faced both by soldiers returning from battle and by those close to them. Readers of the first book will relish the chance to spend more time with the characters, and new readers will find plenty to savor." *(BookLife, Publishers Weekly)*

ALSO AVAILABLE AS AN AUDIO BOOK

The Frozen River

Three strong women make their way in 1950s Canada

The Frozen River completes the trilogy.

English hairdresser, **Ethel Underwood,** is alone after the deaths of her family and her wartime fiancé. Widow and single mother, **Alice Armstrong,** bringing up two daughters, receives an unexpected inheritance that will transform her life. War bride,

Joan Armstrong, is now mother to four small children. All are brought together in a rural Canadian town where they each try to build a future – often in spite of the men in their lives.

Each woman has a different idea of happiness. Will any or all of them achieve it?

ALSO AVAILABLE AS AN AUDIOBOOK

A Greater World

Elizabeth Morton, born into a prosperous family, and **Michael Winterbourne**, a miner, come from different worlds but when they each suffer a life-changing tragedy they're set on a path that intertwines on the deck of the SS Historic, bound for Sydney.

Falling in love should have been the end to all their troubles. But fate and the mysterious **Jack Kidd** make sure it's only the beginning.

ALSO AVAILABLE AS AN AUDIO BOOK

Kurinji Flowers

Married to a man she barely knows. Exiled to a country she doesn't know at all. **Ginny Dunbar** flees a turbulent past only to discover that her future, married to a tea planter, in a colonial hill station, is anything but secure.

An emotional love story set in the dying days of colonial India.

"A sweeping, lush story - the depiction of India in all its colours, smells and vibrancy is pitch-perfect in its depiction." *(Historical Novel Society)*

Letters from a Patchwork Quilt

In 1875, 18-year-old would-be poet, **Jack Brennan**, runs away from home to avoid being forced into the priesthood.

Jack's world is shattered when Mary Ellen, his landlord's daughter, falsely accuses him of fathering the child she is expecting, setting his life on a collision course to disaster.

A touching story of love, loss and thwarted ambition.

"A heartbreaking and moving tale" *Readers' Favorite*

ALSO AVAILABLE AS AN AUDIO BOOK

The Green Ribbons

1900. **Hephzibah Wildman** loses her parents in a tragic accident and is forced to leave home to earn her living as a governess at Ingleton Hall.

A gypsy tells her fortune – "Two men will love you – both will pay the price". An impulsive decision by Hephzibah unleashes a chain of events that lead to dangerous consequences.

A classic Victorian love story, full of twists and turns.

Storms Gather Between Us

Life can change in the matter of a moment...

Since escaping his family's notoriety in Australia **Will Kidd** has spent a decade sailing the seas, never looking back. Content to live the life of a wanderer, everything changes in a single moment when he comes face to face with a ghost from his past on a cloudy beach in Liverpool.

The daughter of an abusive zealot, every step of **Hannah Dawson's** life has been laid out for her...until she meets Will by chance and is set on a new path. Their love is forbidden and forces on all sides divide them, but their bond is undeniable. Now, they will have to fight against all the odds to escape the chains of their histories and find their way back to one another.

"A wonderful read. Very thought-provoking and emotion-inducing, with a lovely ending and memorable characters." (Pursuing Stacie, bookblogger)

"Deeply emotional" (Sally Reads bookblogger)

Printed in Great Britain
by Amazon